Heero Yuy

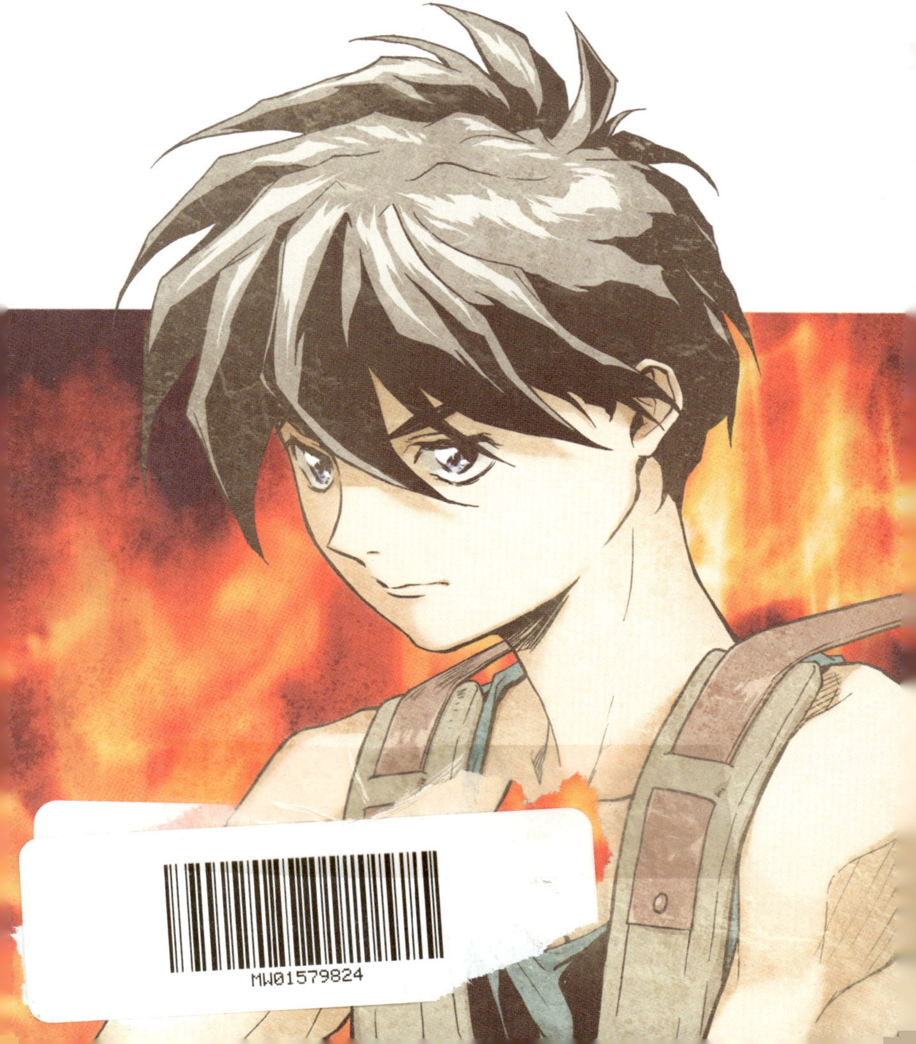

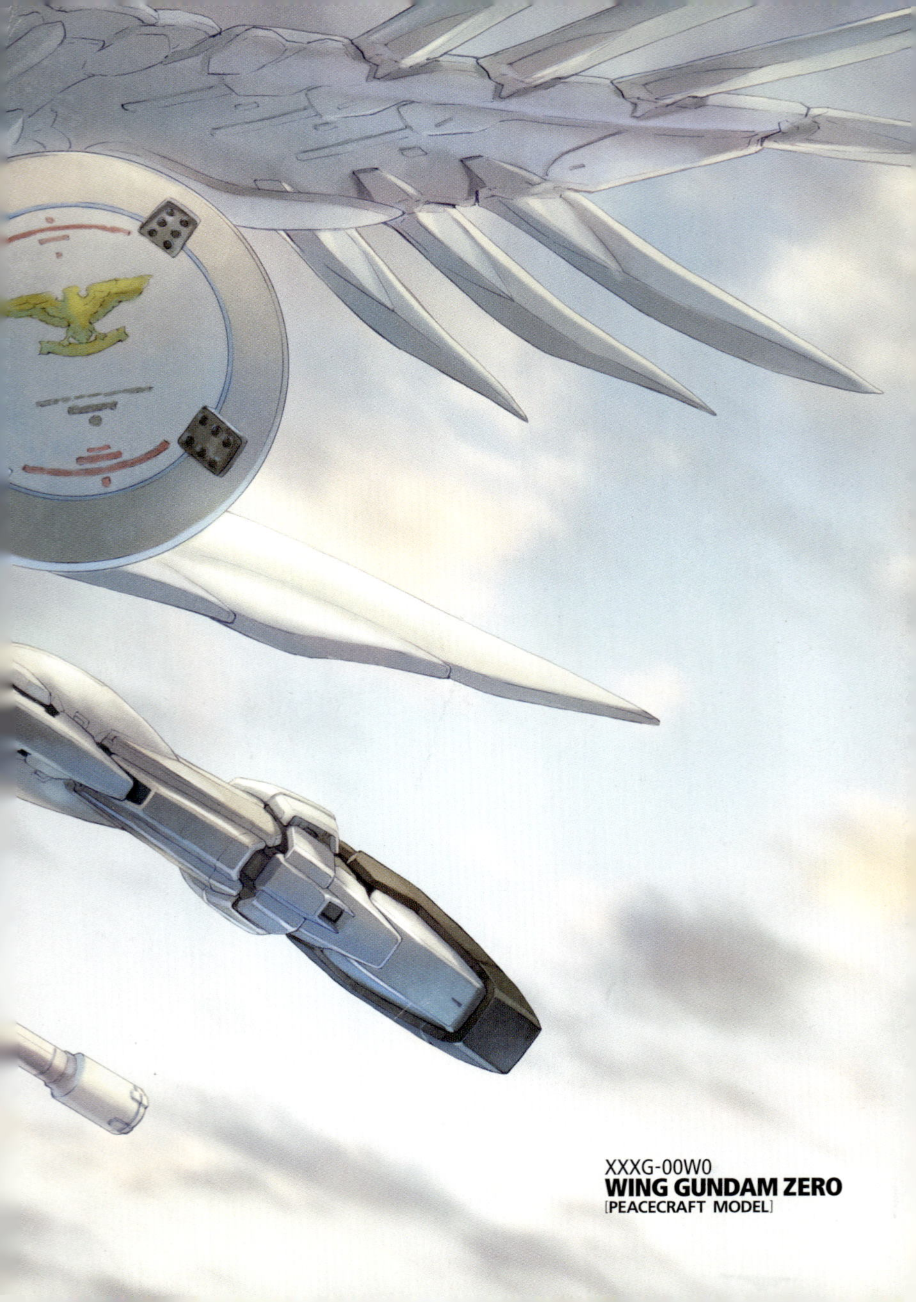

XXXG-00W0
WING GUNDAM ZERO
[PEACECRAFT MODEL]

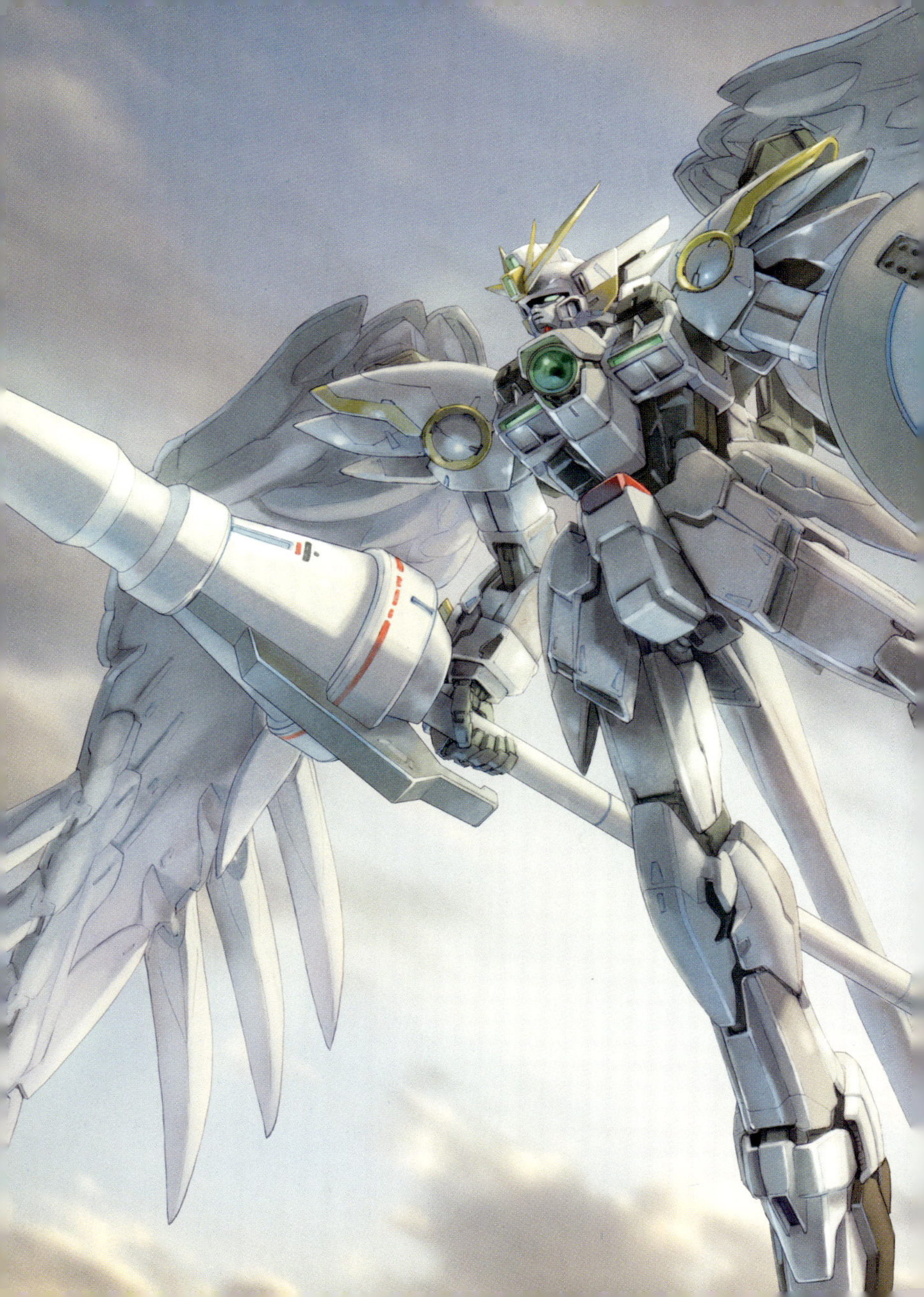

HEAD AND TORSO
WHEN ZERO SYSTEM
IS ACTIVATED

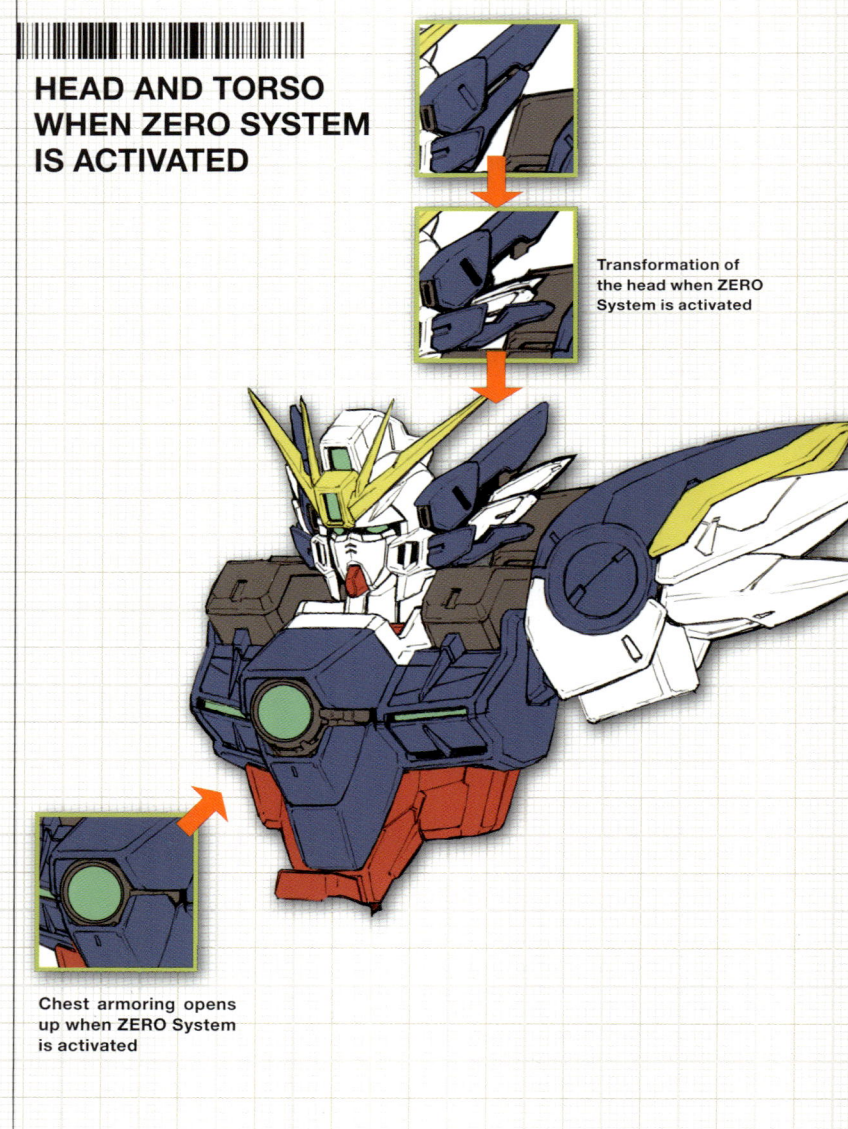

Transformation of the head when ZERO System is activated

Chest armoring opens up when ZERO System is activated

Mobile Suit
GUNDAM WING
Endless Waltz
Glory of the Losers 11

Story
Katsuyuki Sumizawa

Art
Tomofumi Ogasawara

CONTENTS

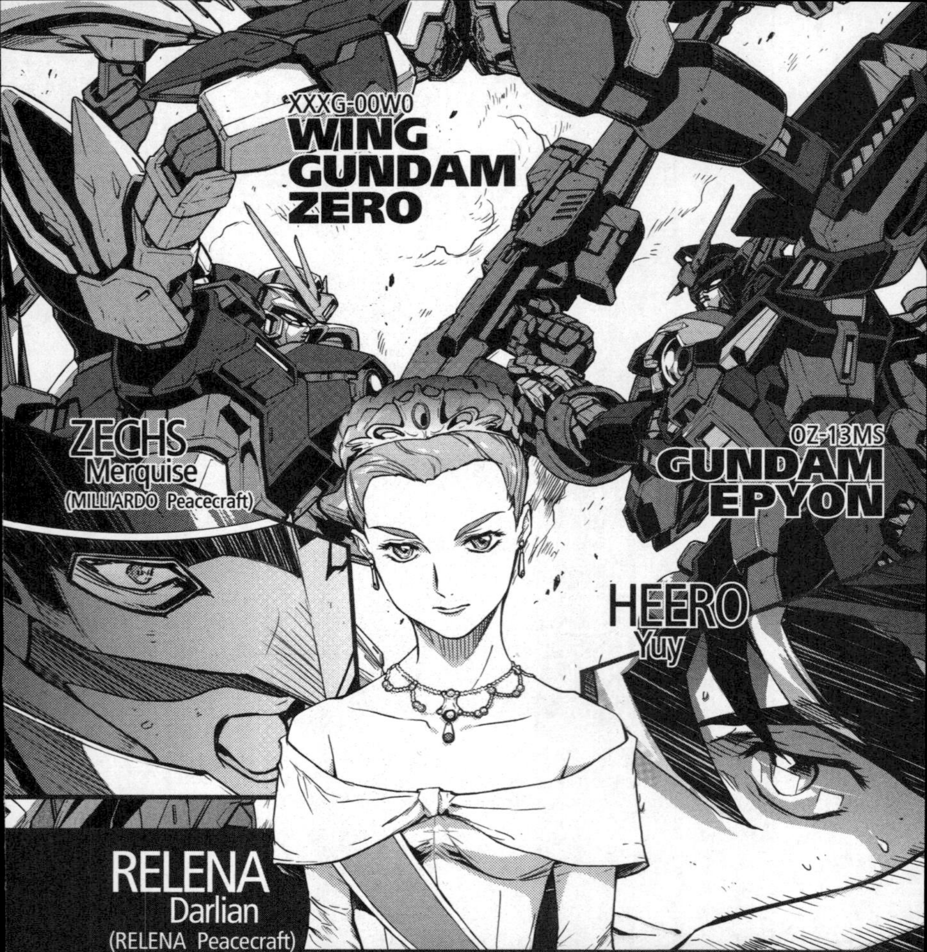
XXXG-00W0
WING GUNDAM ZERO
ZECHS Merquise
(MILLIARDO Peacecraft)
OZ-13MS
GUNDAM EPYON
HEERO Yuy
RELENA Darlian
(RELENA Peacecraft)

OUTLINE

In A.C. 195, the battle between the Gundam pilots and the secret organization OZ enters a new phase. The reborn OZ commences an invasion of the Sanc Kingdom, which had been restored by Relena. Gathering that she's in danger, Zechs heads for the Sanc Kingdom in the Wing Gundam Zero, and Heero sorties in the Gundam Epyon given to him by Treize. Treize watches each of their battles and concludes that neither of their choices connects to the future. As Relena helplessly watches the battle, Dorothy encourages her to declare war against the new OZ. After much agonizing, Relena announces to the world that she will dismantle her country and turn herself over to the Romefeller Foundation.

In the now-dismantled Sanc Kingdom, the Epyon and the Wing Zero confront each other, and the ZERO System on board the Epyon identifies the Wing Zero as an enemy, so Heero initiates an attack. Meanwhile, in space, Duo's Gundam Deathscythe H and Wufei's Altron Gundam launch an assault on the space battleship Libra, which is still under construction ...

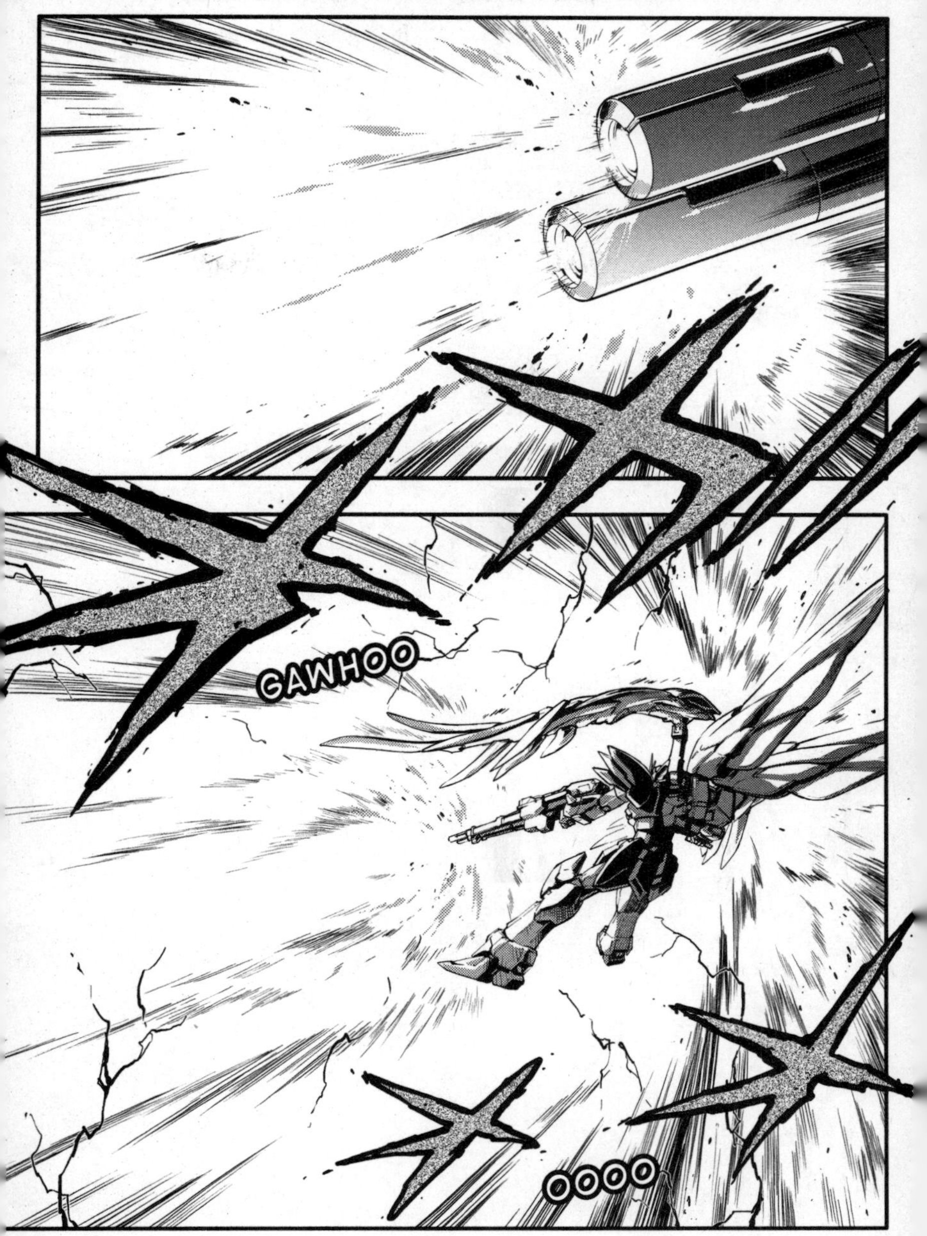
GAWHOO
OOOO

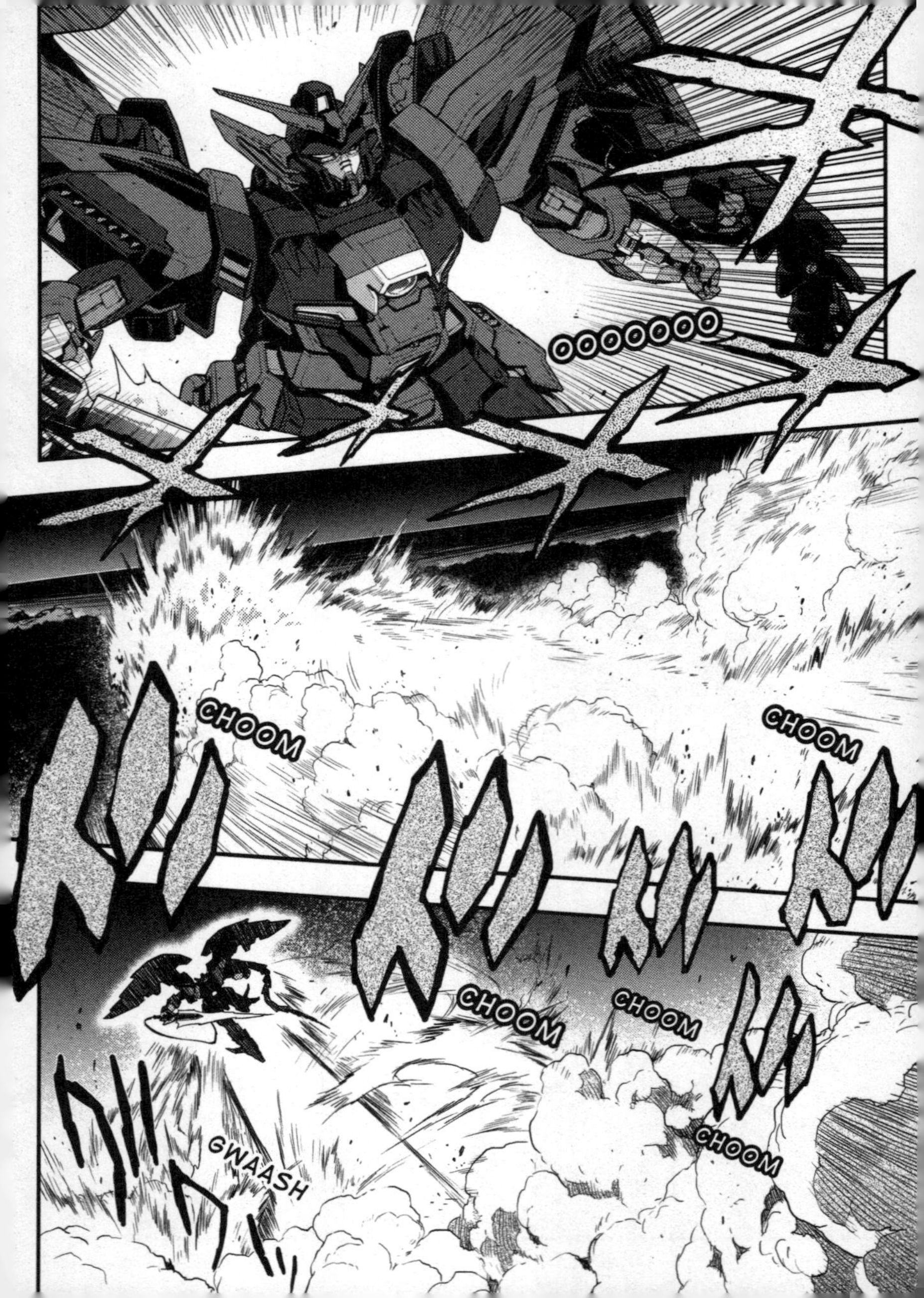
OOOOOOOO
CHOOM
CHOOM
CHOOM
CHOOM
CHOOM
GWAASH

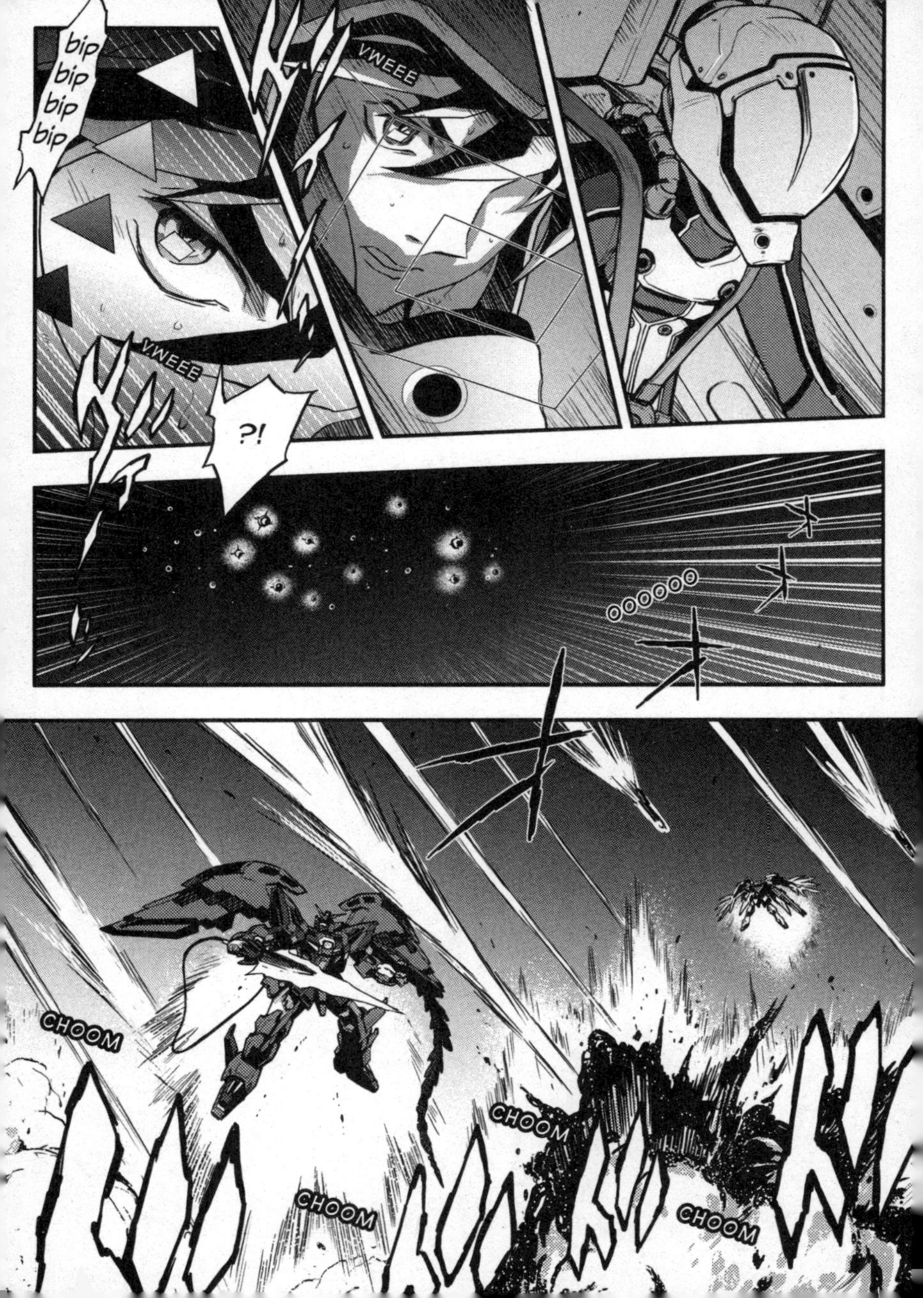

VWEEE
bip bip bip bip
VWEEE
?!
OOOOOO
CHOOM
CHOOM
CHOOM
CHOOM

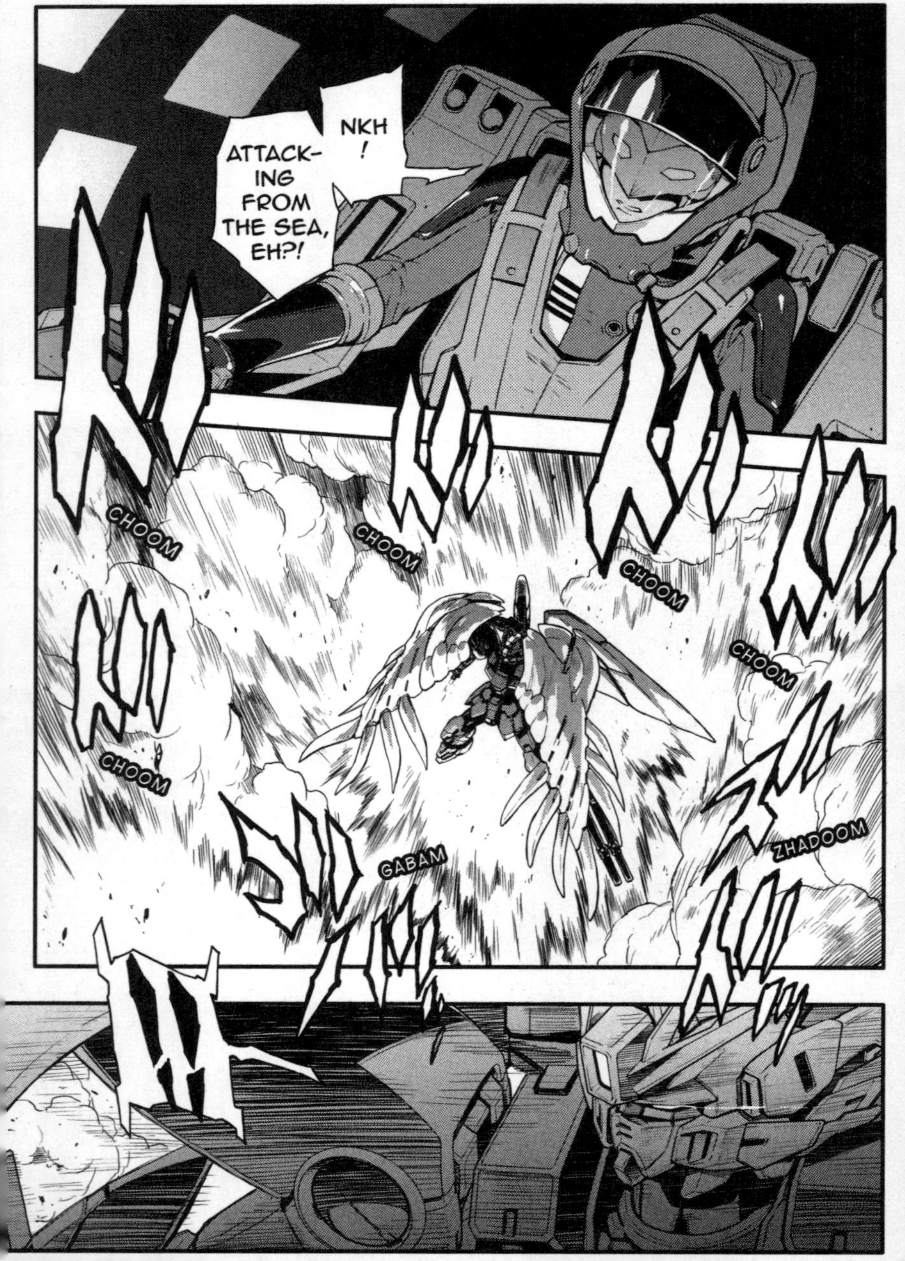
NKH!
ATTACK-ING FROM THE SEA, EH?!
CHOOM
CHOOM
CHOOM
CHOOM
CHOOM
ZHADOOM
GABAM

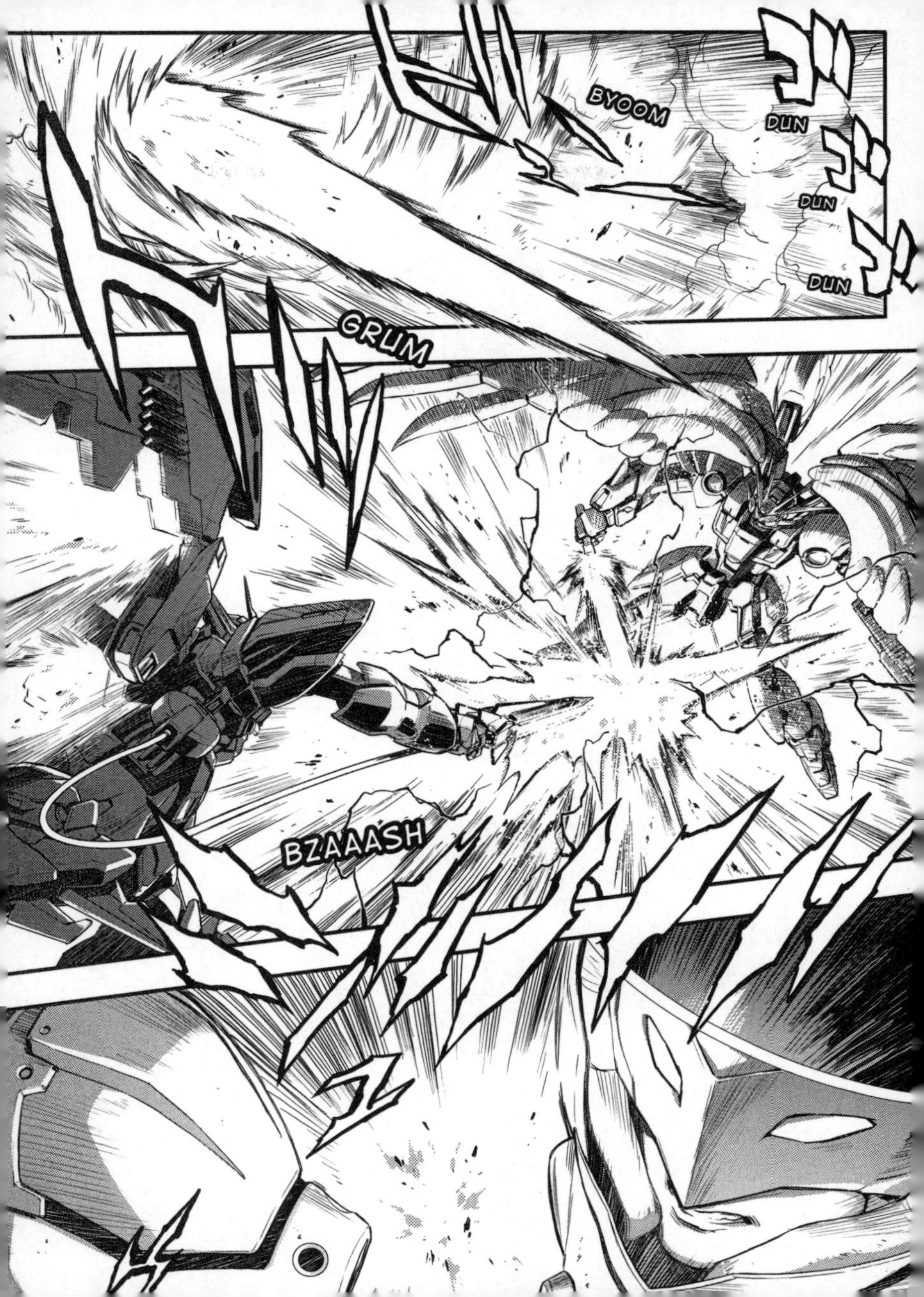
BYOOM
DUN
DUN
DUN
GRUM
BZAAASH

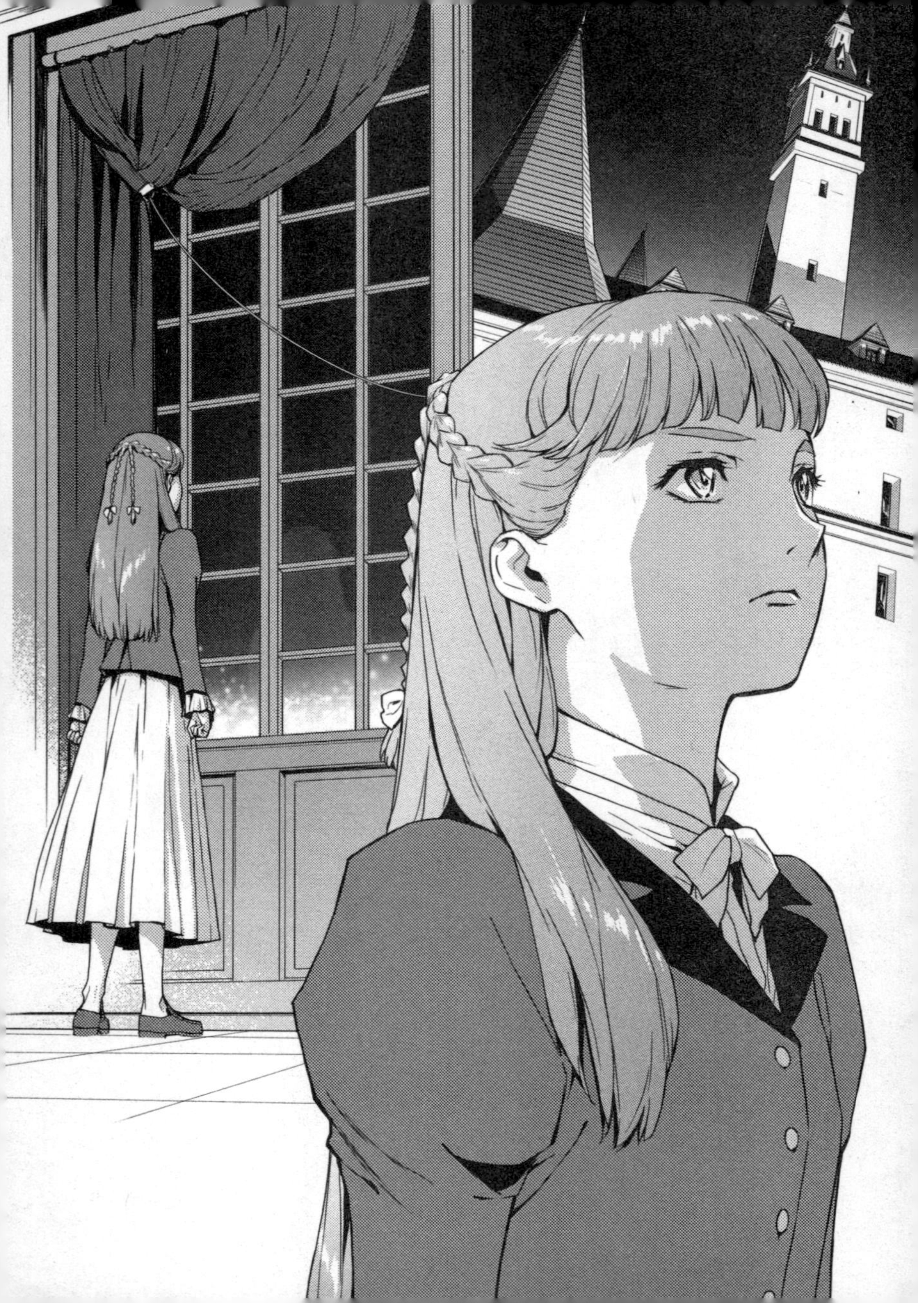

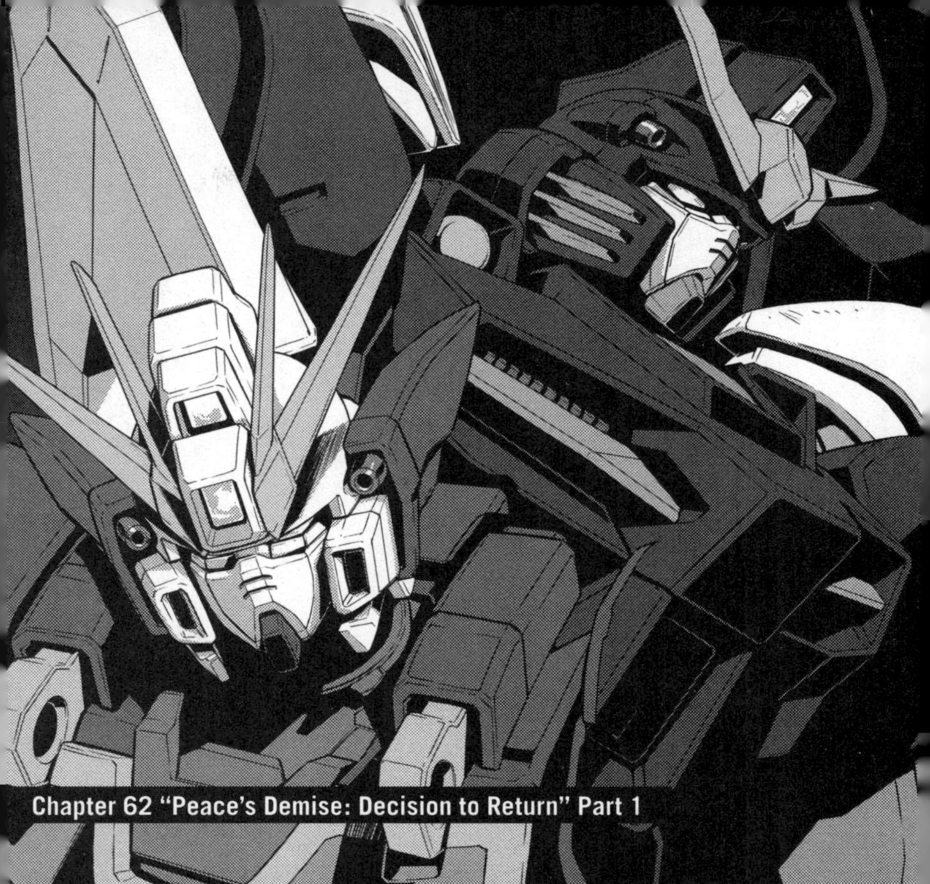

Chapter 62 "Peace's Demise: Decision to Return" Part 1

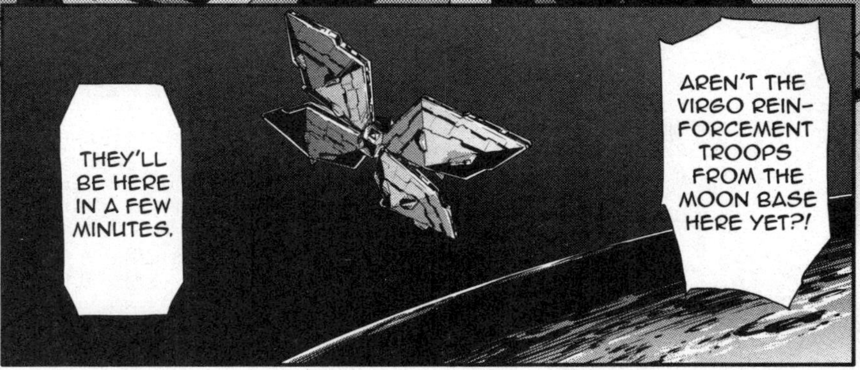
AREN'T THE VIRGO REIN-FORCEMENT TROOPS FROM THE MOON BASE HERE YET?!
THEY'LL BE HERE IN A FEW MINUTES.

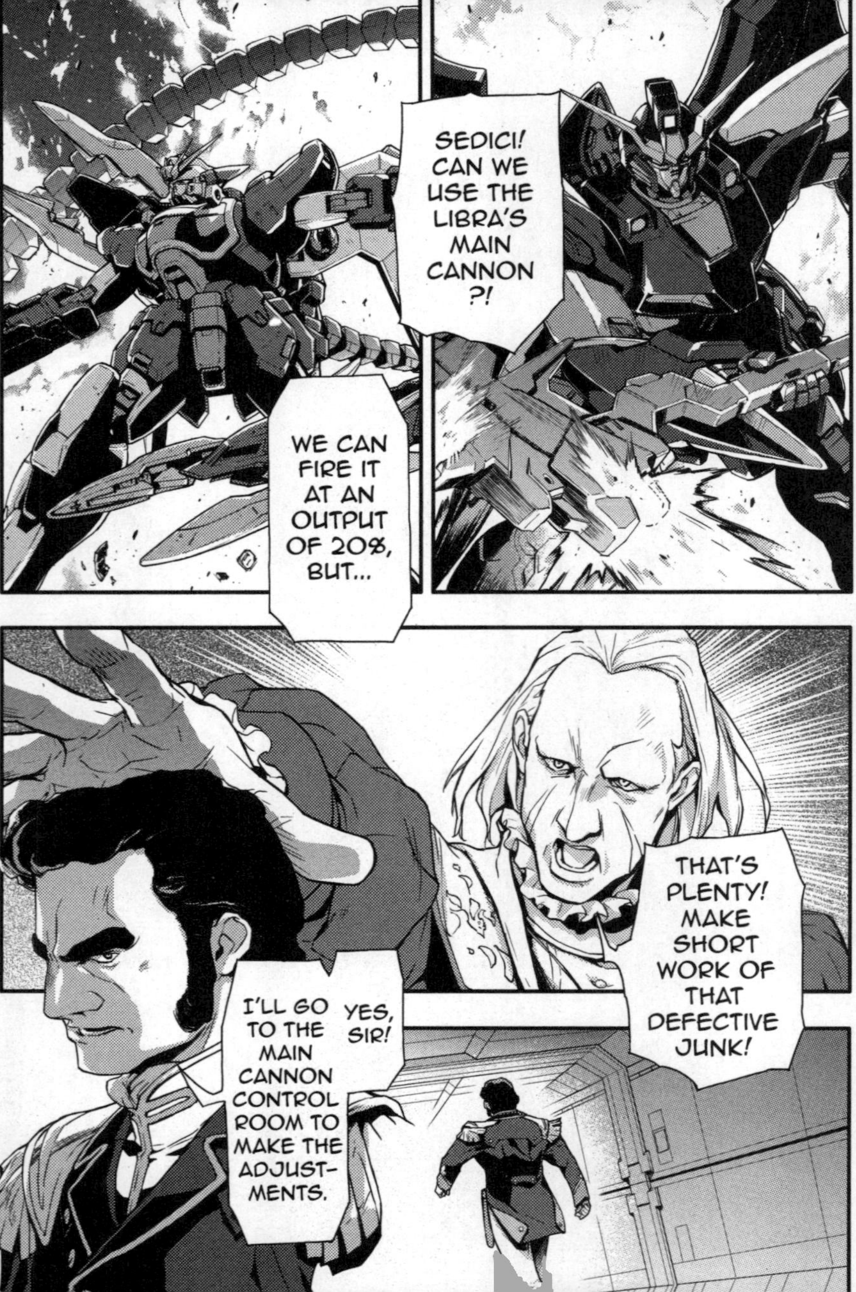
SEDICI! CAN WE USE THE LIBRA'S MAIN CANNON ?!
WE CAN FIRE IT AT AN OUTPUT OF 20%, BUT...
THAT'S PLENTY! MAKE SHORT WORK OF THAT DEFECTIVE JUNK!
YES, SIR!
I'LL GO TO THE MAIN CANNON CONTROL ROOM TO MAKE THE ADJUST-MENTS.

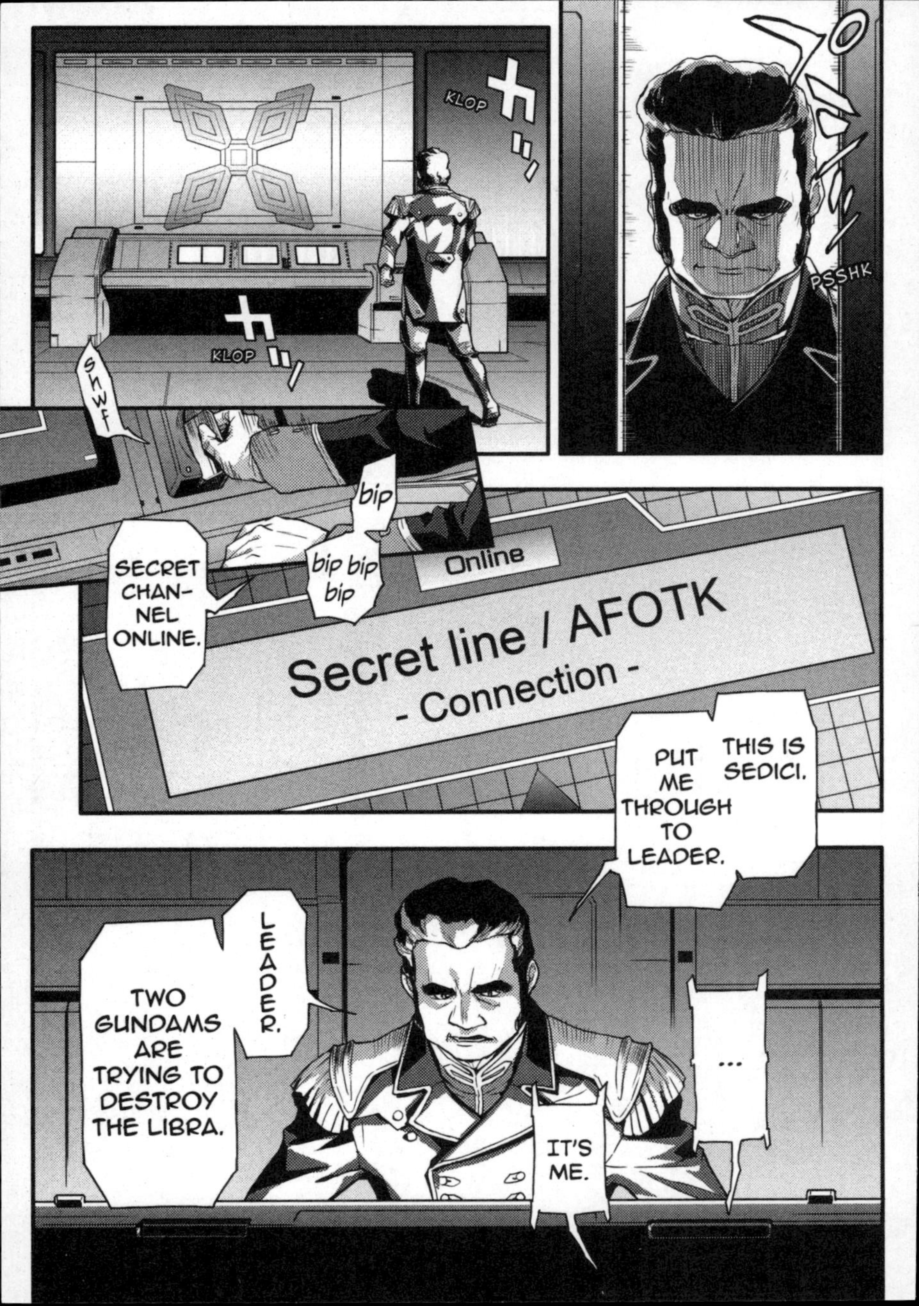
PSSHK
KLOP
KLOP
shwf
bip
bip bip bip
SECRET CHANNEL ONLINE.
Online
Secret line / AFOTK
- Connection -
THIS IS SEDICI.
PUT ME THROUGH TO LEADER.
...
IT'S ME.
LEADER.
TWO GUNDAMS ARE TRYING TO DESTROY THE LIBRA.

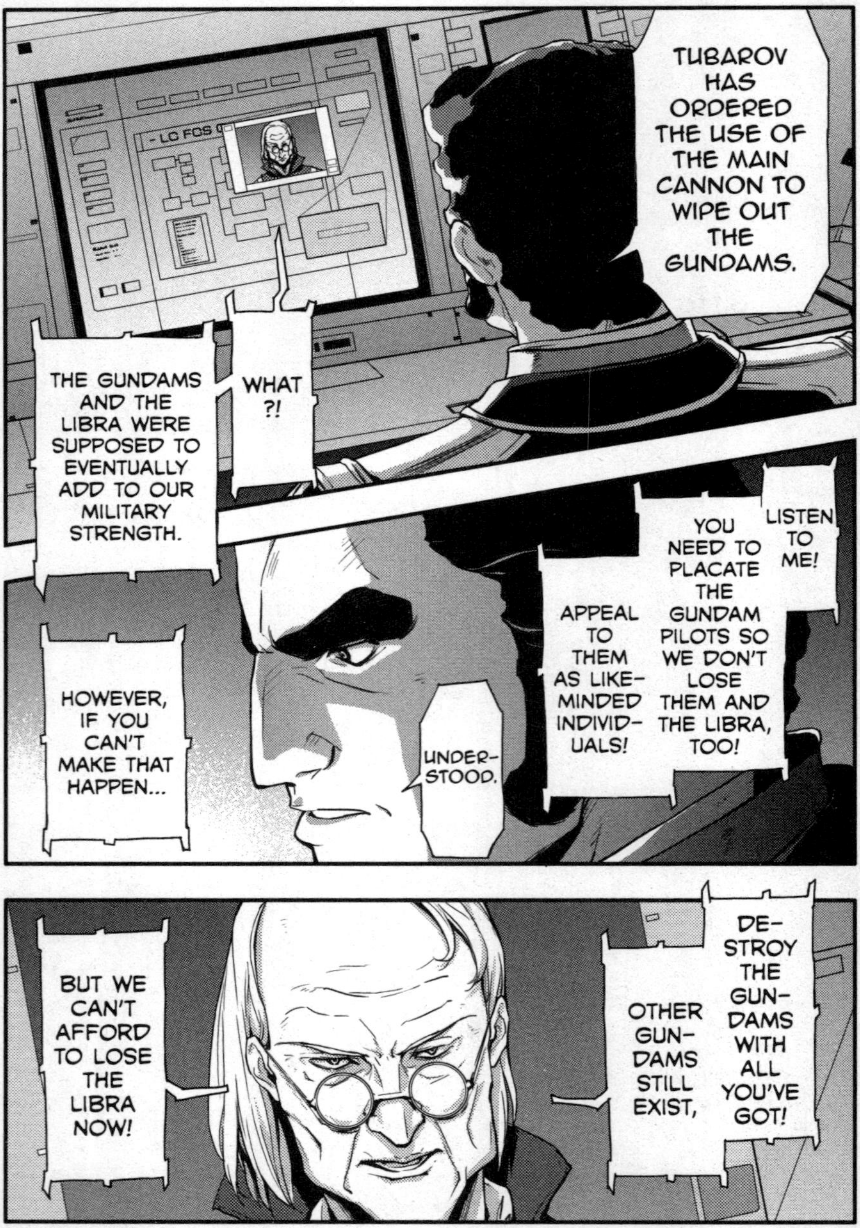
TUBAROV HAS ORDERED THE USE OF THE MAIN CANNON TO WIPE OUT THE GUNDAMS.
WHAT ?!
THE GUNDAMS AND THE LIBRA WERE SUPPOSED TO EVENTUALLY ADD TO OUR MILITARY STRENGTH.
LISTEN TO ME!
YOU NEED TO PLACATE THE GUNDAM PILOTS SO WE DON'T LOSE THEM AND THE LIBRA, TOO!
APPEAL TO THEM AS LIKE-MINDED INDIVID-UALS!
UNDER-STOOD.
HOWEVER, IF YOU CAN'T MAKE THAT HAPPEN...
DE-STROY THE GUN-DAMS WITH ALL YOU'VE GOT!
OTHER GUN-DAMS STILL EXIST,
BUT WE CAN'T AFFORD TO LOSE THE LIBRA NOW!

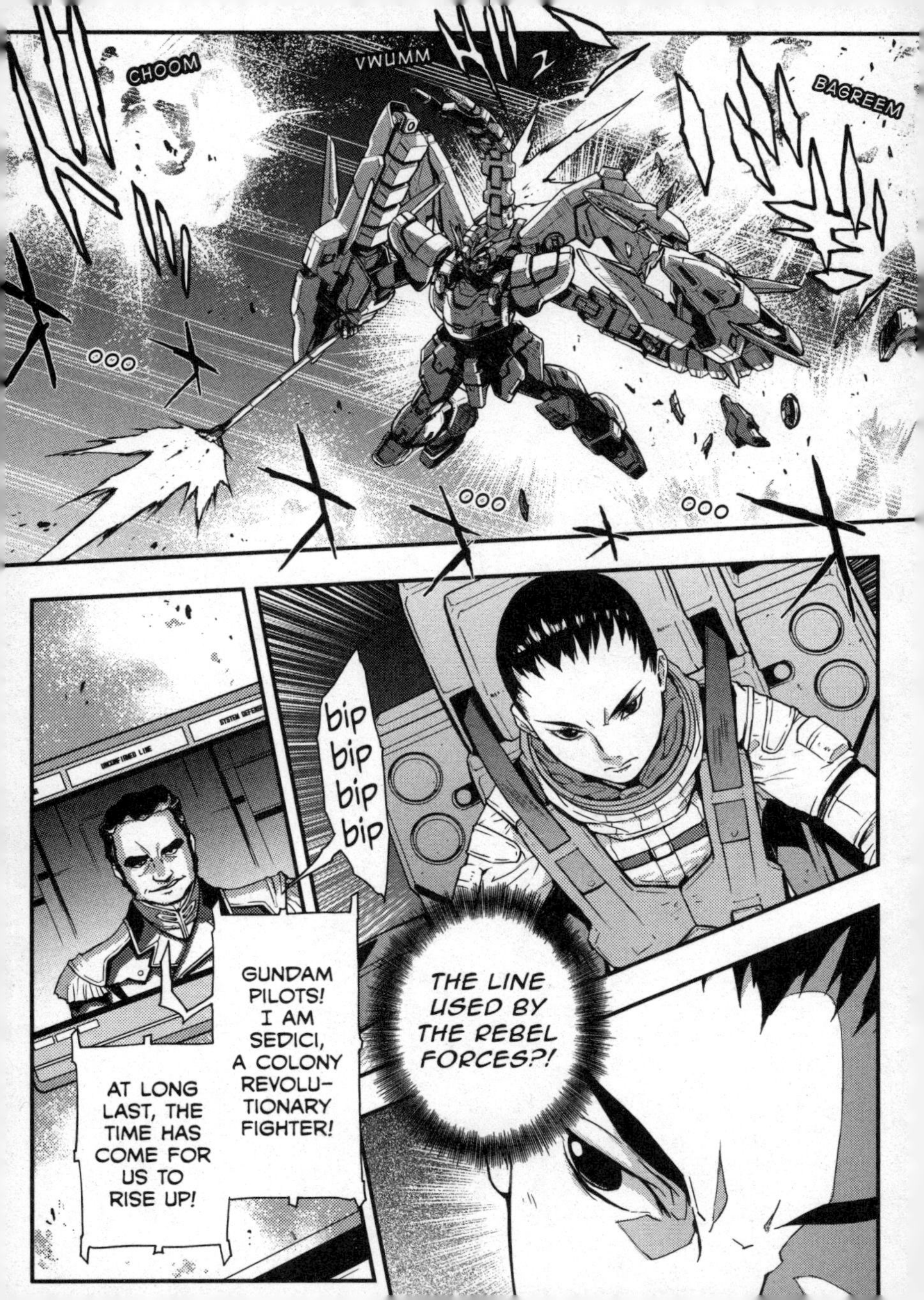
BAGREEM
VWUMM
CHOOM
THE LINE USED BY THE REBEL FORCES?!
bip bip bip bip
GUNDAM PILOTS! I AM SEDICI, A COLONY REVOLUTIONARY FIGHTER!
AT LONG LAST, THE TIME HAS COME FOR US TO RISE UP!

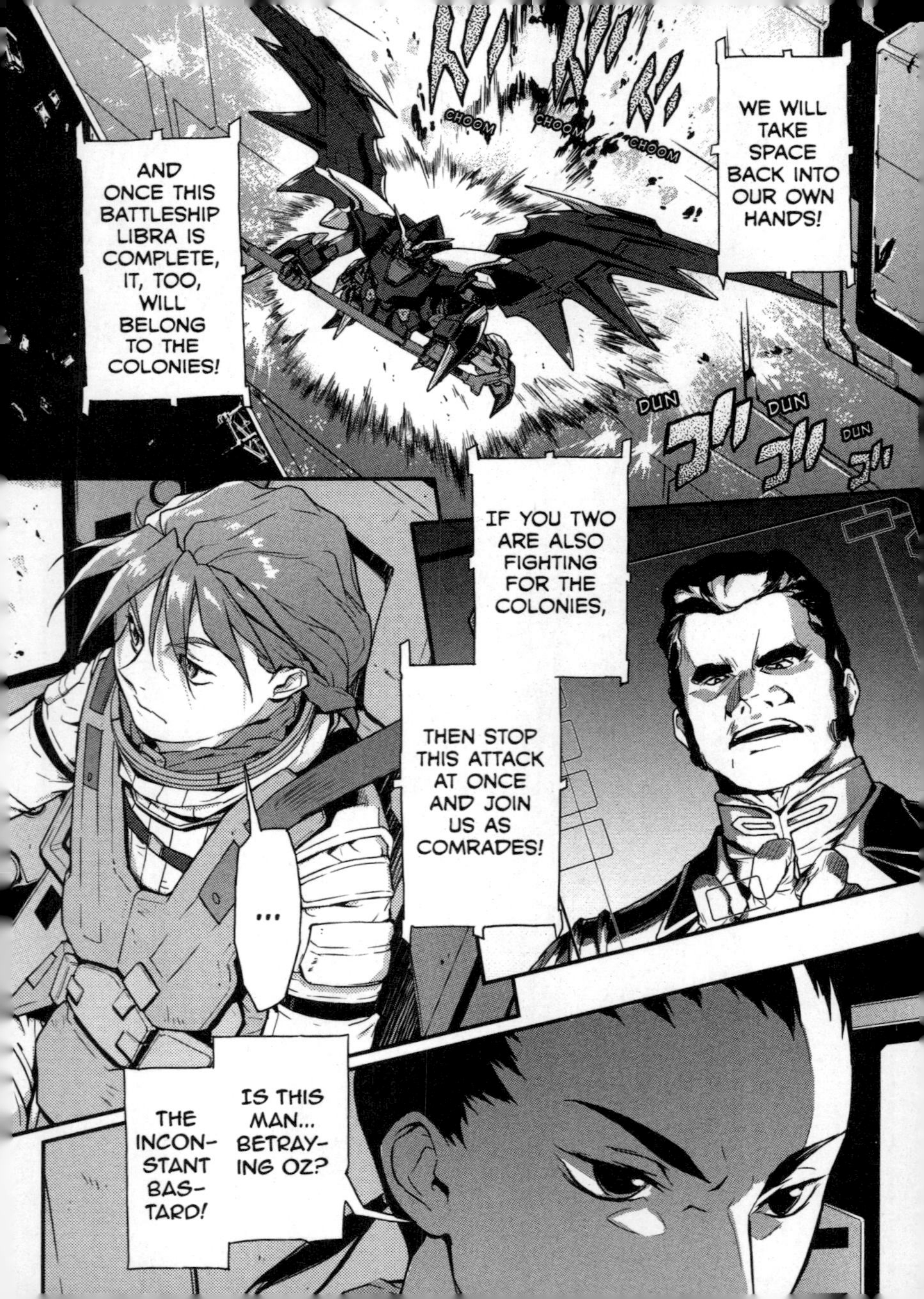
WE WILL TAKE SPACE BACK INTO OUR OWN HANDS!
CHOOM CHOOM CHOOM
AND ONCE THIS BATTLESHIP LIBRA IS COMPLETE, IT, TOO, WILL BELONG TO THE COLONIES!
DUN DUN DUN
IF YOU TWO ARE ALSO FIGHTING FOR THE COLONIES,
THEN STOP THIS ATTACK AT ONCE AND JOIN US AS COMRADES!
...
IS THIS MAN... BETRAYING OZ?
THE INCONSTANT BASTARD!

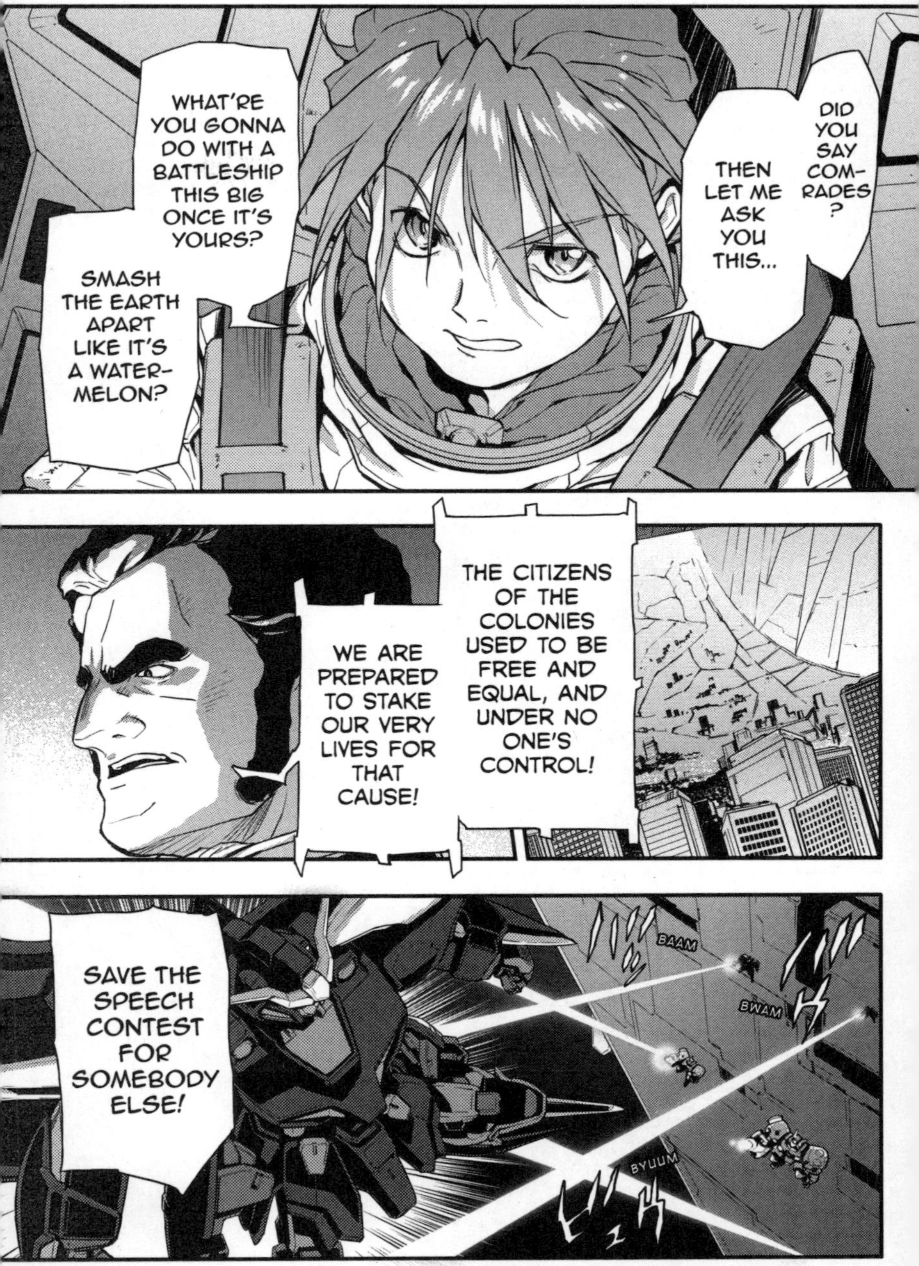
DID YOU SAY COM-RADES?
THEN LET ME ASK YOU THIS...
WHAT'RE YOU GONNA DO WITH A BATTLESHIP THIS BIG ONCE IT'S YOURS?
SMASH THE EARTH APART LIKE IT'S A WATER-MELON?
THE CITIZENS OF THE COLONIES USED TO BE FREE AND EQUAL, AND UNDER NO ONE'S CONTROL!
WE ARE PREPARED TO STAKE OUR VERY LIVES FOR THAT CAUSE!
BAAM
BWAM
SAVE THE SPEECH CONTEST FOR SOMEBODY ELSE!
BYUUM

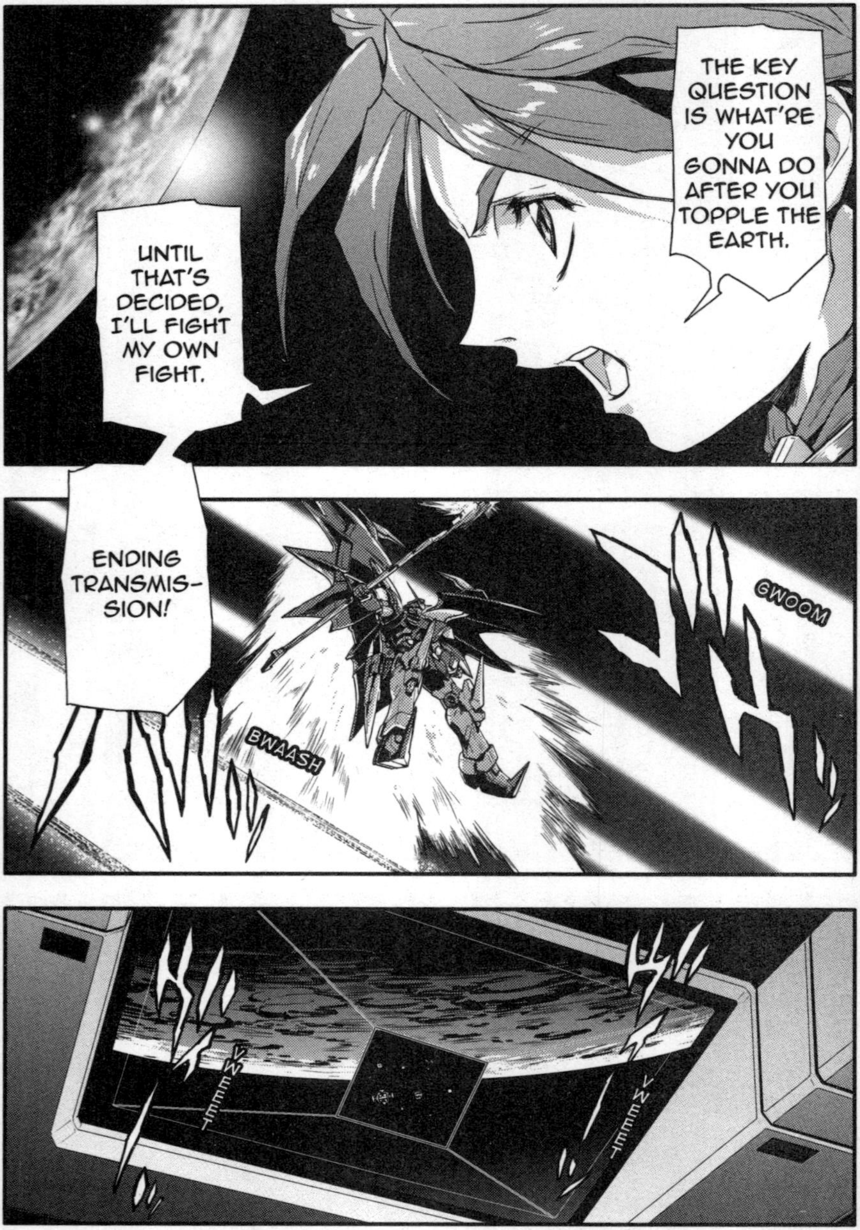
THE KEY QUESTION IS WHAT'RE YOU GONNA DO AFTER YOU TOPPLE THE EARTH.
UNTIL THAT'S DECIDED, I'LL FIGHT MY OWN FIGHT.
ENDING TRANSMIS-SION!
GWOOM
BWAASH
VWEEET
VWEEET

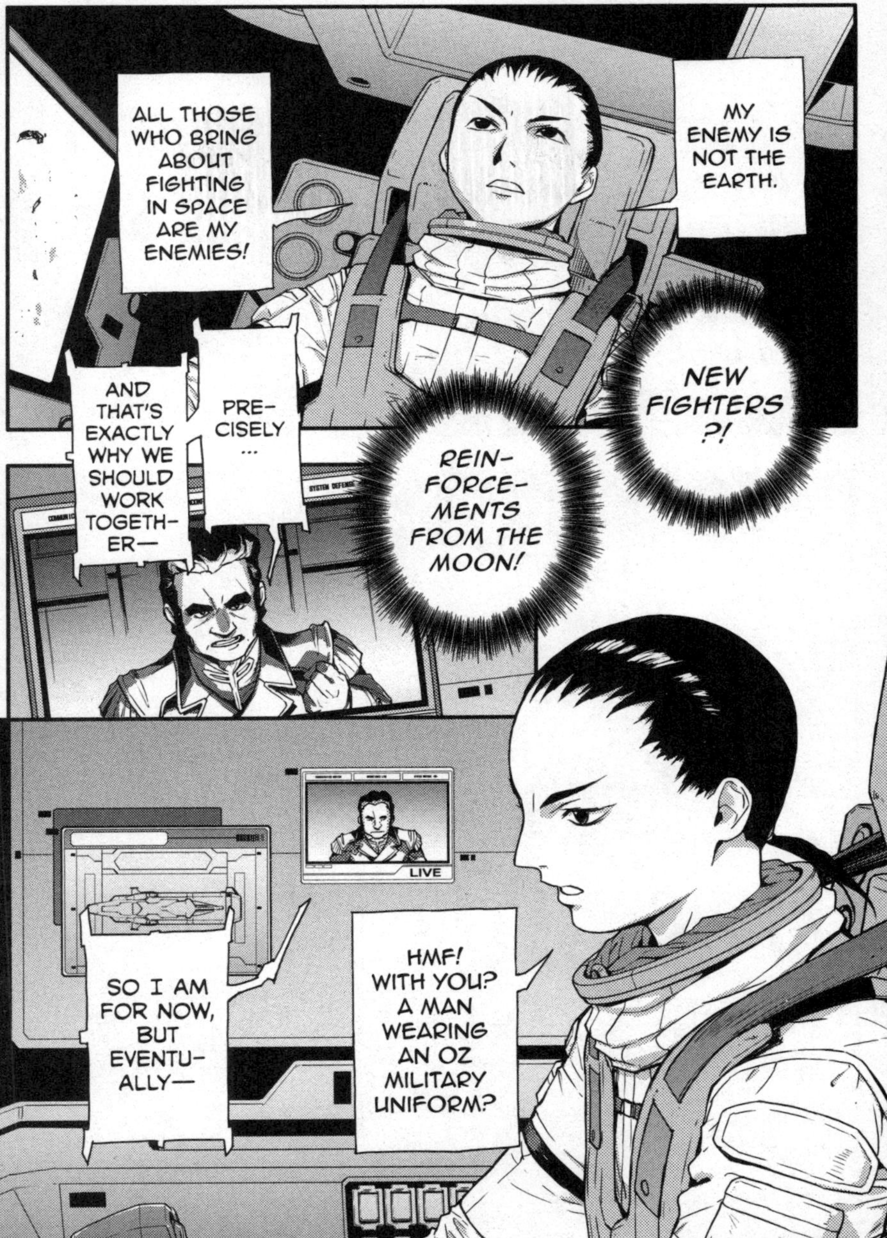
MY ENEMY IS NOT THE EARTH.
ALL THOSE WHO BRING ABOUT FIGHTING IN SPACE ARE MY ENEMIES!
NEW FIGHTERS?!
REIN-FORCE-MENTS FROM THE MOON!
PRE-CISELY...
AND THAT'S EXACTLY WHY WE SHOULD WORK TOGETH-ER—
LIVE
HMF! WITH YOU? A MAN WEARING AN OZ MILITARY UNIFORM?
SO I AM FOR NOW, BUT EVENTU-ALLY—

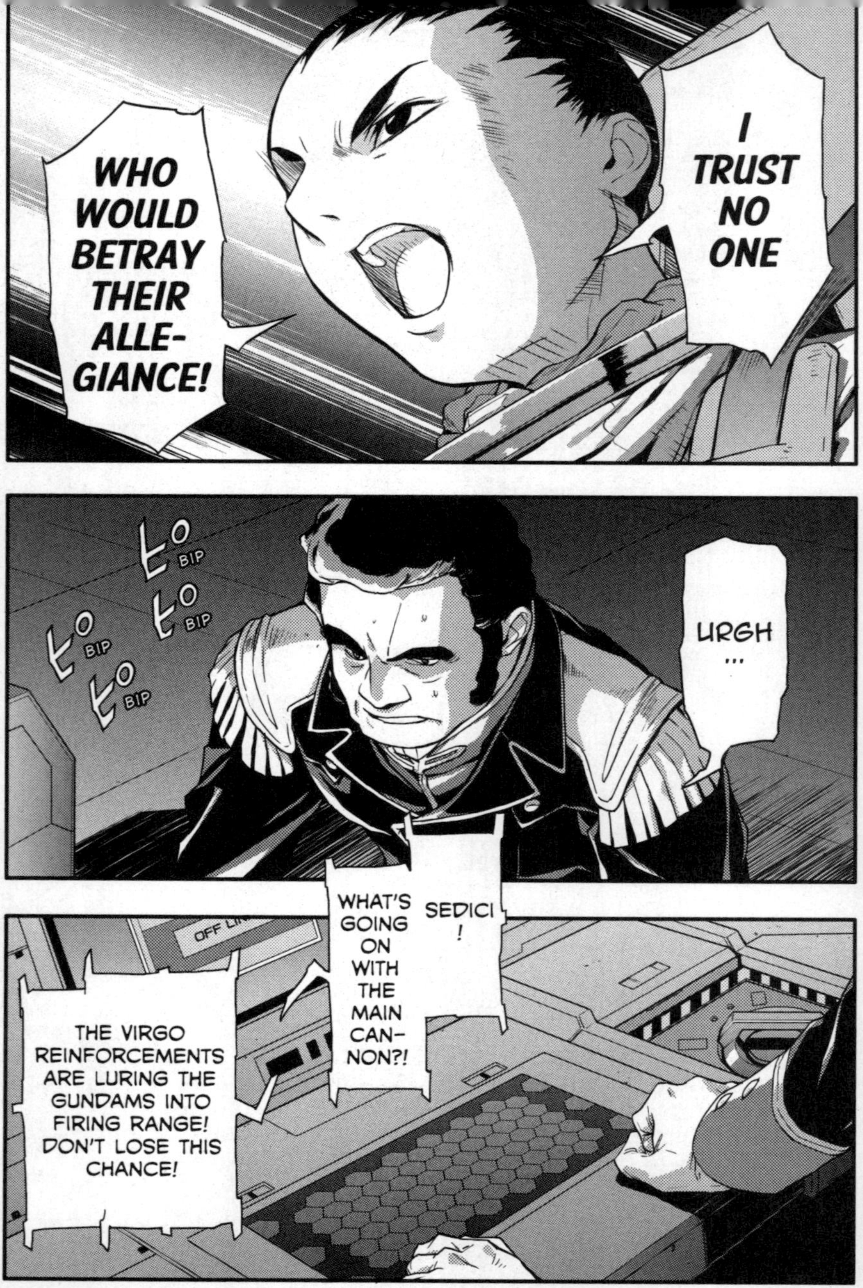
I TRUST NO ONE
WHO WOULD BETRAY THEIR ALLE-GIANCE!
URGH ...
ピ BIP
ピ BIP
ピ BIP
ピ BIP
SEDICI!
WHAT'S GOING ON WITH THE MAIN CAN-NON?!
THE VIRGO REINFORCEMENTS ARE LURING THE GUNDAMS INTO FIRING RANGE! DON'T LOSE THIS CHANCE!

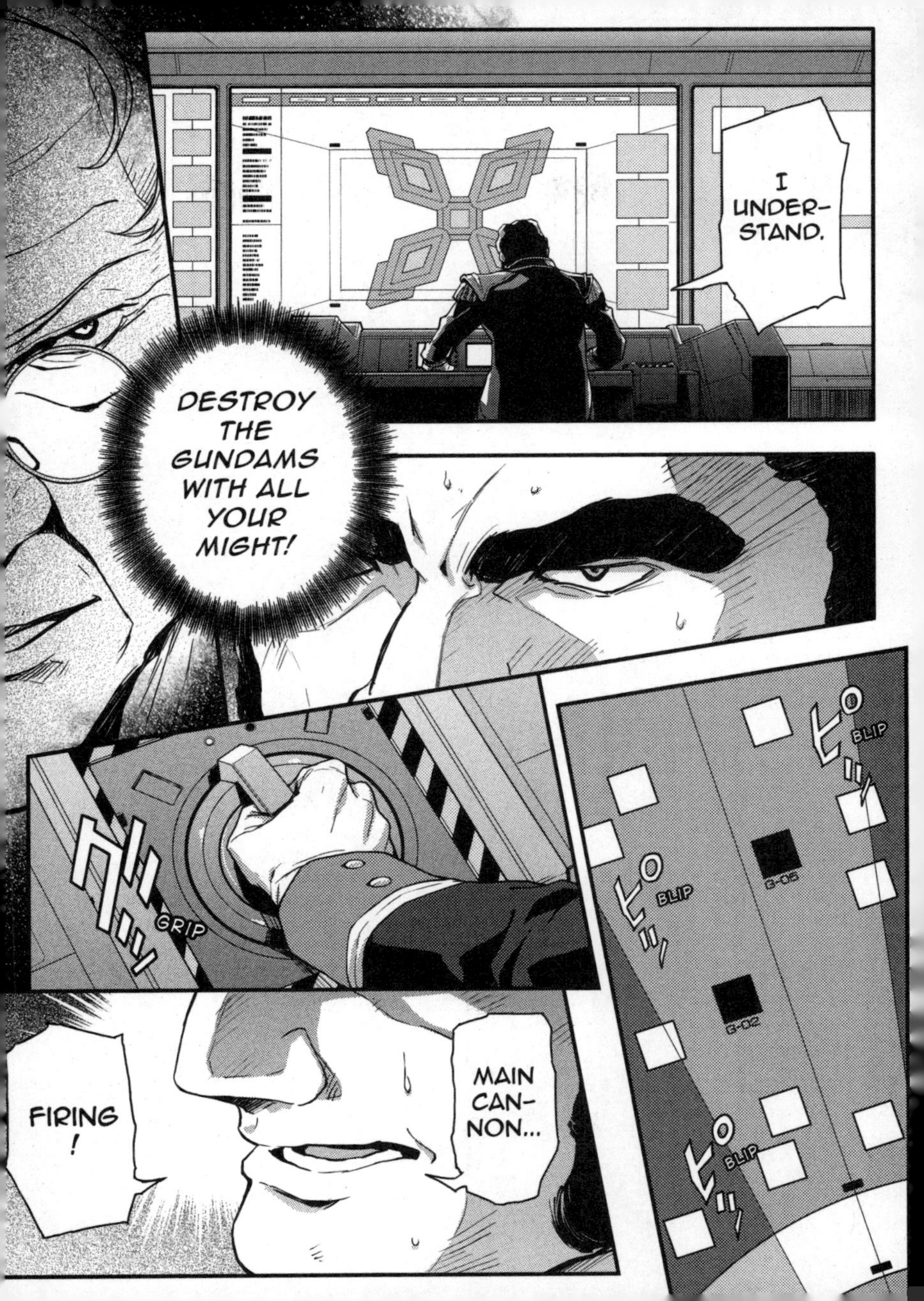

I UNDERSTAND.
DESTROY THE GUNDAMS WITH ALL YOUR MIGHT!
BLIP
G-05
BLIP
G-02
BLIP
GRIP
MAIN CANNON...
FIRING!

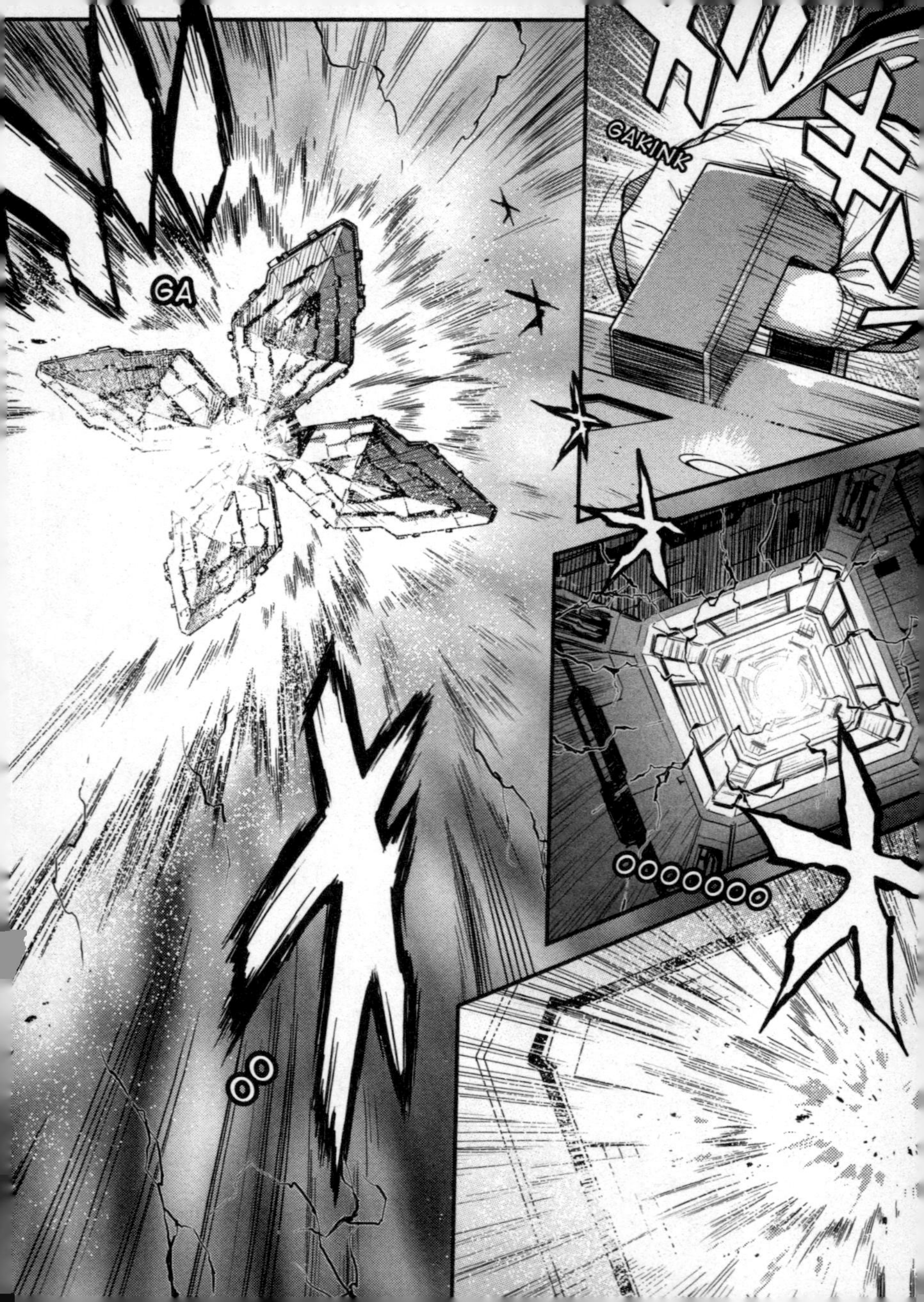
GAKINK
GA
OOOOOOOO
OO

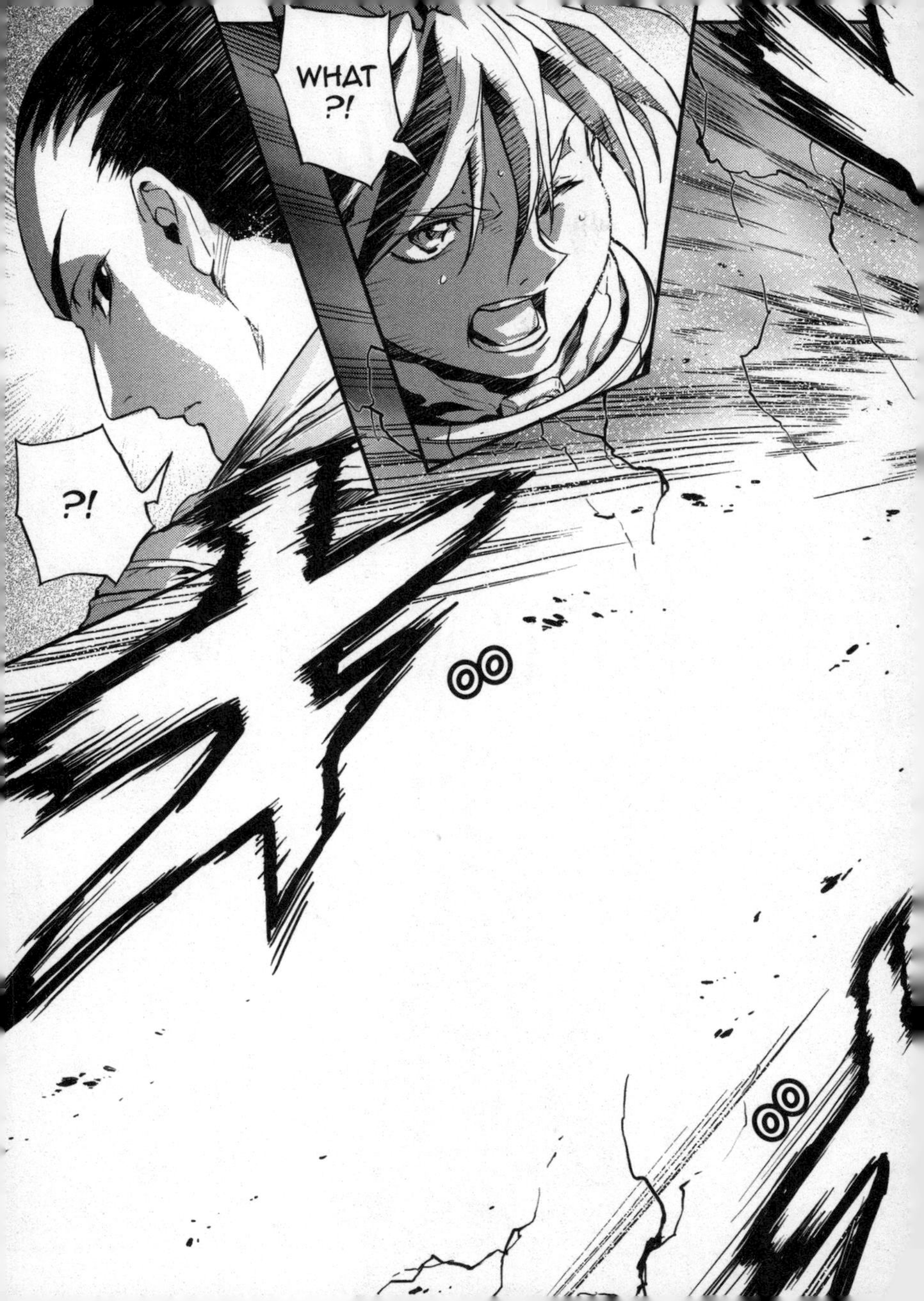
WHAT ?!
?!

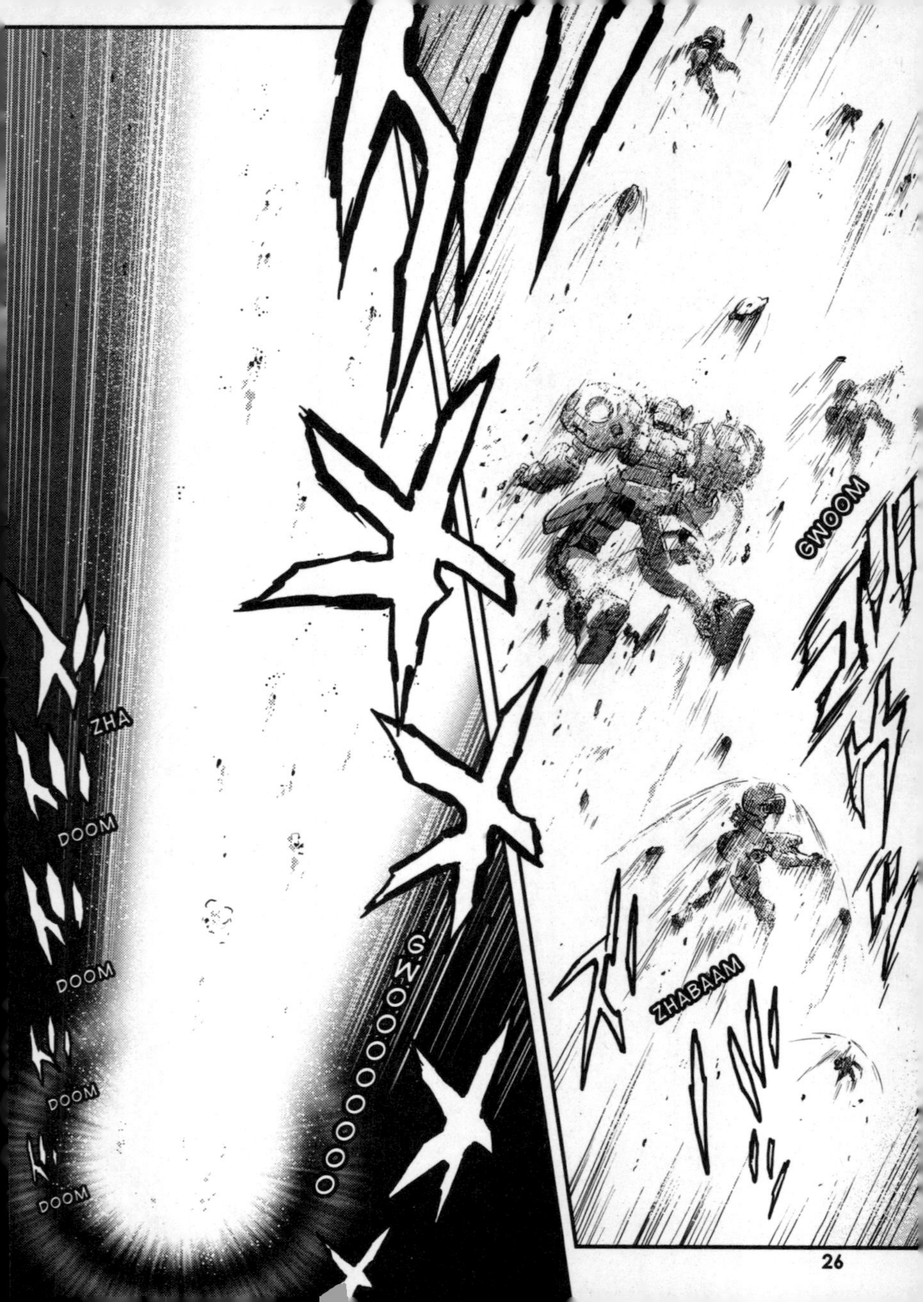
GWOOM
ZHABAAM
GWOOOOOOOOOO
ZHA
DOOM
DOOM
DOOM
DOOM

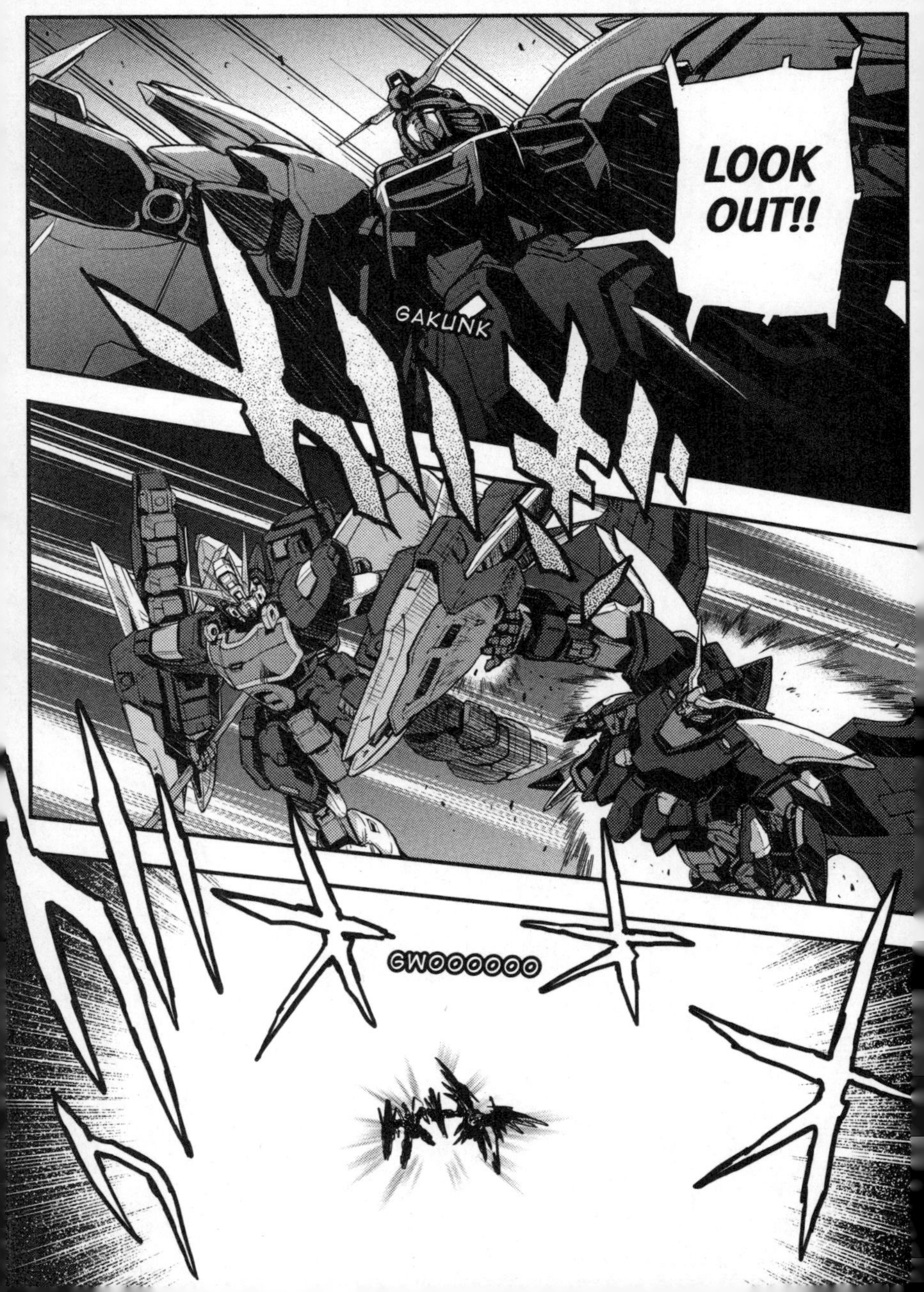
LOOK OUT!!
GAKUNK
GWOOOOOO

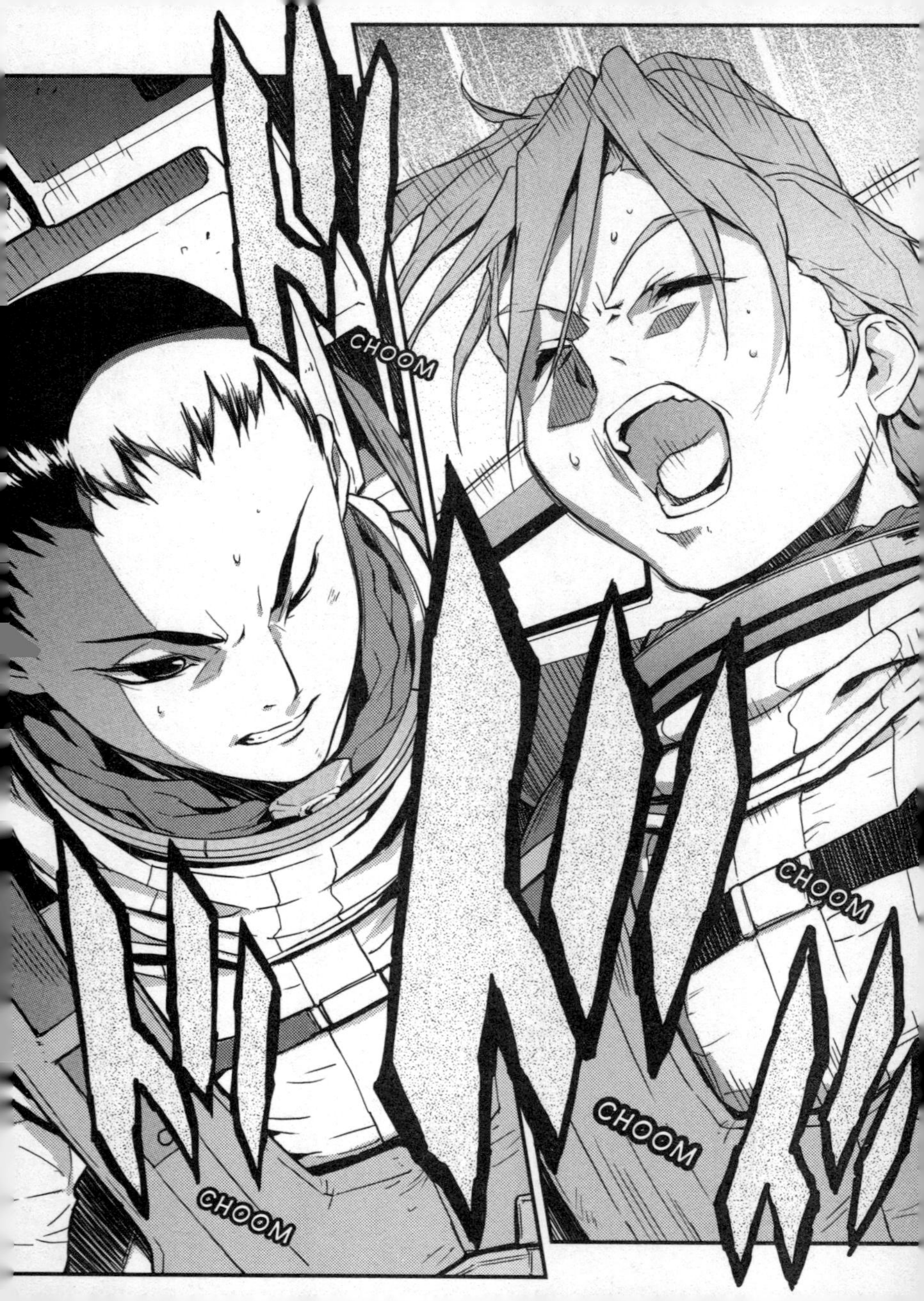
CHOOM
CHOOM
CHOOM
CHOOM

Chapter 63 "Peace's Demise: Decision to Return" Part 2

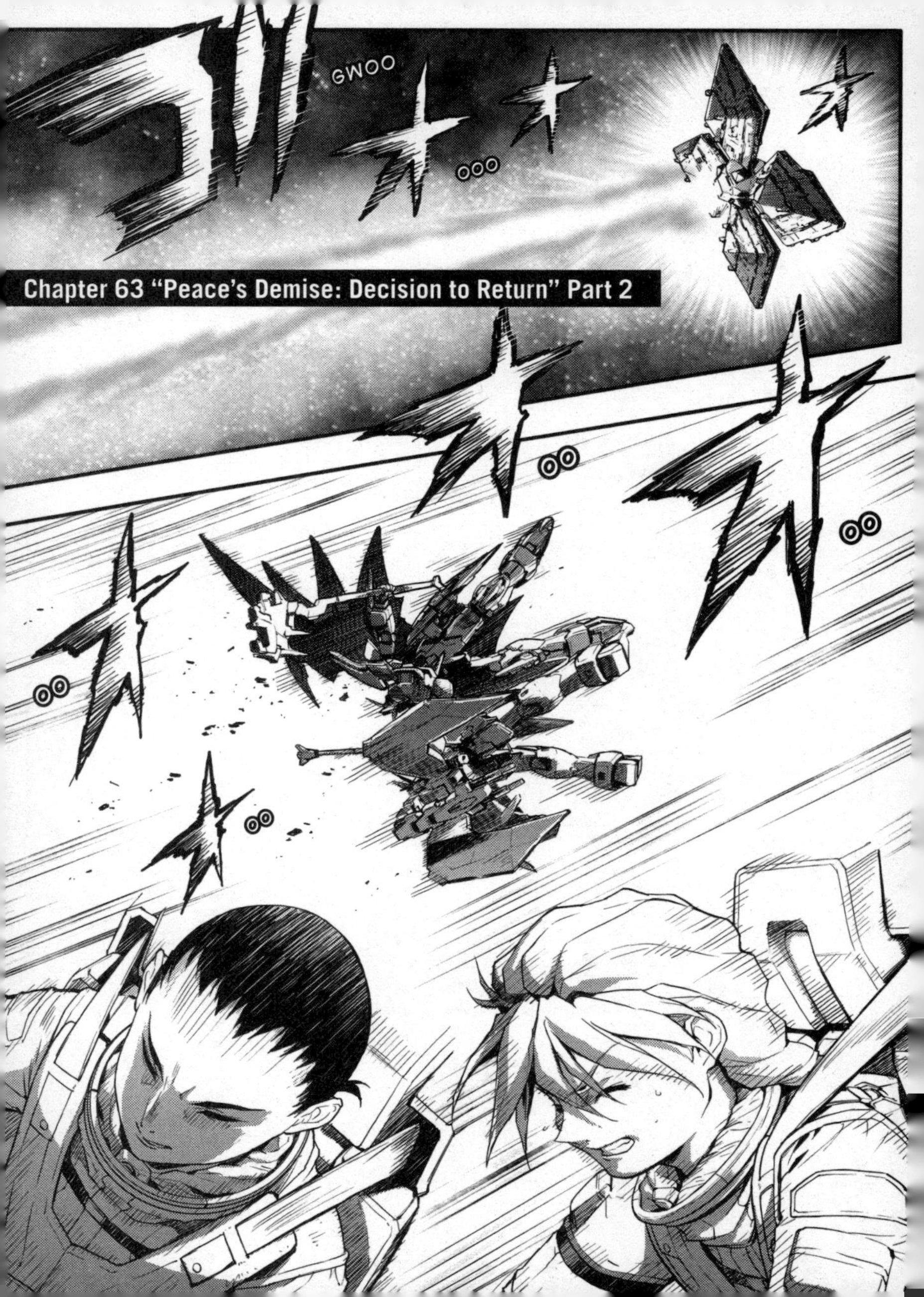
GWOO
OOO
OO
OO
OO
OO

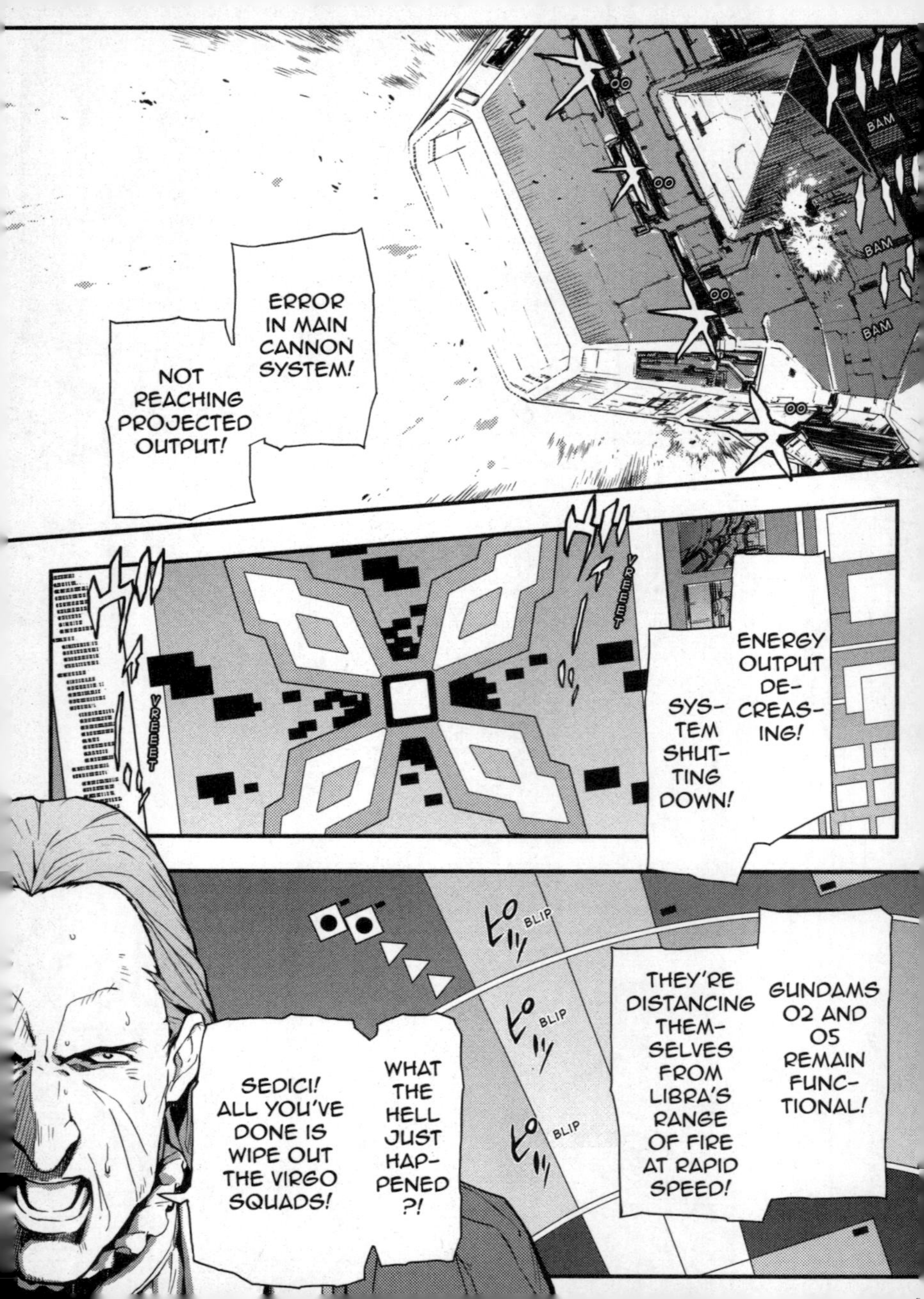
BAM
BAM
BAM
ERROR IN MAIN CANNON SYSTEM!
NOT REACHING PROJECTED OUTPUT!
VREEET
ENERGY OUTPUT DE-CREASING!
SYS-TEM SHUT-TING DOWN!
VREEET
BLIP
BLIP
BLIP
GUNDAMS 02 AND 05 REMAIN FUNC-TIONAL!
THEY'RE DISTANCING THEM-SELVES FROM LIBRA'S RANGE OF FIRE AT RAPID SPEED!
WHAT THE HELL JUST HAP-PENED ?!
SEDICI! ALL YOU'VE DONE IS WIPE OUT THE VIRGO SQUADS!

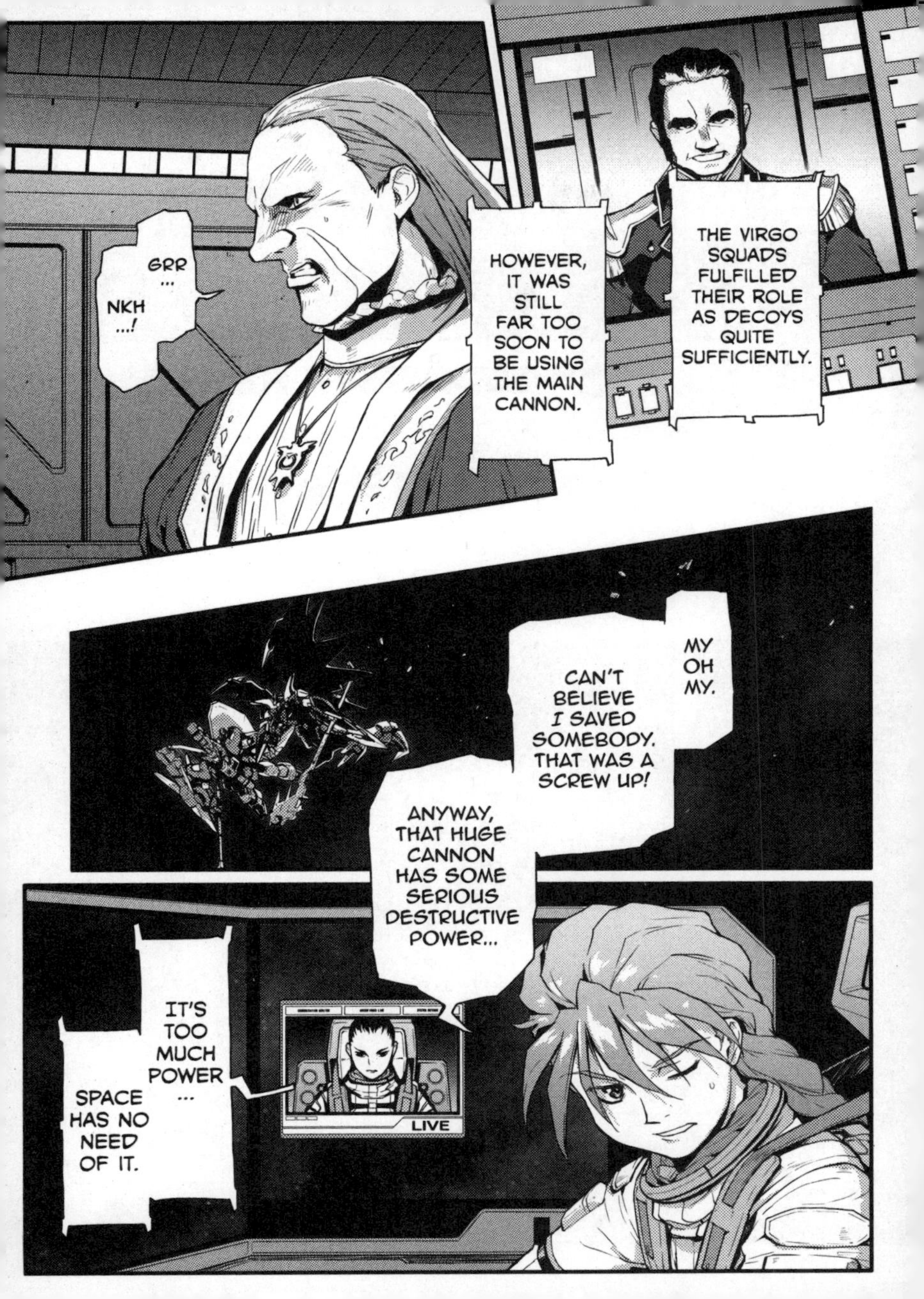
THE VIRGO SQUADS FULFILLED THEIR ROLE AS DECOYS QUITE SUFFICIENTLY.
HOWEVER, IT WAS STILL FAR TOO SOON TO BE USING THE MAIN CANNON.
GRR ...
NKH ...!
MY OH MY.
CAN'T BELIEVE I SAVED SOMEBODY. THAT WAS A SCREW UP!
ANYWAY, THAT HUGE CANNON HAS SOME SERIOUS DESTRUCTIVE POWER...
LIVE
IT'S TOO MUCH POWER ...
SPACE HAS NO NEED OF IT.

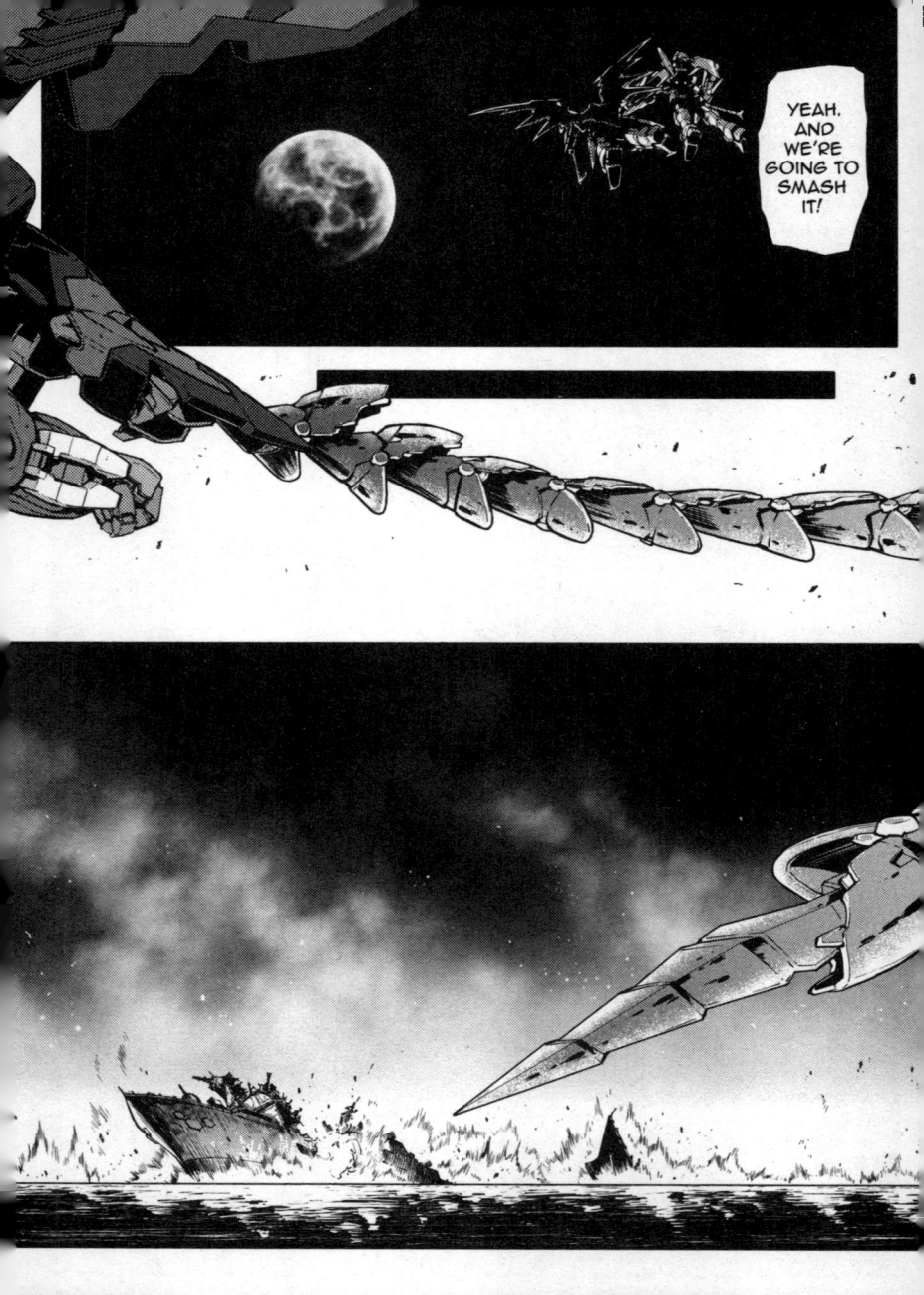

YEAH, AND WE'RE GOING TO SMASH IT!

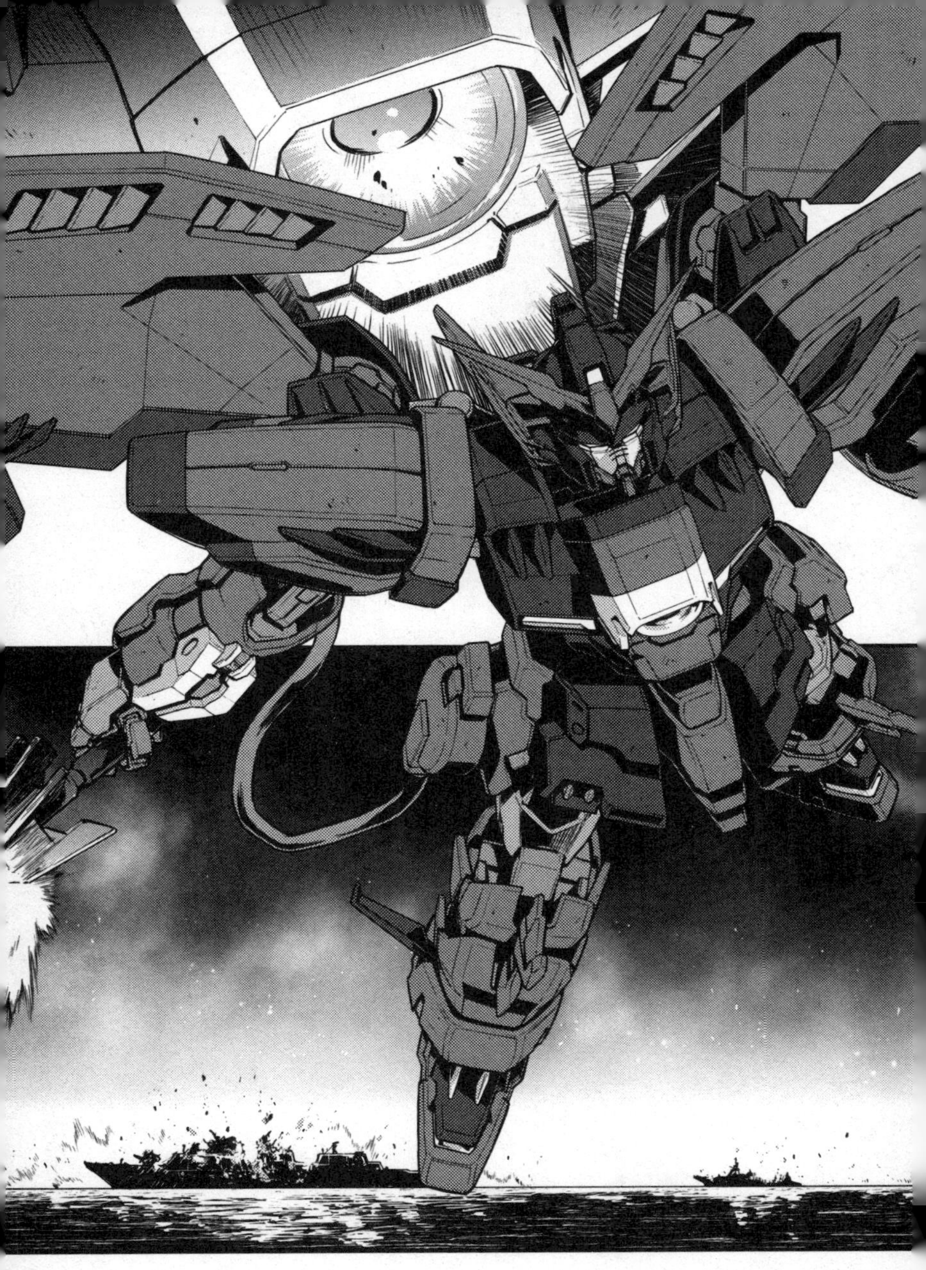

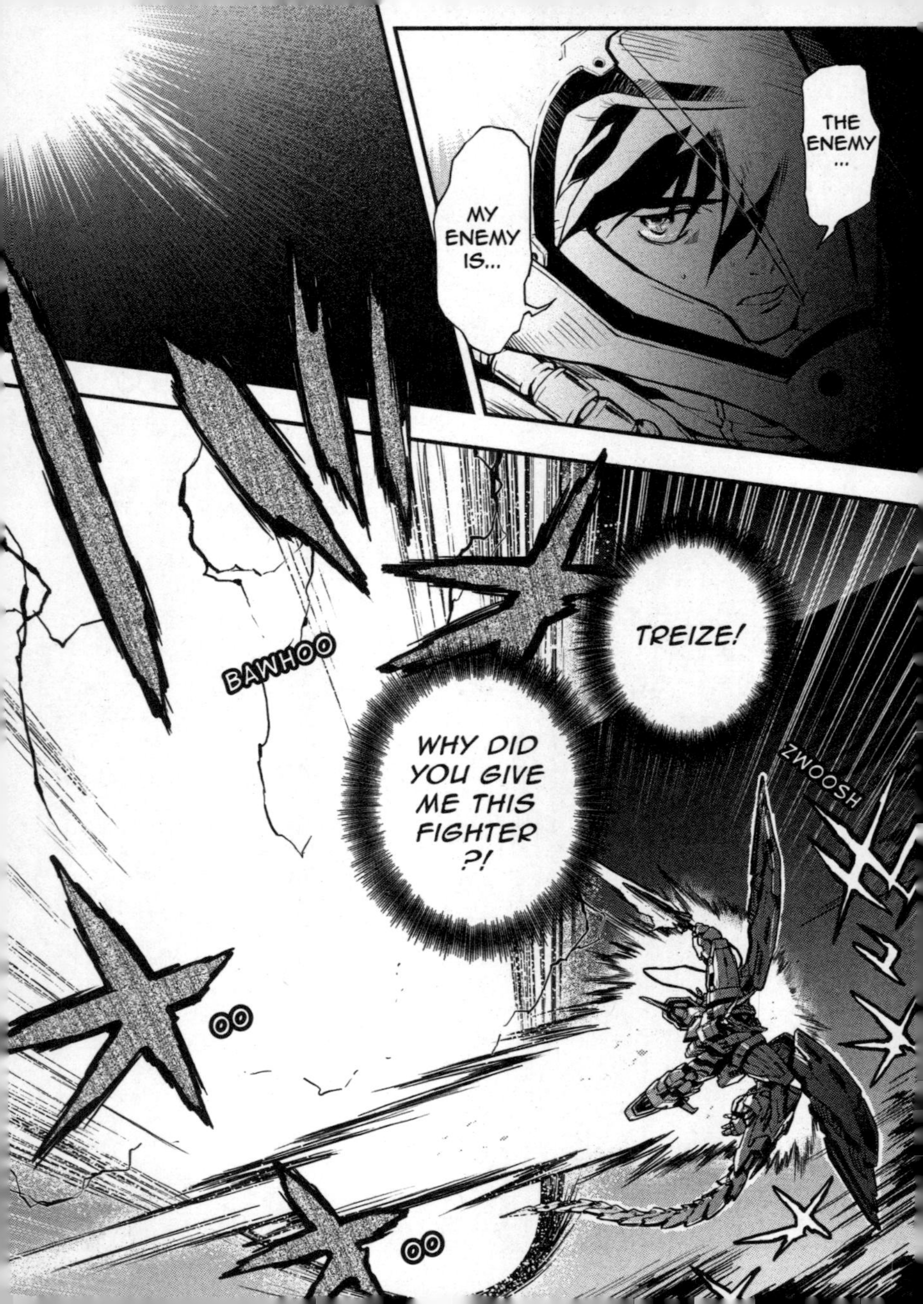
THE ENEMY ...
MY ENEMY IS...
TREIZE!
WHY DID YOU GIVE ME THIS FIGHTER ?!
ZWOOSH
BAWHOO
OO
OO

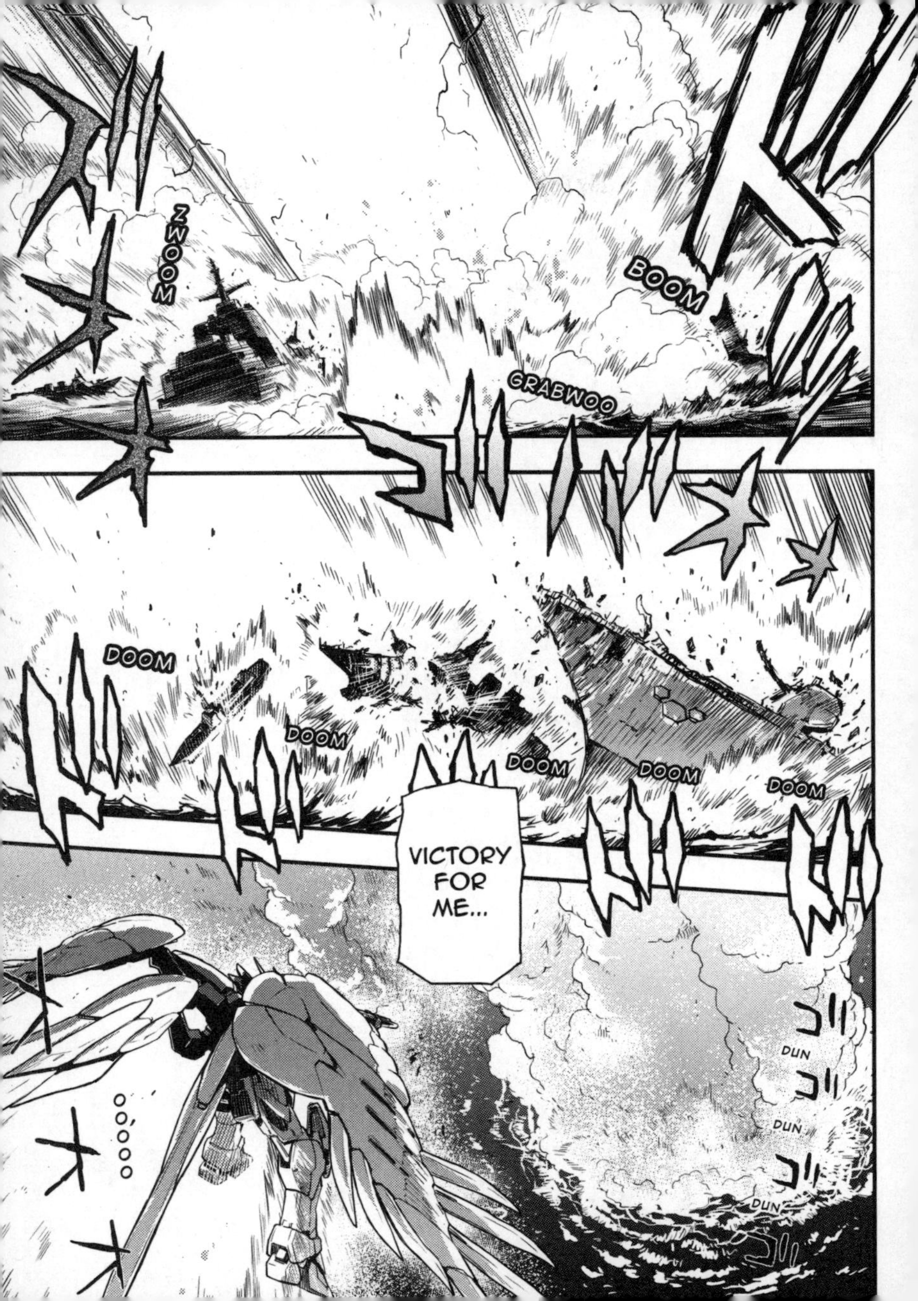
BOOM
GRABWOO
ZWOOM
DOOM
DOOM
DOOM
DOOM
DOOM
VICTORY FOR ME...
DUN
DUN
DUN
OO'OOO

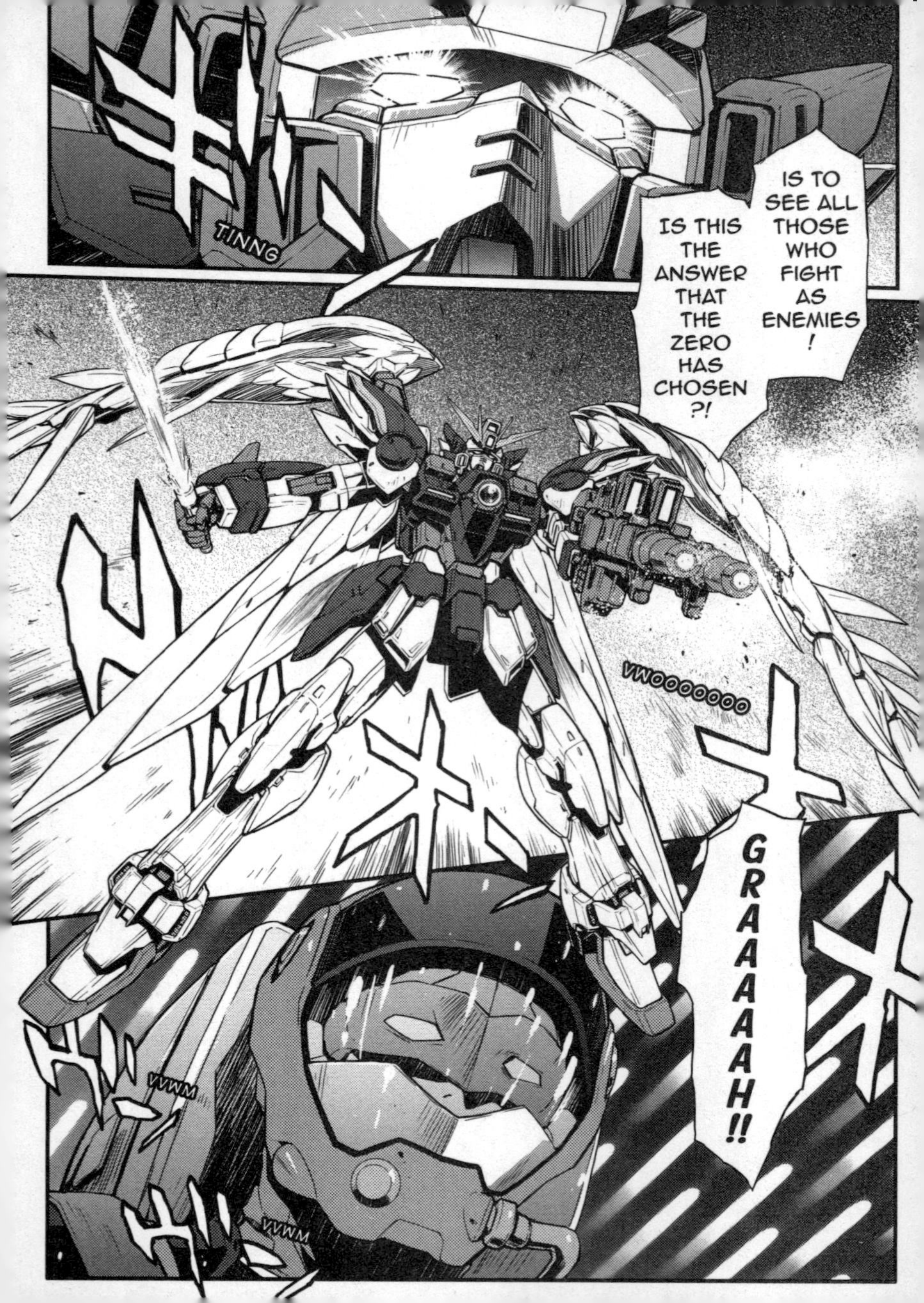
TINNG
IS THIS THE ANSWER THAT THE ZERO HAS CHOSEN ?!
IS TO SEE ALL THOSE WHO FIGHT AS ENEMIES !
VWOOOOOOOO
GRAAAAAAH!!
VVWM
VVWM

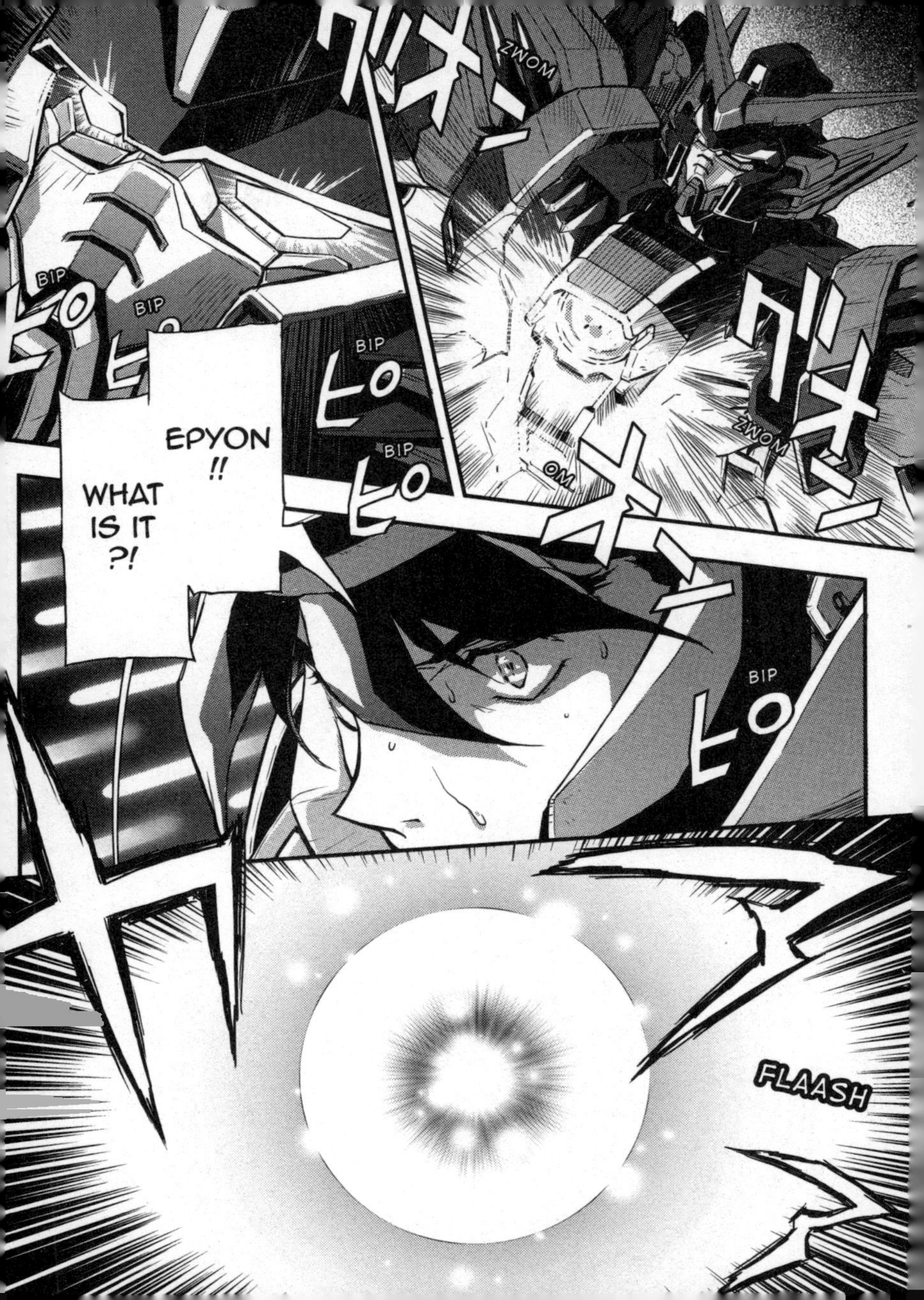
ZWOM
ZWOM
OM
BIP
BIP
BIP
BIP
EPYON !!
WHAT IS IT ?!
BIP
FLAASH

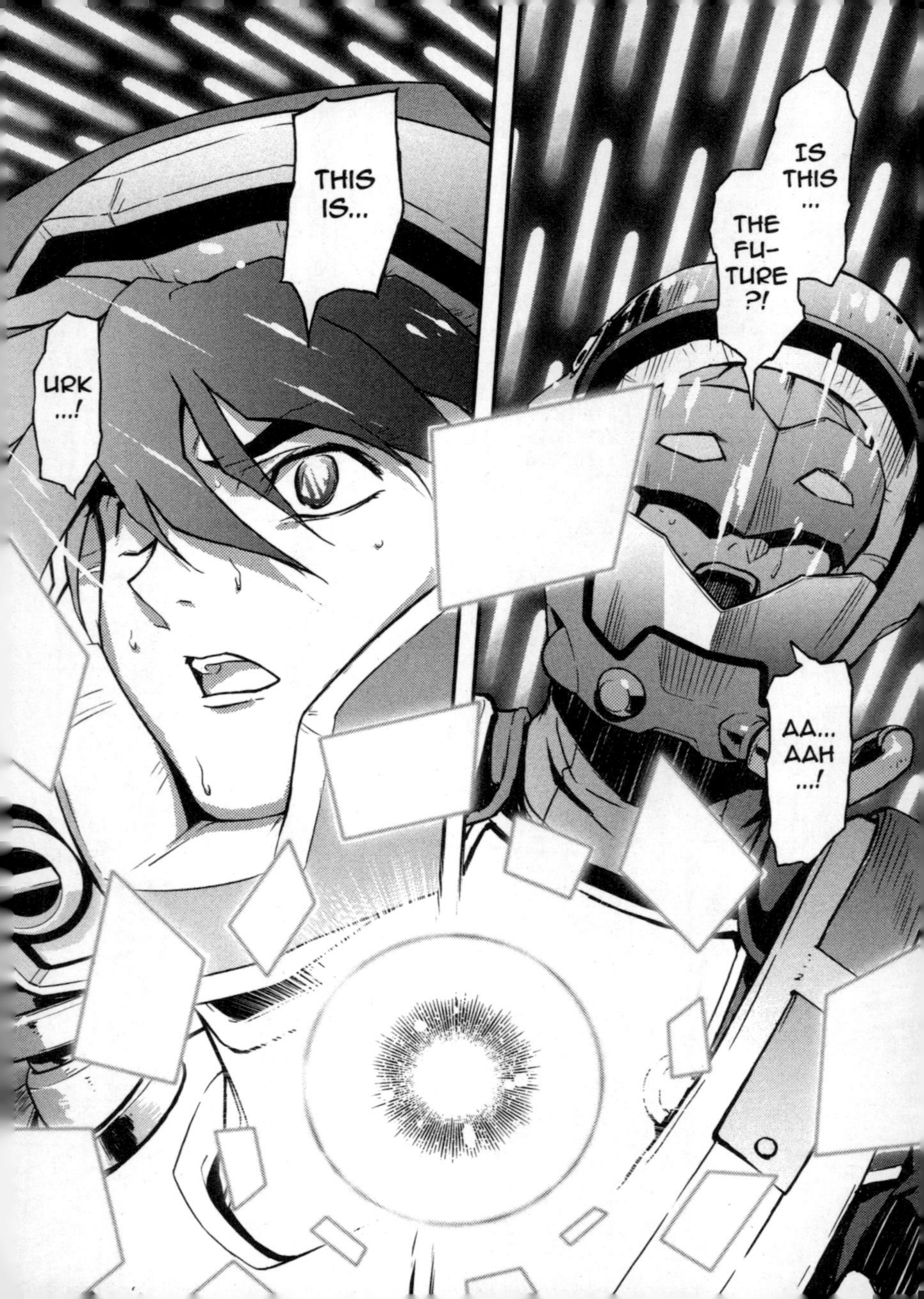
IS THIS ...
THE FU- TURE ?!
AA... AAH ...!
THIS IS...
URK ...!

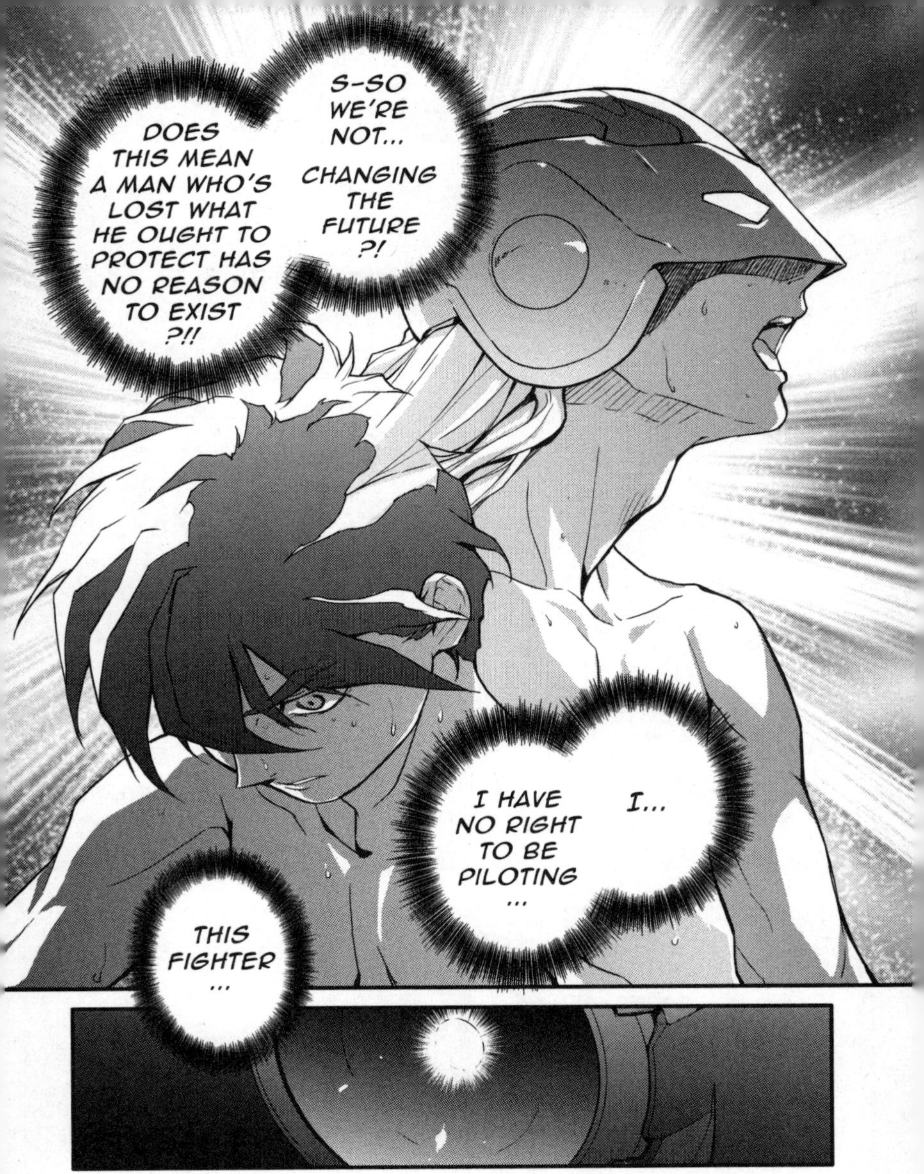
S-SO WE'RE NOT... CHANGING THE FUTURE ?!
DOES THIS MEAN A MAN WHO'S LOST WHAT HE OUGHT TO PROTECT HAS NO REASON TO EXIST ?!!
I...
I HAVE NO RIGHT TO BE PILOTING ...
THIS FIGHTER ...

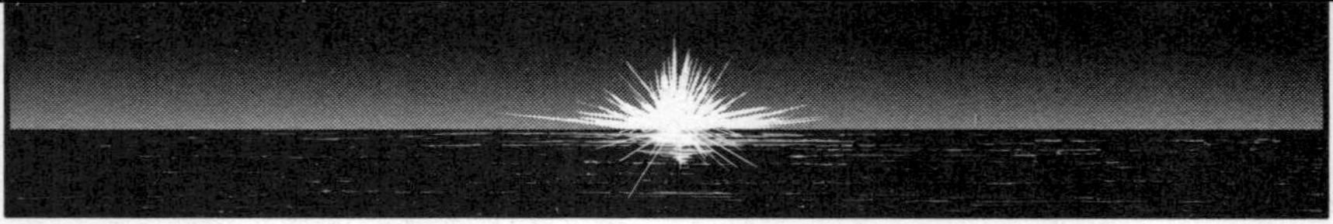
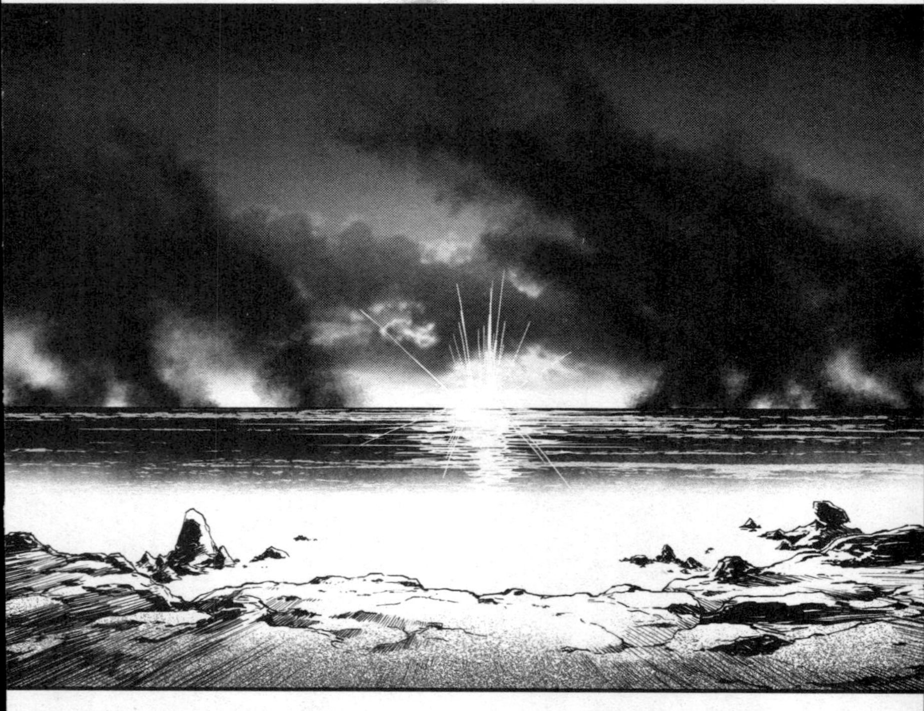
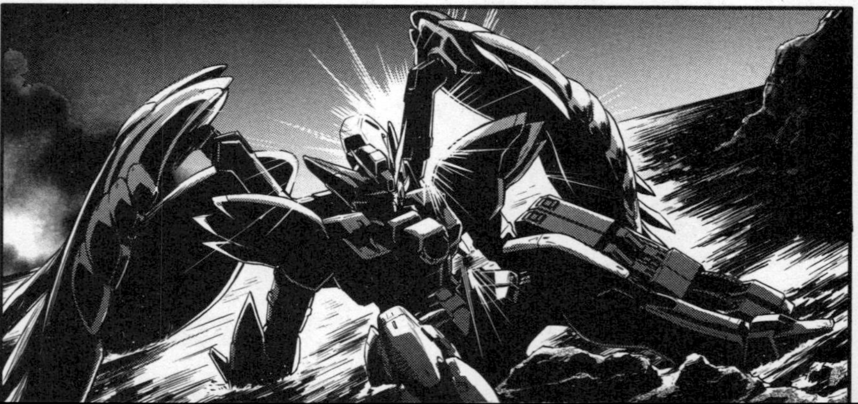

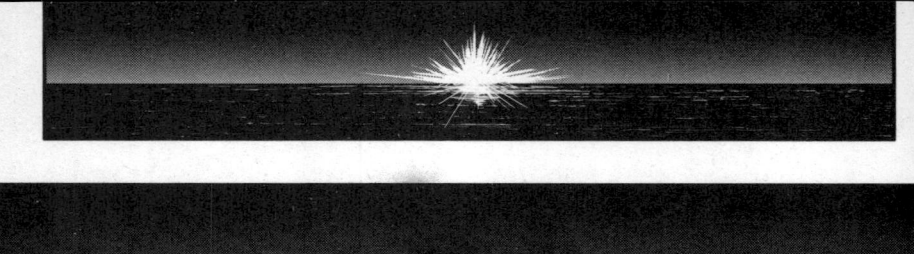

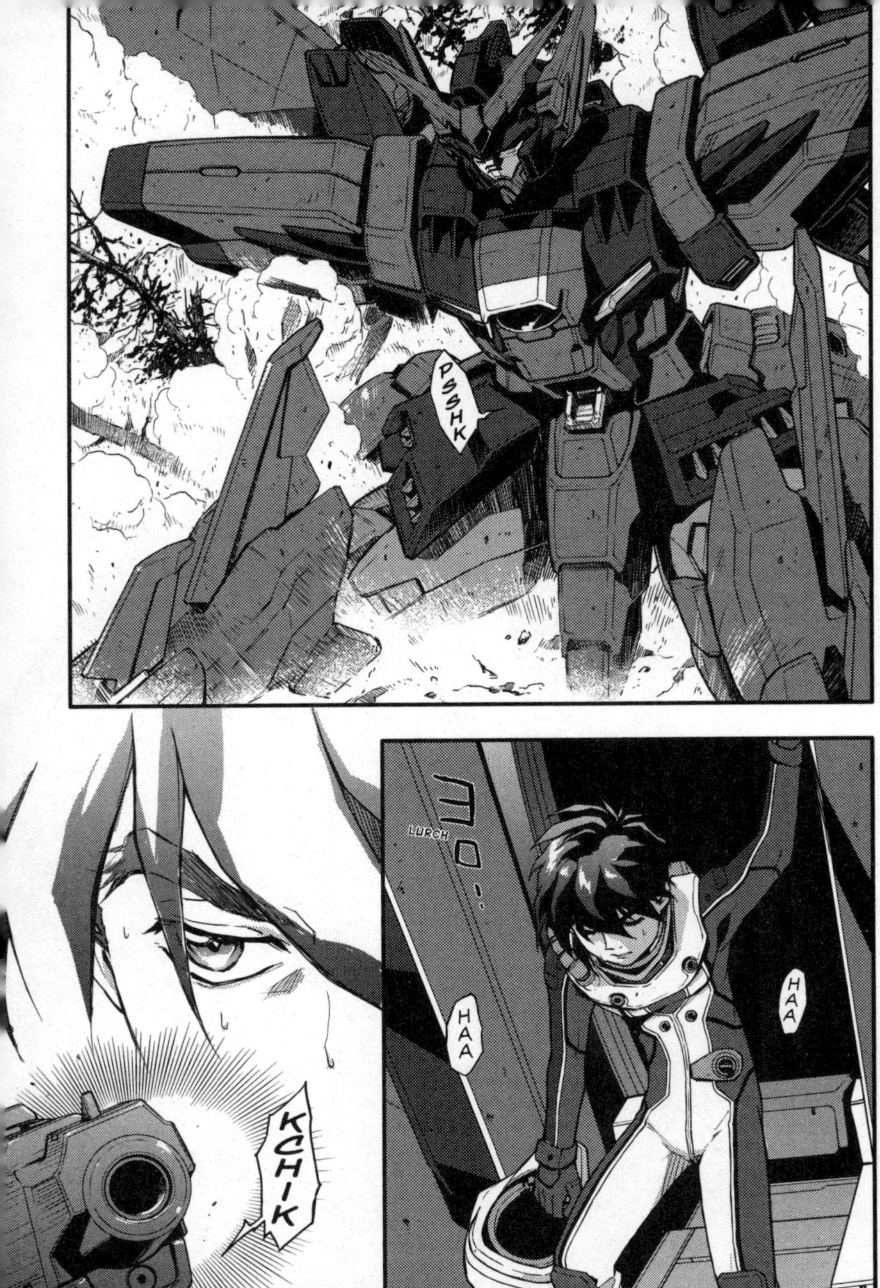
PSSHK
LURCH
HAA
HAA
KCHIK

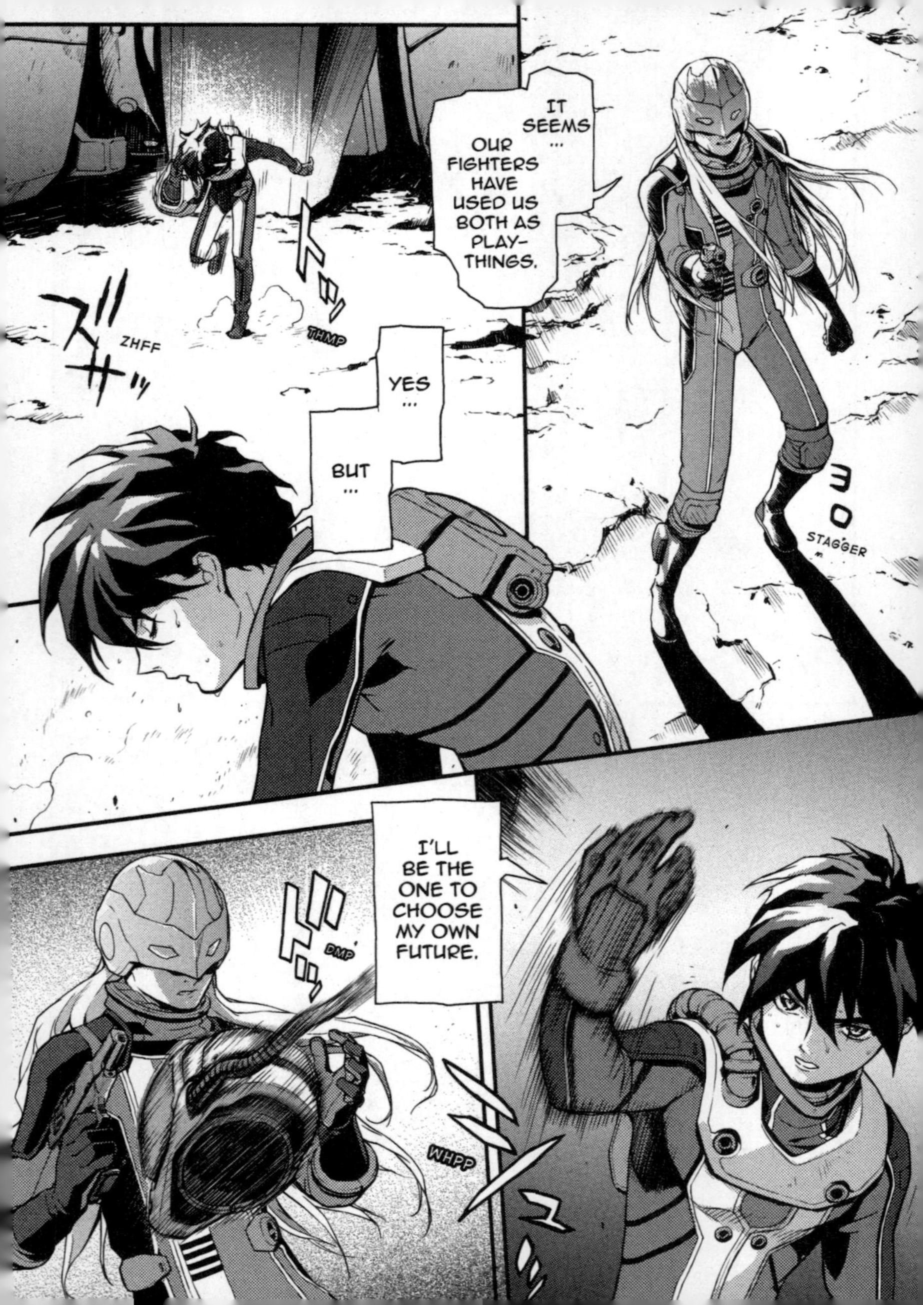
IT SEEMS ...
OUR FIGHTERS HAVE USED US BOTH AS PLAY-THINGS.
STAGGER
THMP
ZHFF
YES ...
BUT ...
I'LL BE THE ONE TO CHOOSE MY OWN FUTURE.
WHPP
DMP

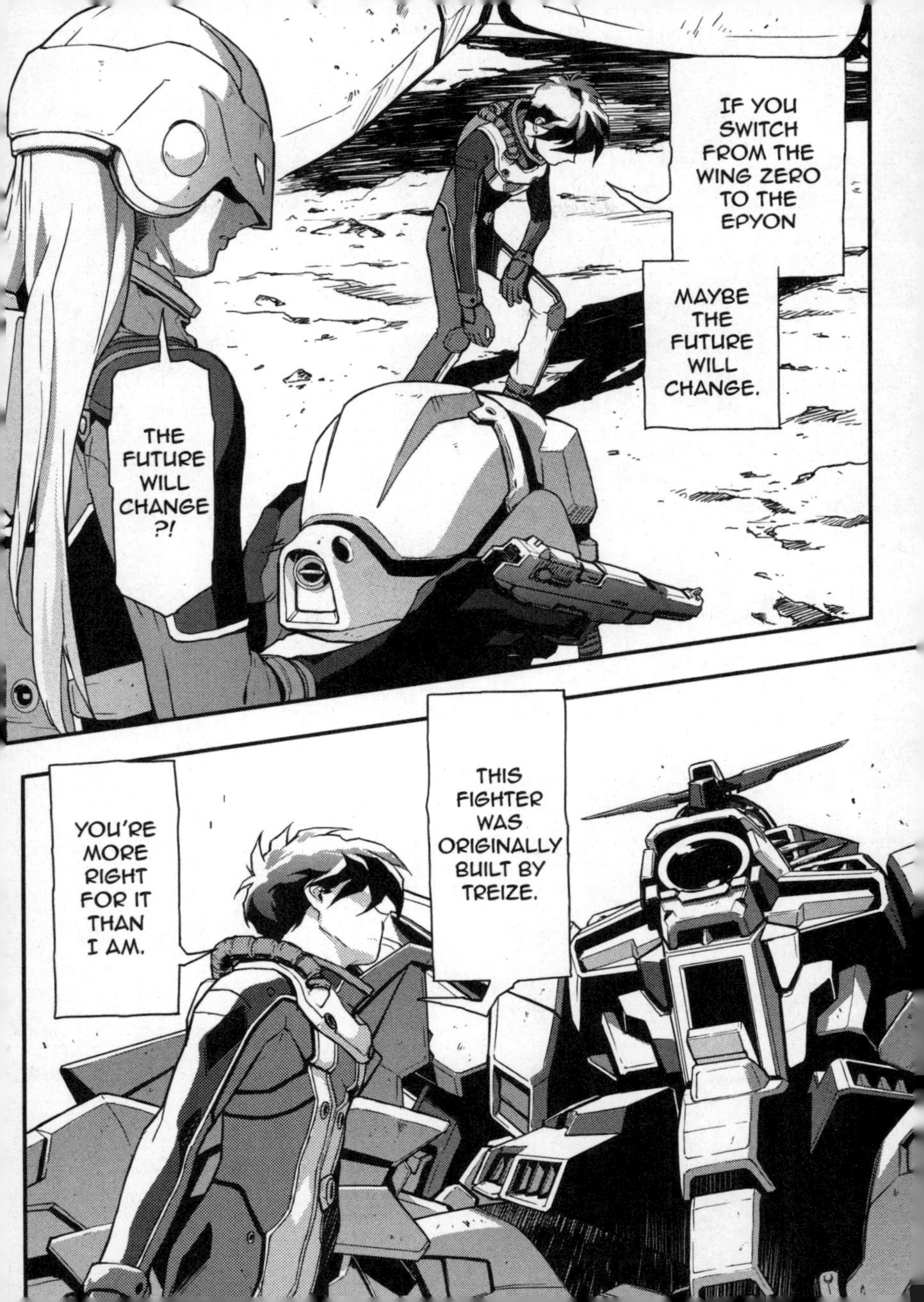
IF YOU SWITCH FROM THE WING ZERO TO THE EPYON
MAYBE THE FUTURE WILL CHANGE.
THE FUTURE WILL CHANGE?!
THIS FIGHTER WAS ORIGINALLY BUILT BY TREIZE.
YOU'RE MORE RIGHT FOR IT THAN I AM.

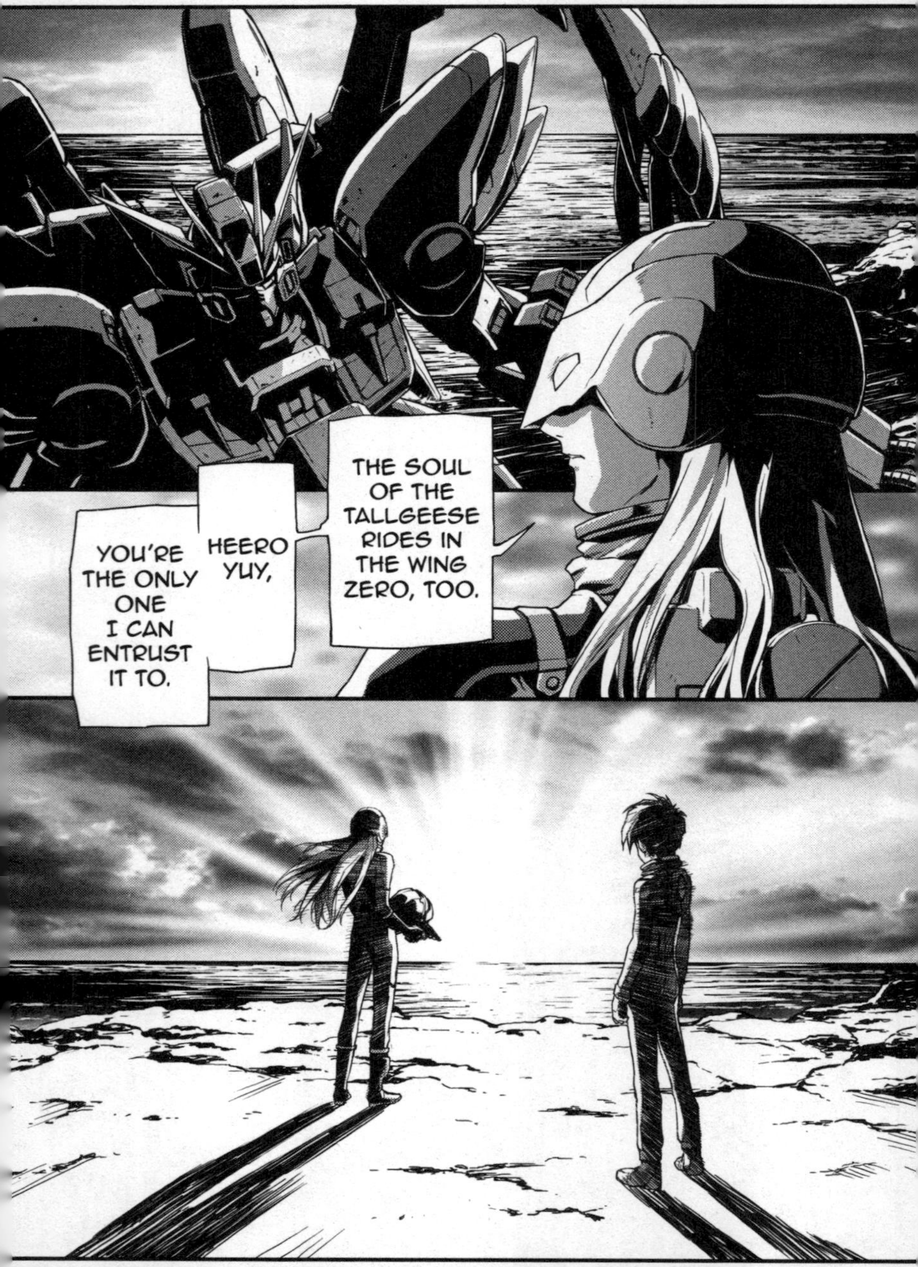
THE SOUL OF THE TALLGEESE RIDES IN THE WING ZERO, TOO.
HEERO YUY,
YOU'RE THE ONLY ONE I CAN ENTRUST IT TO.

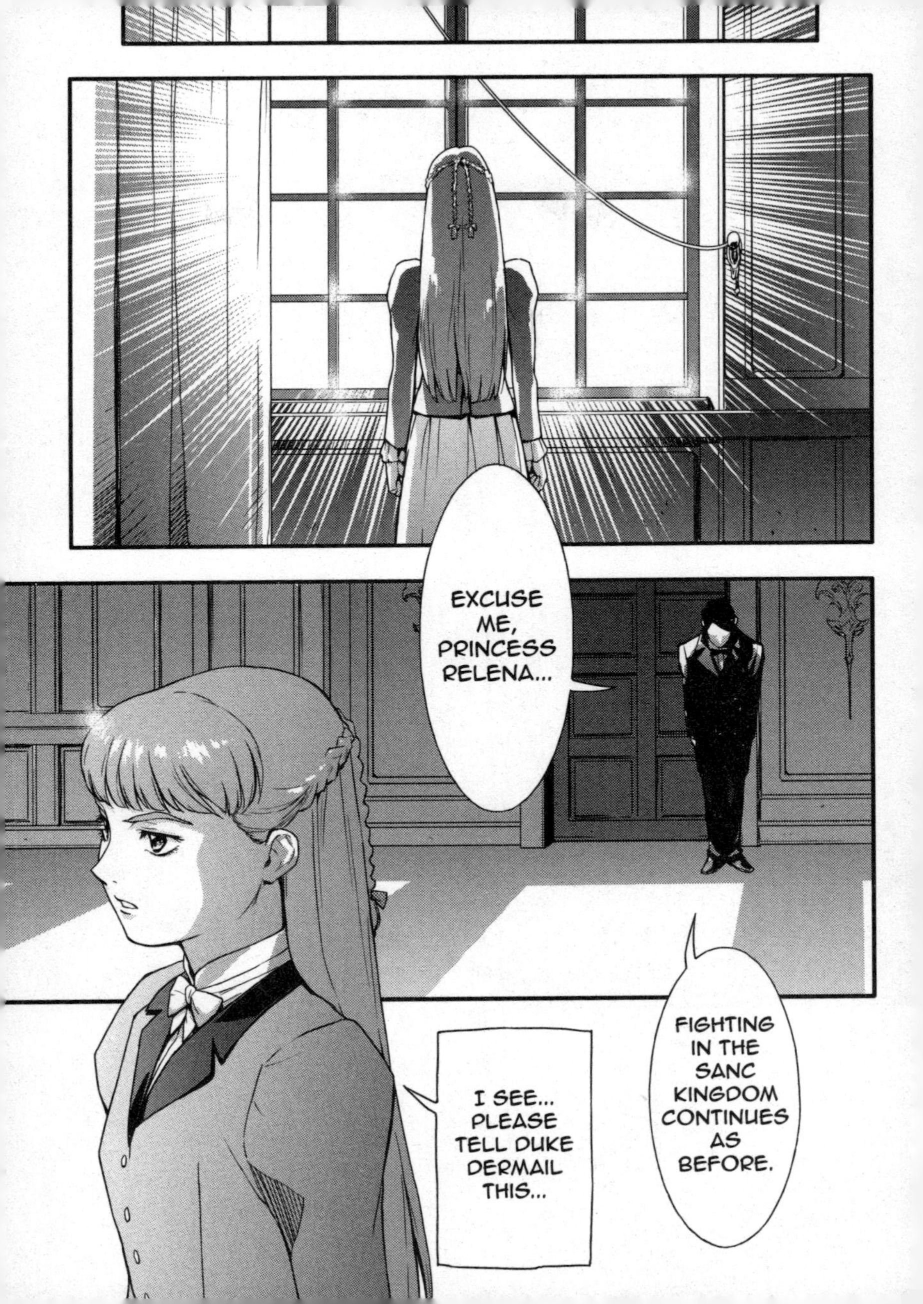
EXCUSE ME, PRINCESS RELENA...
FIGHTING IN THE SANC KINGDOM CONTINUES AS BEFORE.
I SEE... PLEASE TELL DUKE DERMAIL THIS...

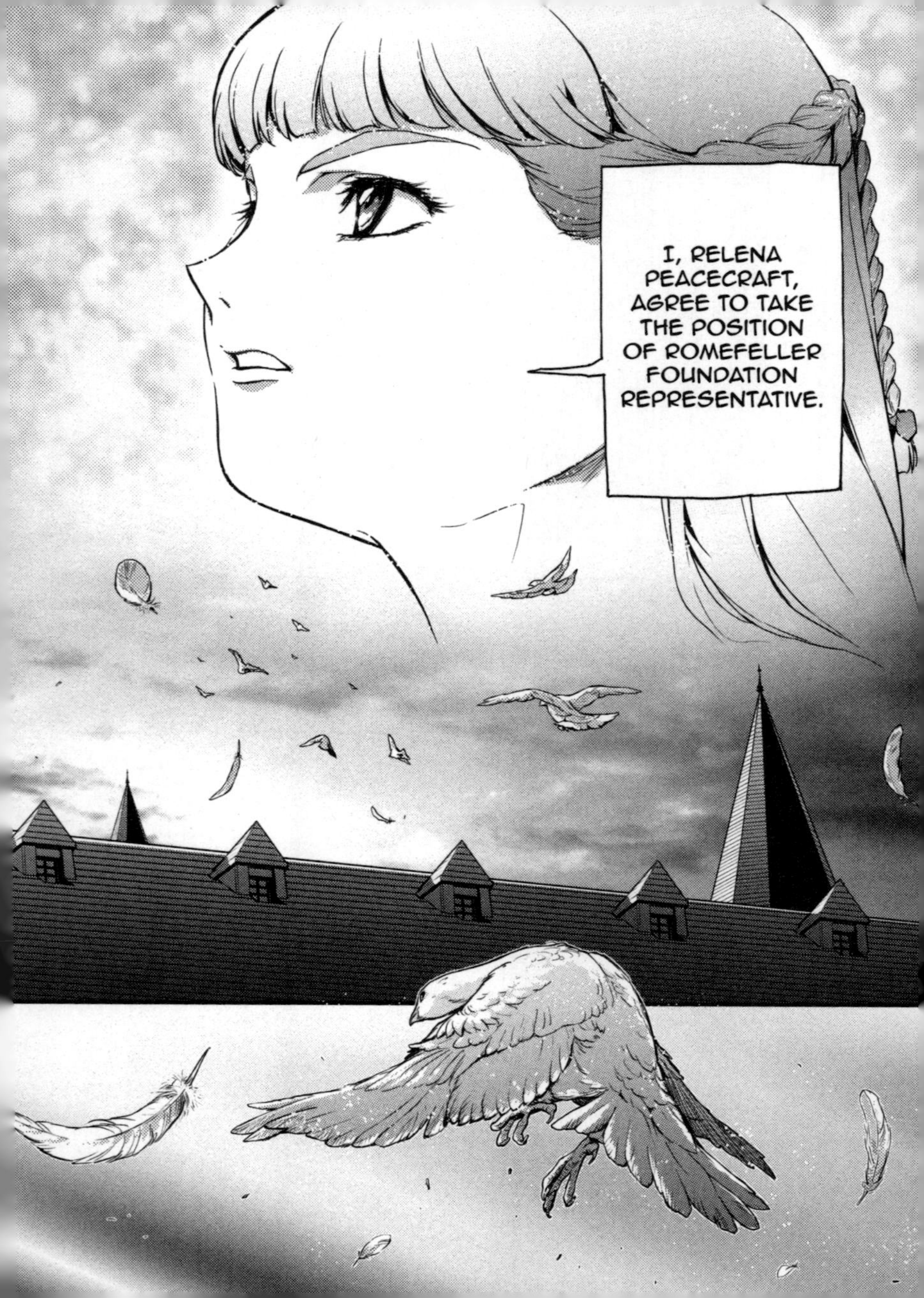
I, RELENA PEACECRAFT, AGREE TO TAKE THE POSITION OF ROMEFELLER FOUNDATION REPRESENTATIVE.

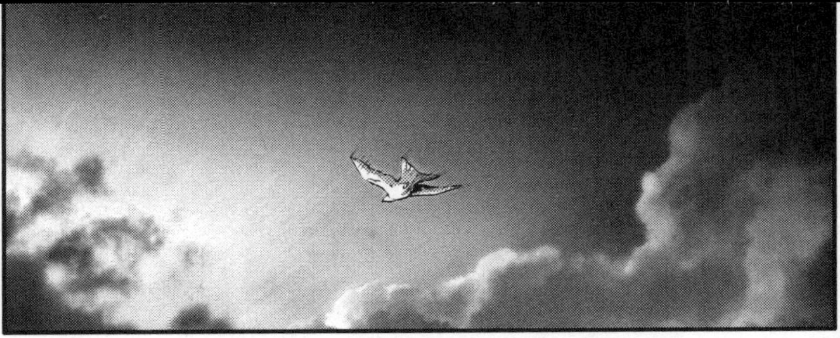

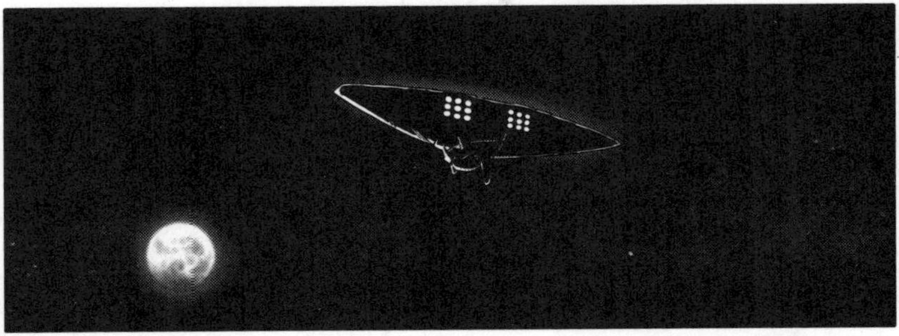

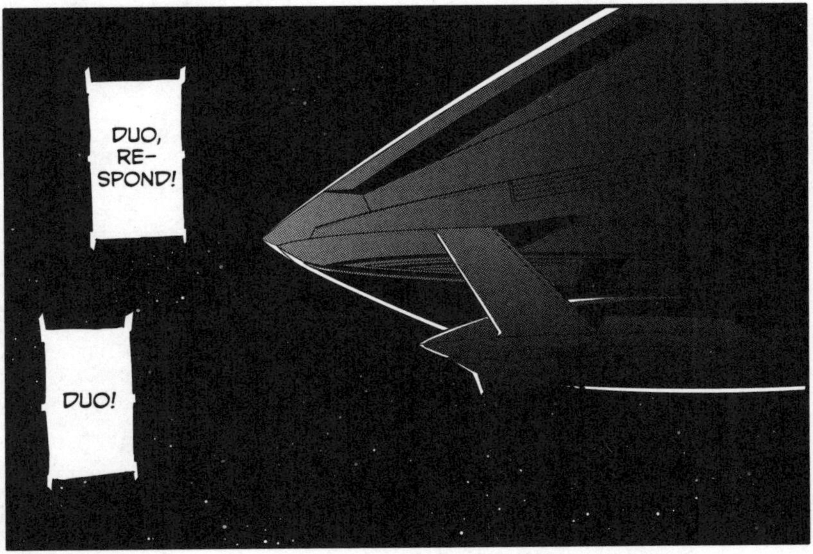
DUO, RE-SPOND!
DUO!

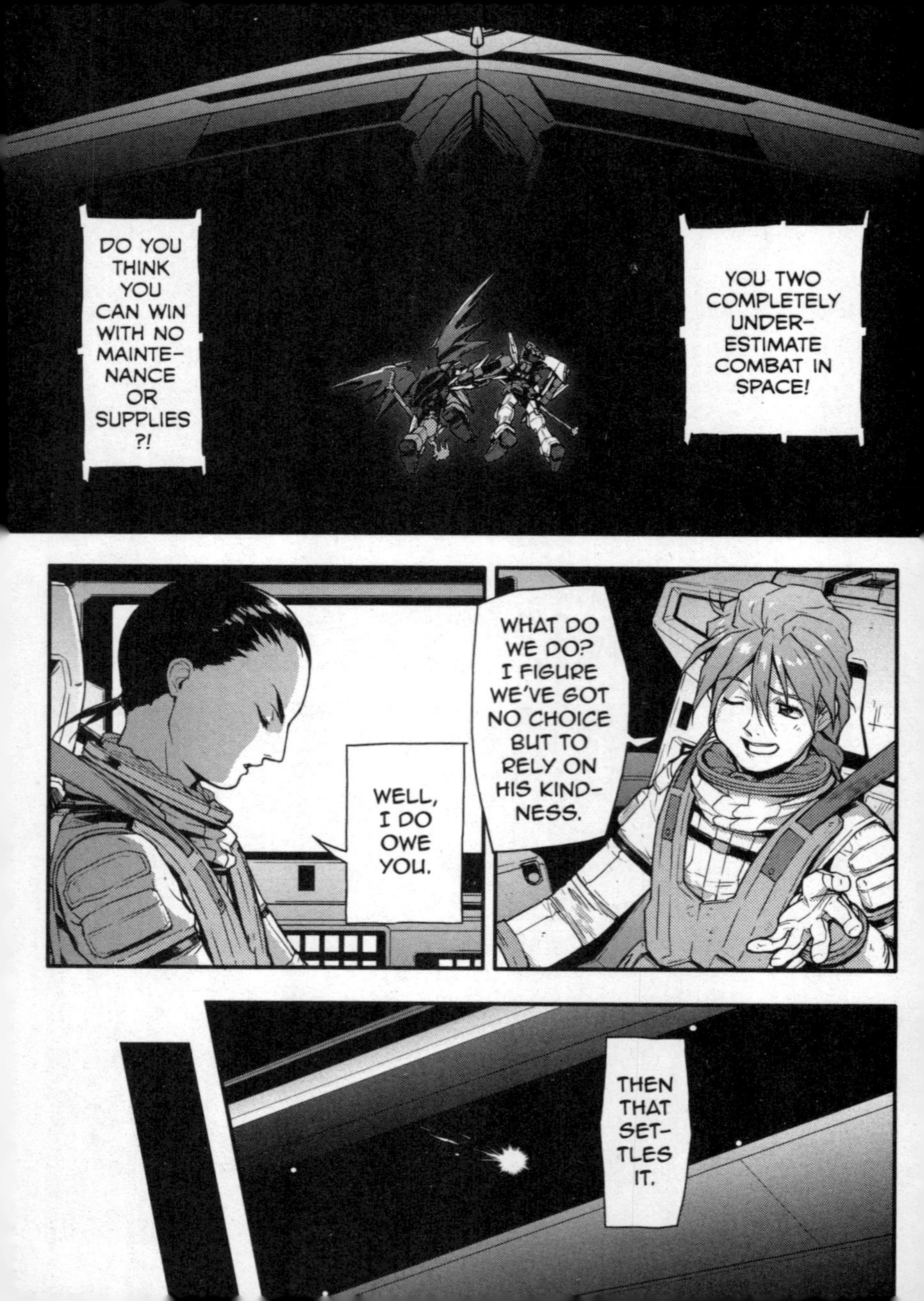
YOU TWO COMPLETELY UNDER-ESTIMATE COMBAT IN SPACE!
DO YOU THINK YOU CAN WIN WITH NO MAINTE-NANCE OR SUPPLIES?!
WHAT DO WE DO? I FIGURE WE'VE GOT NO CHOICE BUT TO RELY ON HIS KIND-NESS.
WELL, I DO OWE YOU.
THEN THAT SET-TLES IT.

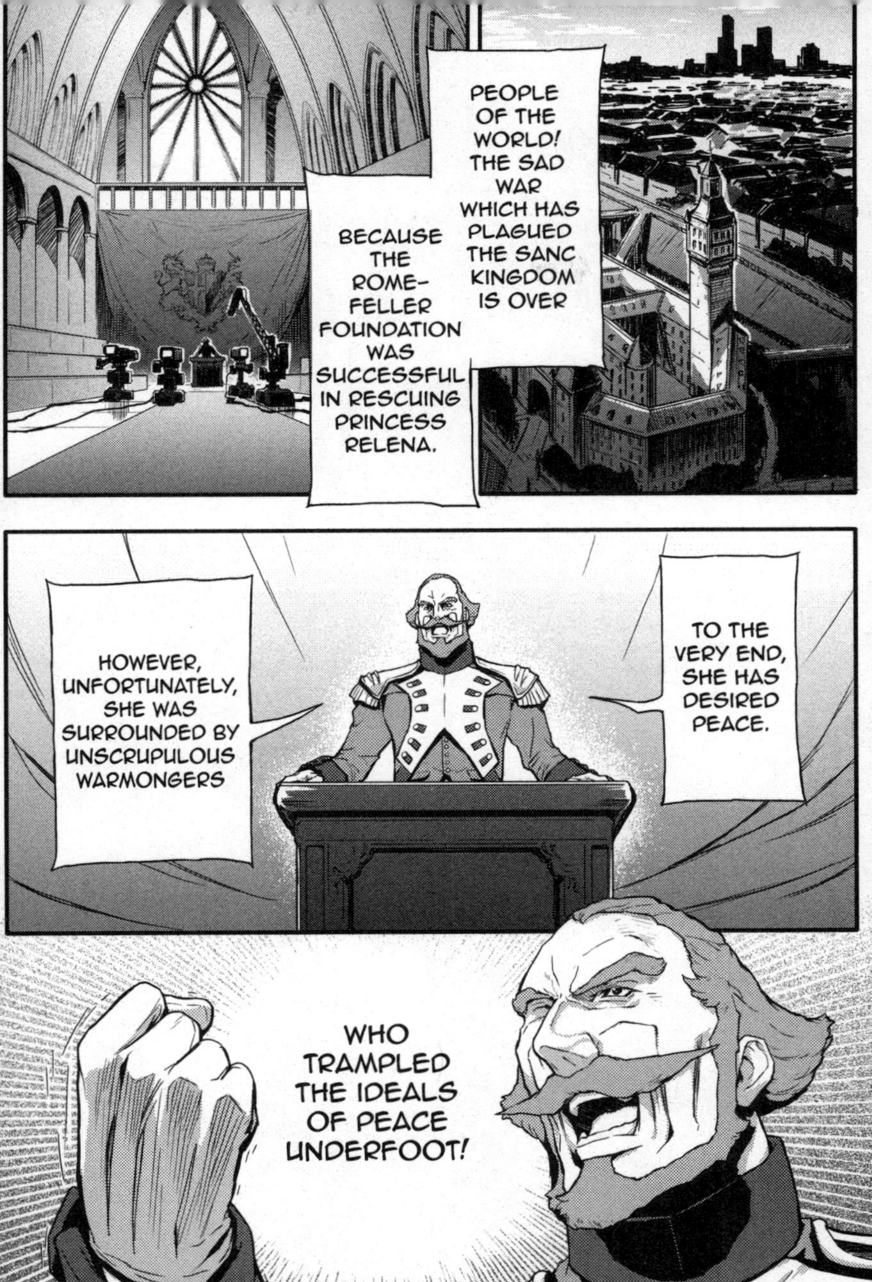
PEOPLE OF THE WORLD! THE SAD WAR WHICH HAS PLAGUED THE SANC KINGDOM IS OVER
BECAUSE THE ROME-FELLER FOUNDATION WAS SUCCESSFUL IN RESCUING PRINCESS RELENA.
TO THE VERY END, SHE HAS DESIRED PEACE.
HOWEVER, UNFORTUNATELY, SHE WAS SURROUNDED BY UNSCRUPULOUS WARMONGERS
WHO TRAMPLED THE IDEALS OF PEACE UNDERFOOT!

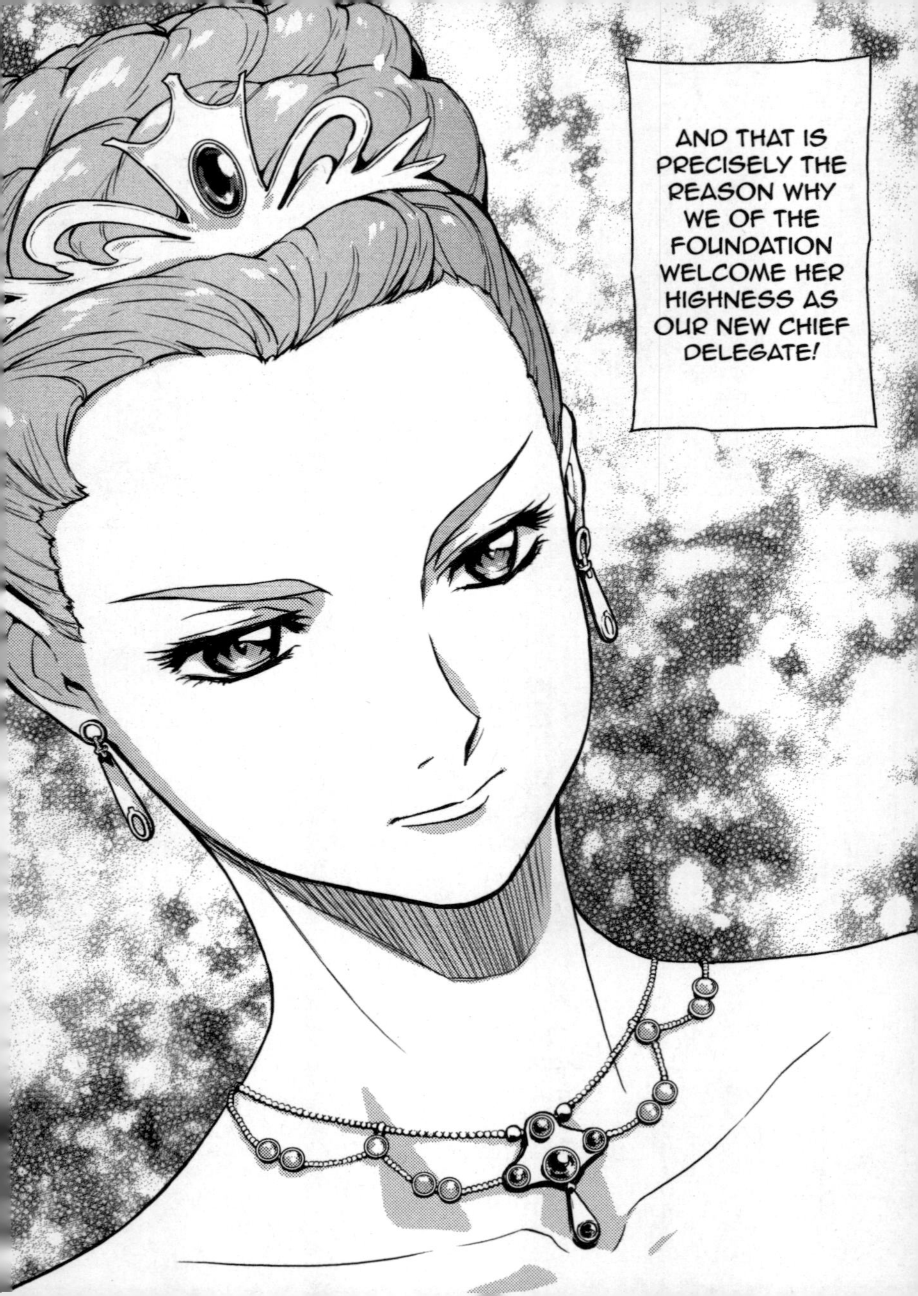
AND THAT IS PRECISELY THE REASON WHY WE OF THE FOUNDATION WELCOME HER HIGHNESS AS OUR NEW CHIEF DELEGATE!

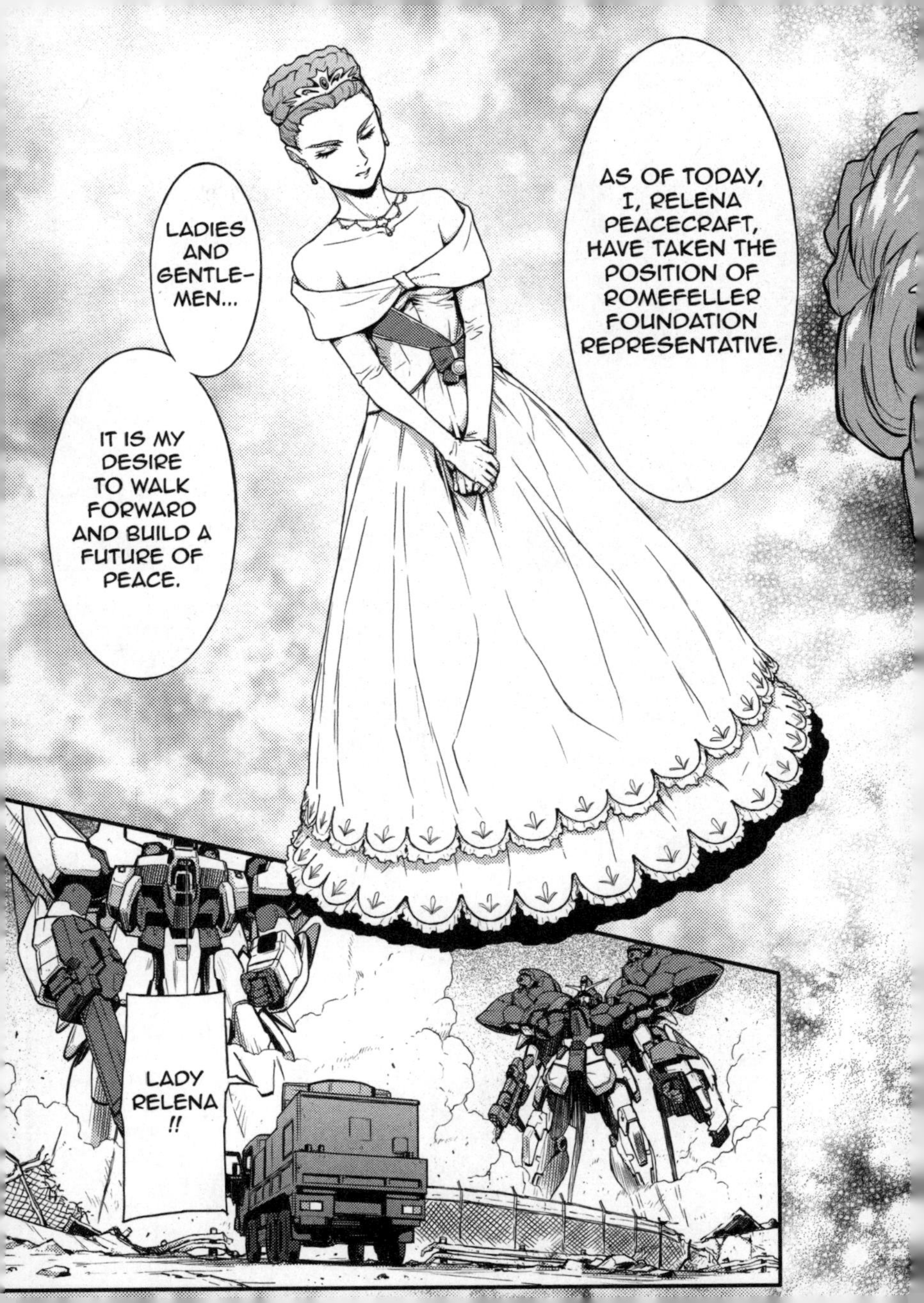
AS OF TODAY, I, RELENA PEACECRAFT, HAVE TAKEN THE POSITION OF ROMEFELLER FOUNDATION REPRESENTATIVE.
LADIES AND GENTLE-MEN...
IT IS MY DESIRE TO WALK FORWARD AND BUILD A FUTURE OF PEACE.
LADY RELENA !!

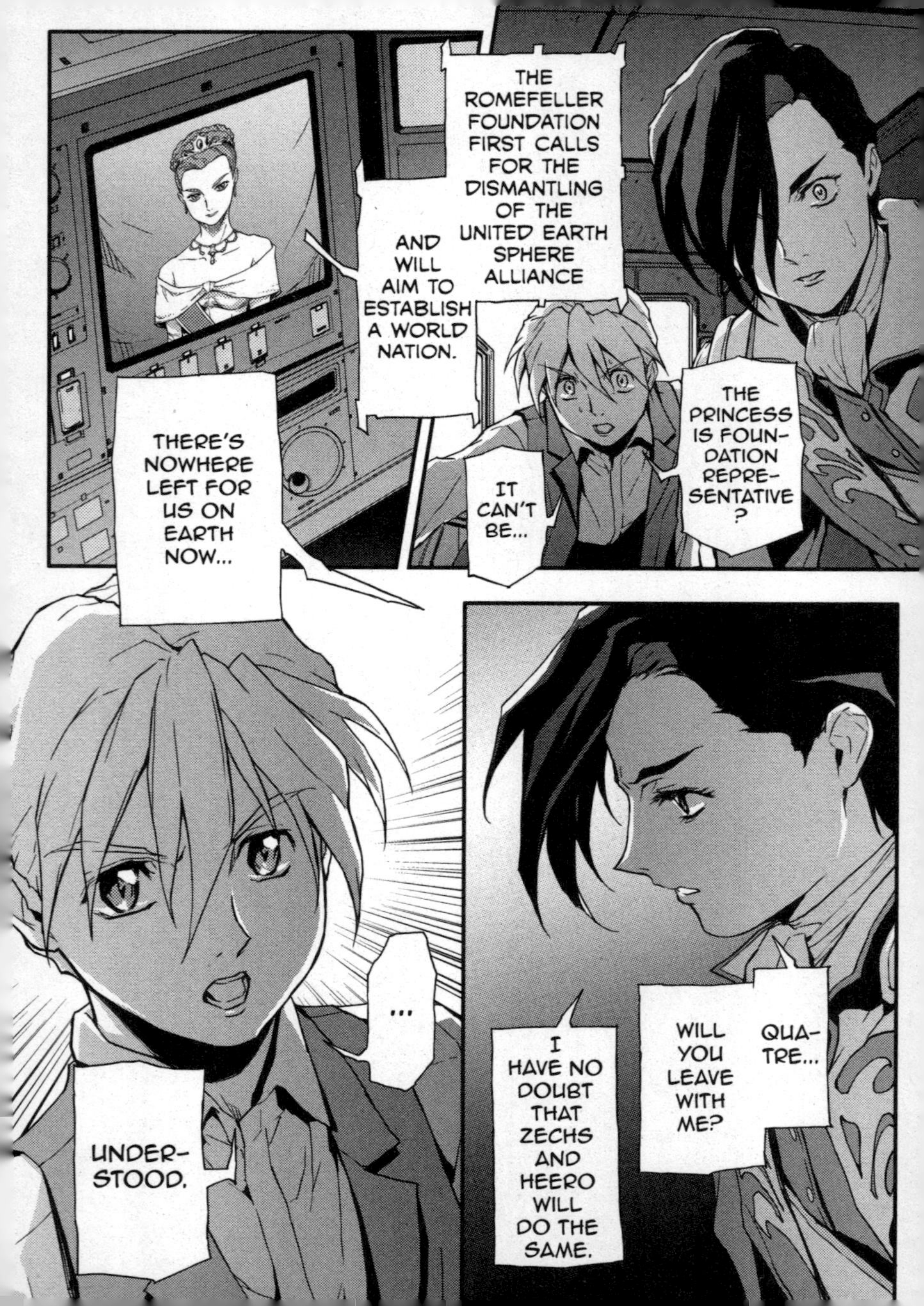

THE ROMEFELLER FOUNDATION FIRST CALLS FOR THE DISMANTLING OF THE UNITED EARTH SPHERE ALLIANCE
AND WILL AIM TO ESTABLISH A WORLD NATION.
THE PRINCESS IS FOUN-DATION REPRE-SENTATIVE?
IT CAN'T BE...
THERE'S NOWHERE LEFT FOR US ON EARTH NOW...
QUA-TRE...
WILL YOU LEAVE WITH ME?
I HAVE NO DOUBT THAT ZECHS AND HEERO WILL DO THE SAME.
...
UNDER-STOOD.

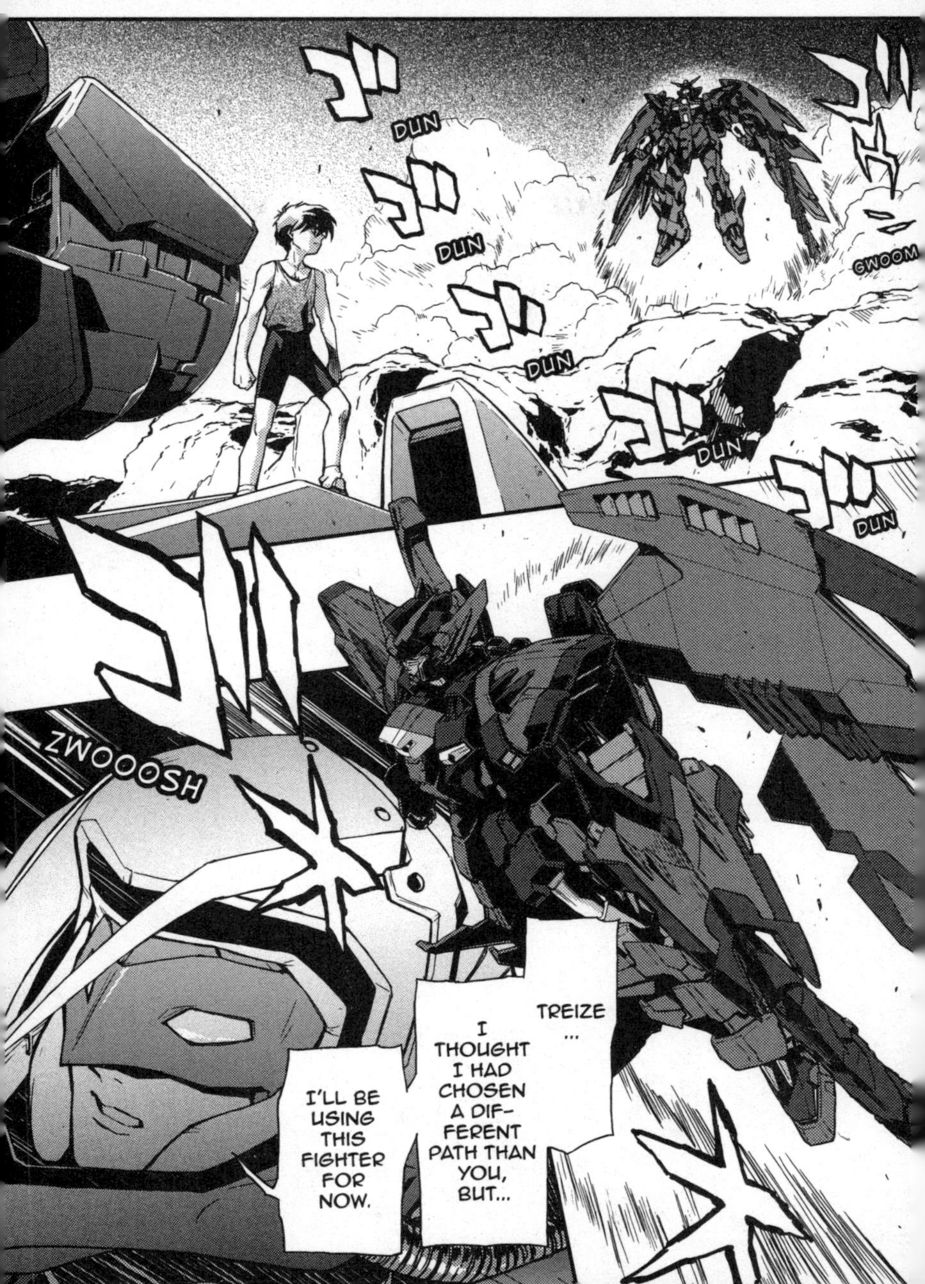
GWOOM
DUN
DUN
DUN
DUN
DUN
DUN
ZWOOOSH
TREIZE ...
I THOUGHT I HAD CHOSEN A DIF-FERENT PATH THAN YOU, BUT...
I'LL BE USING THIS FIGHTER FOR NOW.

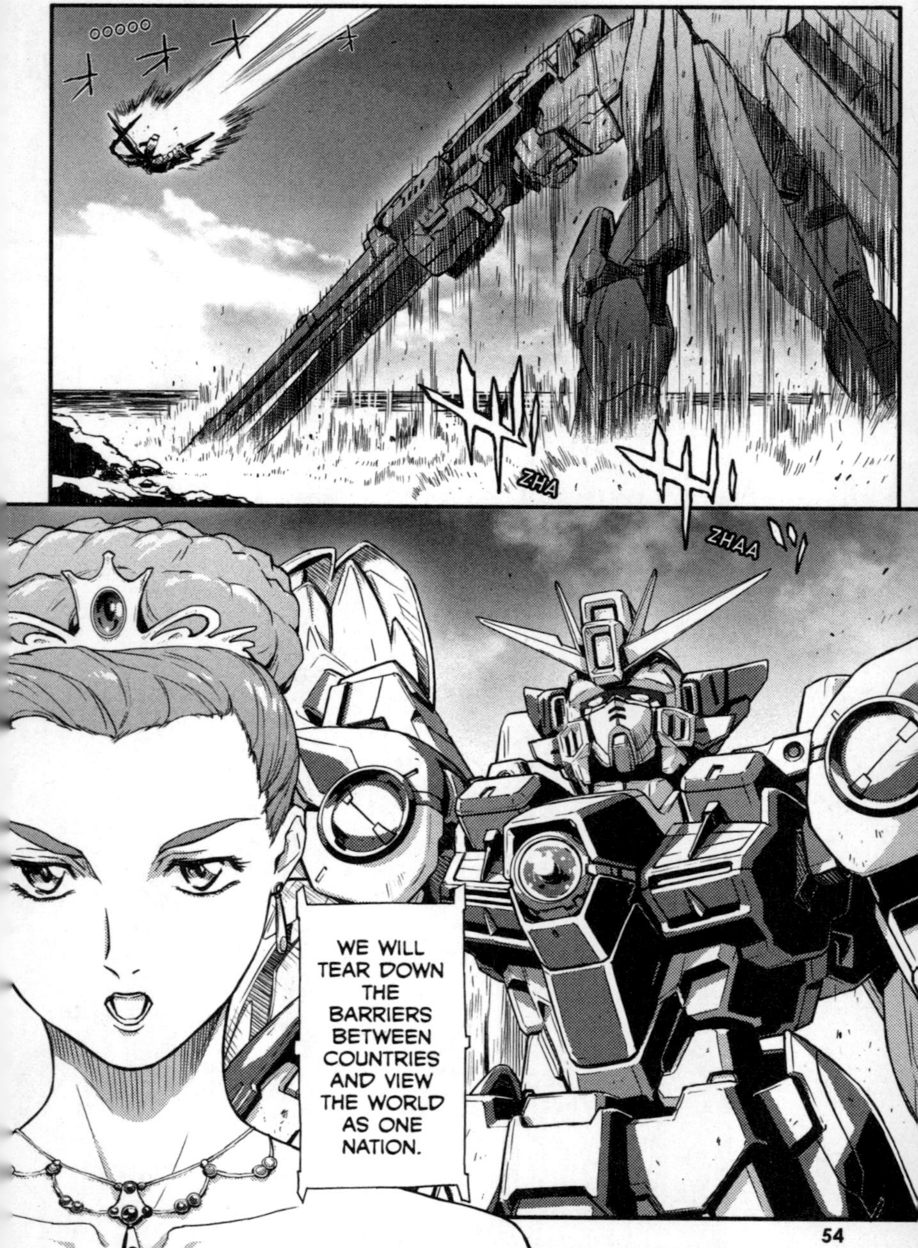
ooooo
オオオオ
ZHA
ZHAA
WE WILL TEAR DOWN THE BARRIERS BETWEEN COUNTRIES AND VIEW THE WORLD AS ONE NATION.

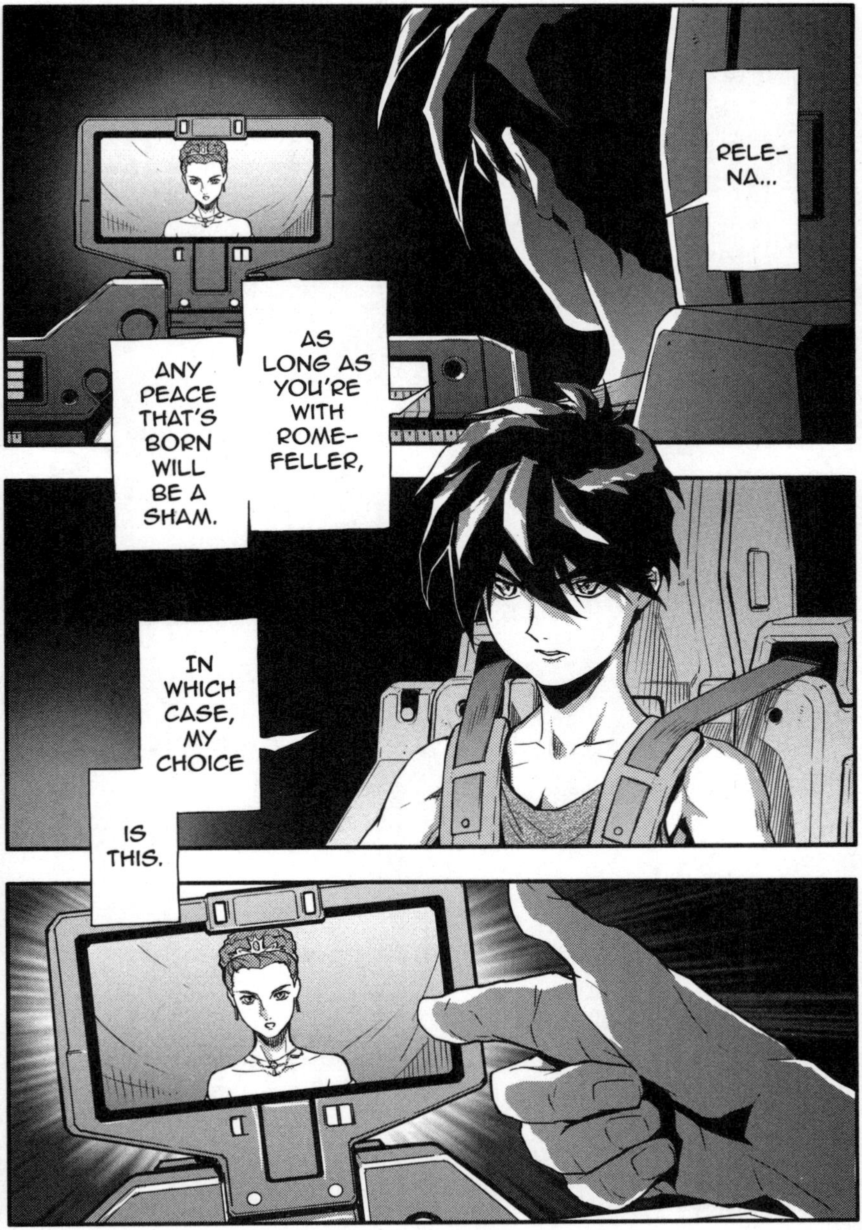
RELE-NA...
AS LONG AS YOU'RE WITH ROME-FELLER,
ANY PEACE THAT'S BORN WILL BE A SHAM.
IN WHICH CASE, MY CHOICE
IS THIS.

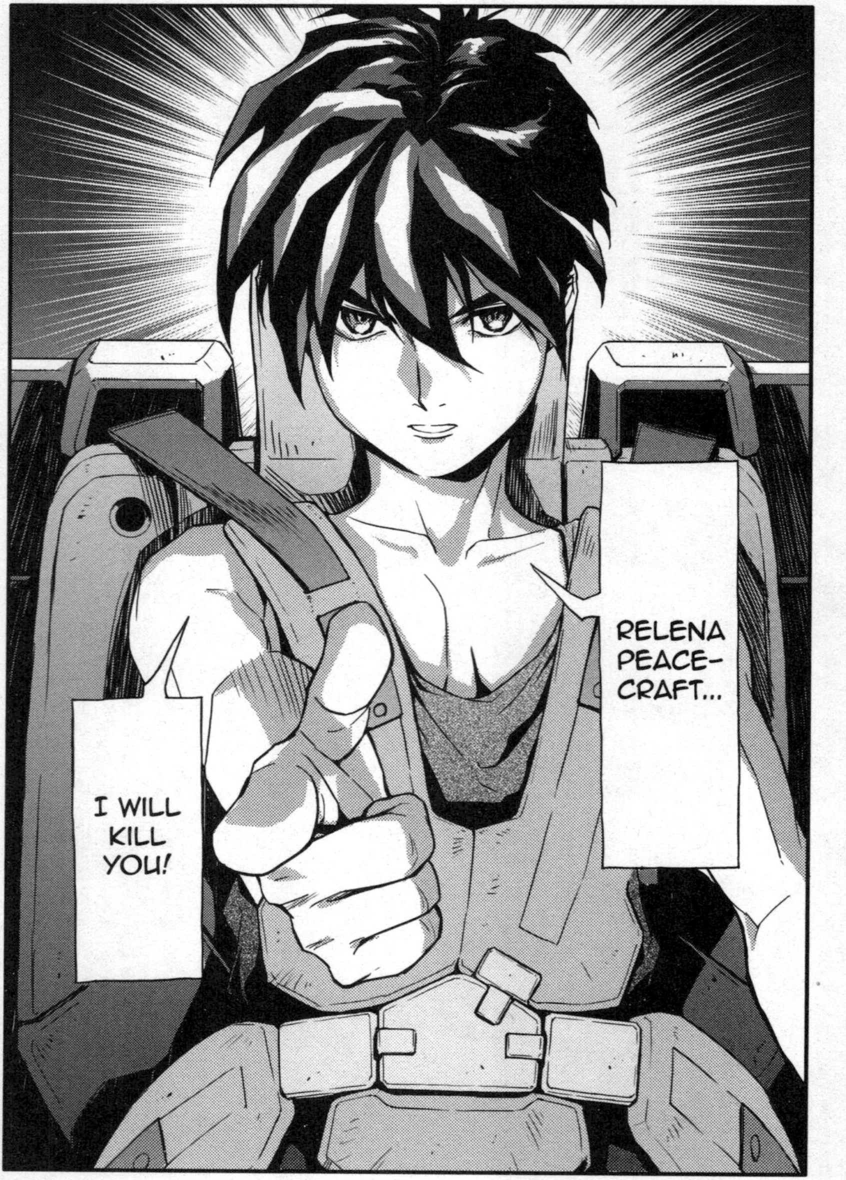
RELENA PEACE-CRAFT...
I WILL KILL YOU!

SLEEVE NOTES:
Endless Waltz

DERMAIL CATALONIA

Acting Leader of the Romefeller Foundation. He is Treize's uncle and Dorothy's grandfather.

A believer in aristocratism, he thinks that administration by the Foundation will lead to peace for the whole Earth Sphere, and so he places the Earth Sphere Alliance under their control, and attempts to placate the colonies. After imprisoning Treize for raising objections to the Foundation's positions, he establishes Relena as Foundation representative, and it looks as if his ideals are about to be fully realized. However...

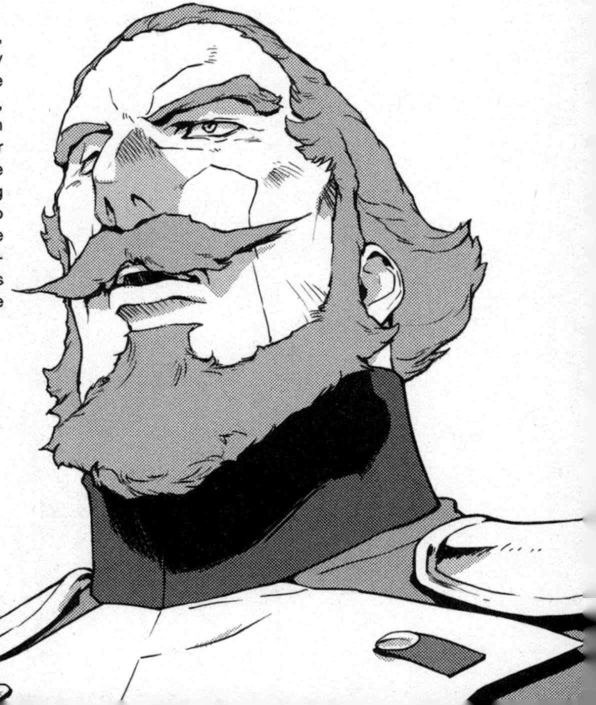

SLEEVE NOTES:
Endless Waltz

TUBAROV BILMON

An OZ engineer who earned the trust of the Romefeller Foundation and conceived the Mobile Doll (MD) system. Placed in charge of OZ's moon base, there he develops and mass produces the MD Virgos, and proceeds with the construction of the space battleship Libra. He believes that what mankind needs is not freedom, but control and order.

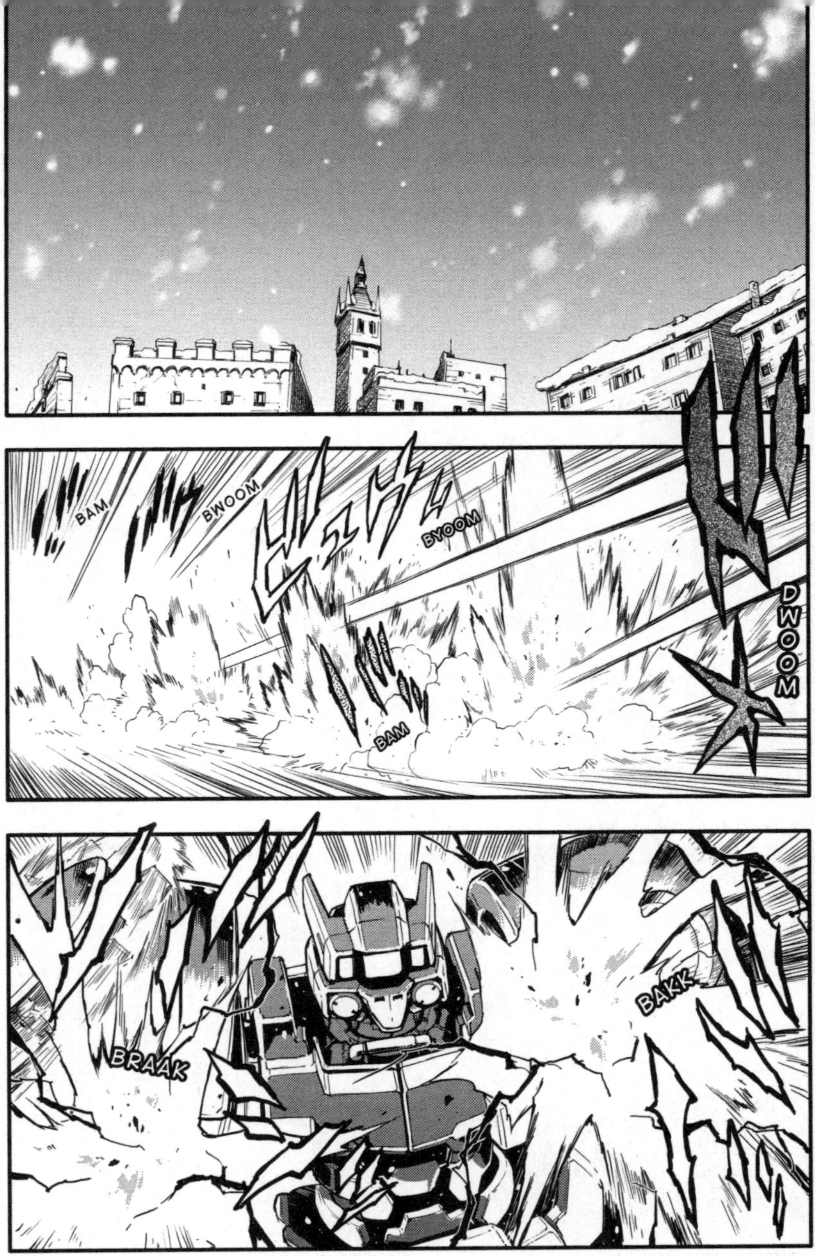
DWOOM
BYOOM
BWOOM
BAM
BAM
BAKK
BRAAK

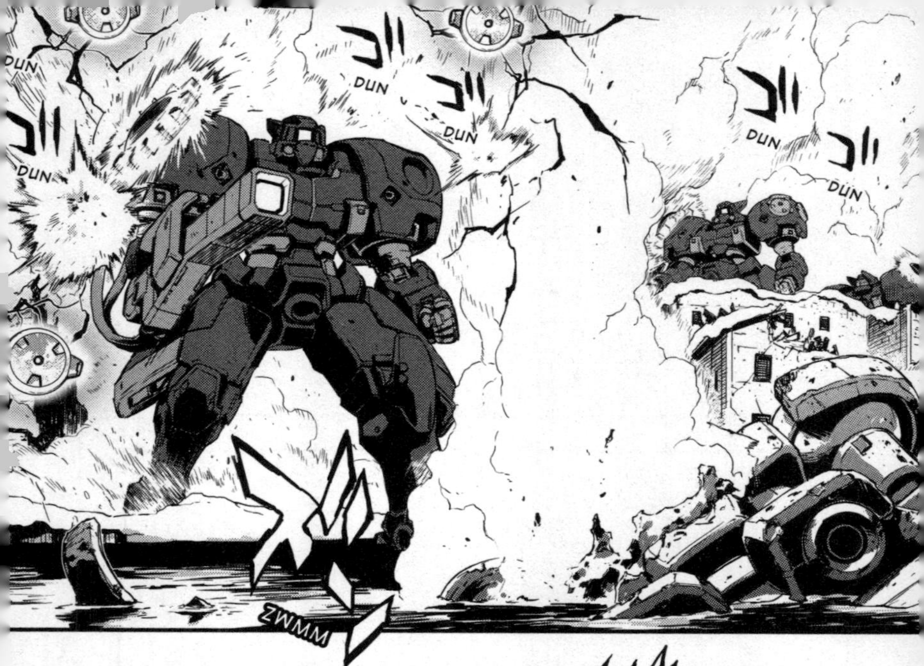
DUN
DUN
DUN
DUN
DUN
DUN
ZWMM

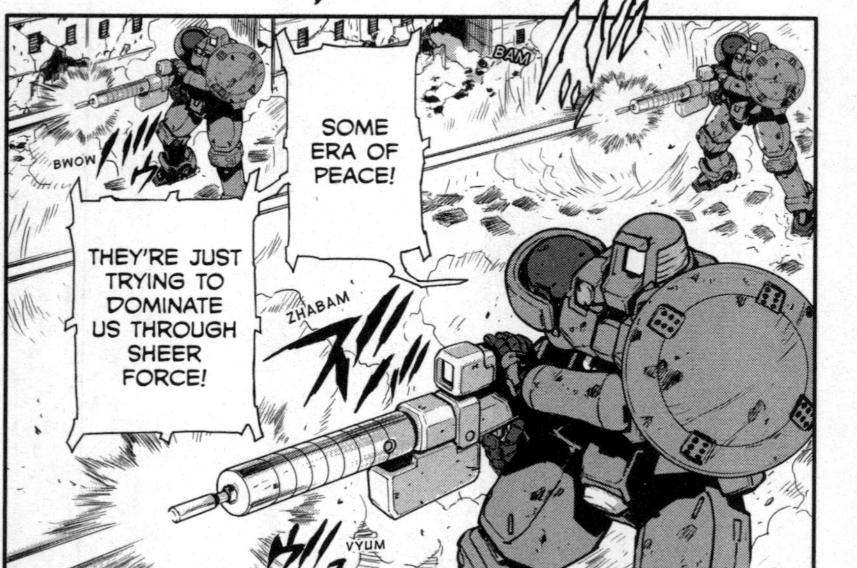
BAM
SOME ERA OF PEACE!
BWOW
THEY'RE JUST TRYING TO DOMINATE US THROUGH SHEER FORCE!
ZHABAM
VYUM

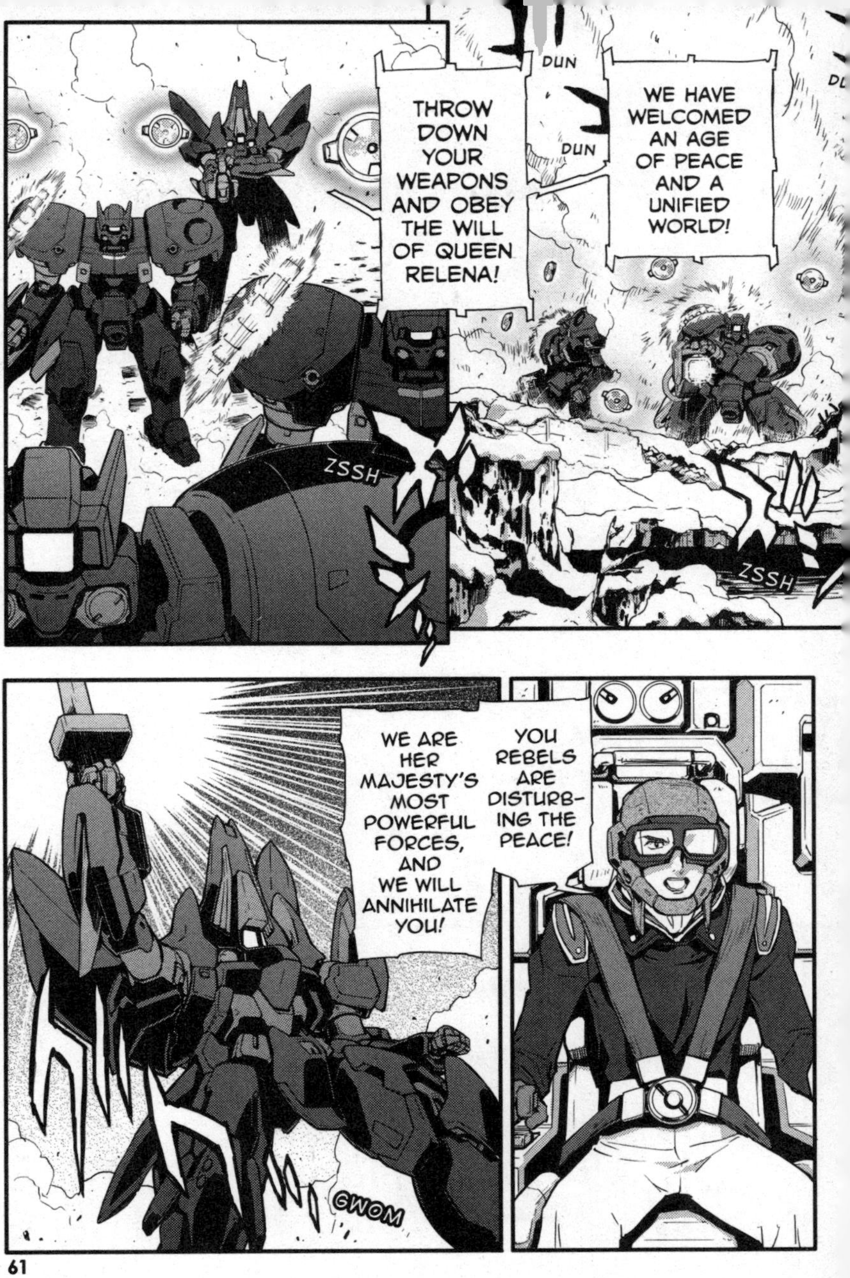
WE HAVE WELCOMED AN AGE OF PEACE AND A UNIFIED WORLD!
DUN
DUN
THROW DOWN YOUR WEAPONS AND OBEY THE WILL OF QUEEN RELENA!
ZSSH
ZSSH
YOU REBELS ARE DISTURBING THE PEACE!
WE ARE HER MAJESTY'S MOST POWERFUL FORCES, AND WE WILL ANNIHILATE YOU!
GWOM

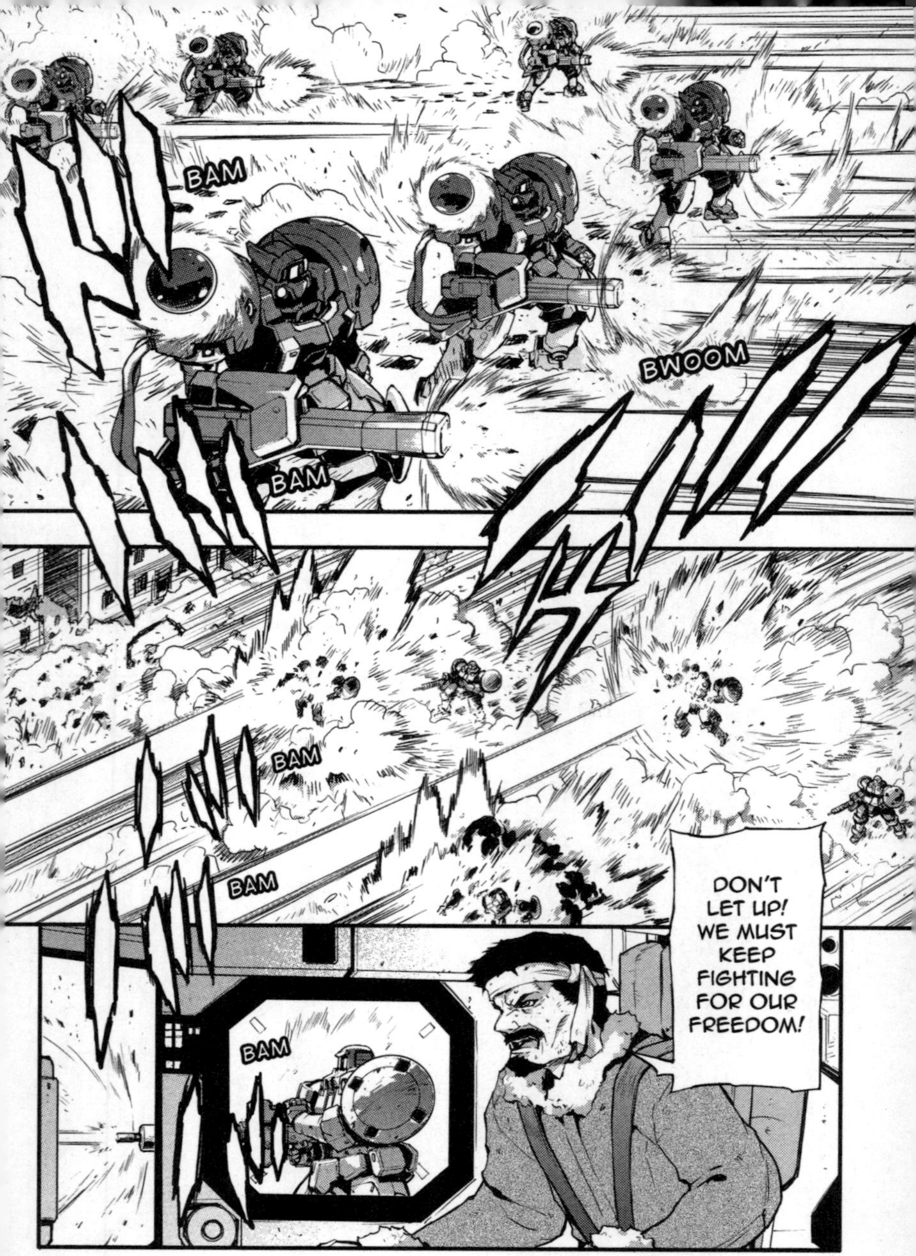
BWOOM
BAM
BAM
BAM
BAM
DON'T LET UP! WE MUST KEEP FIGHTING FOR OUR FREEDOM!
BAM

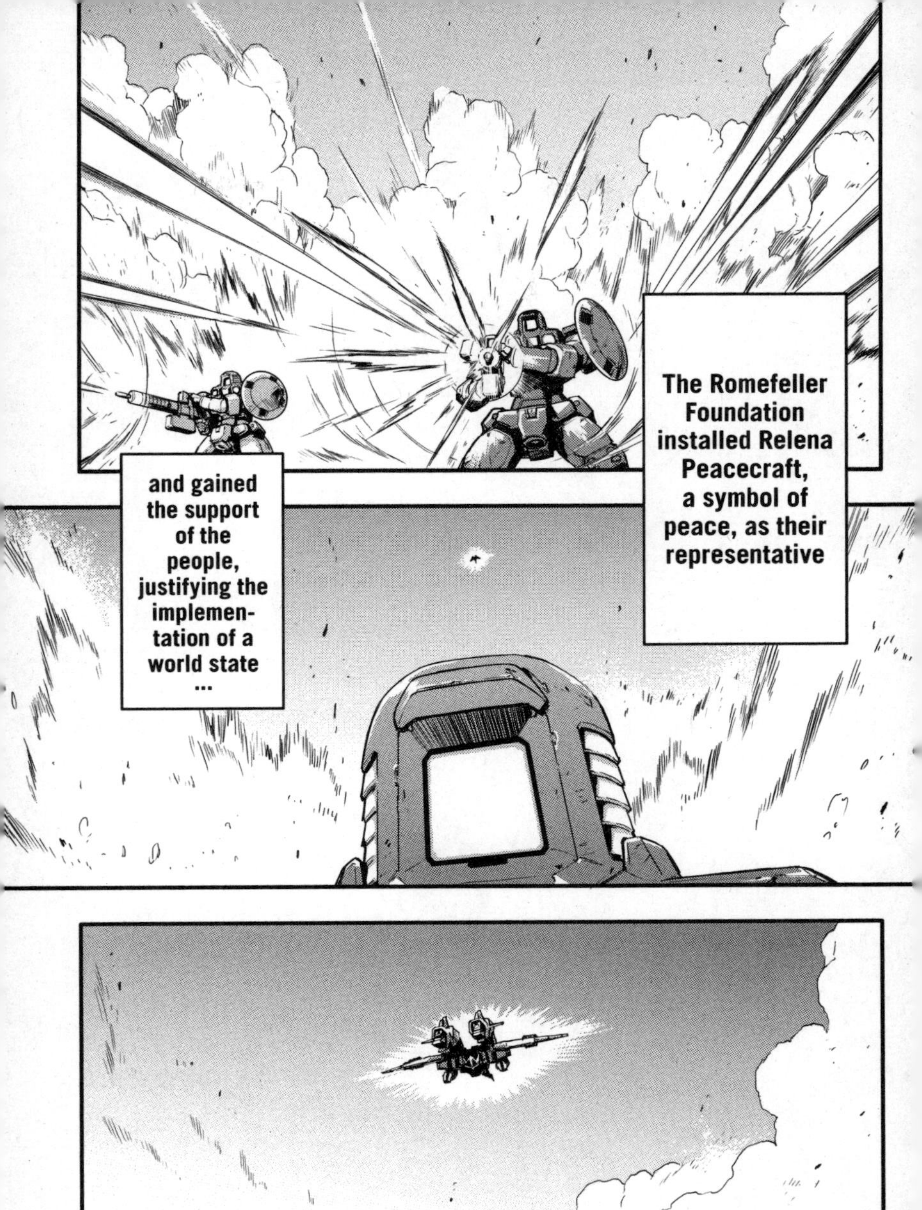
The Romefeller Foundation installed Relena Peacecraft, a symbol of peace, as their representative
and gained the support of the people, justifying the implemen-tation of a world state ...

Chapter 64 "Future Choice: Regicide"

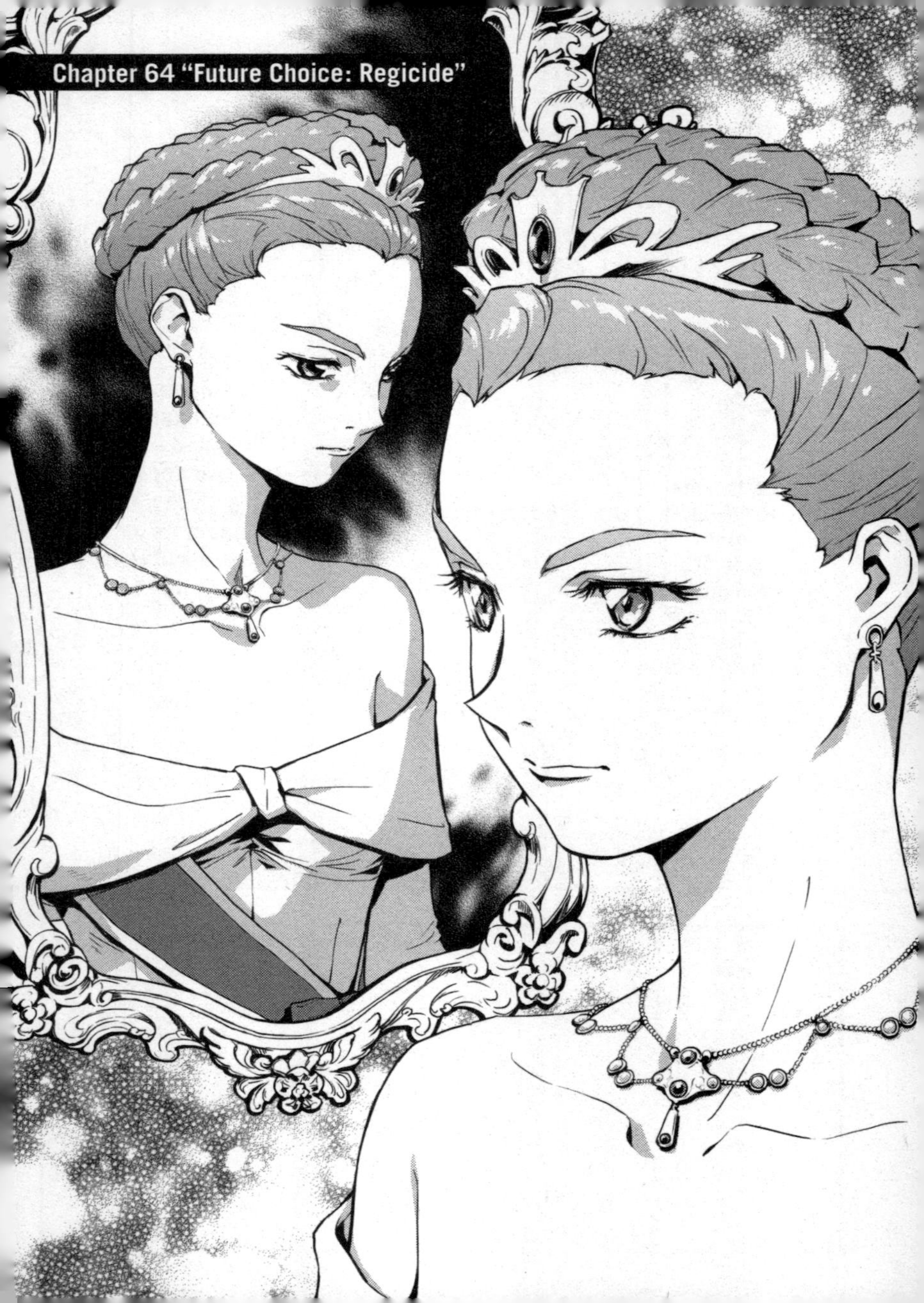

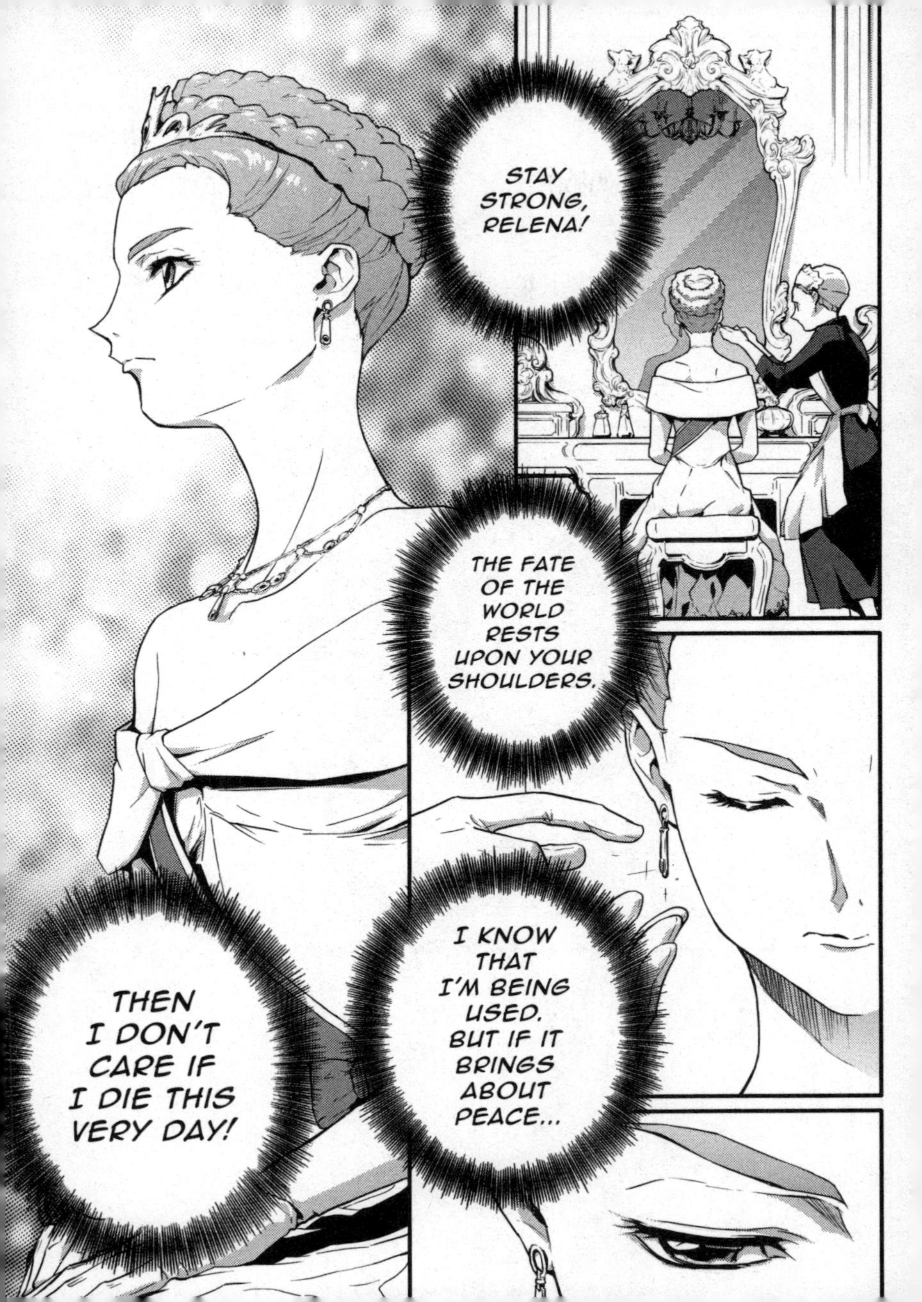
STAY STRONG, RELENA!
THE FATE OF THE WORLD RESTS UPON YOUR SHOULDERS.
I KNOW THAT I'M BEING USED. BUT IF IT BRINGS ABOUT PEACE...
THEN I DON'T CARE IF I DIE THIS VERY DAY!

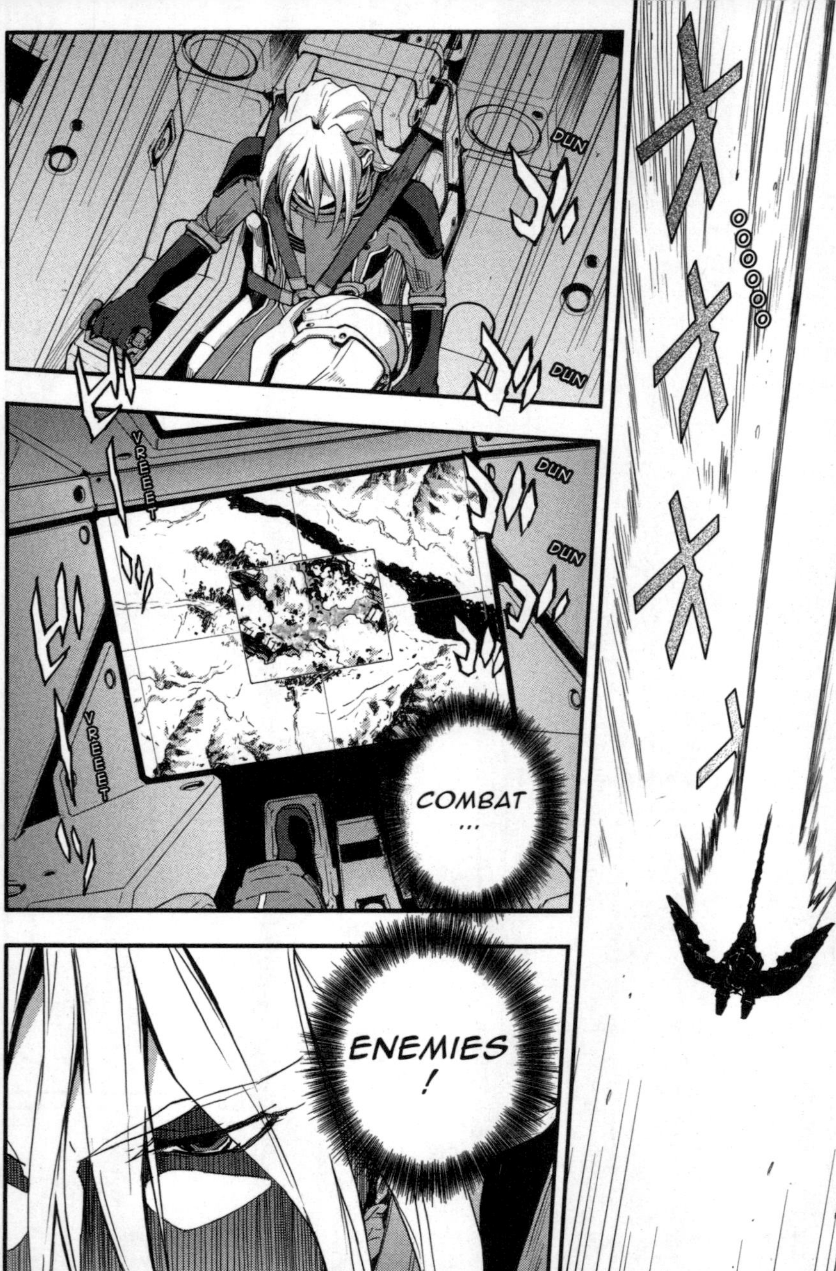
OOOOOOO
DUN
DUN
VREEEET
DUN
DUN
VREEEET
COMBAT ...
ENEMIES !

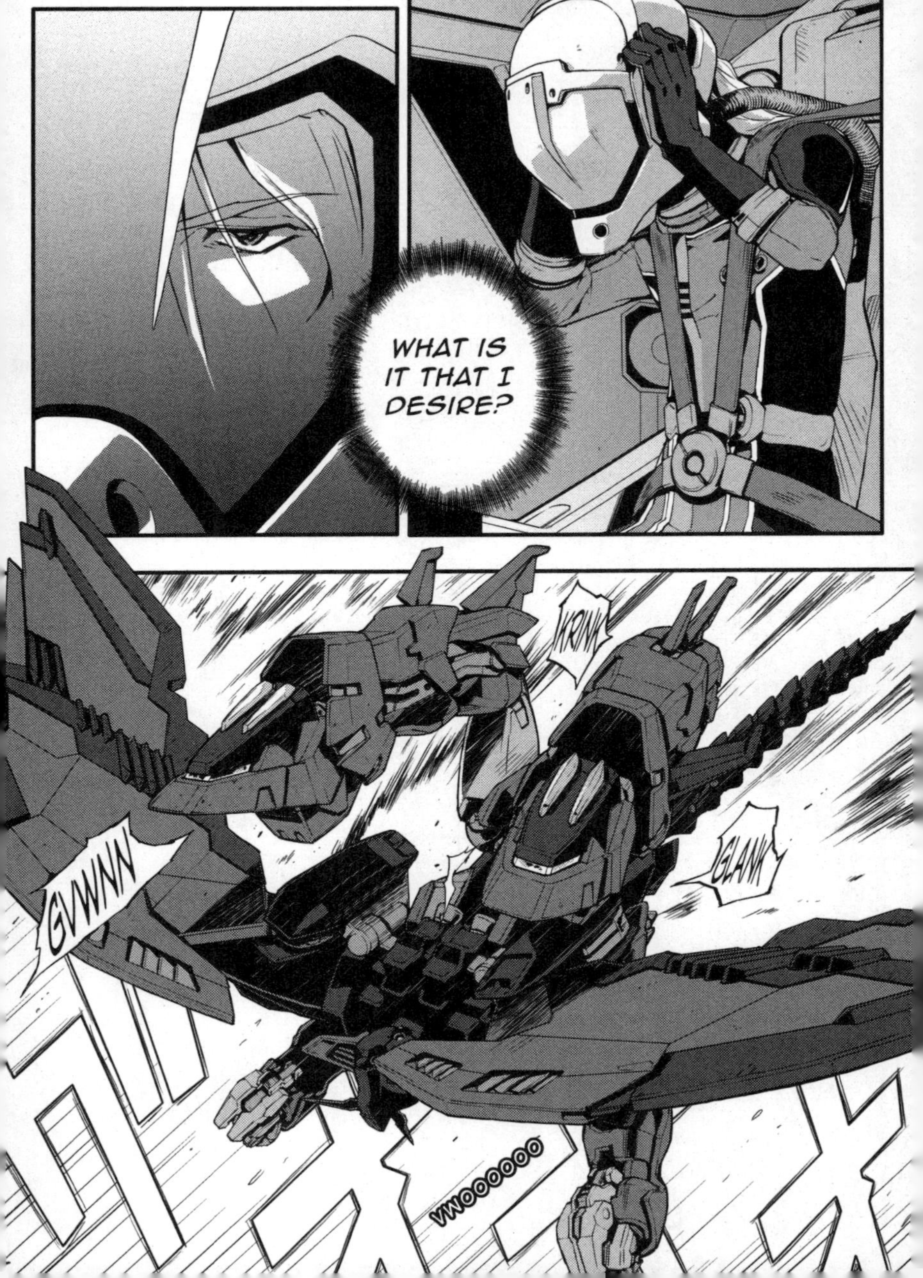
WHAT IS IT THAT I DESIRE?
KRINK
GLANK
GVWNN
VWOOOOOO

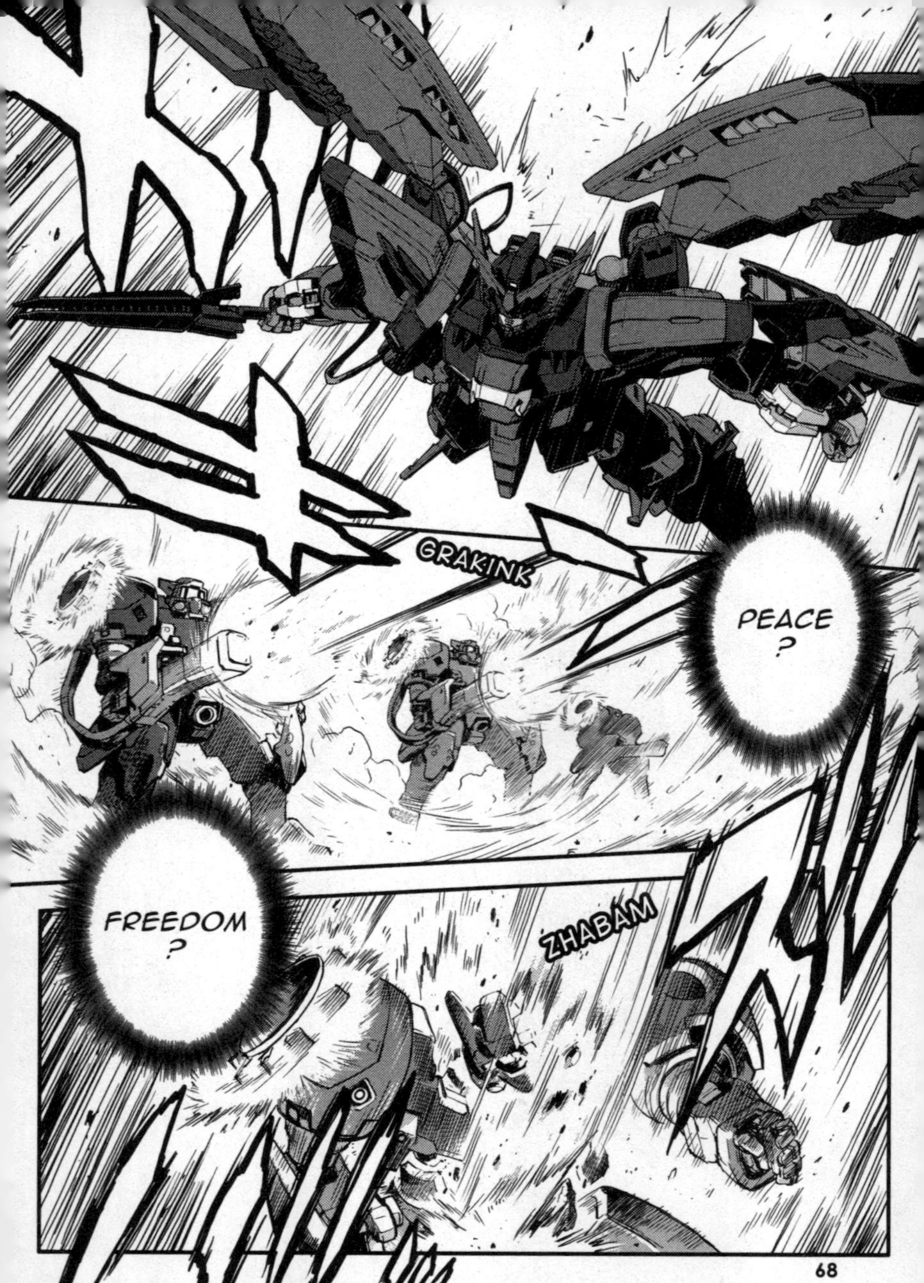
PEACE ?
GRAKINK
ZHABAM
FREEDOM ?

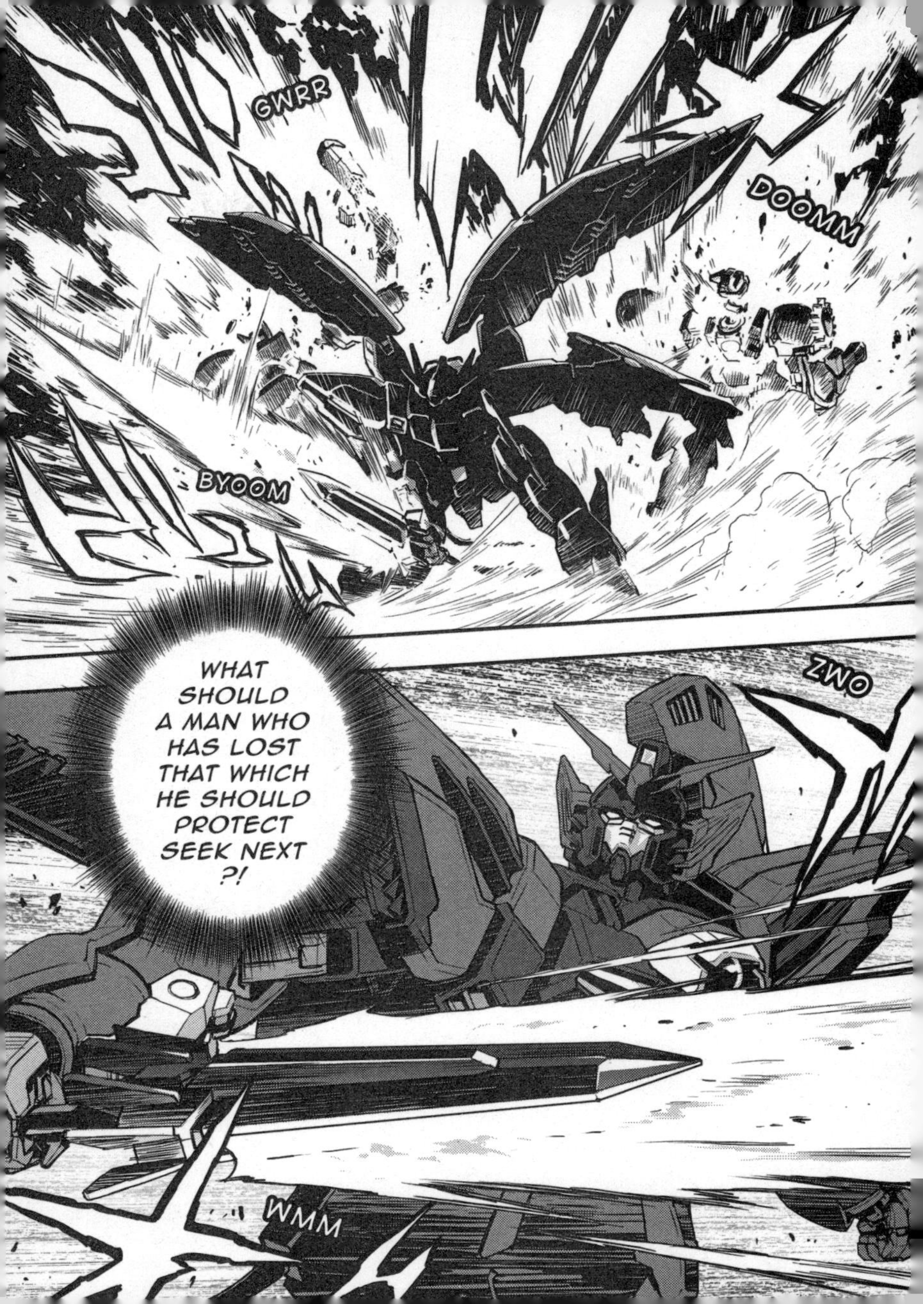
DOOMM
GWRR
BYOOM
ZWO
WHAT SHOULD A MAN WHO HAS LOST THAT WHICH HE SHOULD PROTECT SEEK NEXT ?!
WMM

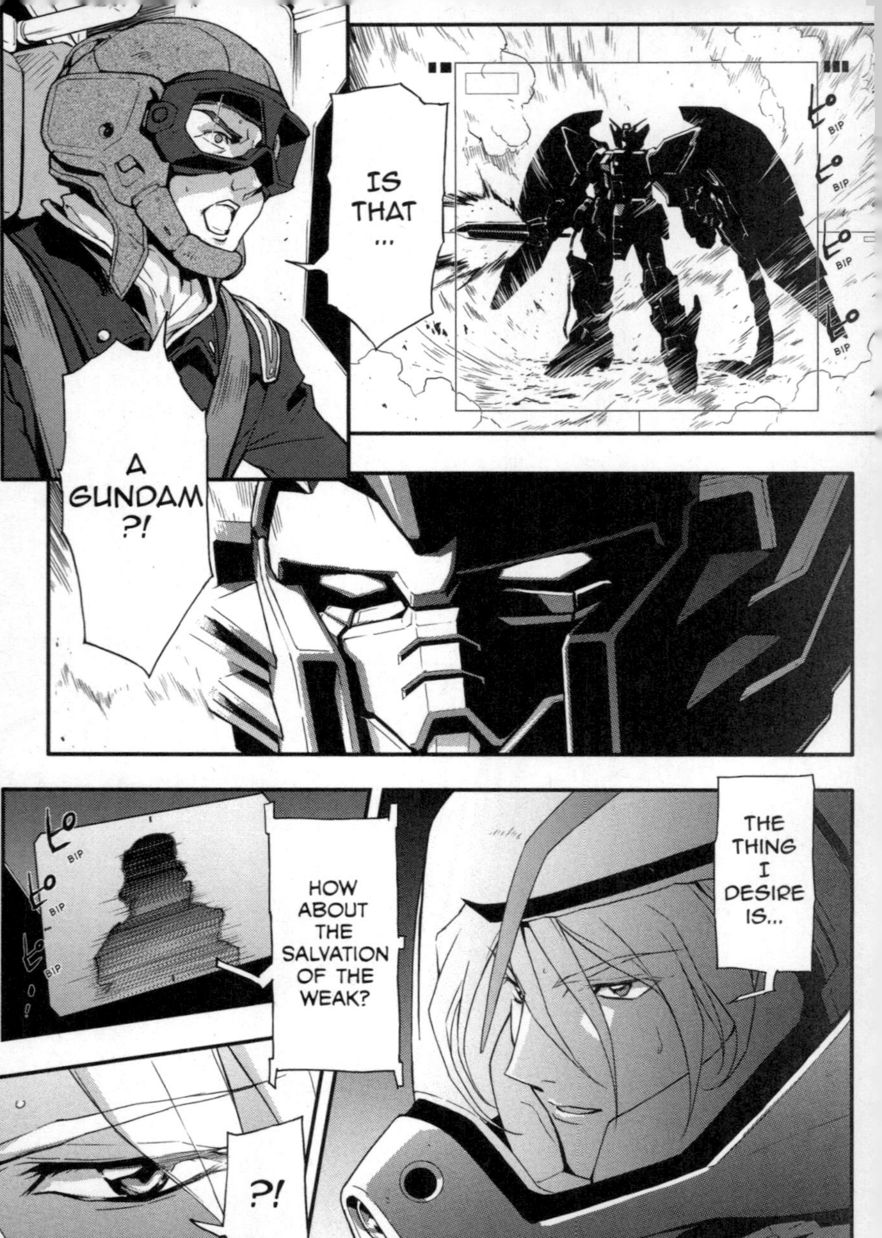
BIP
BIP
BIP
BIP
IS THAT ...
A GUNDAM ?!
THE THING I DESIRE IS...
BIP
BIP
BIP
HOW ABOUT THE SALVATION OF THE WEAK?
?!

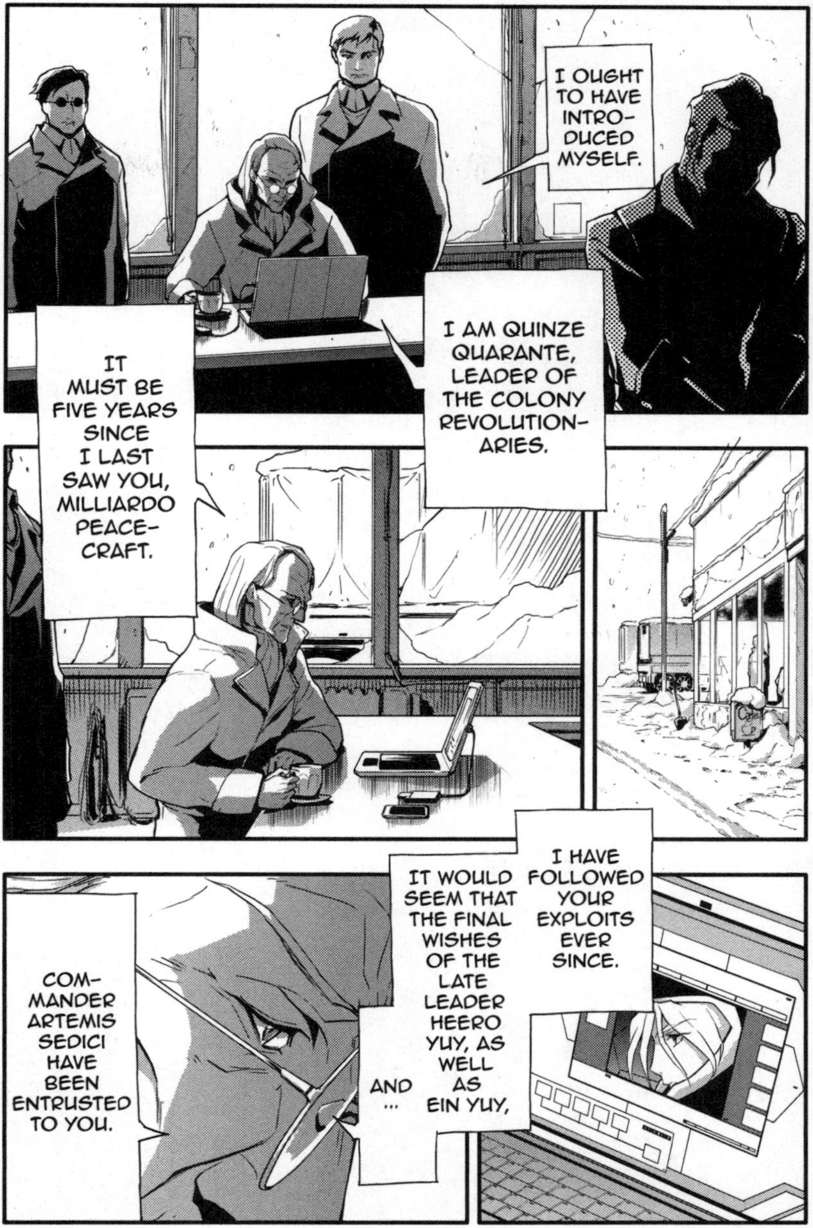
I OUGHT TO HAVE INTRO-DUCED MYSELF.
I AM QUINZE QUARANTE, LEADER OF THE COLONY REVOLUTION-ARIES.
IT MUST BE FIVE YEARS SINCE I LAST SAW YOU, MILLIARDO PEACE-CRAFT.
I HAVE FOLLOWED YOUR EXPLOITS EVER SINCE.
IT WOULD SEEM THAT THE FINAL WISHES OF THE LATE LEADER HEERO YUY, AS WELL AS EIN YUY,
AND ...
COM-MANDER ARTEMIS SEDICI HAVE BEEN ENTRUSTED TO YOU.

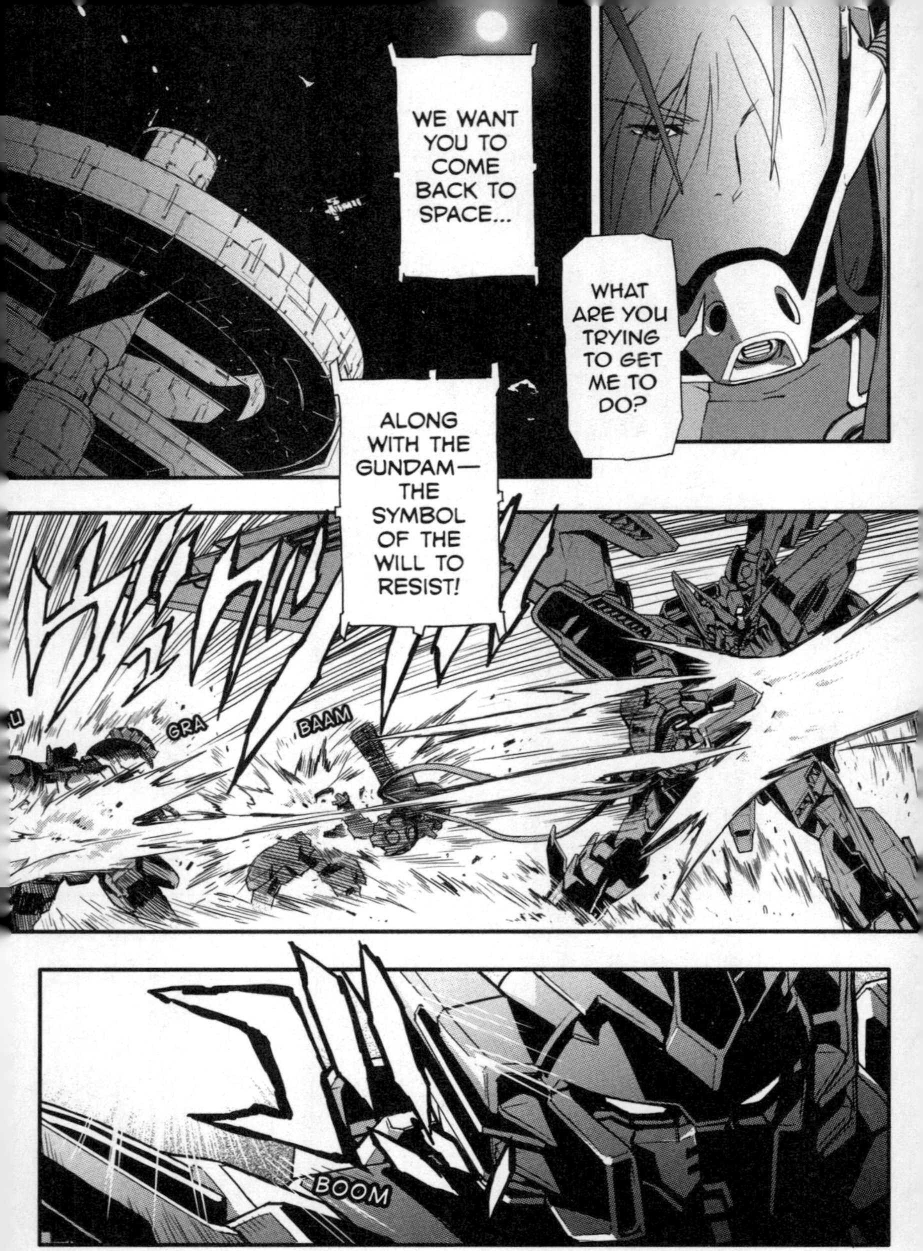
WHAT ARE YOU TRYING TO GET ME TO DO?
WE WANT YOU TO COME BACK TO SPACE...
ALONG WITH THE GUNDAM—THE SYMBOL OF THE WILL TO RESIST!
BAAM
GRA
BOOM

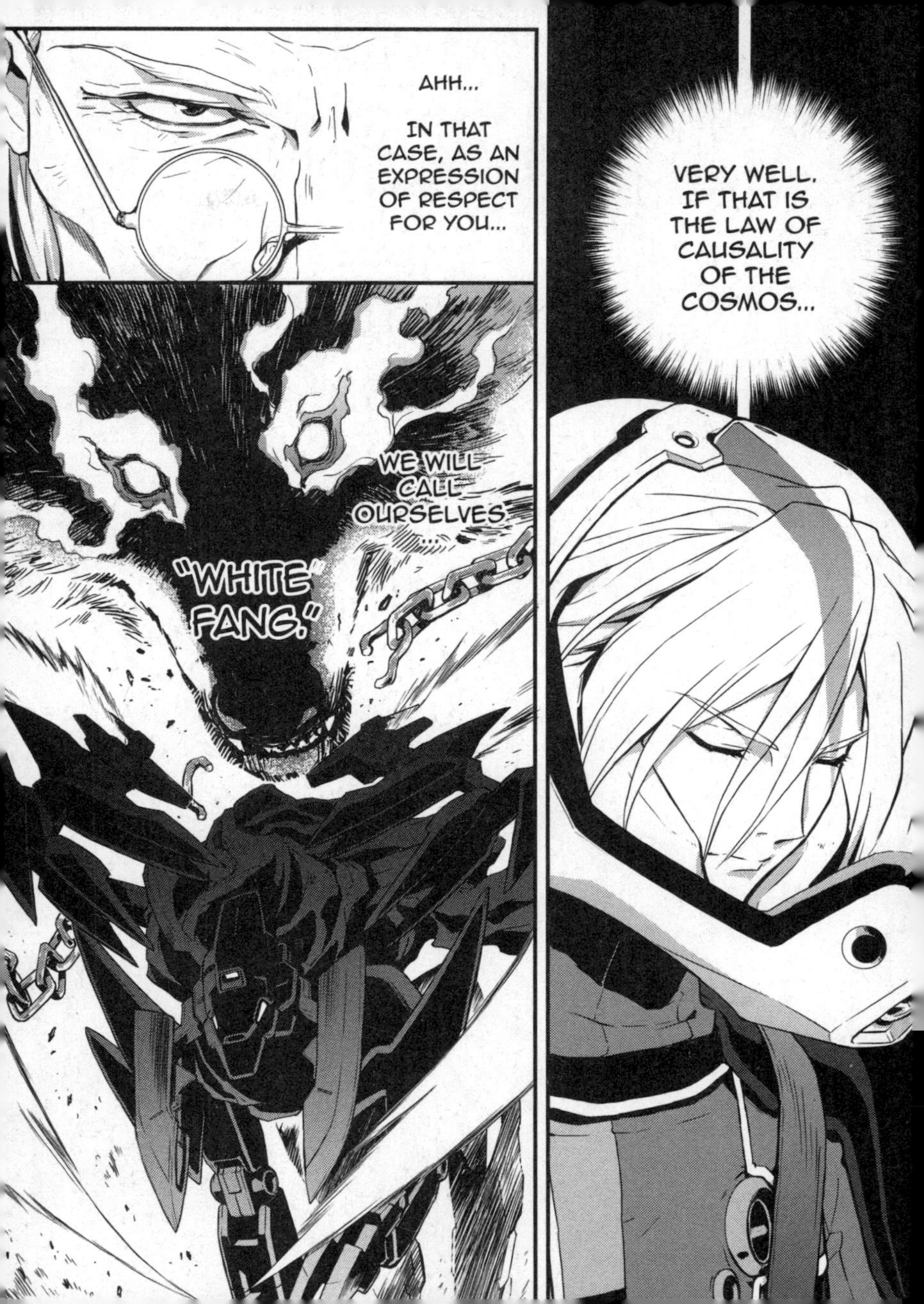
VERY WELL. IF THAT IS THE LAW OF CAUSALITY OF THE COSMOS...
AHH...
IN THAT CASE, AS AN EXPRESSION OF RESPECT FOR YOU...
WE WILL CALL OURSELVES...
"WHITE" FANG."

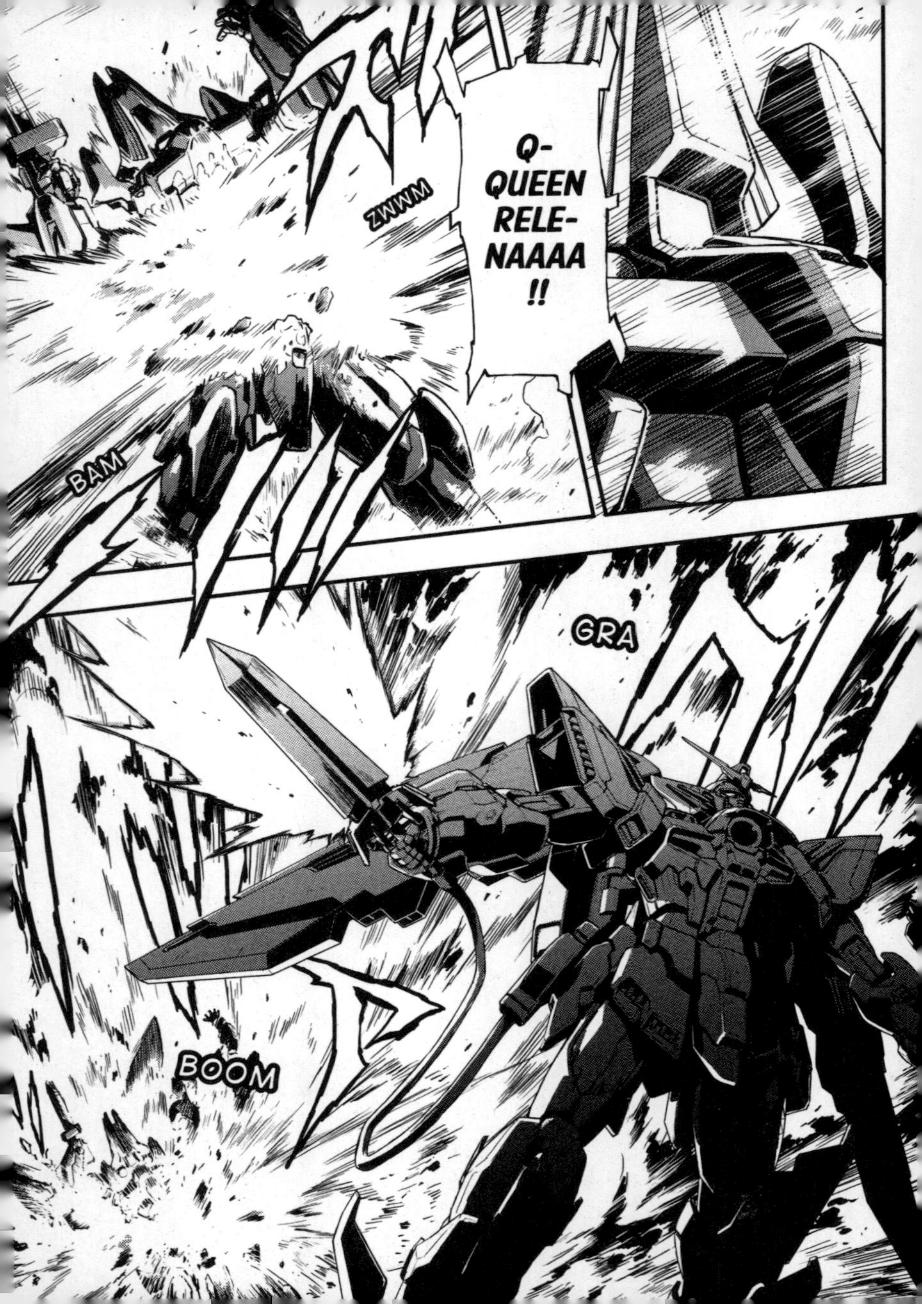
Q-
QUEEN
RELE-
NAAAA
!!
ZWWM
BAM
GRA
BOOM

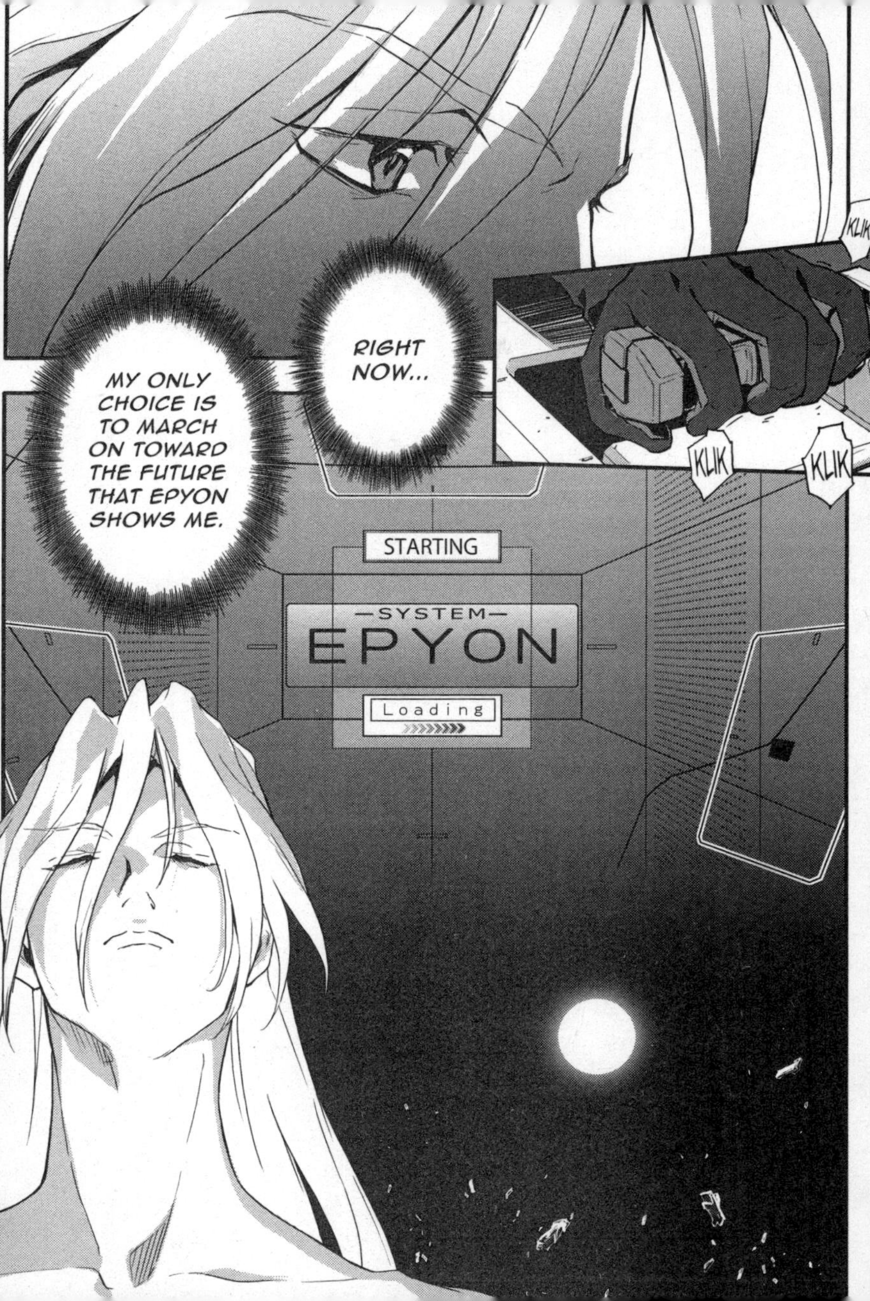
KLIK
KLIK
KLIK
RIGHT NOW...
MY ONLY CHOICE IS TO MARCH ON TOWARD THE FUTURE THAT EPYON SHOWS ME.
STARTING
—SYSTEM— EPYON
Loading

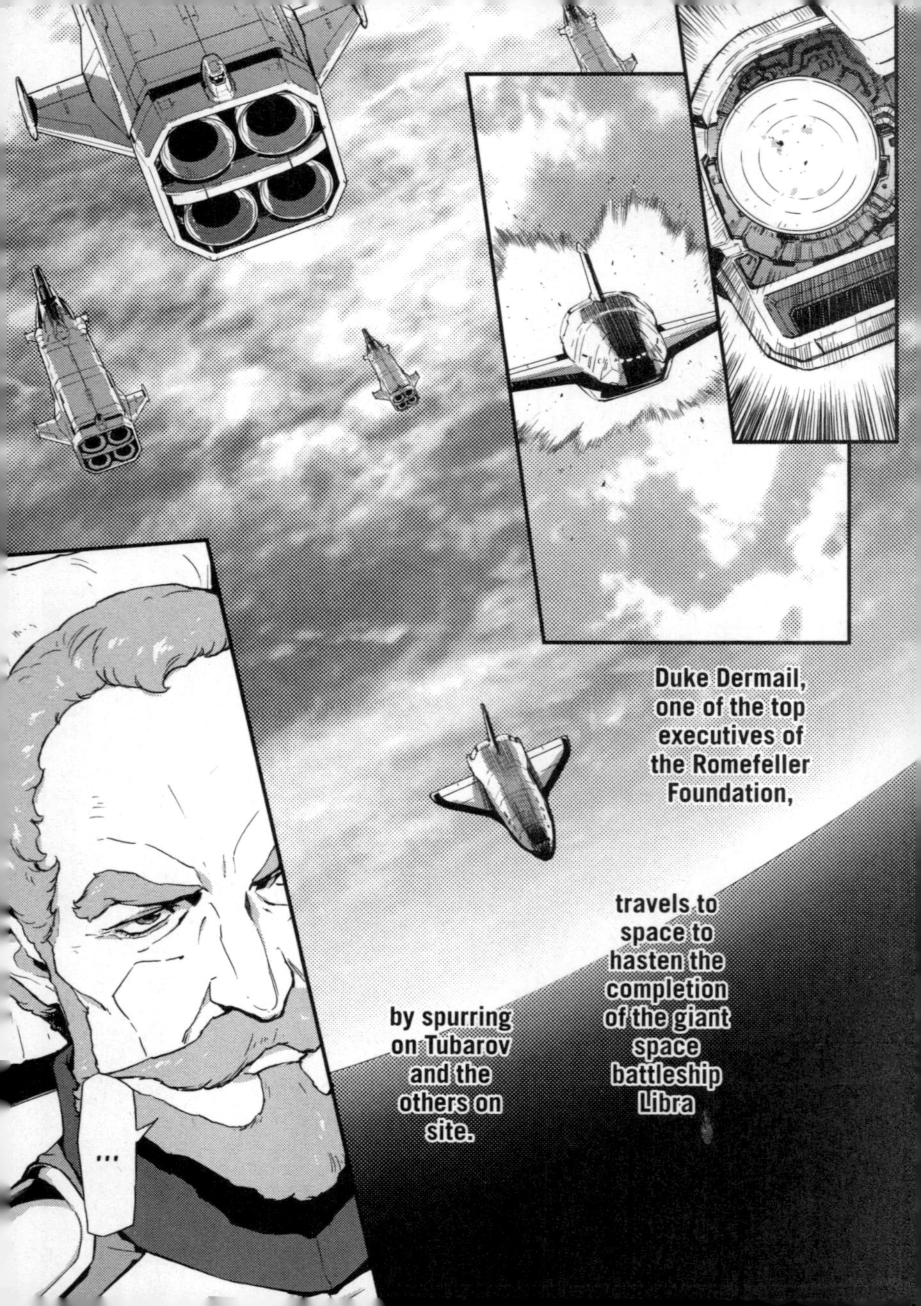
Duke Dermail, one of the top executives of the Romefeller Foundation,
travels to space to hasten the completion of the giant space battleship Libra
by spurring on Tubarov and the others on site.
...

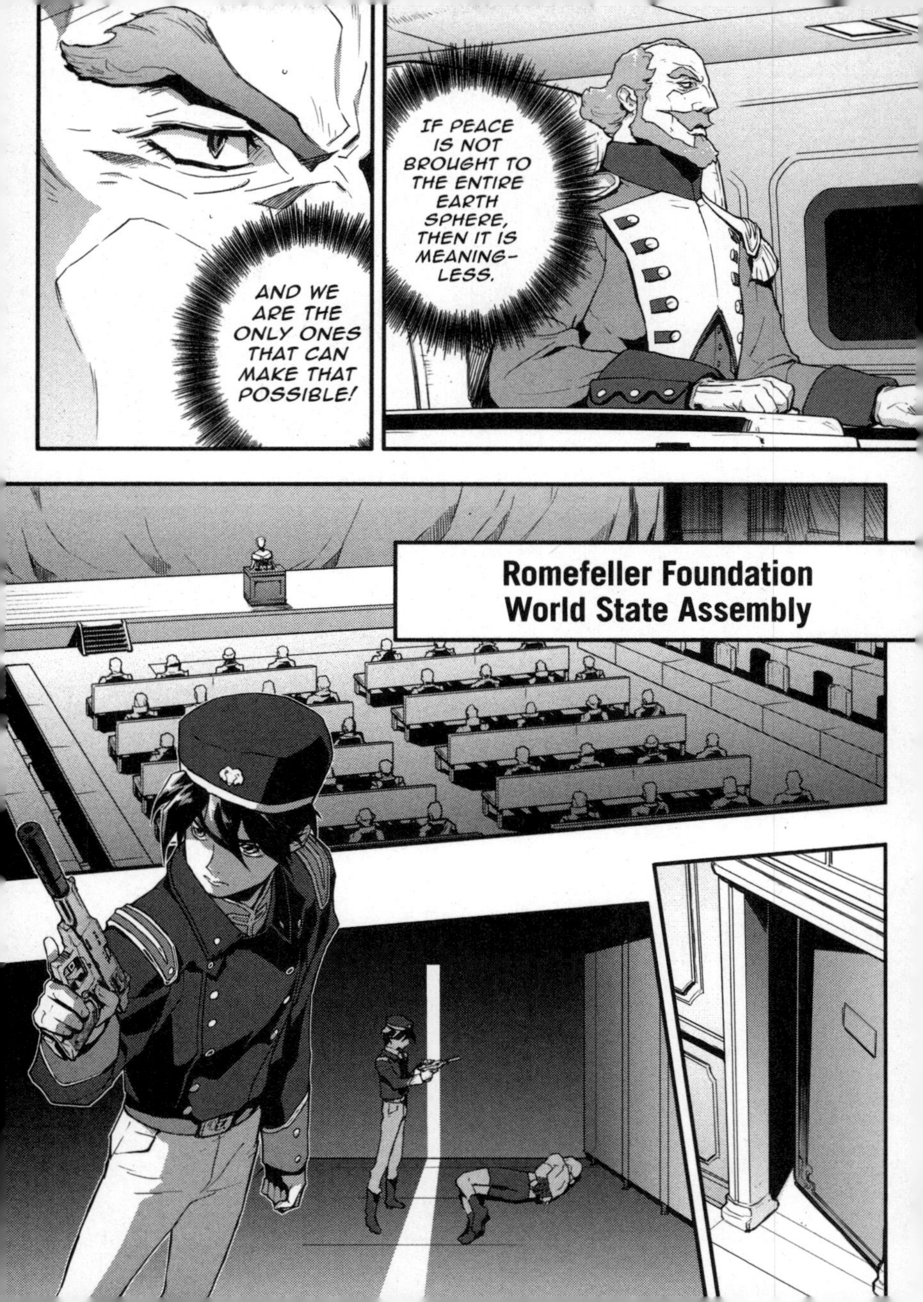
IF PEACE IS NOT BROUGHT TO THE ENTIRE EARTH SPHERE, THEN IT IS MEANING-LESS.
AND WE ARE THE ONLY ONES THAT CAN MAKE THAT POSSIBLE!
Romefeller Foundation World State Assembly

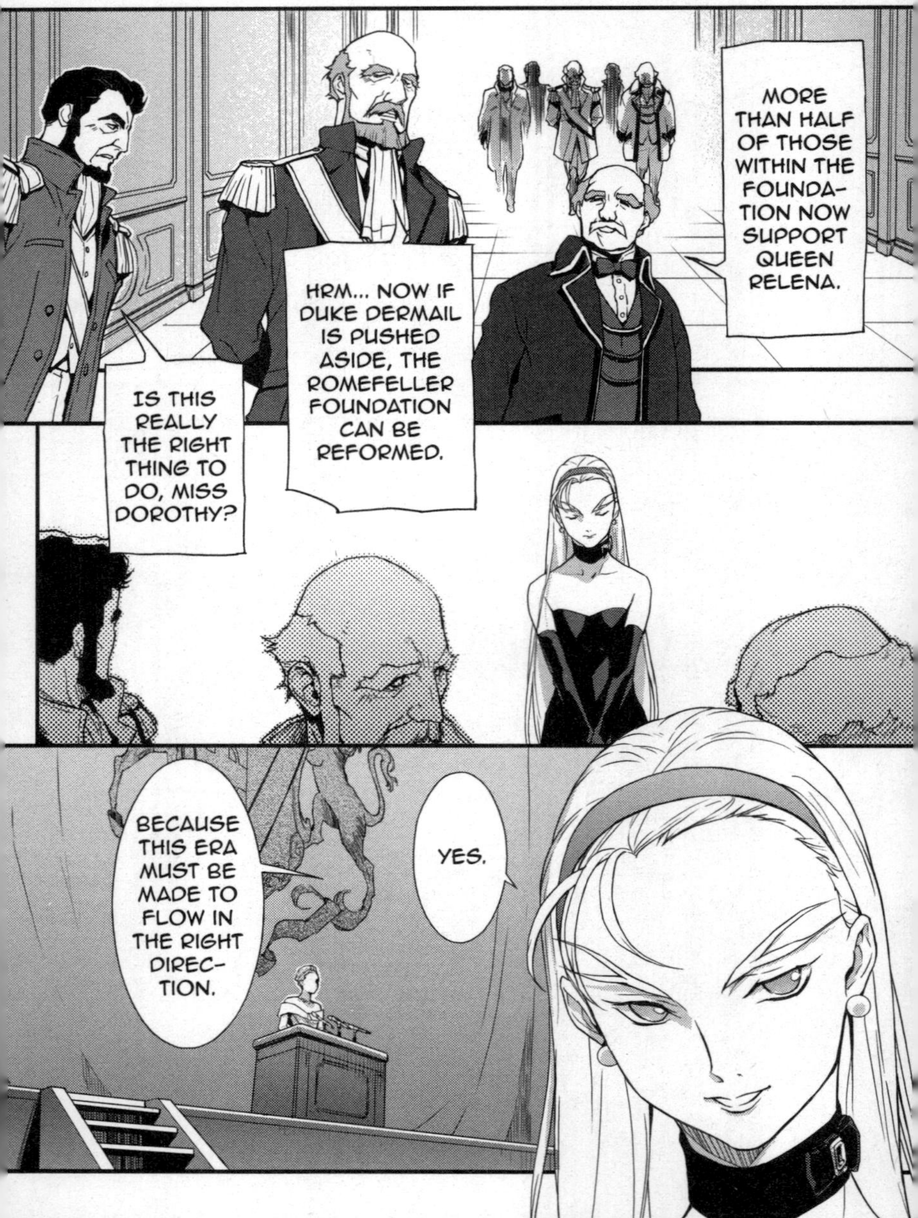
MORE THAN HALF OF THOSE WITHIN THE FOUNDA-TION NOW SUPPORT QUEEN RELENA.
HRM... NOW IF DUKE DERMAIL IS PUSHED ASIDE, THE ROMEFELLER FOUNDATION CAN BE REFORMED.
IS THIS REALLY THE RIGHT THING TO DO, MISS DOROTHY?
YES.
BECAUSE THIS ERA MUST BE MADE TO FLOW IN THE RIGHT DIREC-TION.

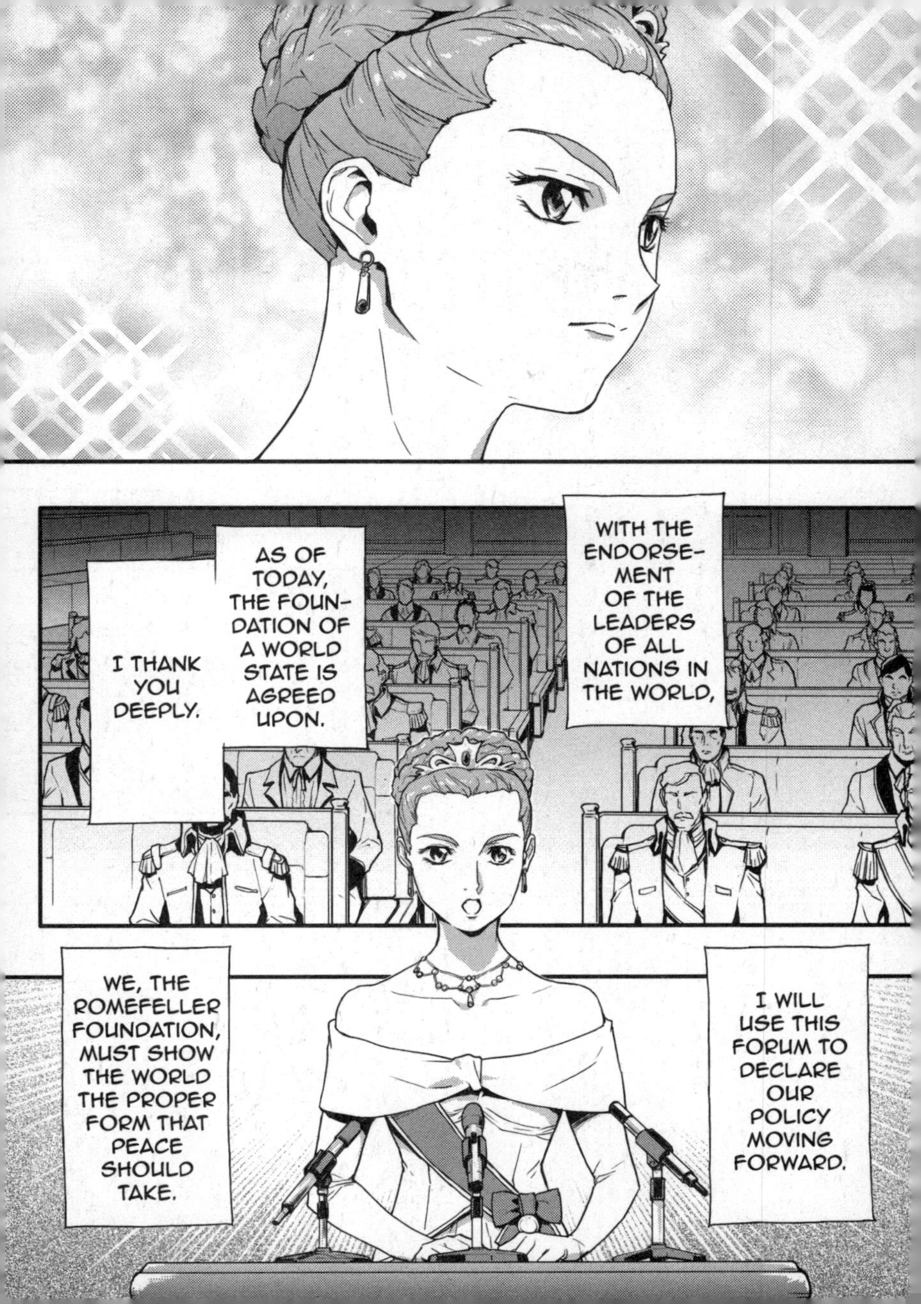
WITH THE ENDORSEMENT OF THE LEADERS OF ALL NATIONS IN THE WORLD,
AS OF TODAY, THE FOUNDATION OF A WORLD STATE IS AGREED UPON.
I THANK YOU DEEPLY.
I WILL USE THIS FORUM TO DECLARE OUR POLICY MOVING FORWARD.
WE, THE ROMEFELLER FOUNDATION, MUST SHOW THE WORLD THE PROPER FORM THAT PEACE SHOULD TAKE.

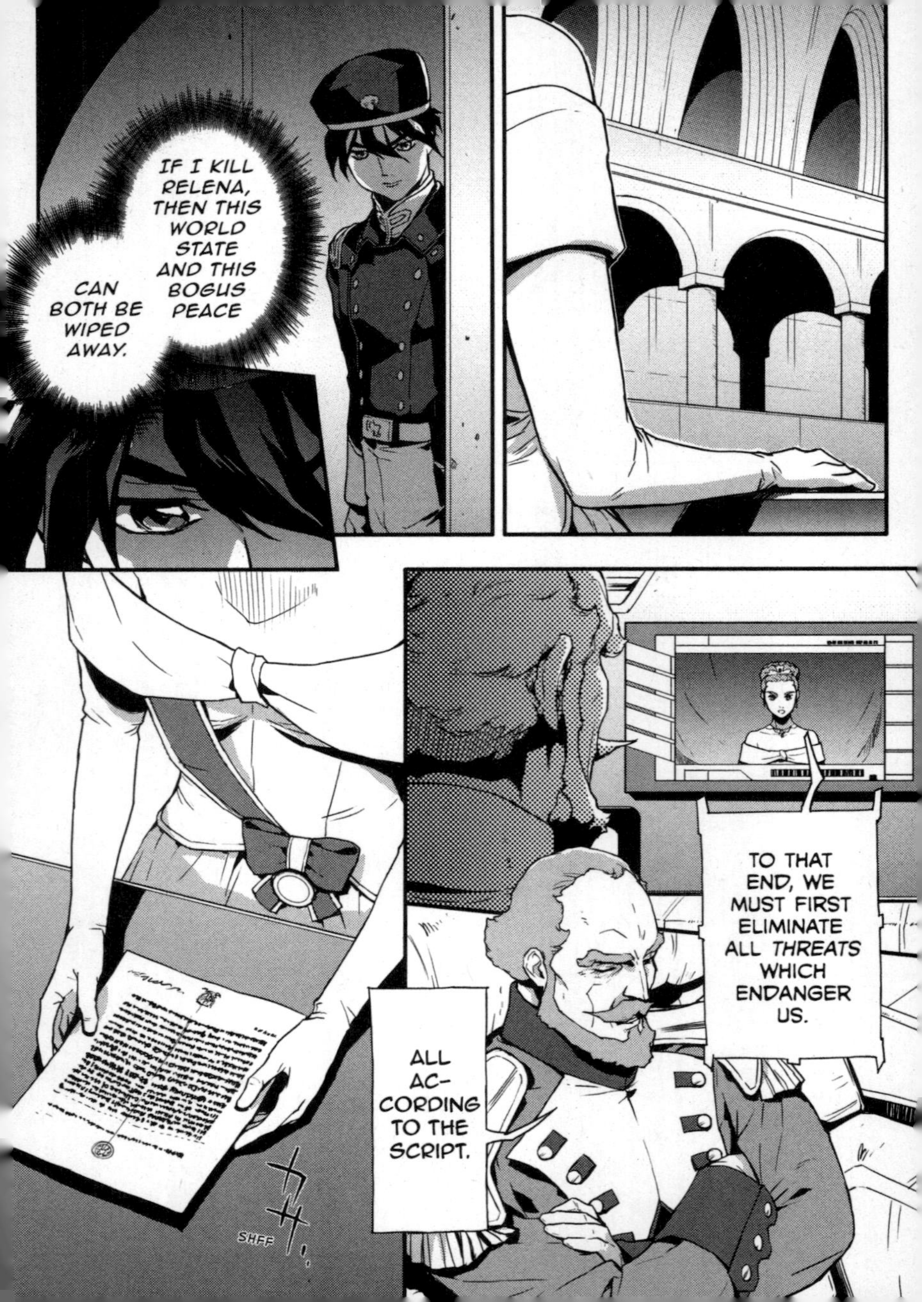
IF I KILL RELENA, THEN THIS WORLD STATE AND THIS BOGUS PEACE CAN BOTH BE WIPED AWAY.
TO THAT END, WE MUST FIRST ELIMINATE ALL *THREATS* WHICH ENDANGER US.
ALL AC-CORDING TO THE SCRIPT.
SHFF

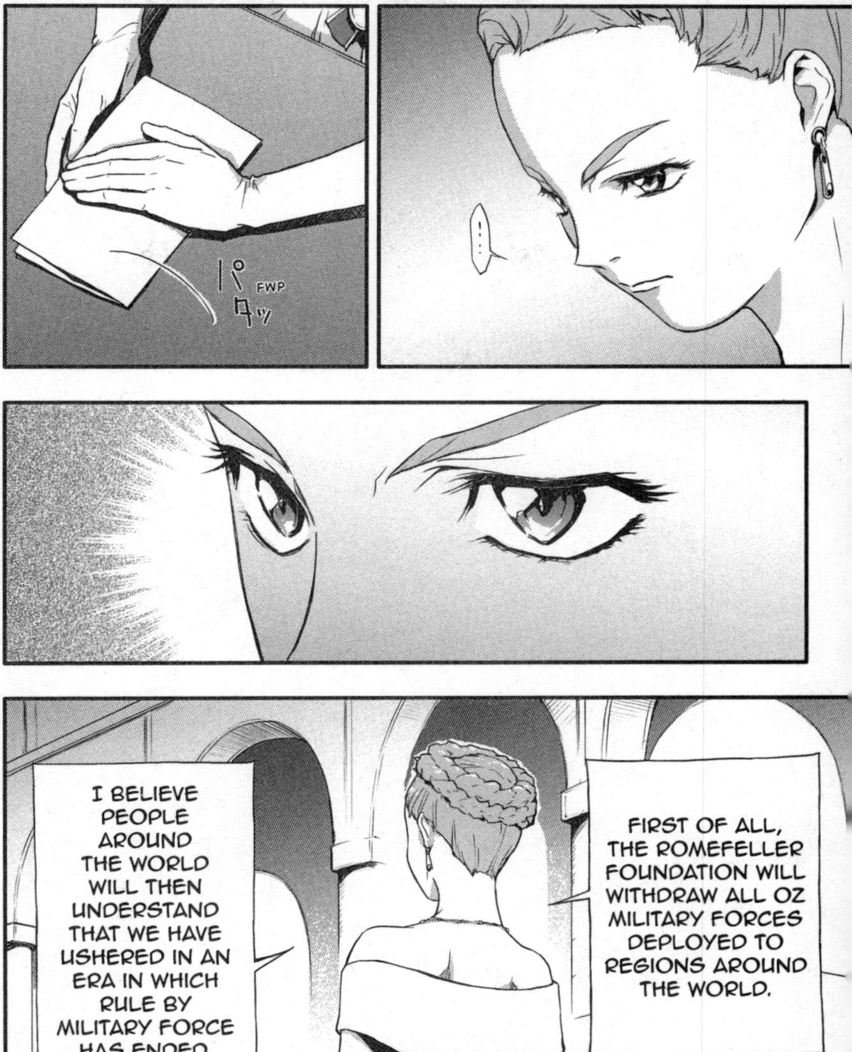
!...
パタッ
FWP
FIRST OF ALL, THE ROMEFELLER FOUNDATION WILL WITHDRAW ALL OZ MILITARY FORCES DEPLOYED TO REGIONS AROUND THE WORLD.
I BELIEVE PEOPLE AROUND THE WORLD WILL THEN UNDERSTAND THAT WE HAVE USHERED IN AN ERA IN WHICH RULE BY MILITARY FORCE HAS ENDED.

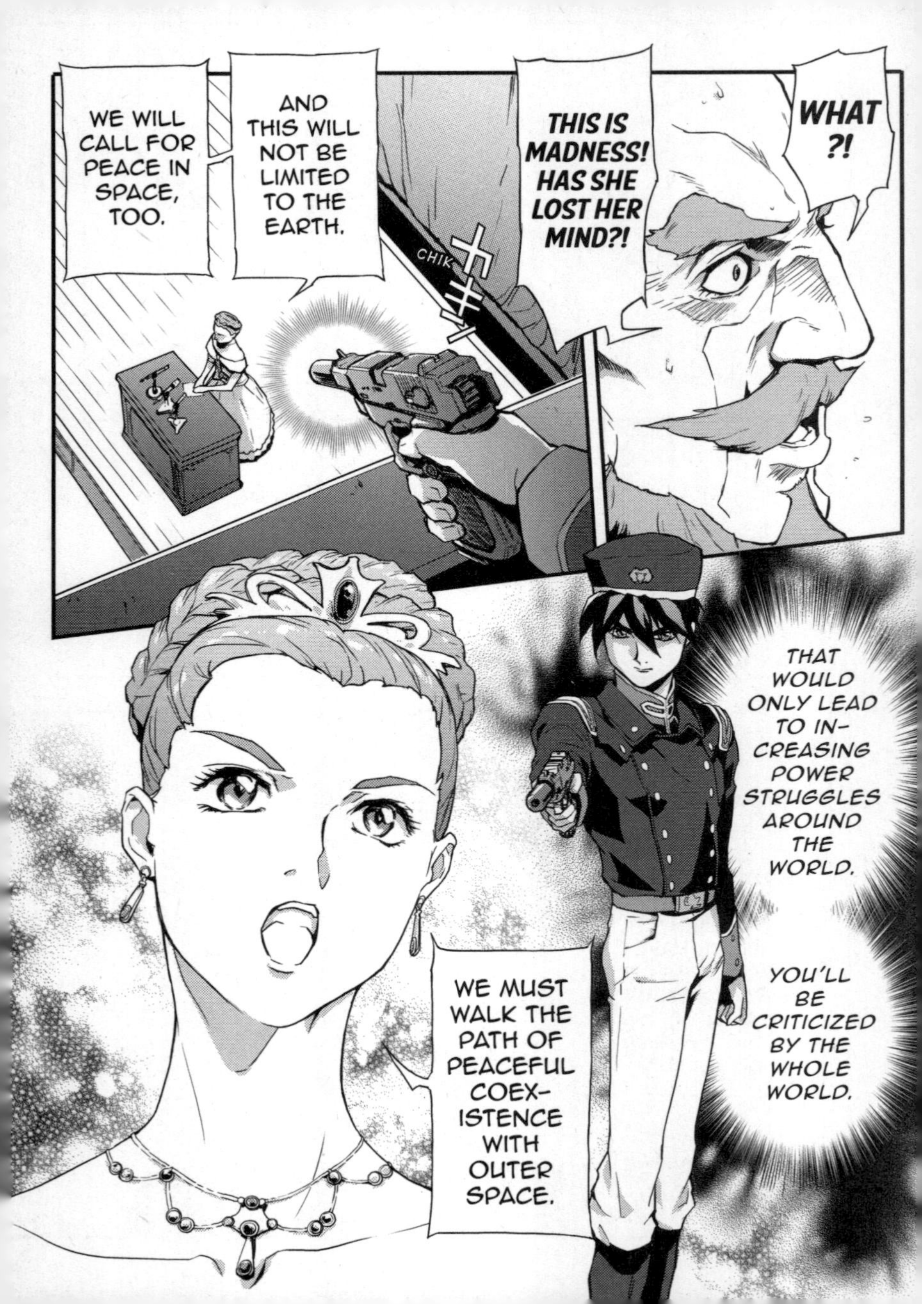
WHAT ?!
THIS IS MADNESS! HAS SHE LOST HER MIND?!
CHIK
AND THIS WILL NOT BE LIMITED TO THE EARTH.
WE WILL CALL FOR PEACE IN SPACE, TOO.
THAT WOULD ONLY LEAD TO IN-CREASING POWER STRUGGLES AROUND THE WORLD.
YOU'LL BE CRITICIZED BY THE WHOLE WORLD.
WE MUST WALK THE PATH OF PEACEFUL COEX-ISTENCE WITH OUTER SPACE.

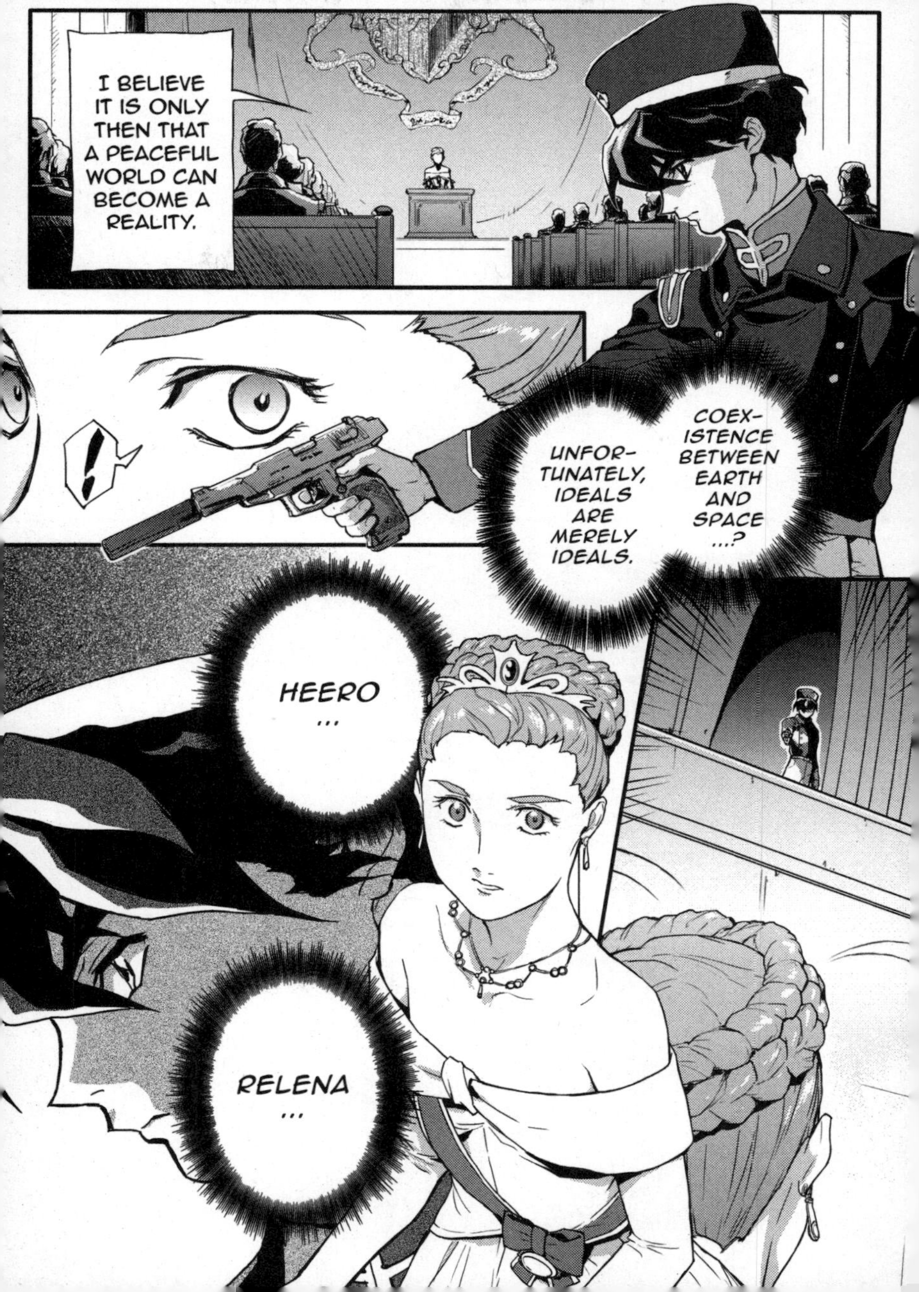
I BELIEVE IT IS ONLY THEN THAT A PEACEFUL WORLD CAN BECOME A REALITY.
COEX-ISTENCE BETWEEN EARTH AND SPACE ...?
UNFOR-TUNATELY, IDEALS ARE MERELY IDEALS.
!
HEERO ...
RELENA ...

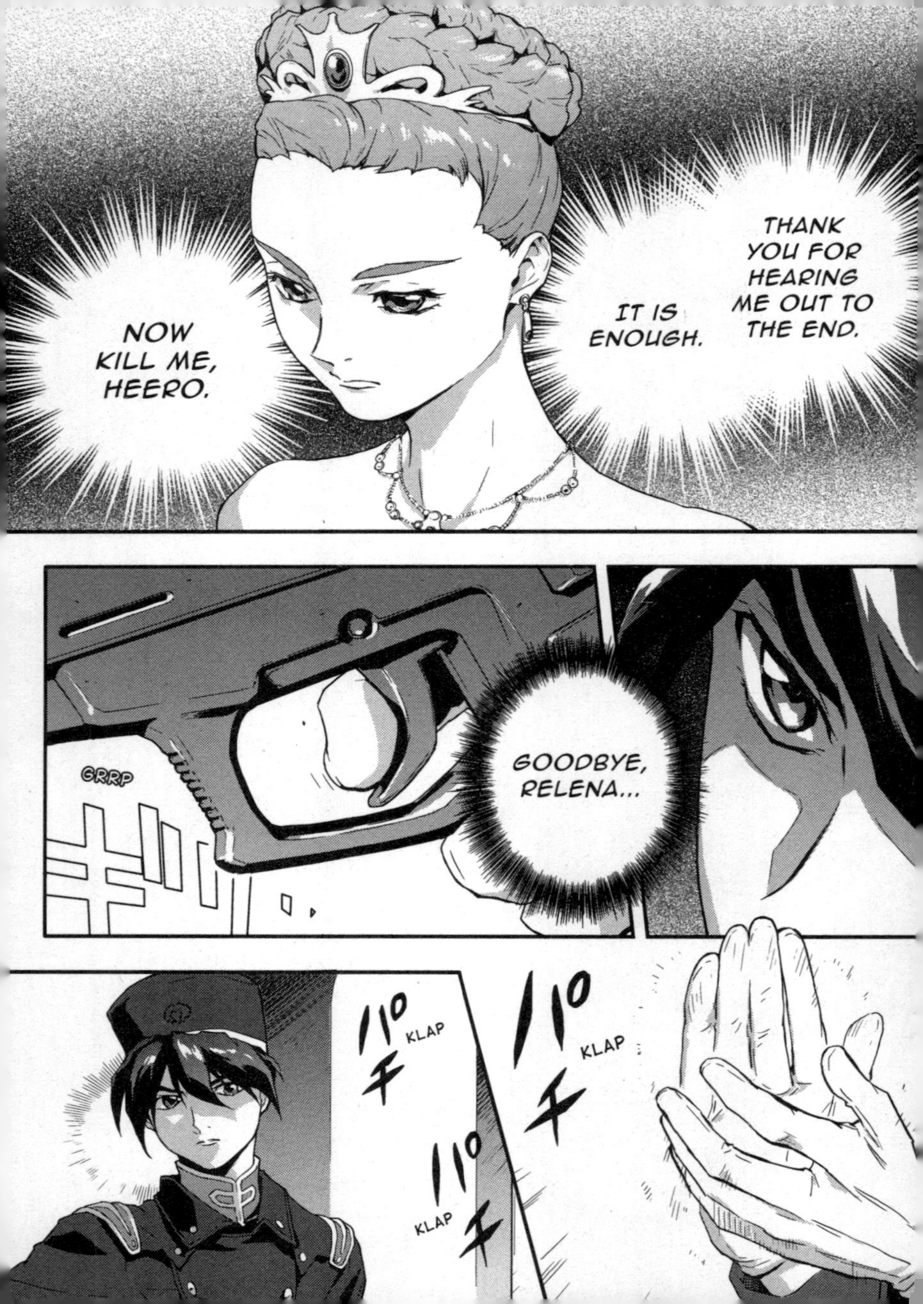

THANK YOU FOR HEARING ME OUT TO THE END.
IT IS ENOUGH.
NOW KILL ME, HEERO.
GOODBYE, RELENA...
GRRP
KLAP
KLAP
KLAP

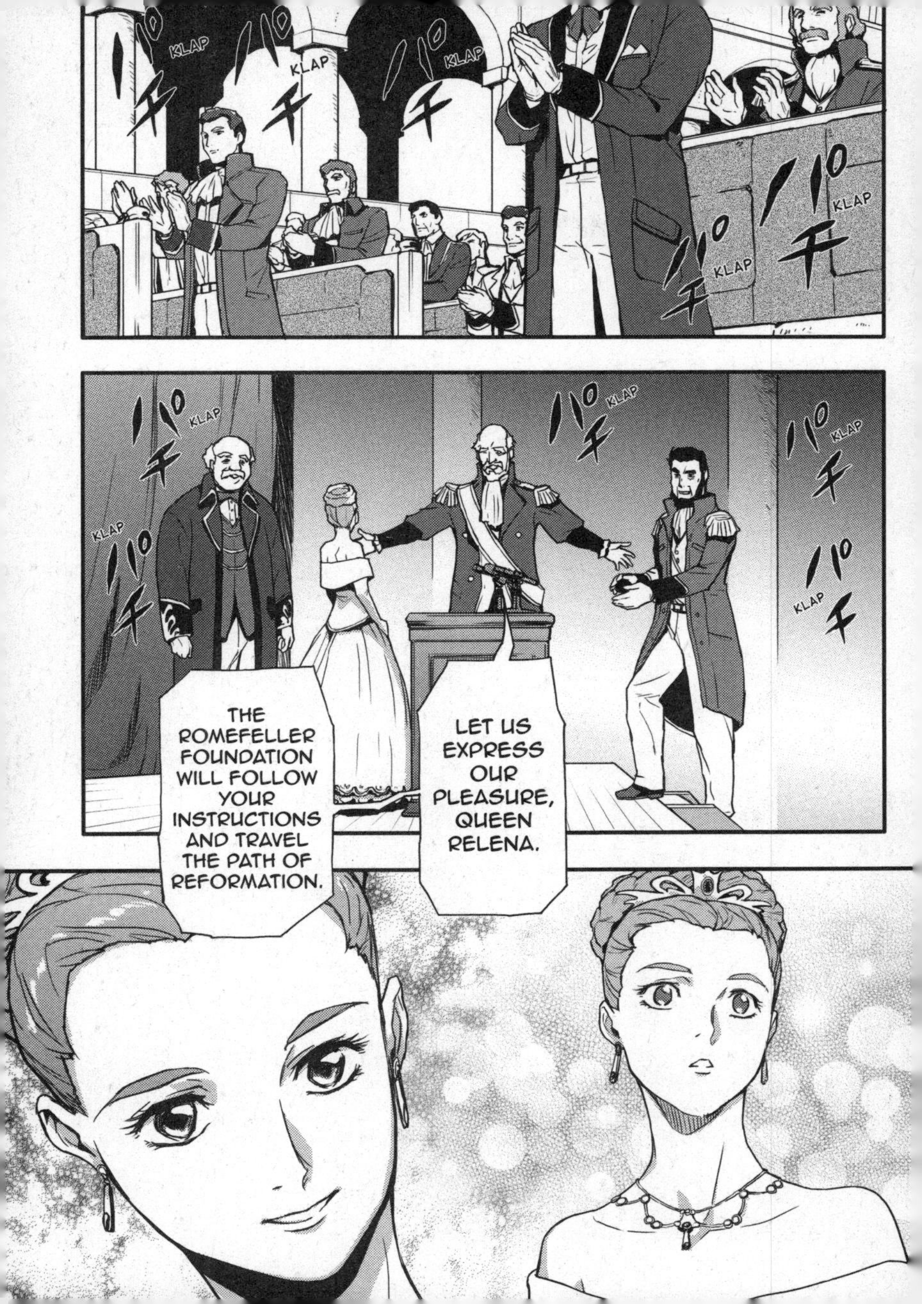
パチ
KLAP
パチ
KLAP
パチ
KLAP
パチ
KLAP
パチ
KLAP
パチ
KLAP
パチ
KLAP
パチ
KLAP
パチ
KLAP
パチ
KLAP
LET US EXPRESS OUR PLEASURE, QUEEN RELENA.
THE ROMEFELLER FOUNDATION WILL FOLLOW YOUR INSTRUCTIONS AND TRAVEL THE PATH OF REFORMATION.

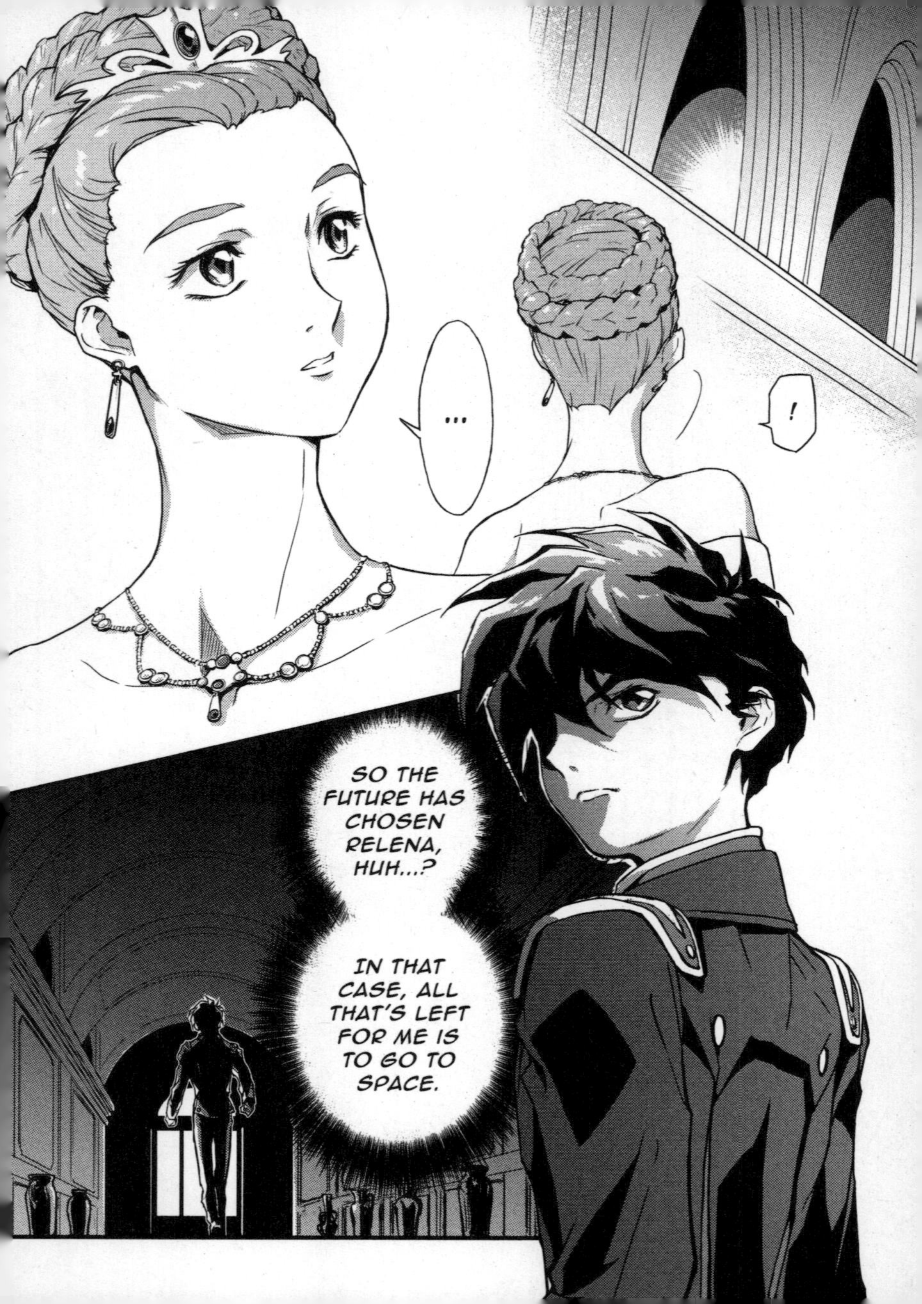
!
...
SO THE FUTURE HAS CHOSEN RELENA, HUH...?
IN THAT CASE, ALL THAT'S LEFT FOR ME IS TO GO TO SPACE.

SLEEVE NOTES:
Endless Waltz

QUINZE QUARANTE

Leader of the colony revolutionaries, he watched and waited for the opportunity to revolt while Sedici and other comrades were in hiding within OZ. He met Zechs five years earlier when Zechs was cooperating with the colony rebel army after his surrender. With a direct descendant of the Peacecraft royal family (Zechs) and a symbol of resistance (a Gundam) in his hands, Quinze takes audacious action against the world state. Also, his brother Tomas was a genius who created the "ZERO System" when he was a student, and he was killed by the tyranny of the United Earth Sphere Alliance.

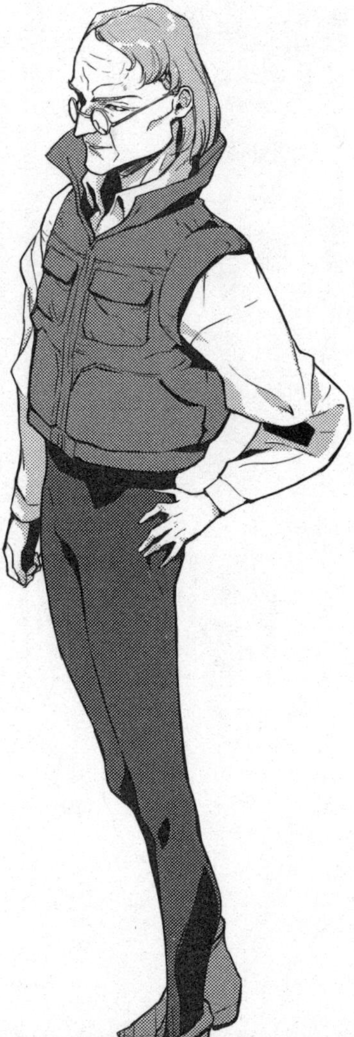

SLEEVE NOTES:
Endless Waltz

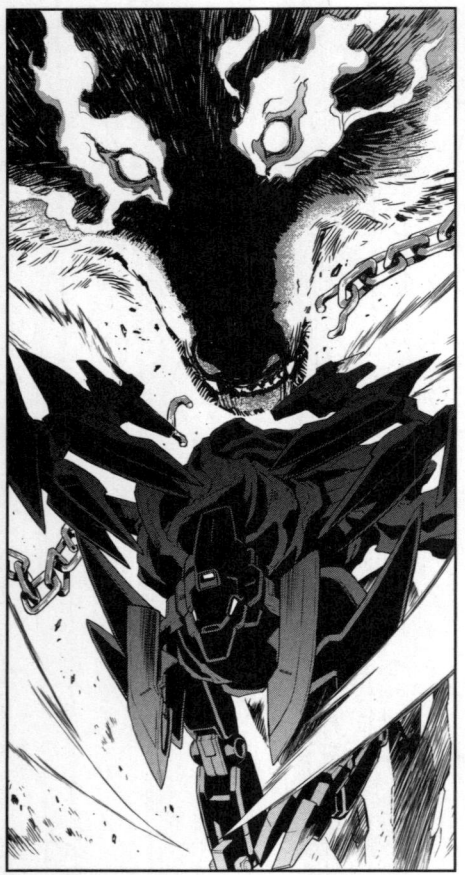

MS "MAOH"

When Quinze invites Zechs to join the activities of the revolutionaries, he names their organization "White Fang." This is in reference to the MS "Maoh" which Zechs once piloted when he was a rebel army test pilot. The Maoh ran on four legs and was specialized for high speeds, and its weapon was called the "White Fang." It exhibited fearsome power in close-range combat.

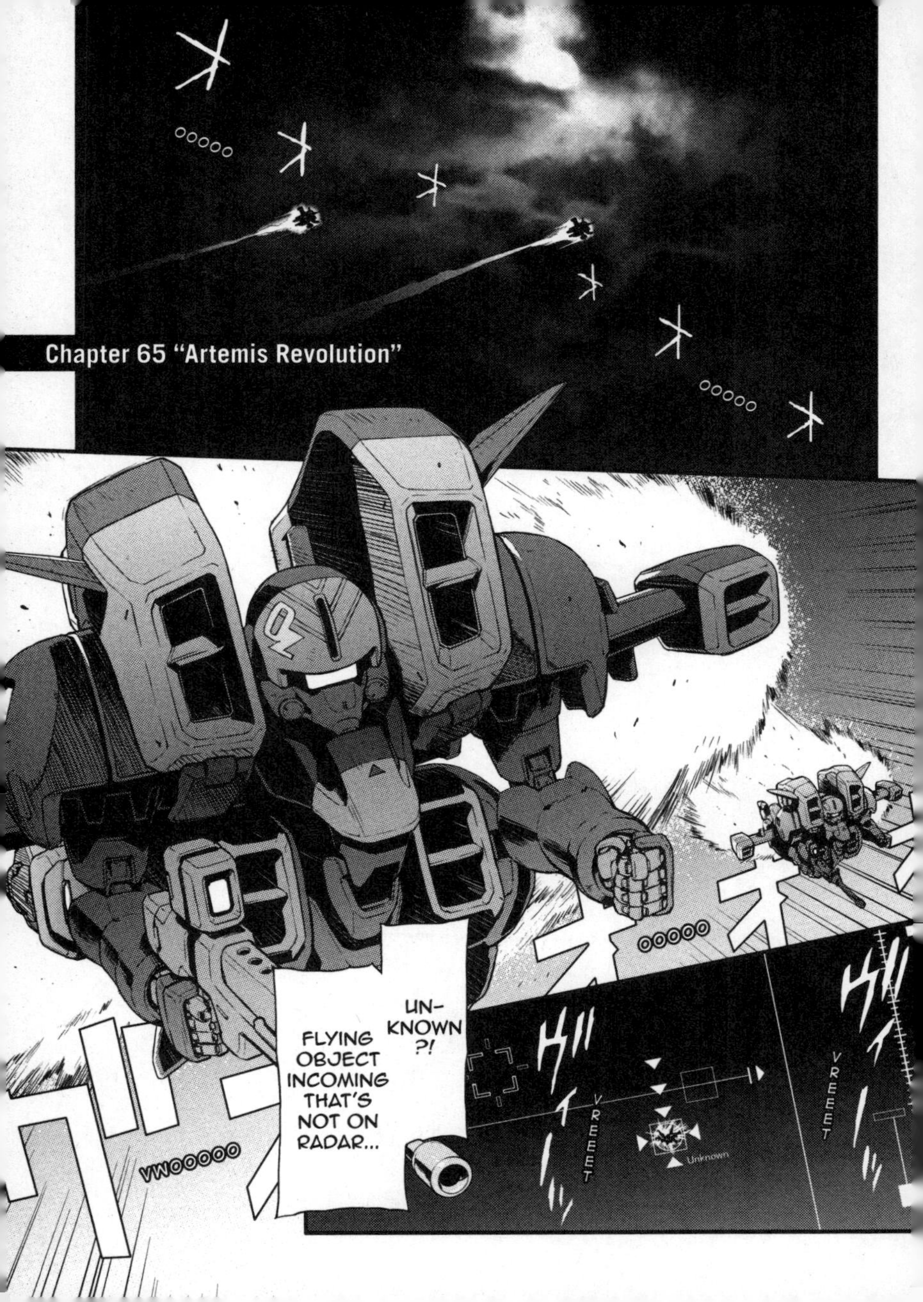
Chapter 65 "Artemis Revolution"
ooooo
ooooo
ooooo
UN-KNOWN ?!
FLYING OBJECT INCOMING THAT'S NOT ON RADAR...
VREEET
VREEET
Unknown
VWOOOOOO

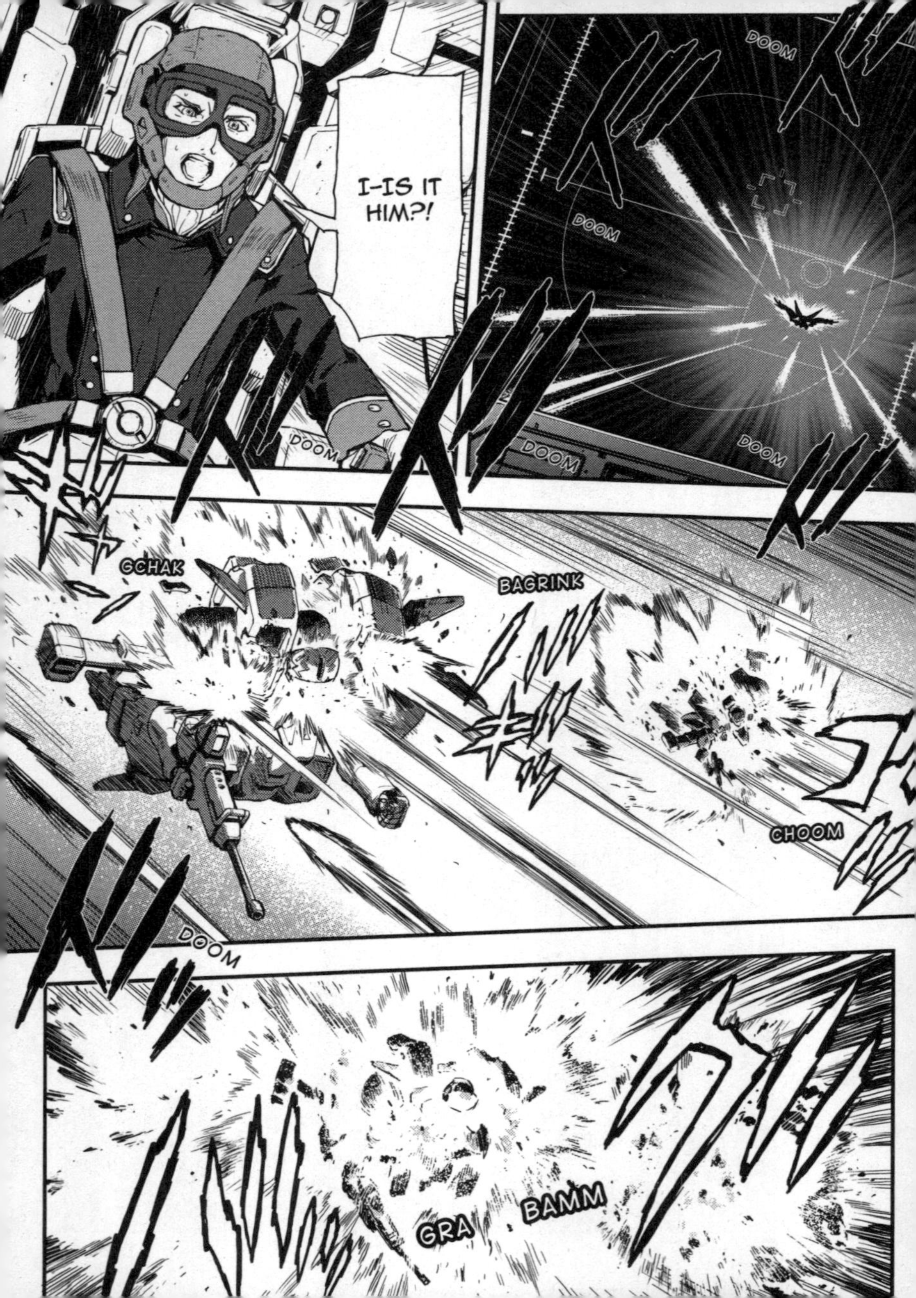
DOOM
DOOM
DOOM
DOOM
I-IS IT HIM?!
DOOM
BAGRINK
GCHAK
CHOOM
DOOM
GRA BAMM

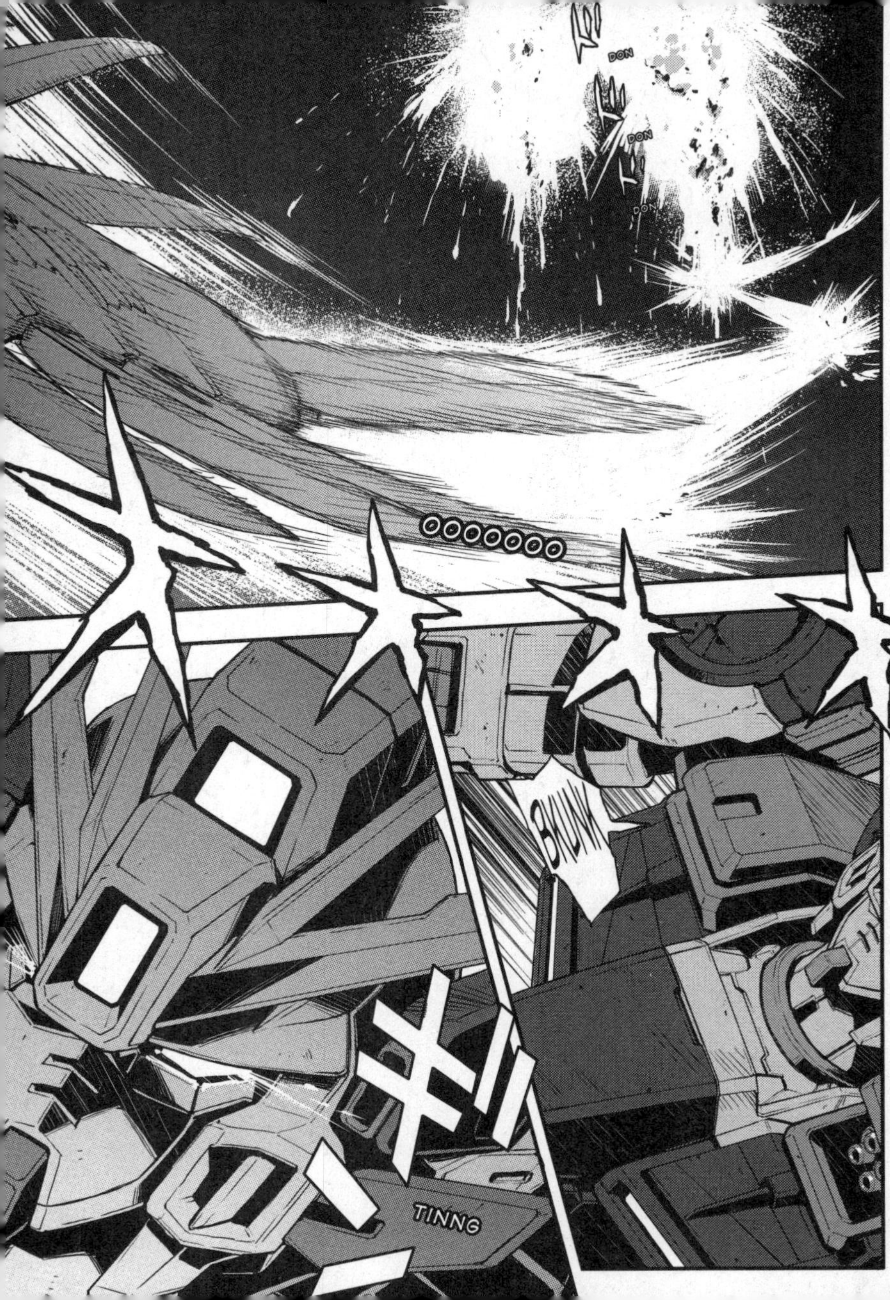
DON
DON
DON
OOOOOOOO
BKUNK
TINNG

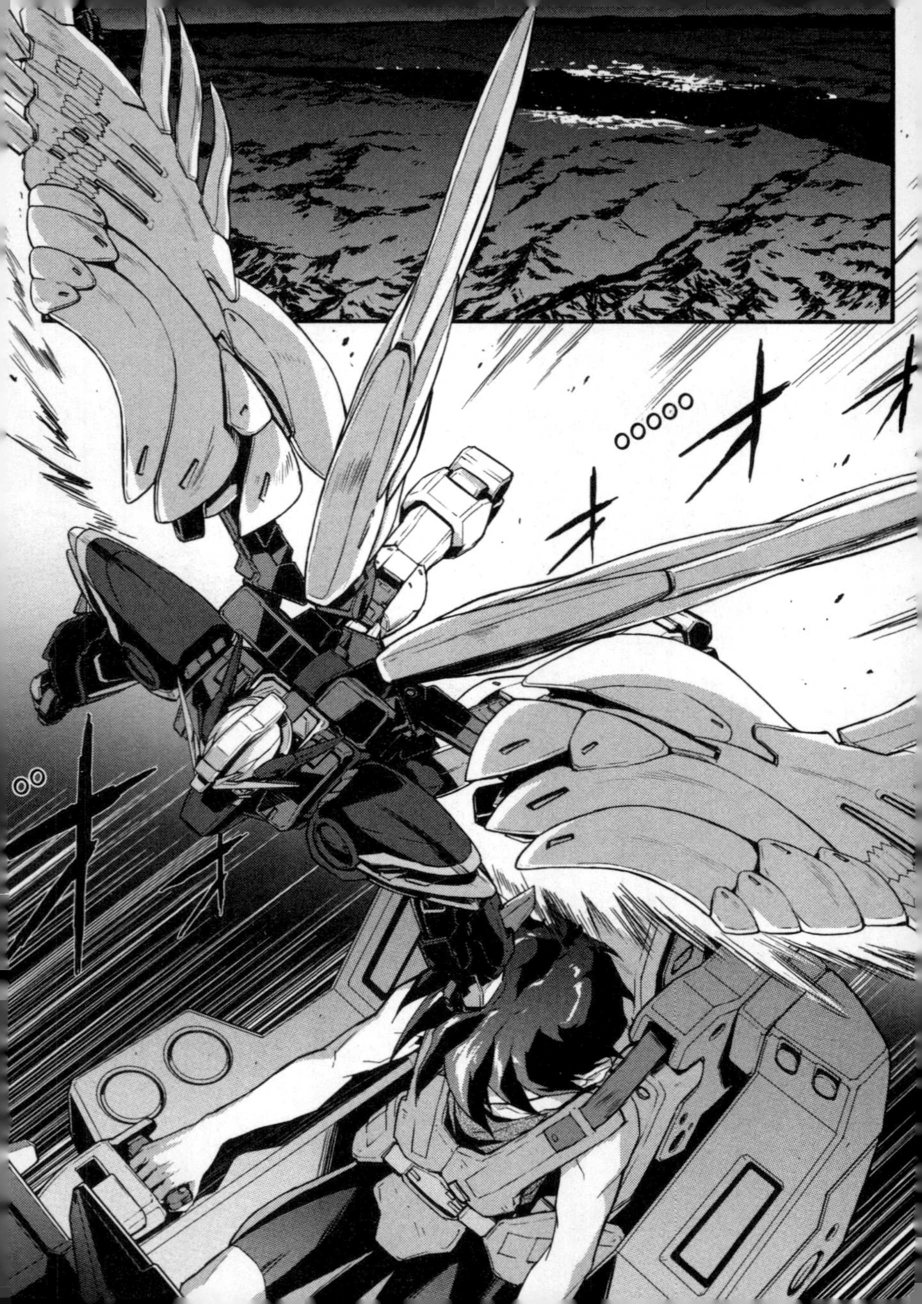
OOOOO
OO

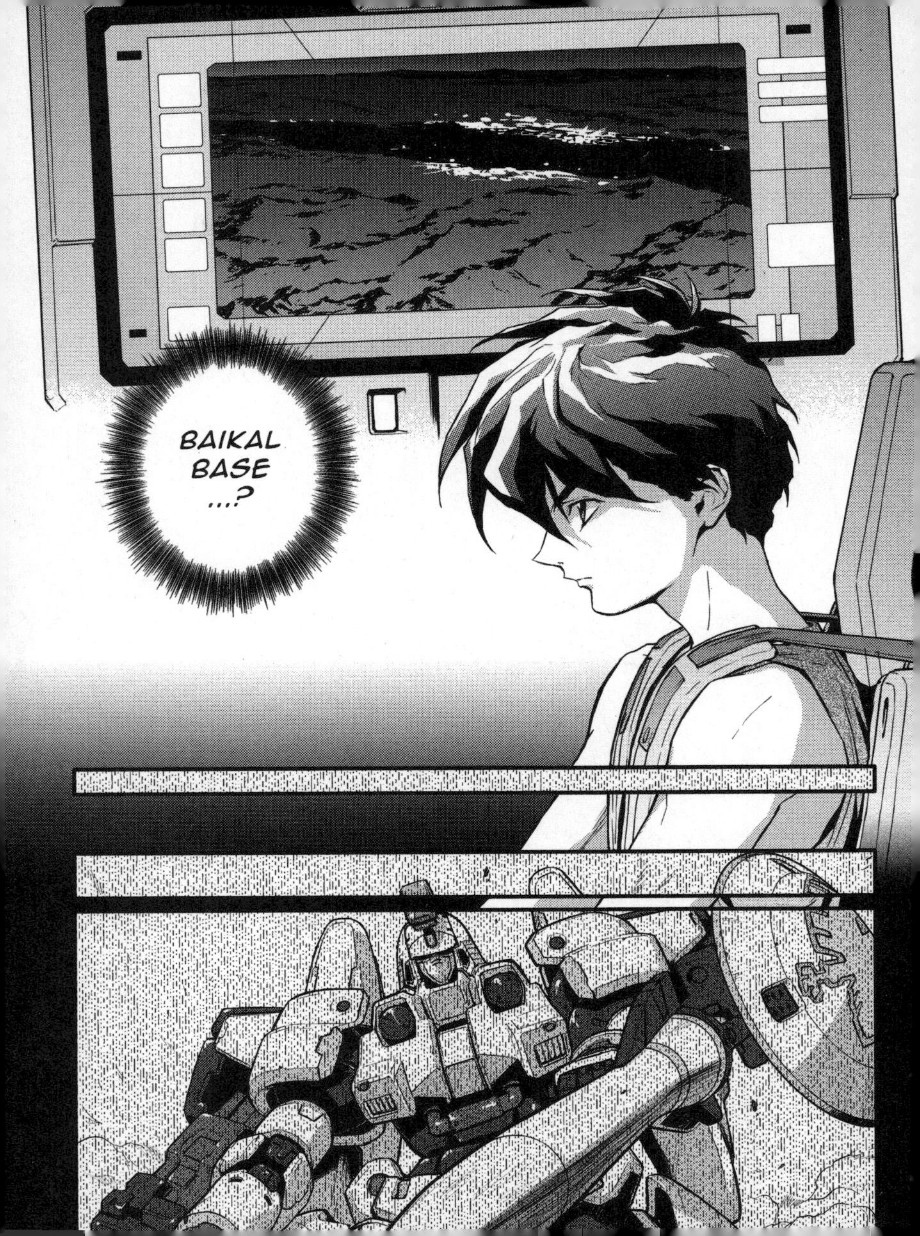
BAIKAL BASE ...?

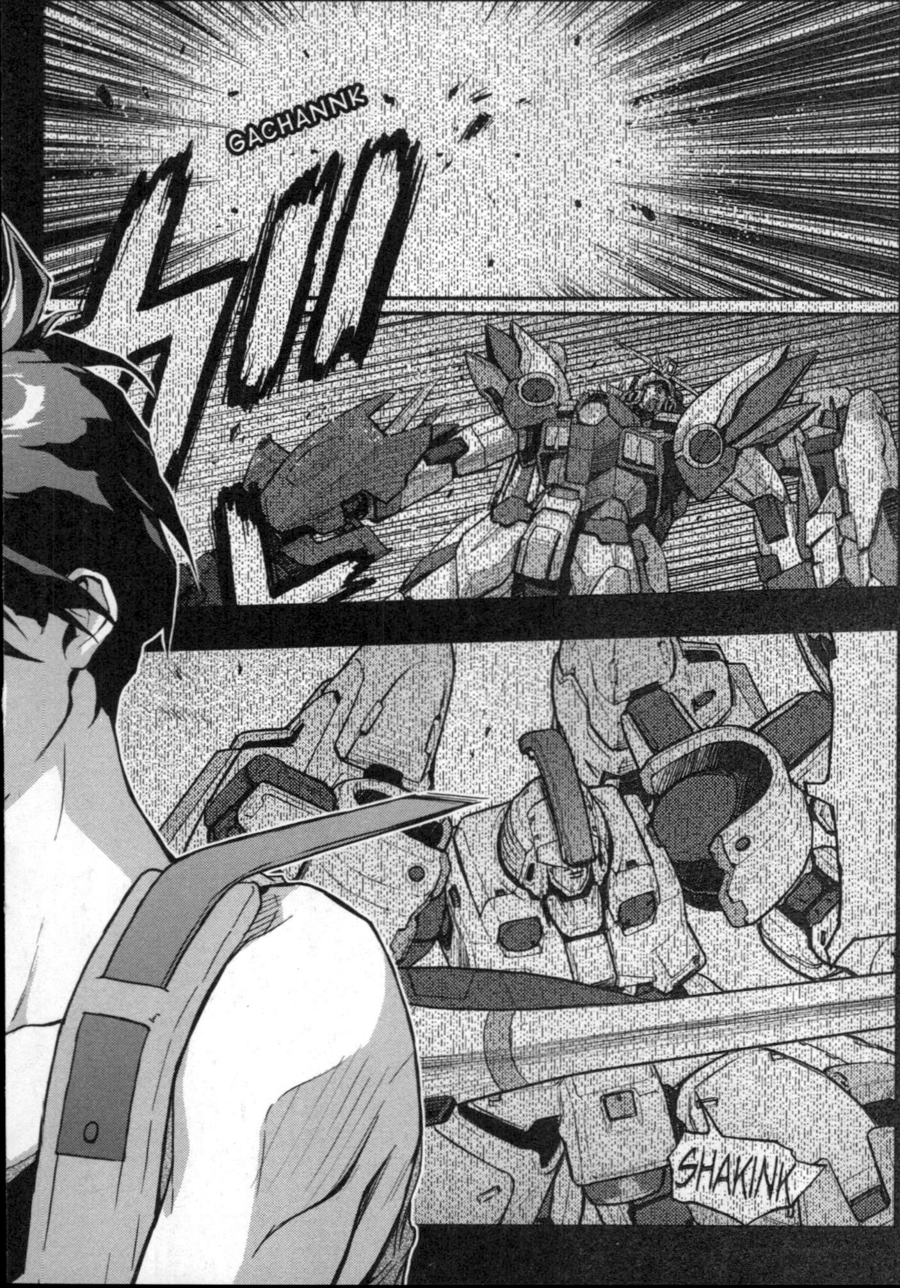
GACHANNK
SHAKINK

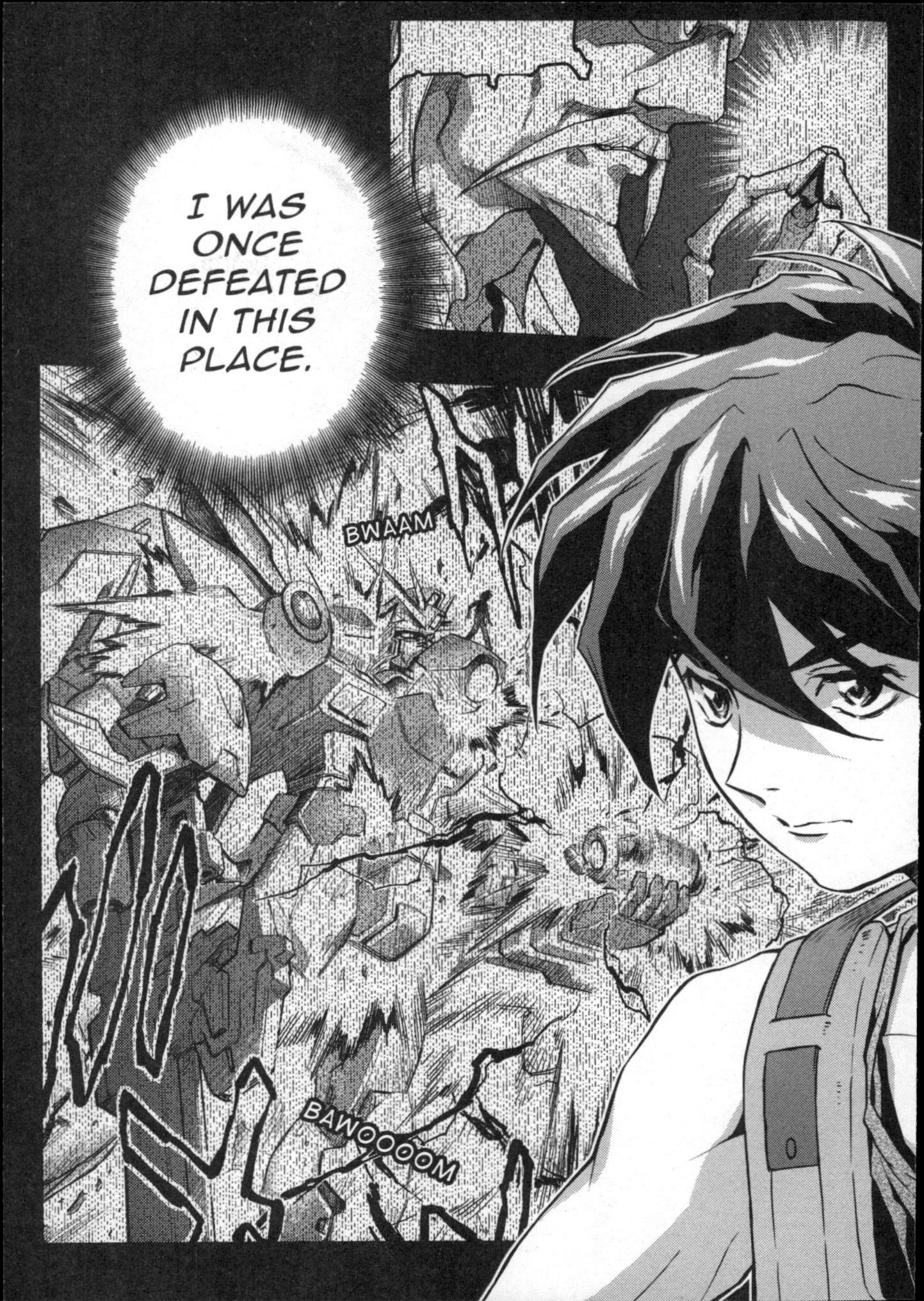
I WAS ONCE DEFEATED IN THIS PLACE.
BWAAM
BAWOOOOOM

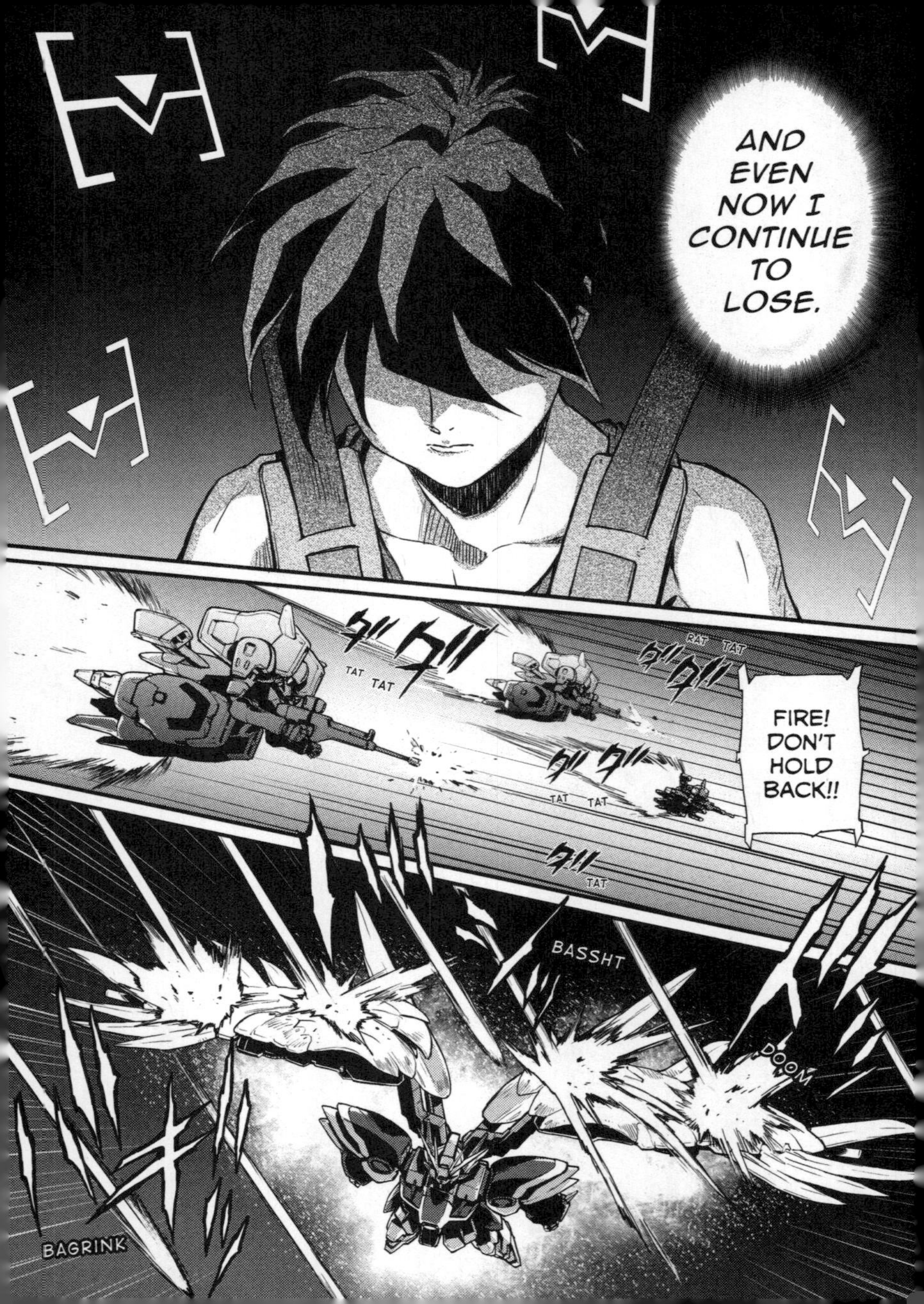
AND EVEN NOW I CONTINUE TO LOSE.
FIRE! DON'T HOLD BACK!!
RAT TAT
TAT TAT
TAT TAT
TAT
BASSHT
DOOM
BAGRINK

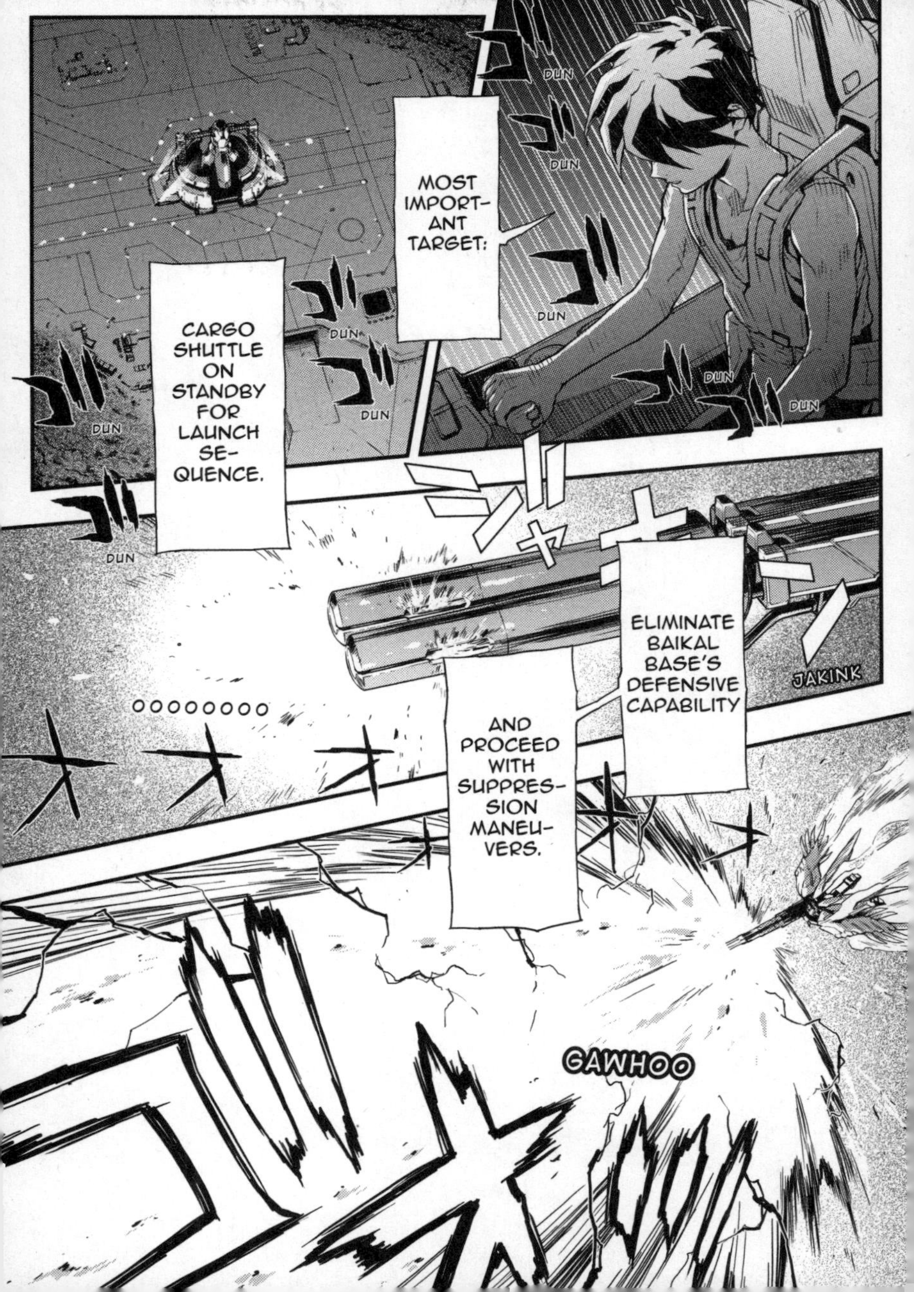
DUN
DUN
MOST IMPORTANT TARGET:
DUN
DUN
DUN
CARGO SHUTTLE ON STANDBY FOR LAUNCH SEQUENCE.
DUN
DUN
DUN
DUN
JAKINK
ELIMINATE BAIKAL BASE'S DEFENSIVE CAPABILITY
AND PROCEED WITH SUPPRESSION MANEUVERS.
OOOOOOOO
GAWHOO

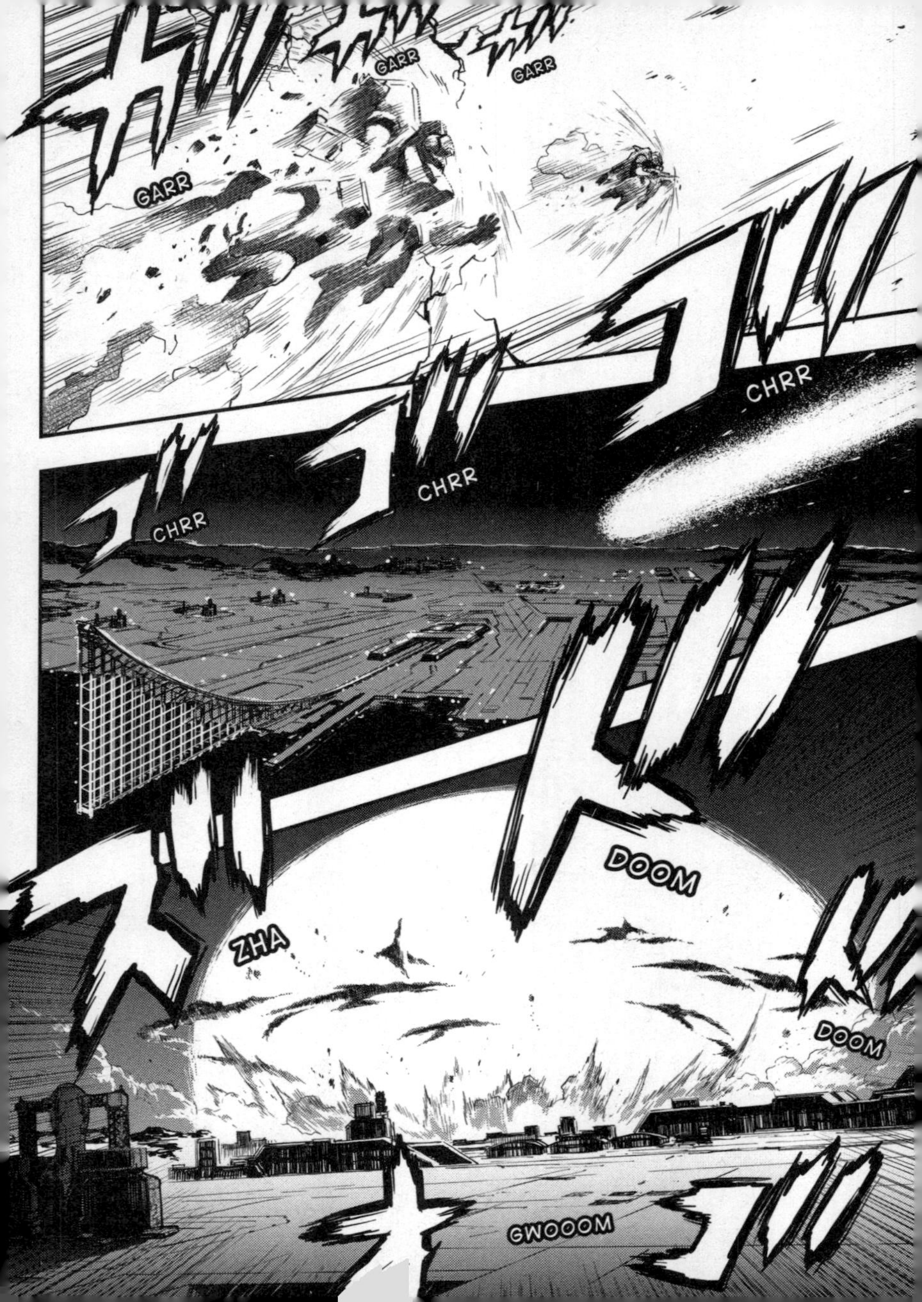
GARR
GARR
GARR
CHRR
CHRR
CHRR
DOOM
ZHA
DOOM
GWOOOM

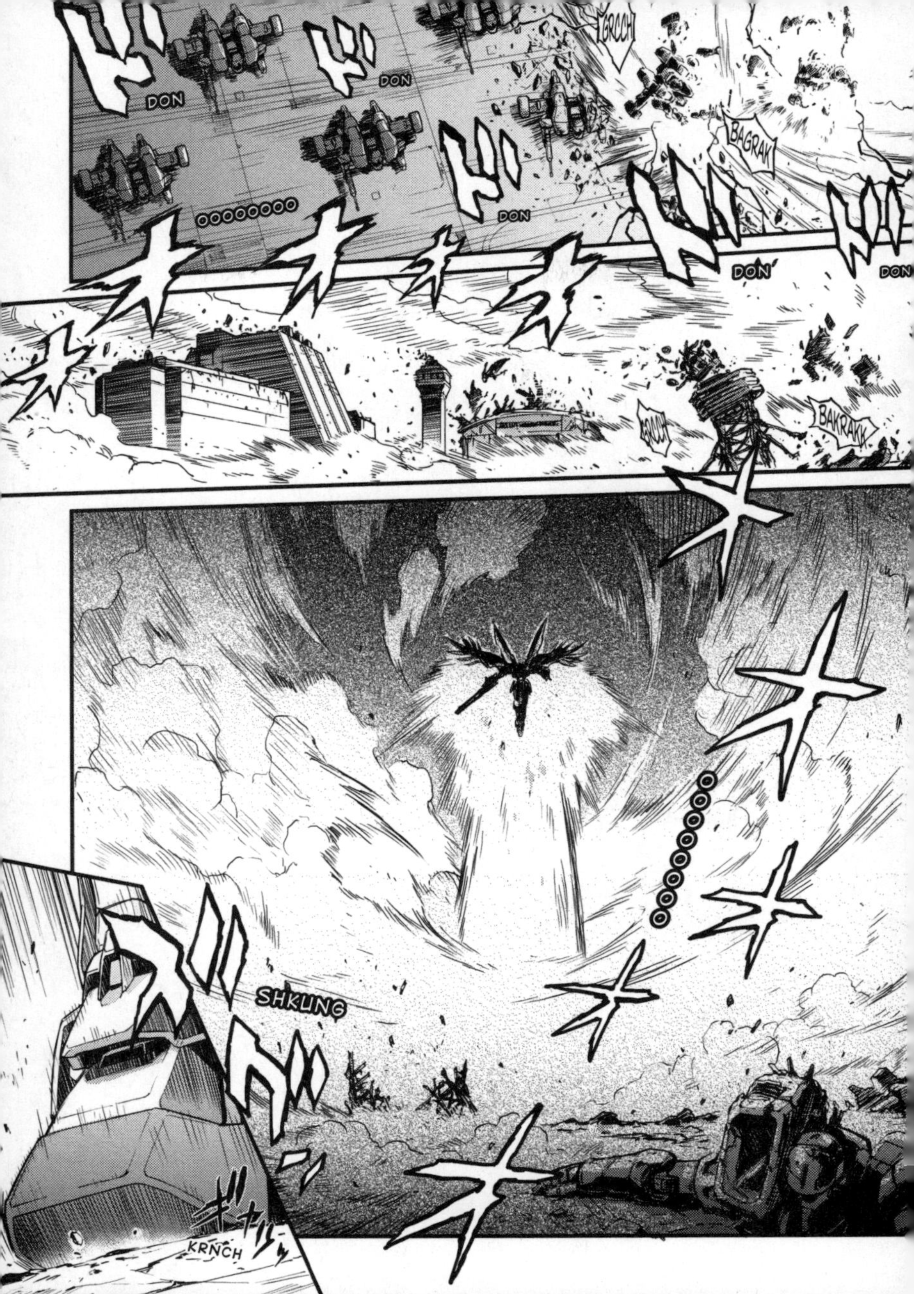
DON
DON
BAGRAK
GRCCH
DON
DON
DON
OOOOOOOO
DON
BAKRAKK
GRCCH
OOOOOOOO
SHKLING
KRNCH

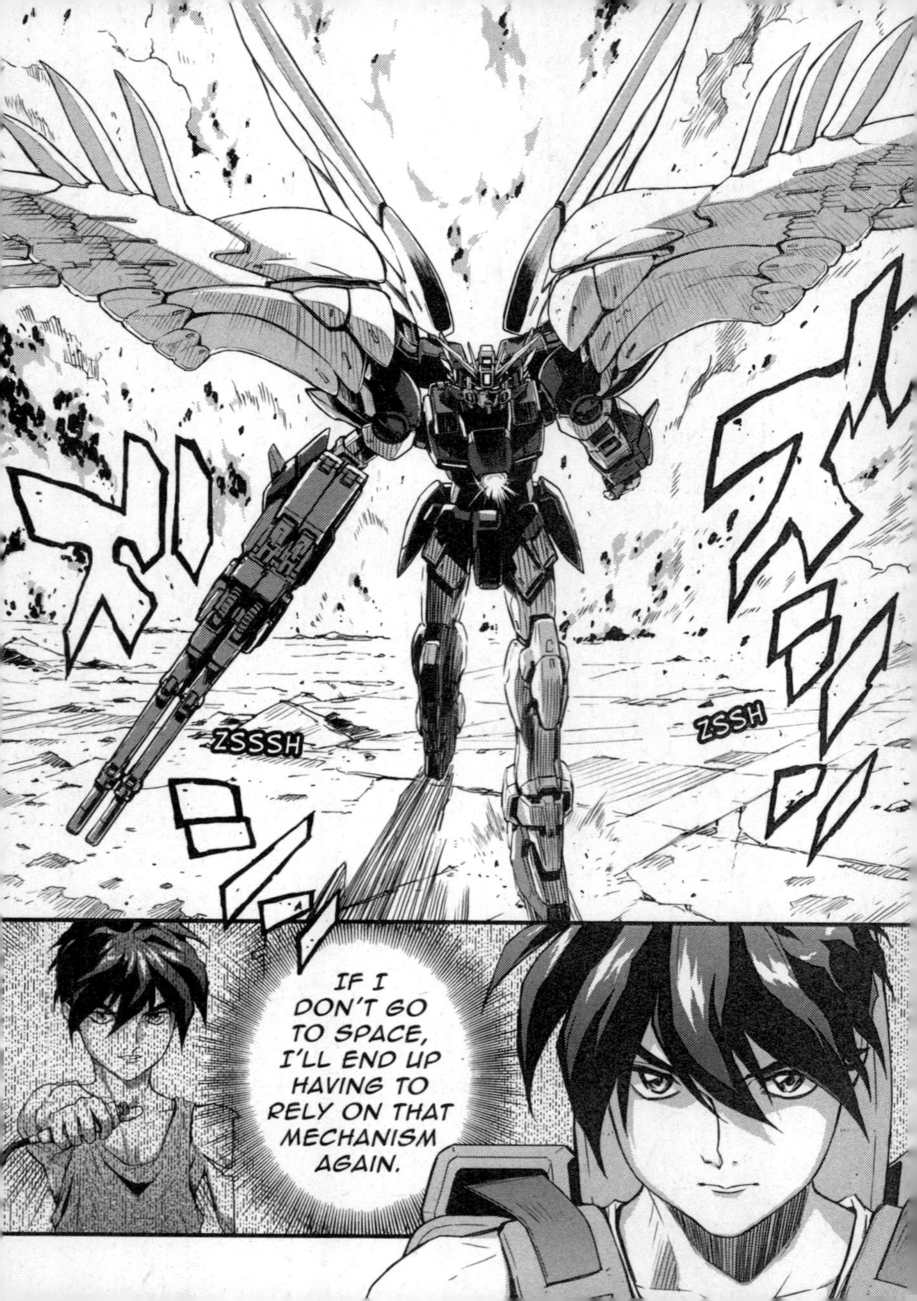
ZSSH
ZSSSH
IF I DON'T GO TO SPACE, I'LL END UP HAVING TO RELY ON THAT MECHANISM AGAIN.

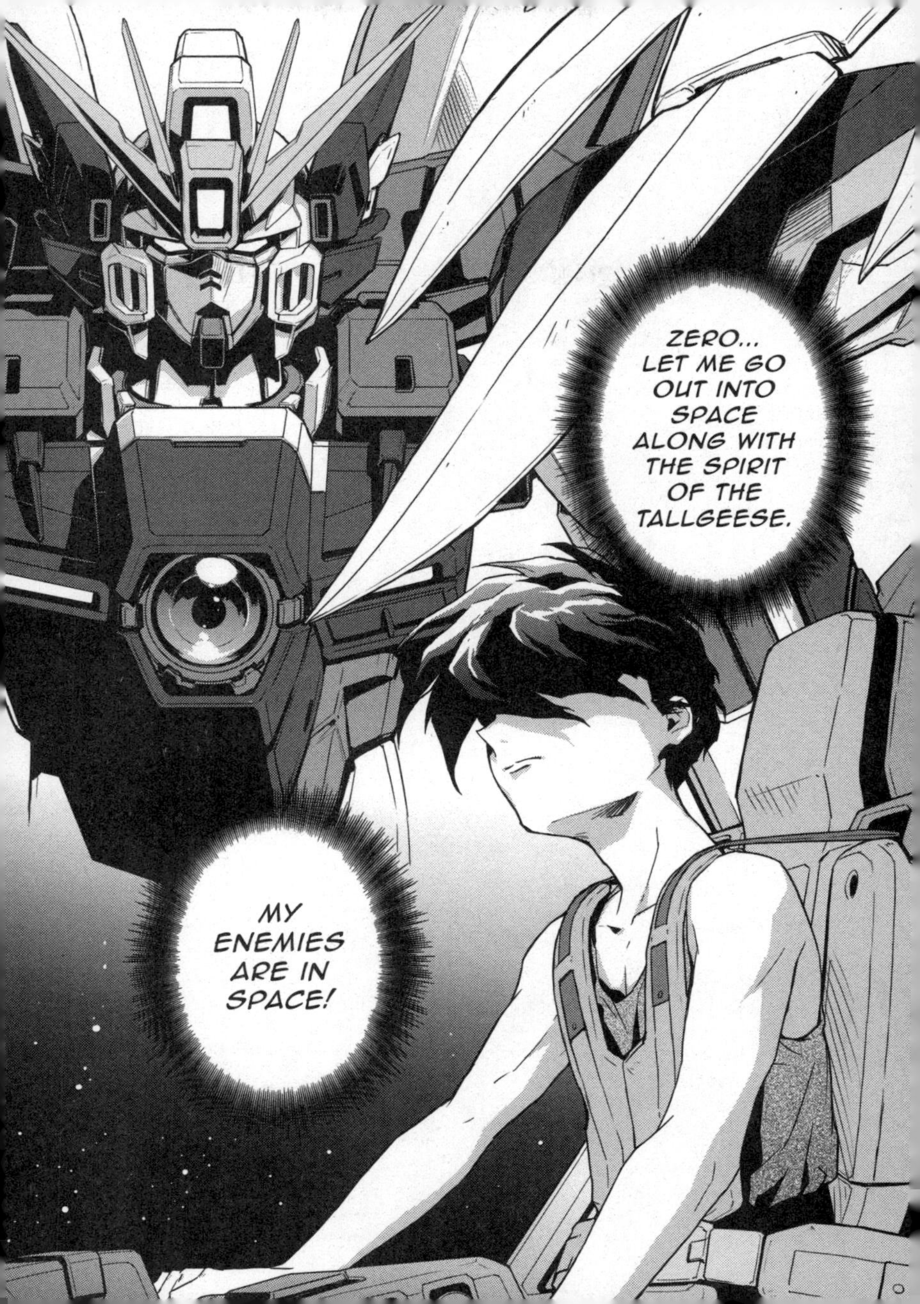
ZERO... LET ME GO OUT INTO SPACE ALONG WITH THE SPIRIT OF THE TALLGEESE.
MY ENEMIES ARE IN SPACE!

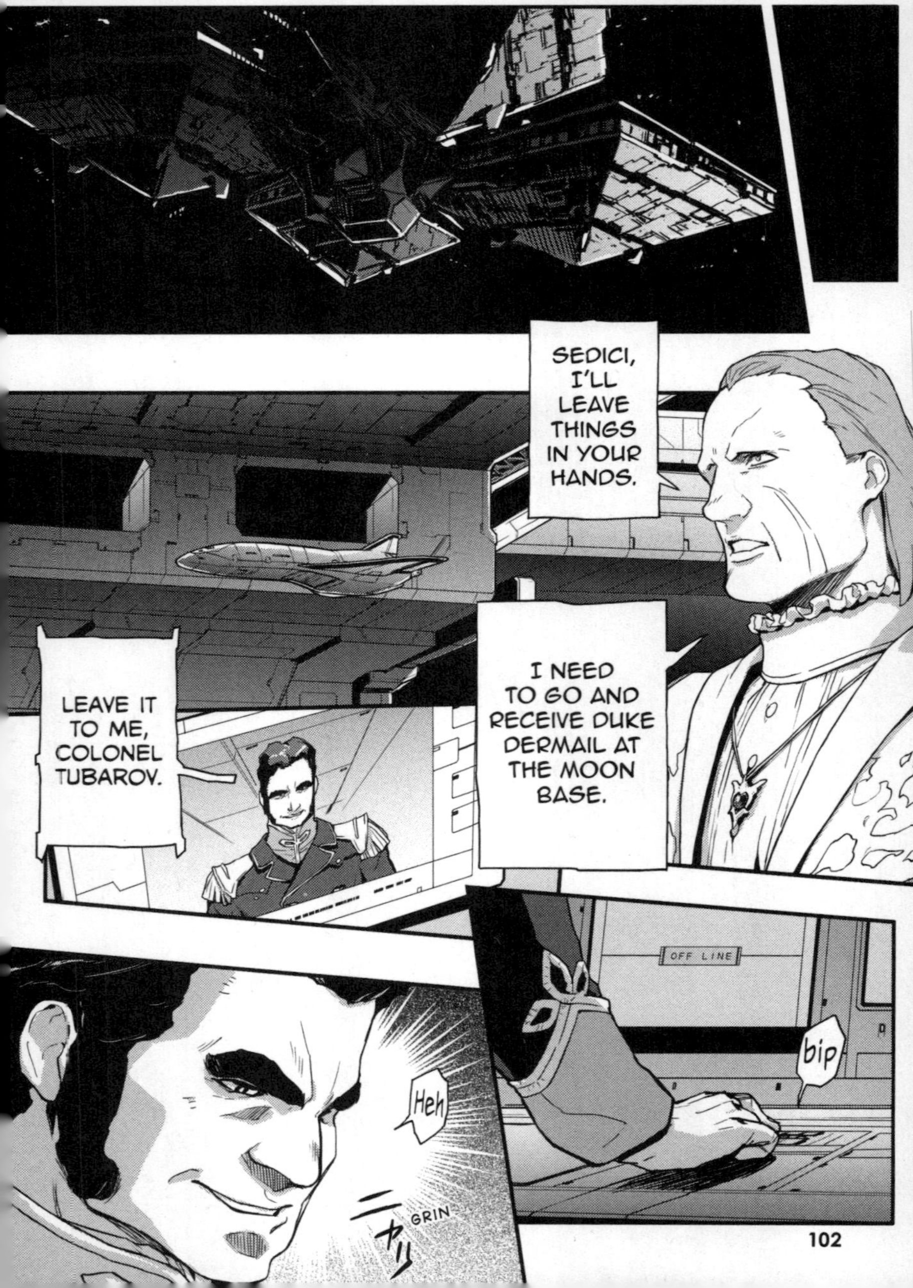
SEDICI, I'LL LEAVE THINGS IN YOUR HANDS.
I NEED TO GO AND RECEIVE DUKE DERMAIL AT THE MOON BASE.
LEAVE IT TO ME, COLONEL TUBAROV.
OFF LINE
bip
Heh
ニヤリ
GRIN

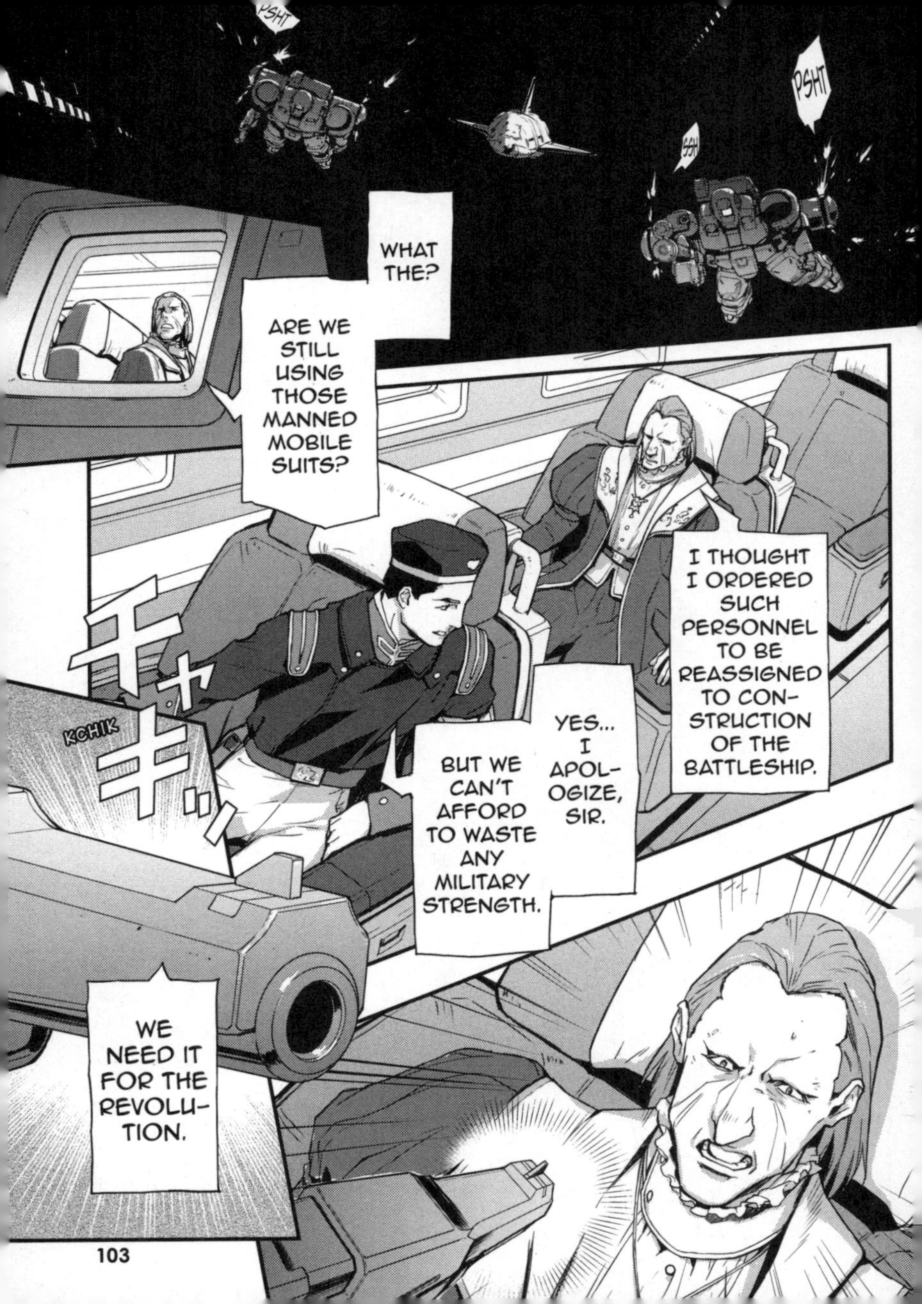
PSHT
SSH
PSHT
WHAT THE?
ARE WE STILL USING THOSE MANNED MOBILE SUITS?
I THOUGHT I ORDERED SUCH PERSONNEL TO BE REASSIGNED TO CON-STRUCTION OF THE BATTLESHIP.
YES... I APOL-OGIZE, SIR.
BUT WE CAN'T AFFORD TO WASTE ANY MILITARY STRENGTH.
チャキッ
KCHIK
WE NEED IT FOR THE REVOLU-TION.

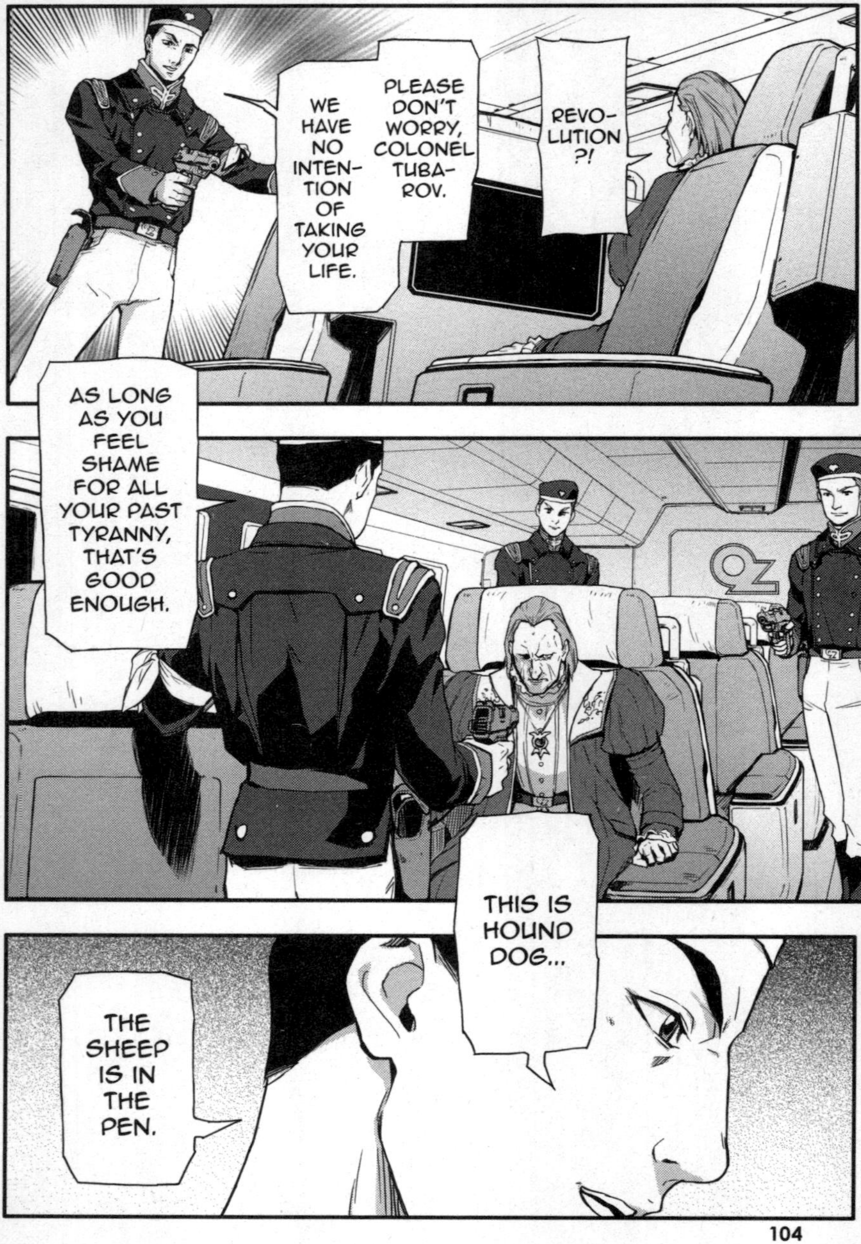
REVO-LUTION?!
PLEASE DON'T WORRY, COLONEL TUBA-ROV.
WE HAVE NO INTEN-TION OF TAKING YOUR LIFE.
AS LONG AS YOU FEEL SHAME FOR ALL YOUR PAST TYRANNY, THAT'S GOOD ENOUGH.
THIS IS HOUND DOG...
THE SHEEP IS IN THE PEN.

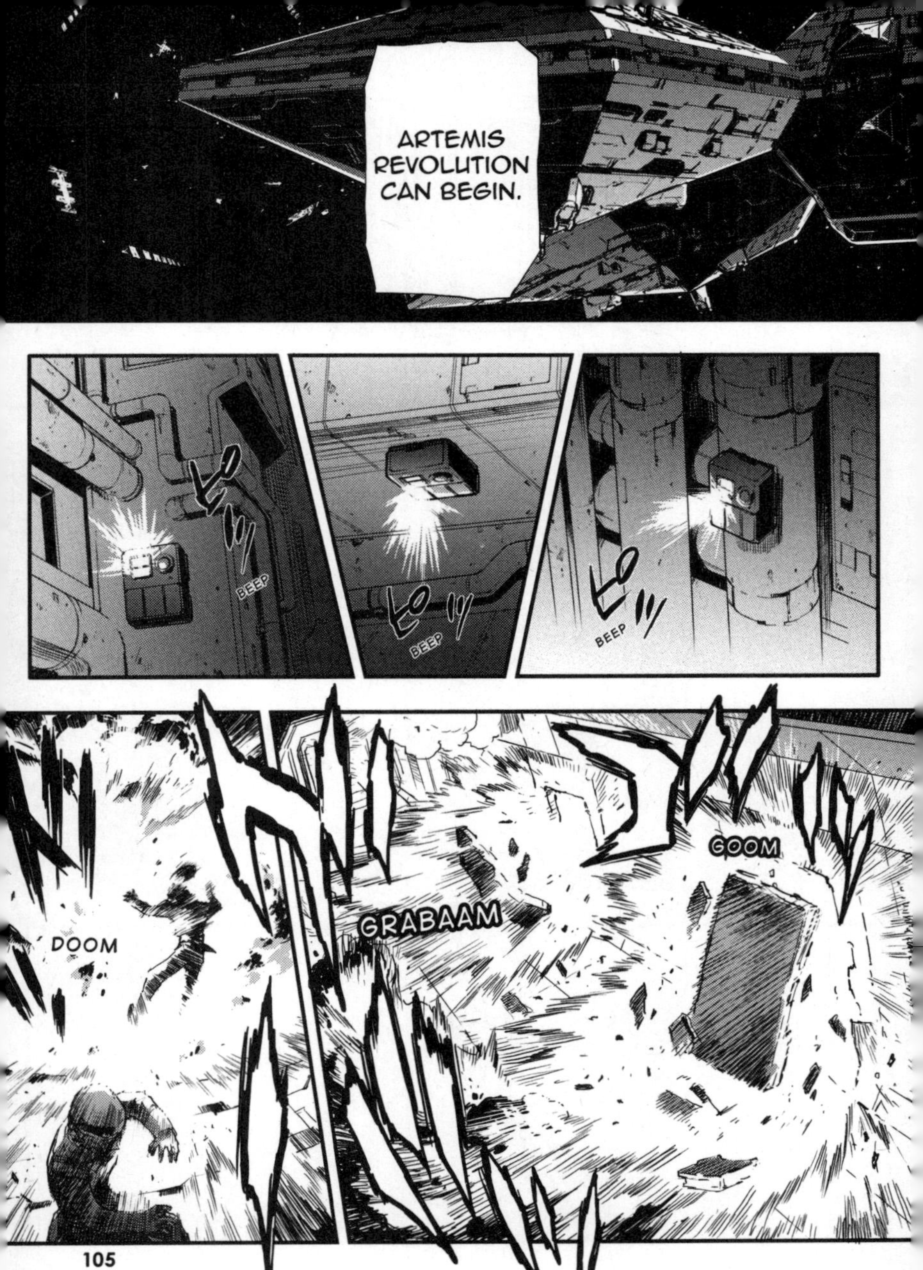
ARTEMIS REVOLUTION CAN BEGIN.
BEEP
BEEP
BEEP
GOOM
GRABAAM
DOOM

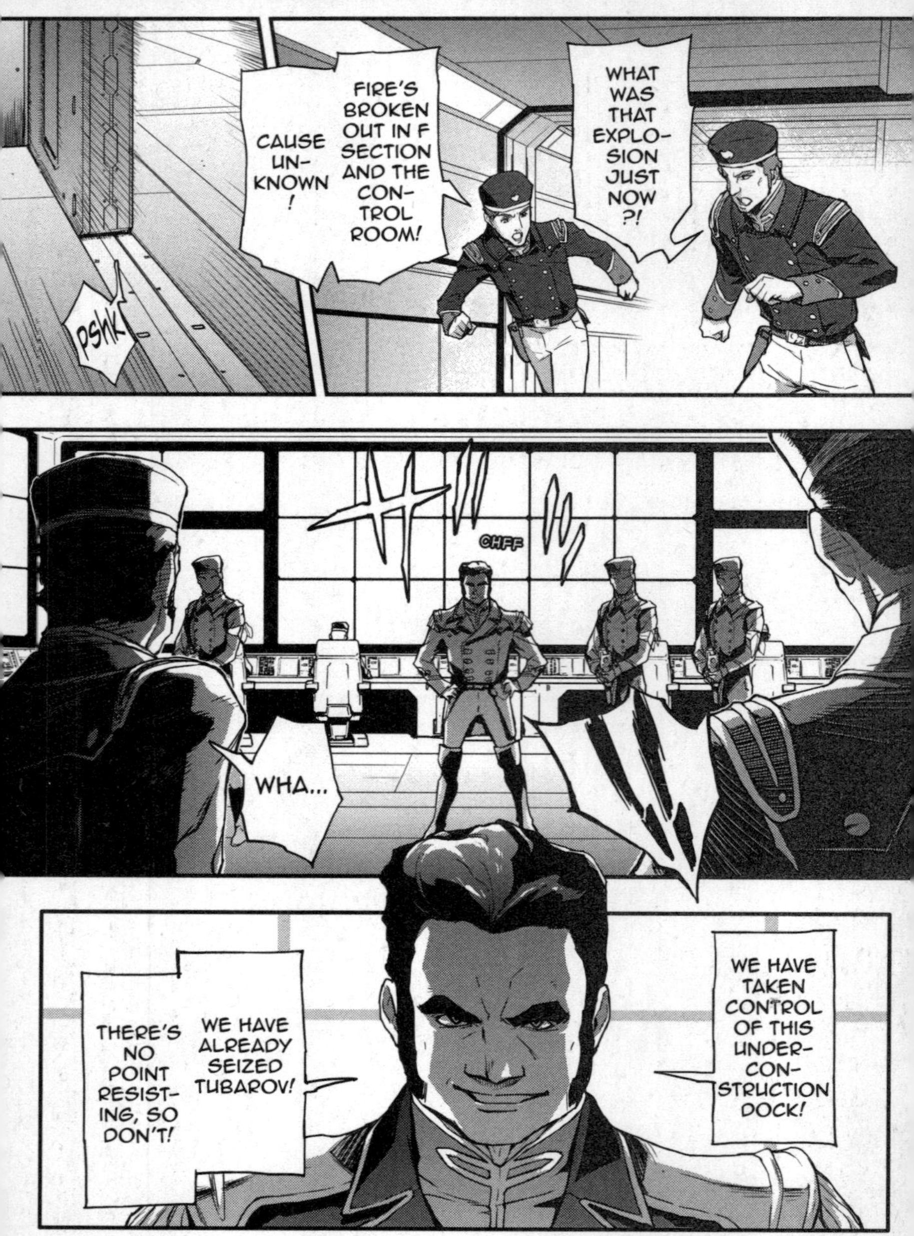
WHAT WAS THAT EXPLOSION JUST NOW?!
FIRE'S BROKEN OUT IN F SECTION AND THE CONTROL ROOM!
CAUSE UNKNOWN!
pshk
CHFF
WHA...
WE HAVE TAKEN CONTROL OF THIS UNDER-CONSTRUCTION DOCK!
WE HAVE ALREADY SEIZED TUBAROV!
THERE'S NO POINT RESISTING, SO DON'T!

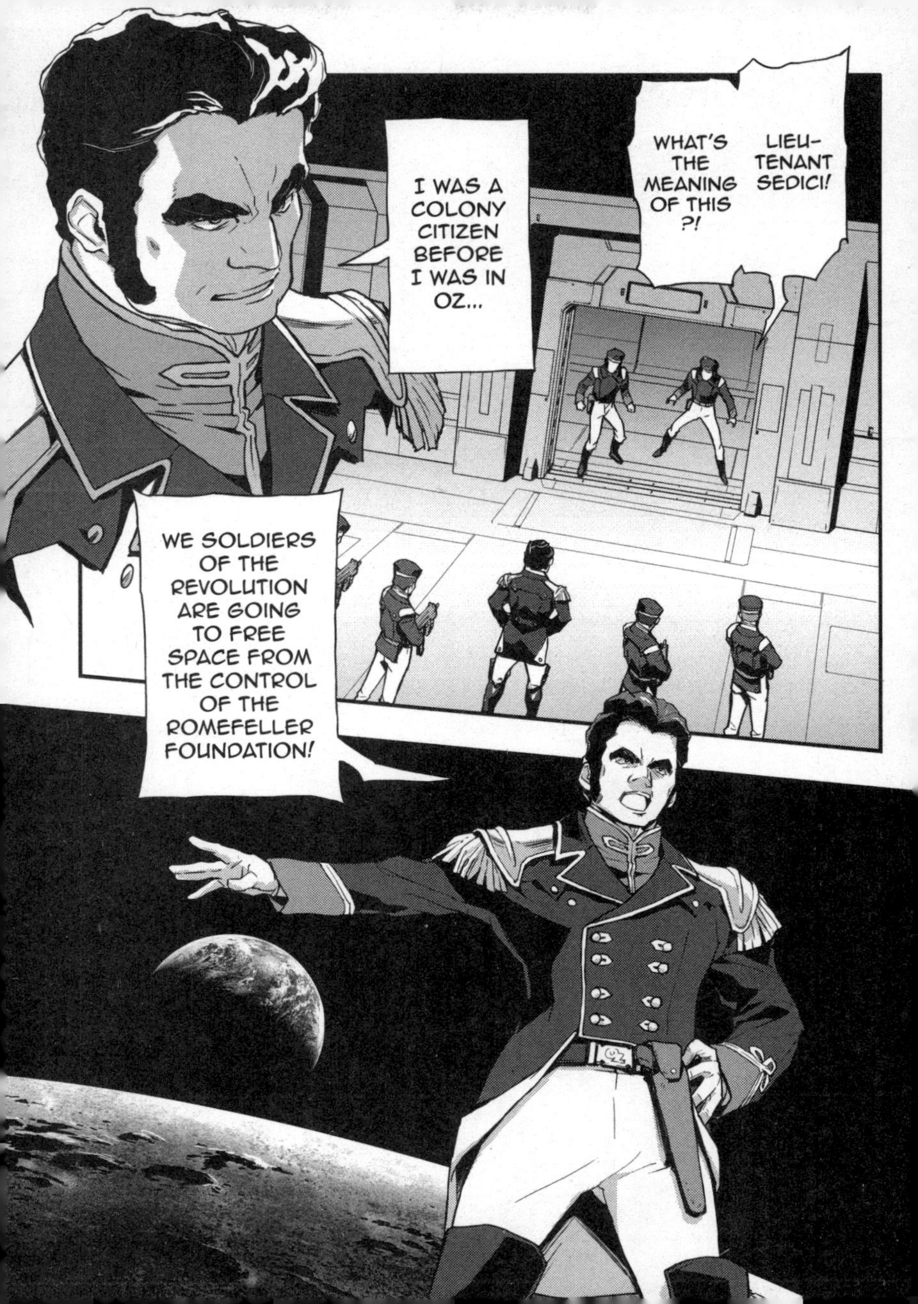
LIEU-TENANT SEDICI!
WHAT'S THE MEANING OF THIS?!
I WAS A COLONY CITIZEN BEFORE I WAS IN OZ...
WE SOLDIERS OF THE REVOLUTION ARE GOING TO FREE SPACE FROM THE CONTROL OF THE ROMEFELLER FOUNDATION!

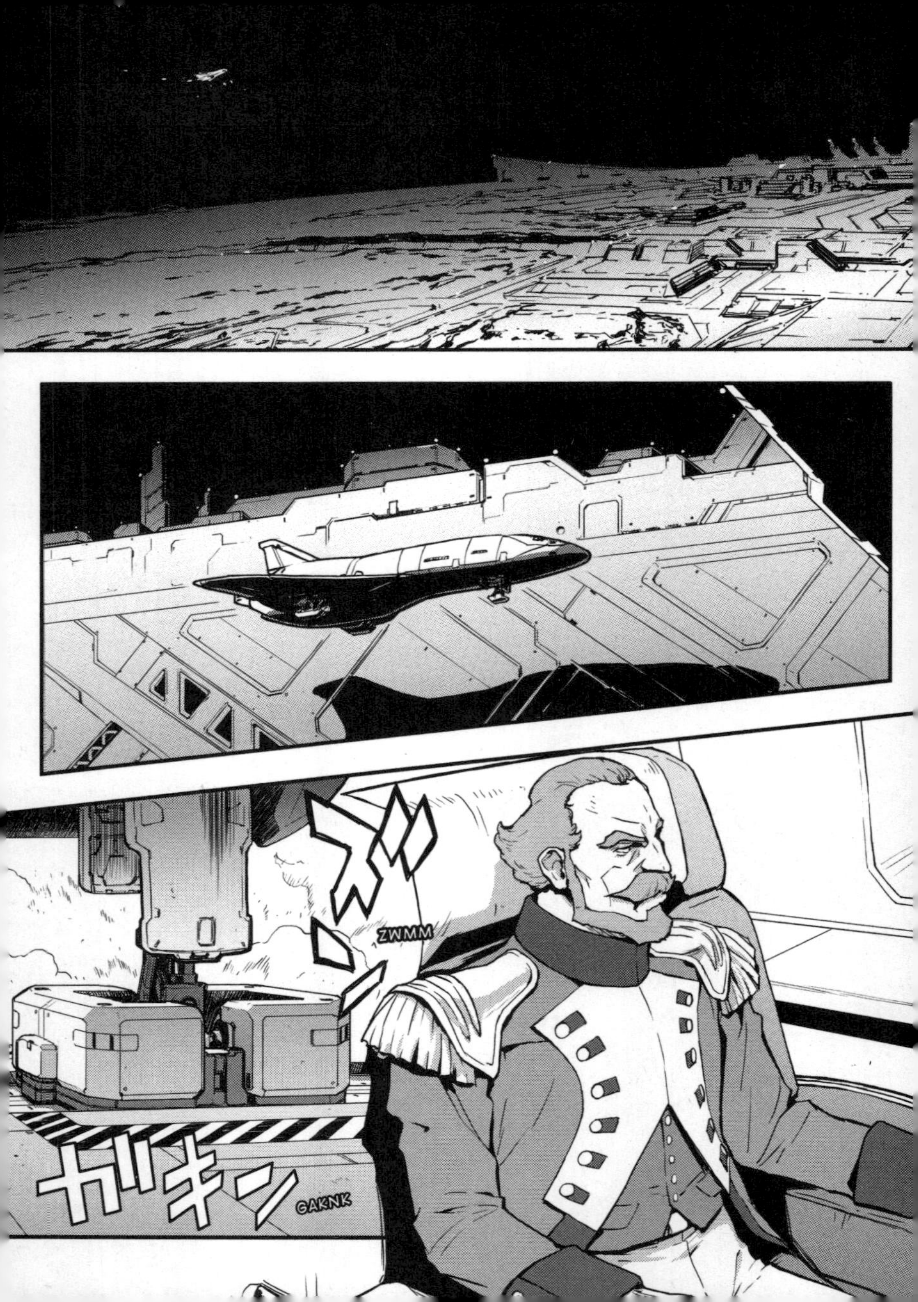
ZWMM
ガキン
GAKNK

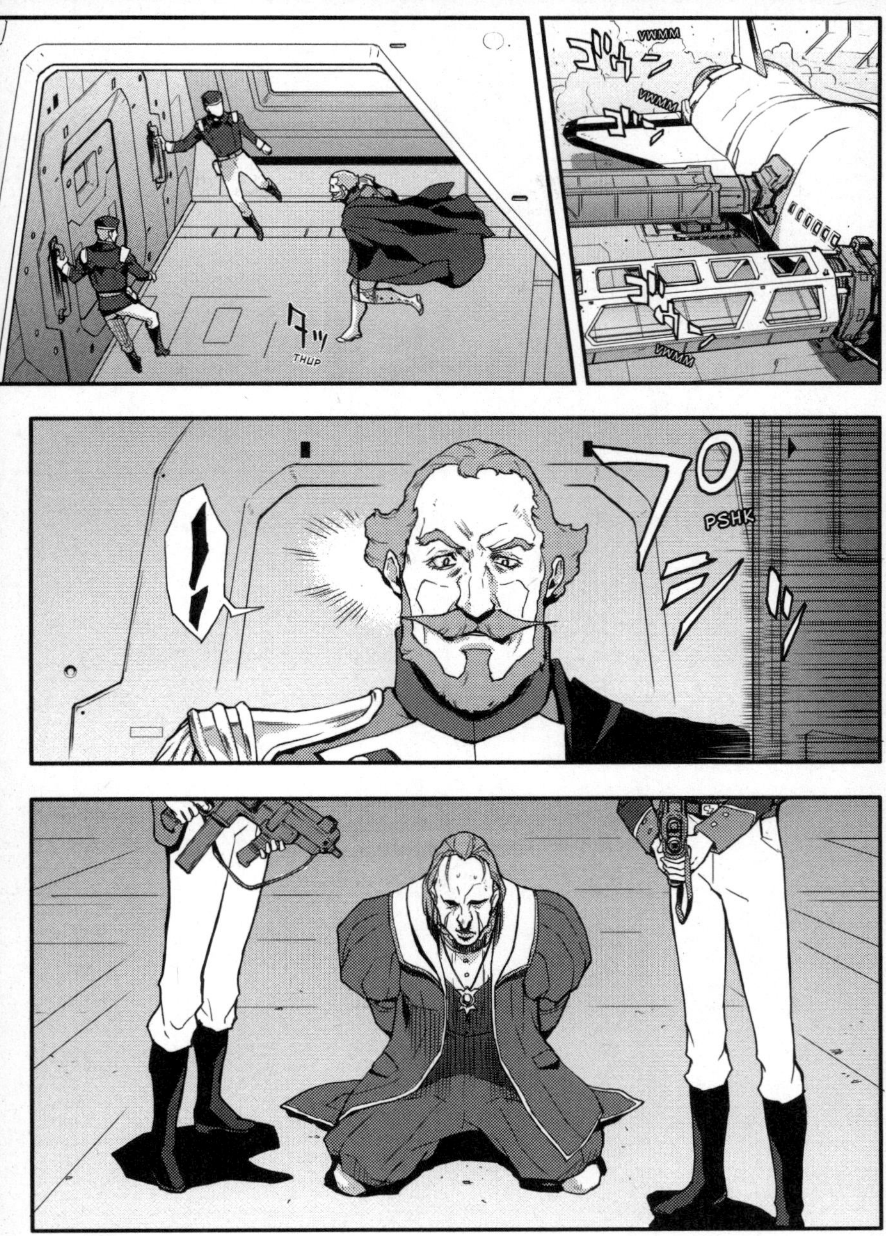
VWMM
VWMM
VWMM
タッ
THUP
PSHK
!

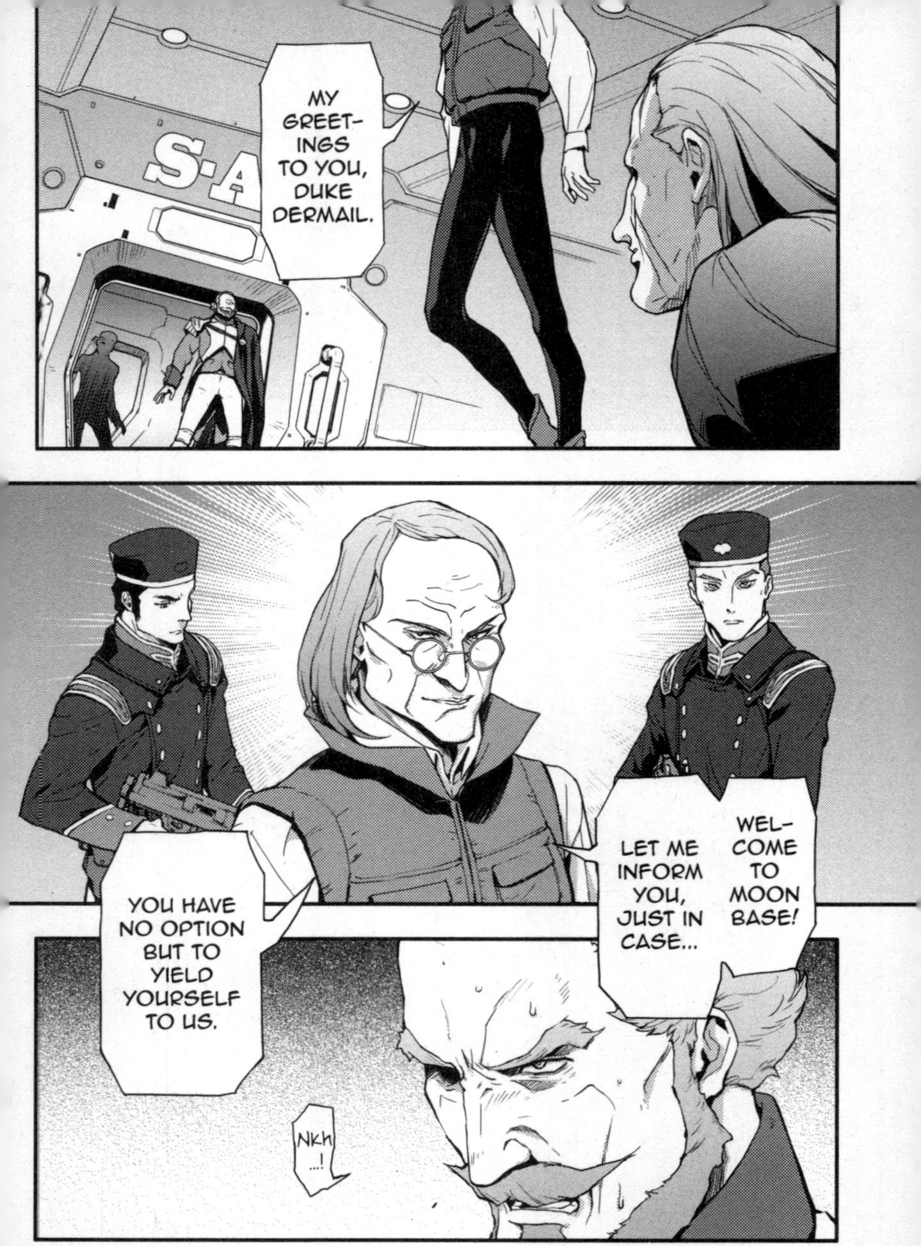
MY GREETINGS TO YOU, DUKE DERMAIL.
WELCOME TO MOON BASE!
LET ME INFORM YOU, JUST IN CASE...
YOU HAVE NO OPTION BUT TO YIELD YOURSELF TO US.
Nkh ...!

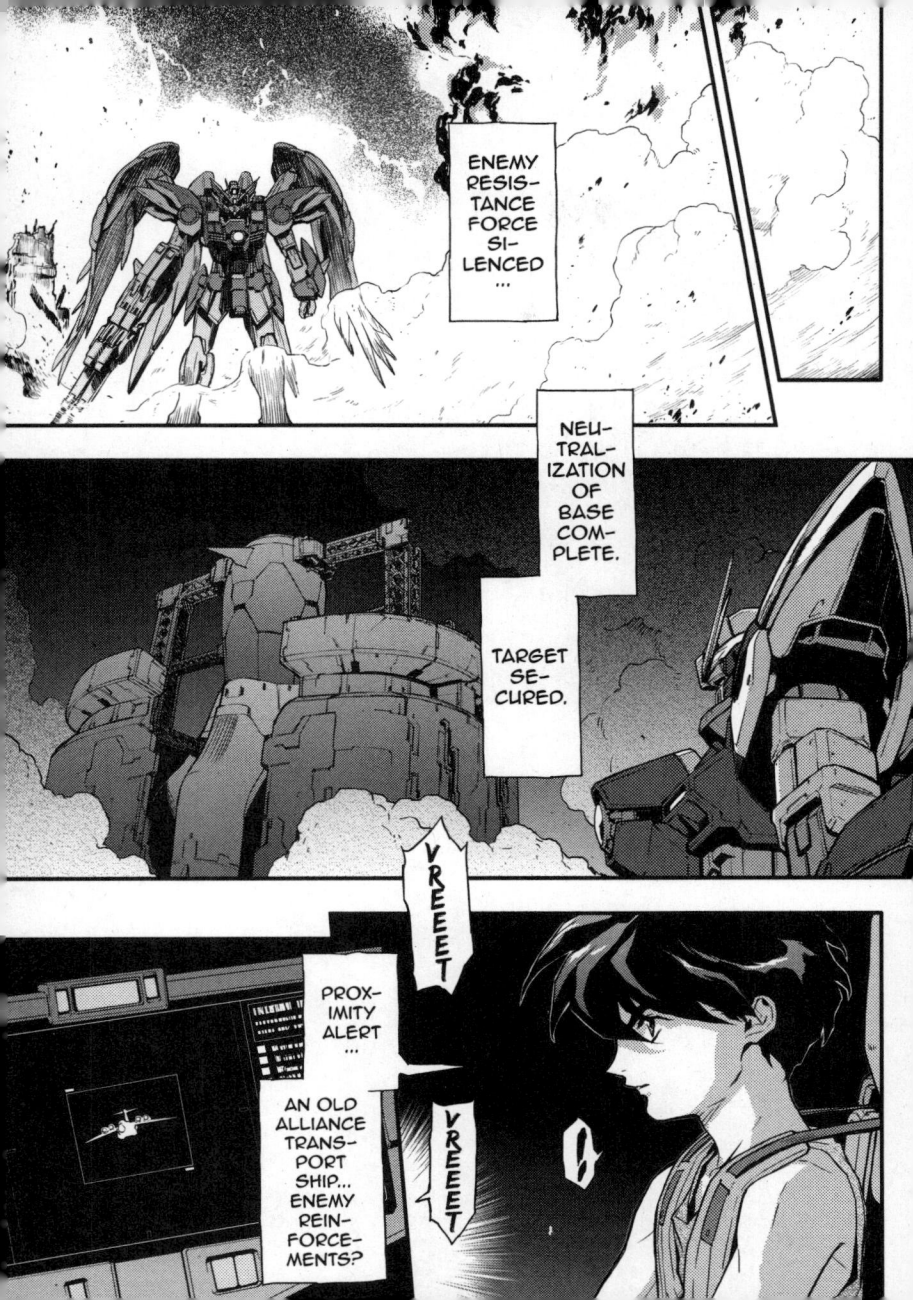

ENEMY RESISTANCE FORCE SILENCED...

NEUTRALIZATION OF BASE COMPLETE.

TARGET SECURED.

VREEET

PROXIMITY ALERT...

AN OLD ALLIANCE TRANSPORT SHIP... ENEMY REINFORCEMENTS?

VREEET

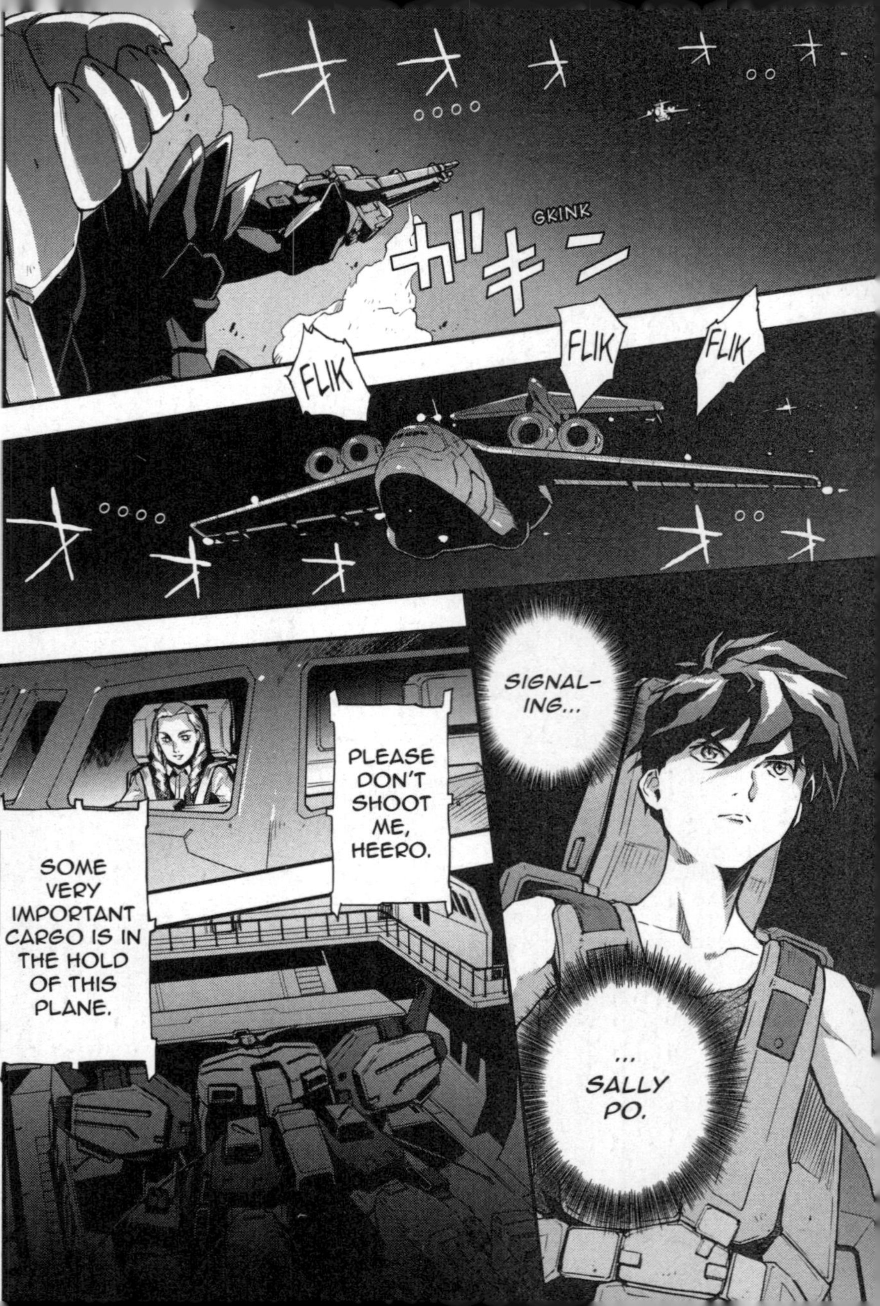
GKINK
ガキン
FLIK
FLIK
FLIK
SIGNAL-ING...
... SALLY PO.
PLEASE DON'T SHOOT ME, HEERO.
SOME VERY IMPORTANT CARGO IS IN THE HOLD OF THIS PLANE.

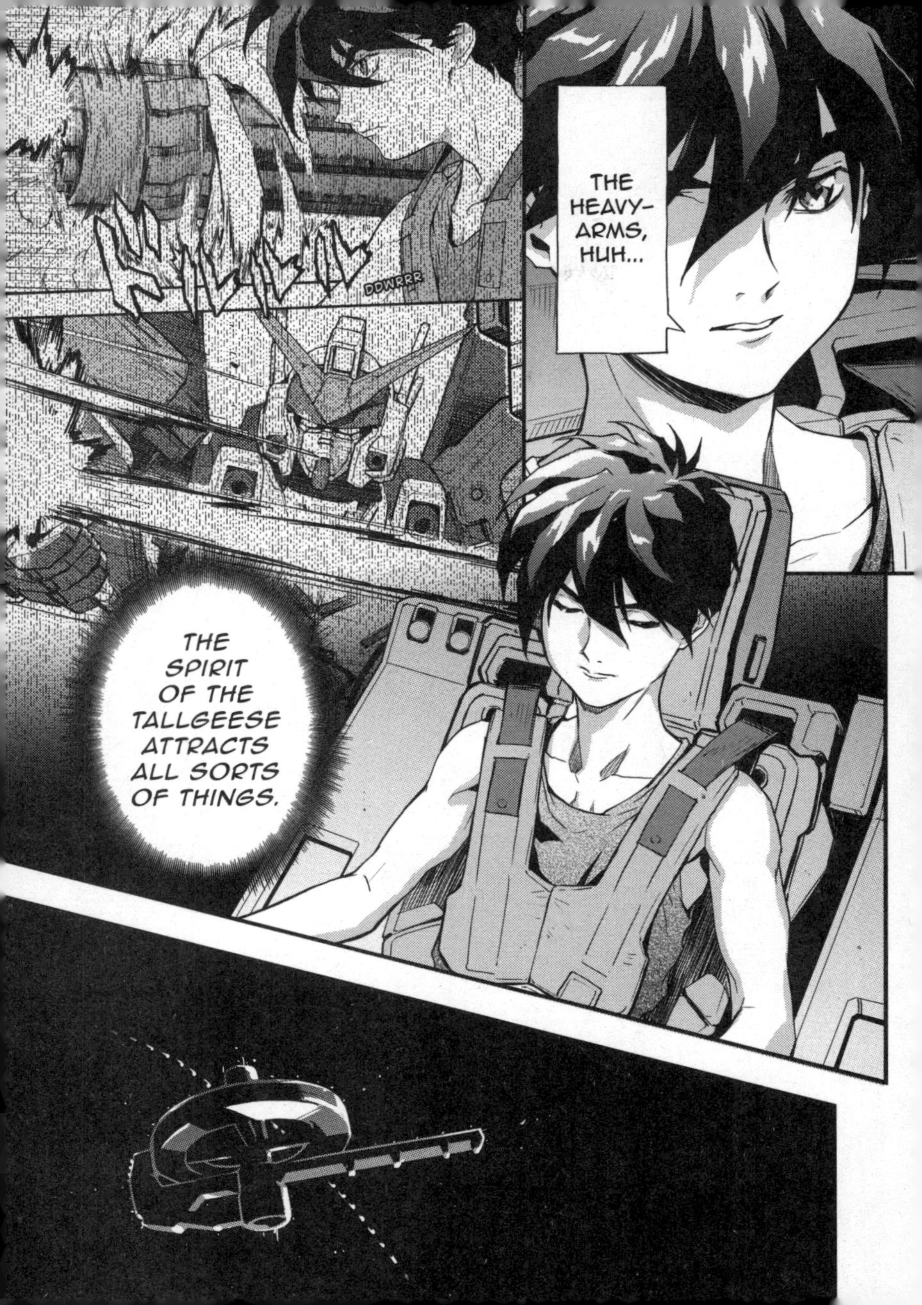
THE HEAVY-ARMS, HUH...
DDWRRR
THE SPIRIT OF THE TALLGEESE ATTRACTS ALL SORTS OF THINGS.

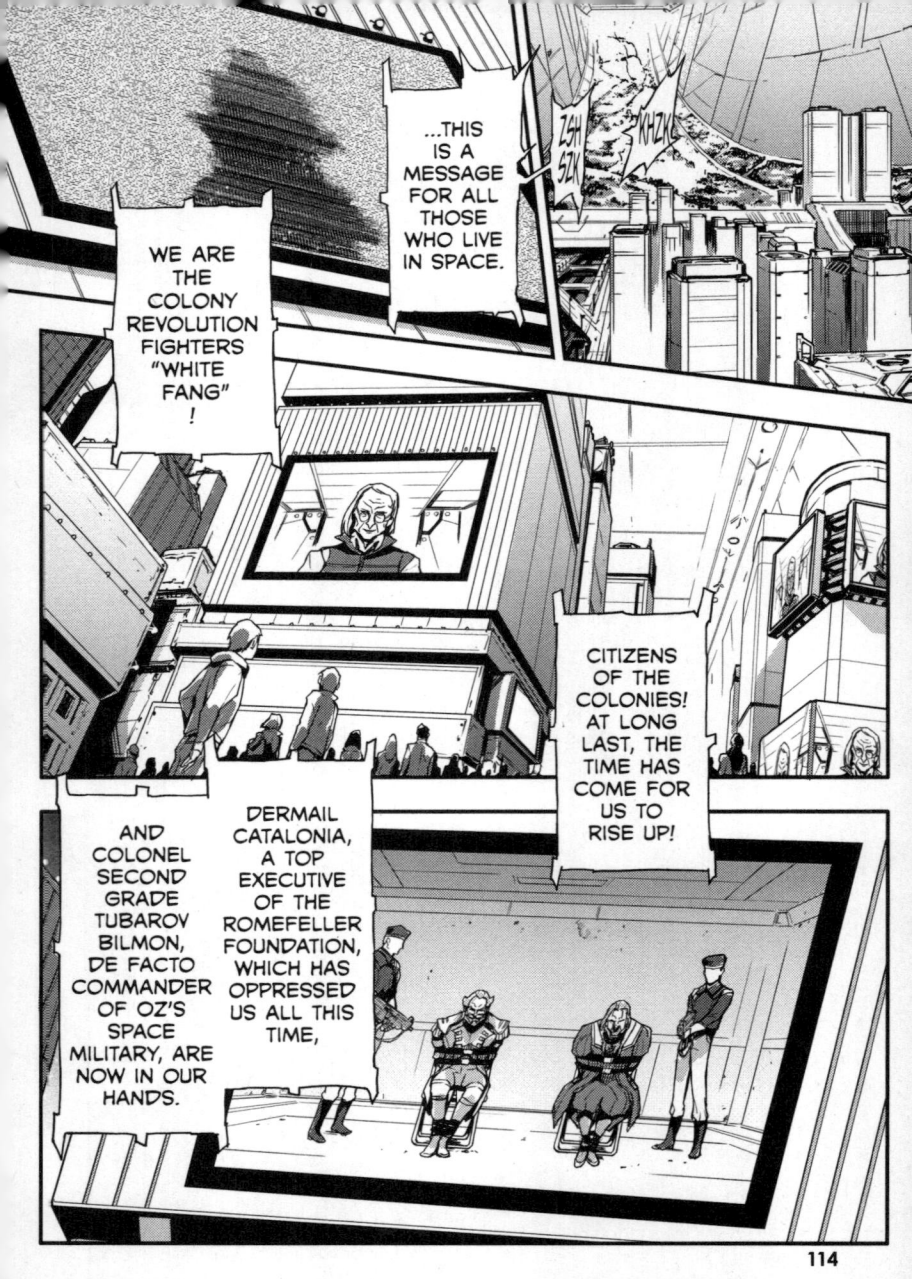

...THIS IS A MESSAGE FOR ALL THOSE WHO LIVE IN SPACE.

WE ARE THE COLONY REVOLUTION FIGHTERS "WHITE FANG"!

CITIZENS OF THE COLONIES! AT LONG LAST, THE TIME HAS COME FOR US TO RISE UP!

DERMAIL CATALONIA, A TOP EXECUTIVE OF THE ROMEFELLER FOUNDATION, WHICH HAS OPPRESSED US ALL THIS TIME,

AND COLONEL SECOND GRADE TUBAROV BILMON, DE FACTO COMMANDER OF OZ'S SPACE MILITARY, ARE NOW IN OUR HANDS.

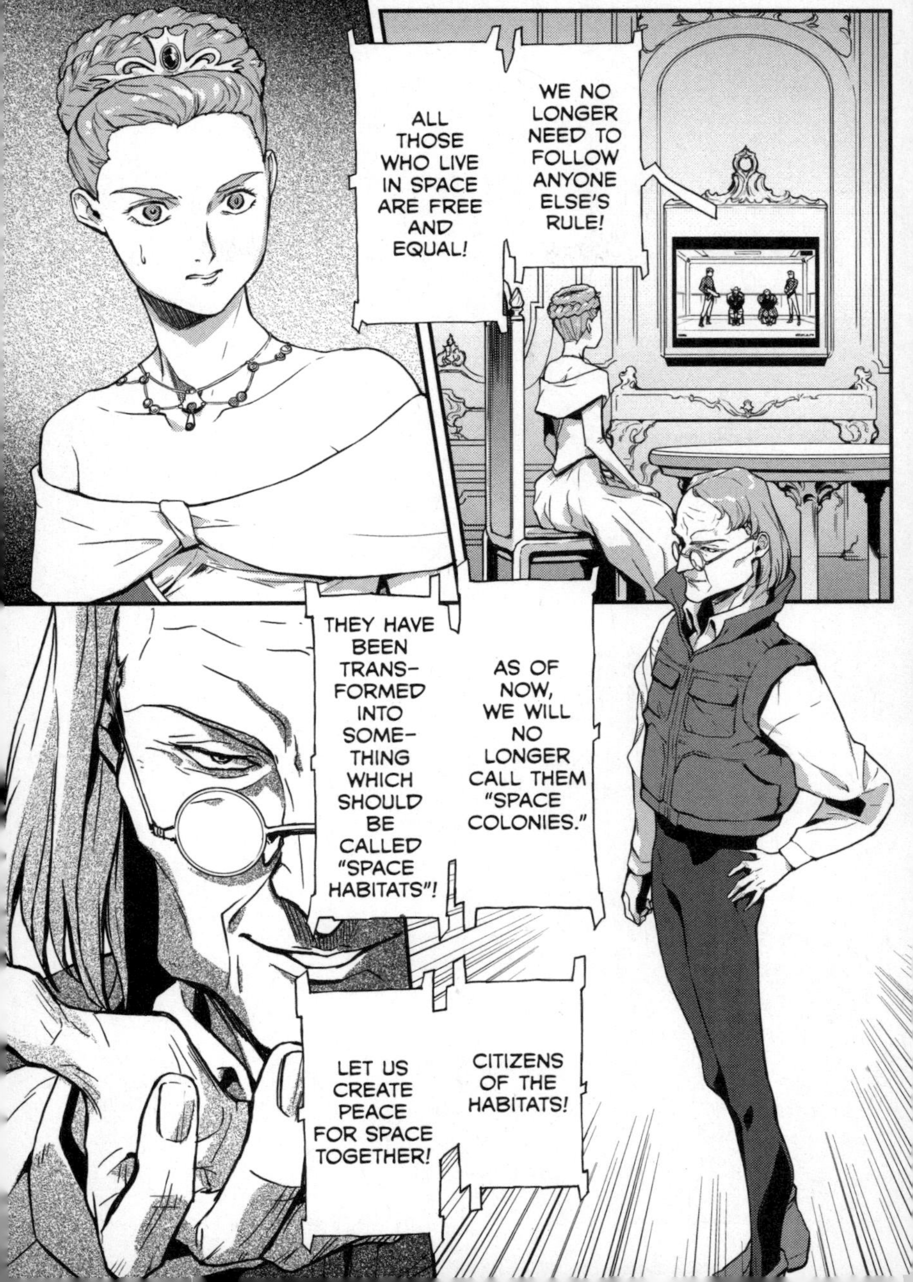
WE NO LONGER NEED TO FOLLOW ANYONE ELSE'S RULE!
ALL THOSE WHO LIVE IN SPACE ARE FREE AND EQUAL!
AS OF NOW, WE WILL NO LONGER CALL THEM "SPACE COLONIES."
THEY HAVE BEEN TRANS-FORMED INTO SOME-THING WHICH SHOULD BE CALLED "SPACE HABITATS"!
CITIZENS OF THE HABITATS!
LET US CREATE PEACE FOR SPACE TOGETHER!

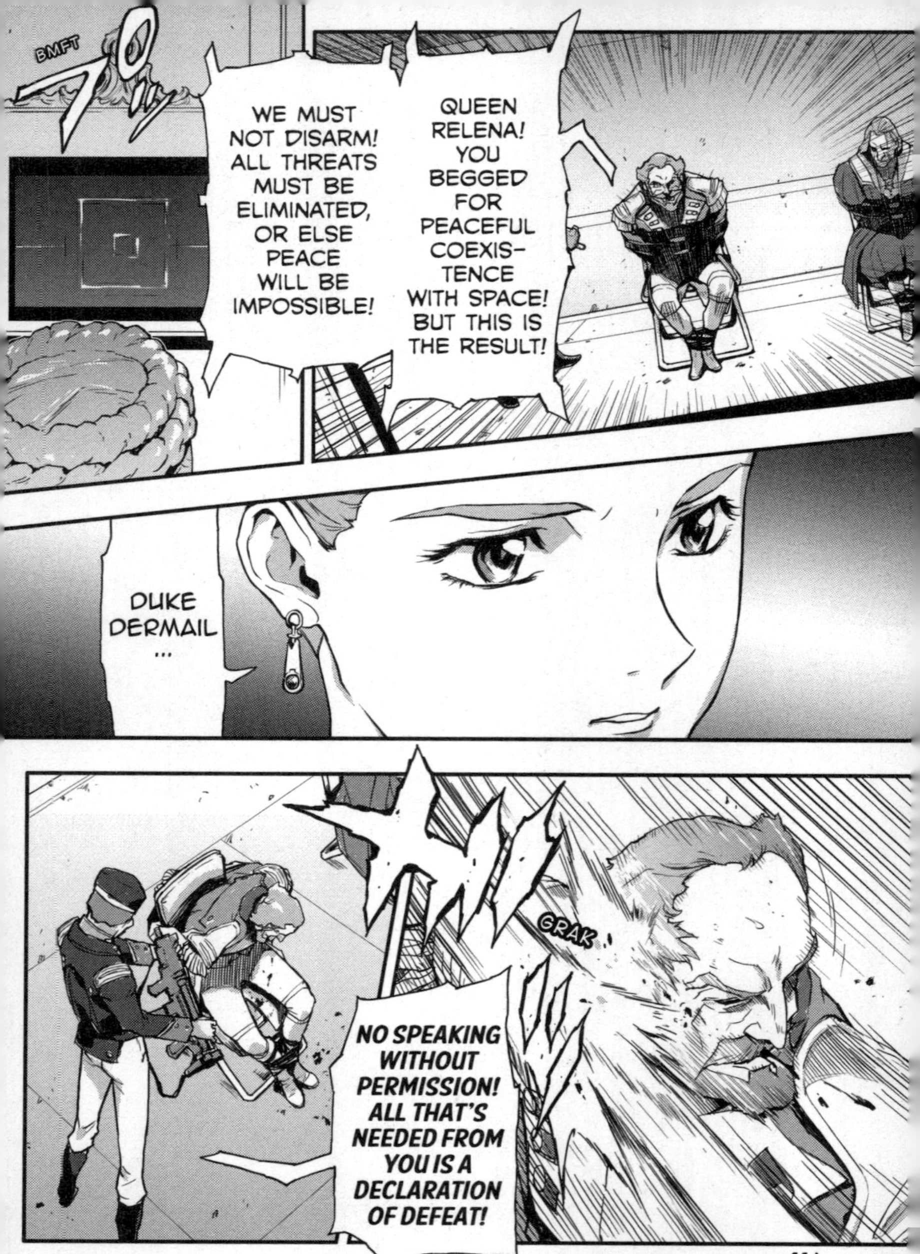
QUEEN RELENA! YOU BEGGED FOR PEACEFUL COEXIS-TENCE WITH SPACE! BUT THIS IS THE RESULT!
WE MUST NOT DISARM! ALL THREATS MUST BE ELIMINATED, OR ELSE PEACE WILL BE IMPOSSIBLE!
BMFT
DUKE DERMAIL ...
GRAK
NO SPEAKING WITHOUT PERMISSION! ALL THAT'S NEEDED FROM YOU IS A DECLARATION OF DEFEAT!

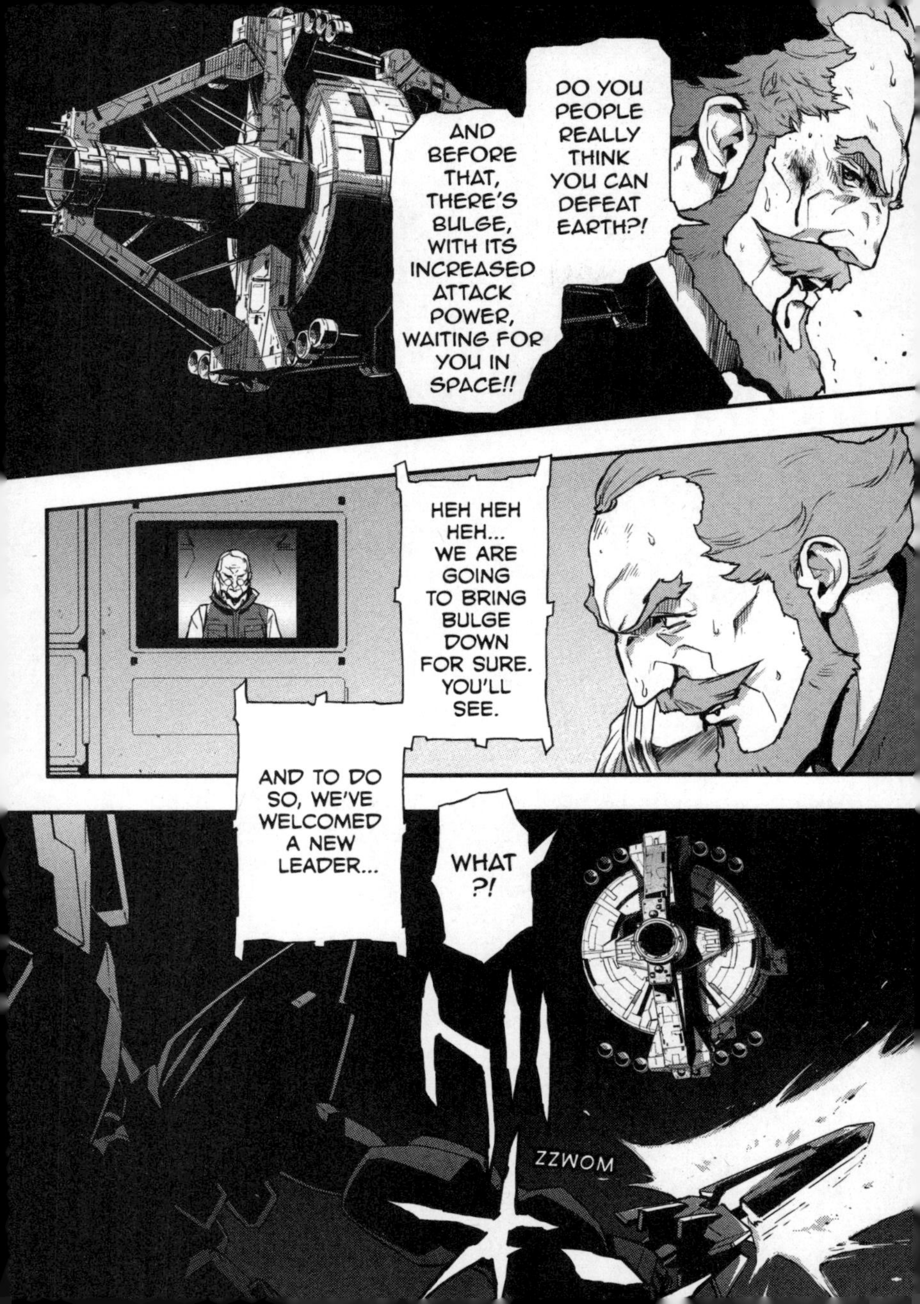
DO YOU PEOPLE REALLY THINK YOU CAN DEFEAT EARTH?!
AND BEFORE THAT, THERE'S BULGE, WITH ITS INCREASED ATTACK POWER, WAITING FOR YOU IN SPACE!!
HEH HEH HEH... WE ARE GOING TO BRING BULGE DOWN FOR SURE. YOU'LL SEE.
AND TO DO SO, WE'VE WELCOMED A NEW LEADER...
WHAT?!
ZZWOM

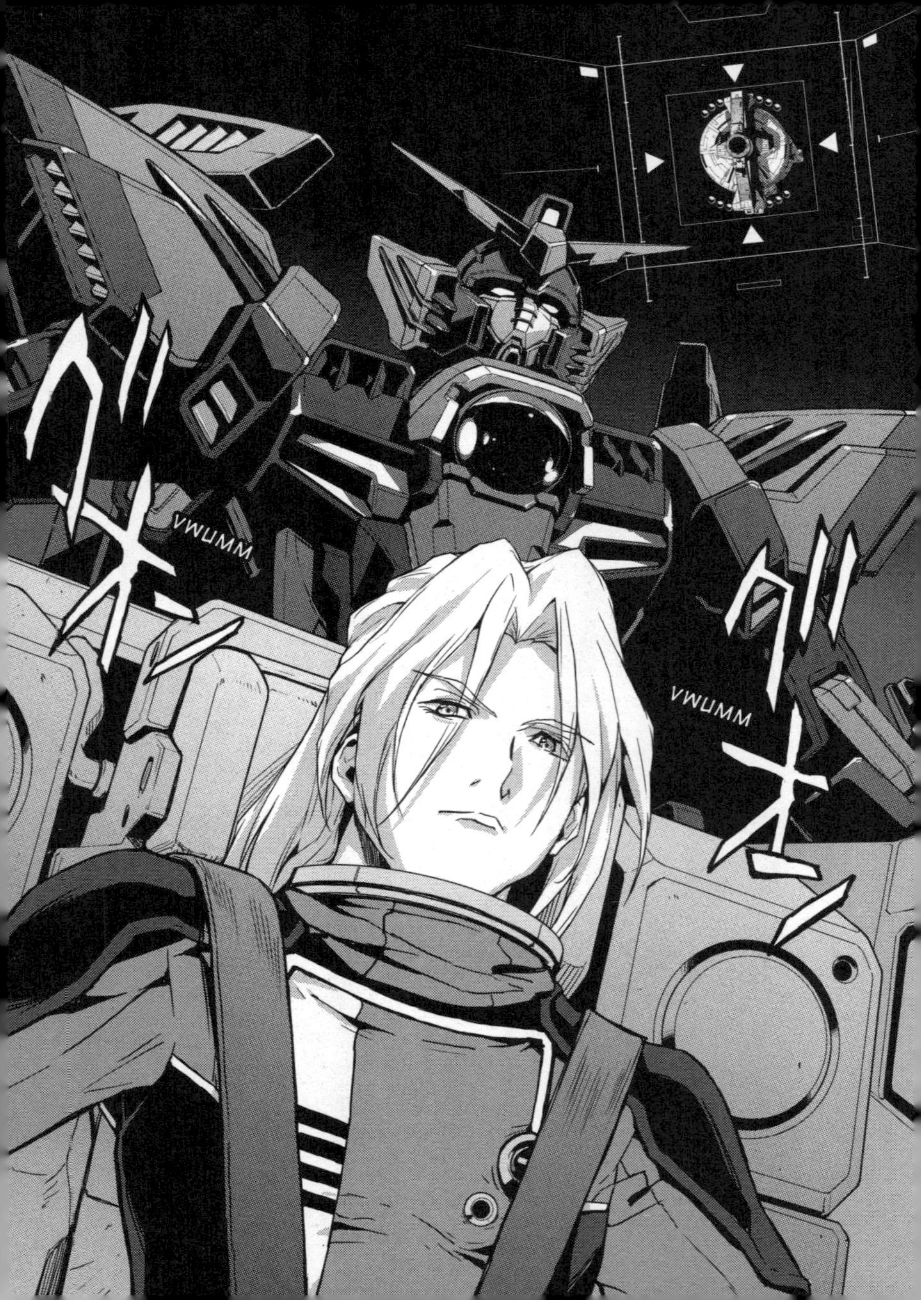
VWUMM
VWUMM

SLEEVE NOTES:
Endless Waltz

SEDICI

An OZ officer under Tubarov, and in charge of the construction of the massive space battleship Libra. He is revealed to be a colony revolutionary. It's as though he is destined to fight against the United Earth Sphere Alliance because of his bloodline, since his grandfather fought alongside Relena's great-aunt Katrina, and his mother Artemis was a rebel army commander who fought along with Quinze and Zechs in Moon War II.

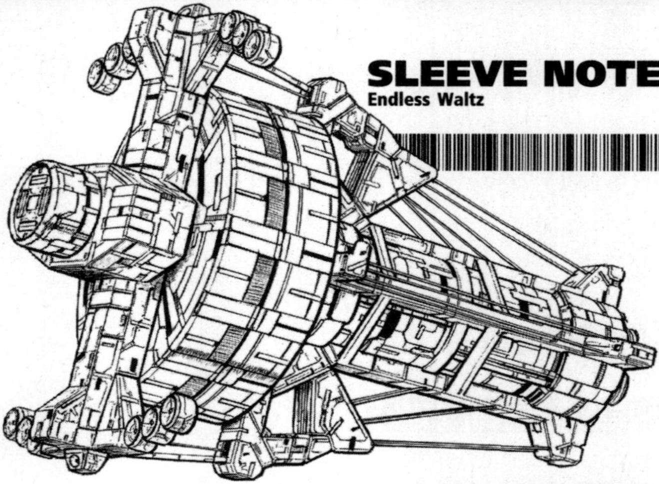

SLEEVE NOTES:
Endless Waltz

SPACE FORTRESS BULGE

A mobile space fortress built by the Earth Sphere Alliance's Space Force. Heero's step-father Seis Clark designed it, and it was completed in A.C. 186. Construction costs were placed entirely on the colonies, which garnered strong animosity among colony citizens. There is a spaceport and cargo hold in its core, and the central cylinder is an artificial gravity block. It travels via six gigantic rocket engines.

SPACE FORTRESS BULGE UPGRADED

Bulge's upgraded form, equipped with a colossal beam cannon called the "Bulge Cannon." At maximum output, it can destroy a colony with a single blast. Repeated fire is also possible at an output of about 10%. When the beam cannon is in use, propulsion functions are halted. The Bulge Cannon is directly connected to the generators and is fixed in place, so to aim, execution of attitude control for the entire fortress is necessary.

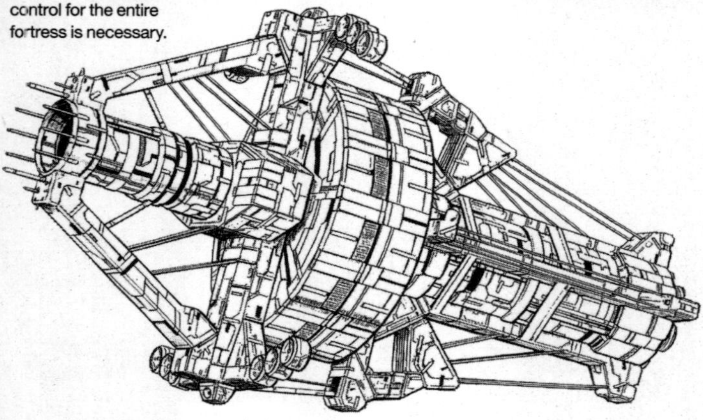

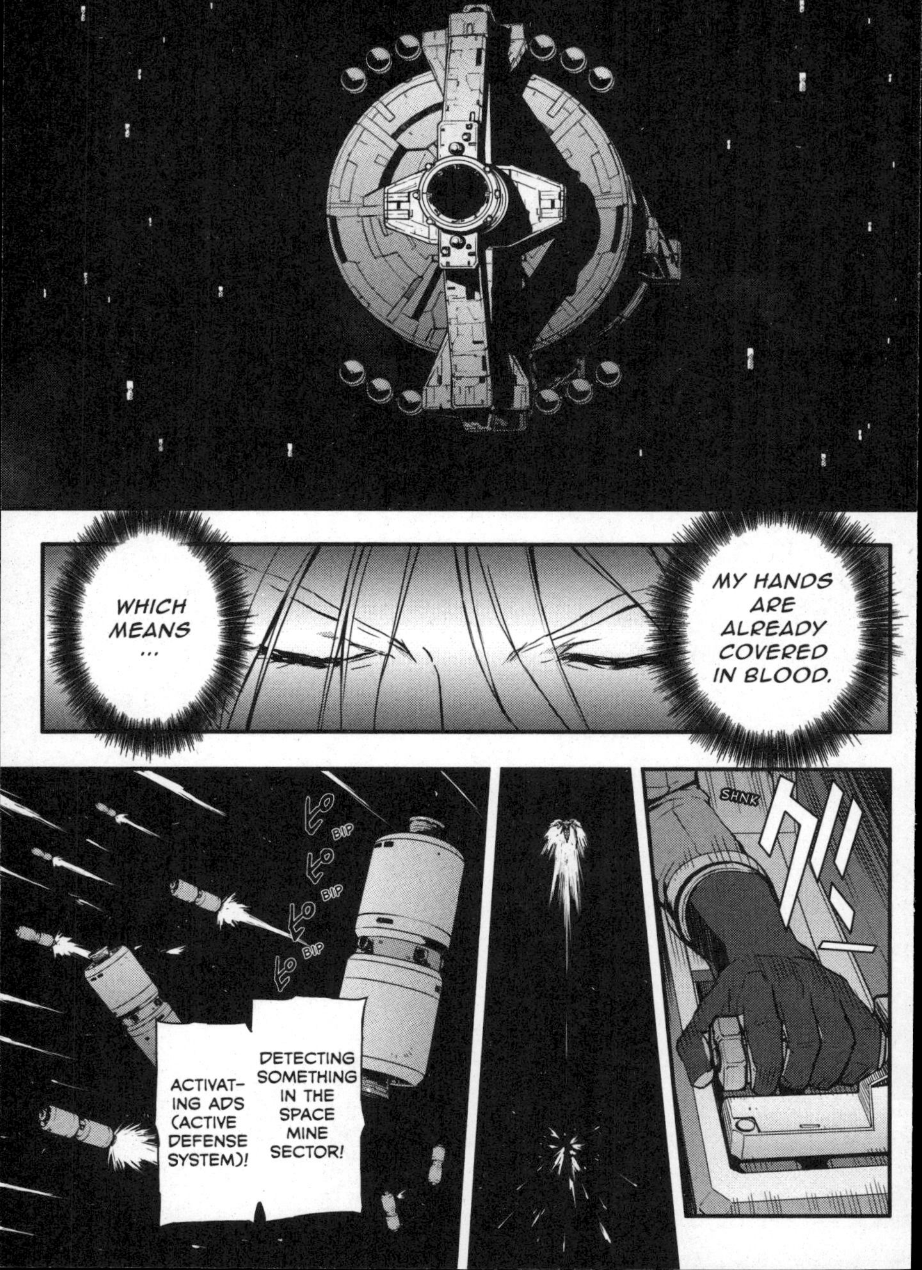
MY HANDS ARE ALREADY COVERED IN BLOOD.
WHICH MEANS ...
SHNK
BIP
BIP
BIP
DETECTING SOMETHING IN THE SPACE MINE SECTOR!
ACTIVAT-ING ADS (ACTIVE DEFENSE SYSTEM)!

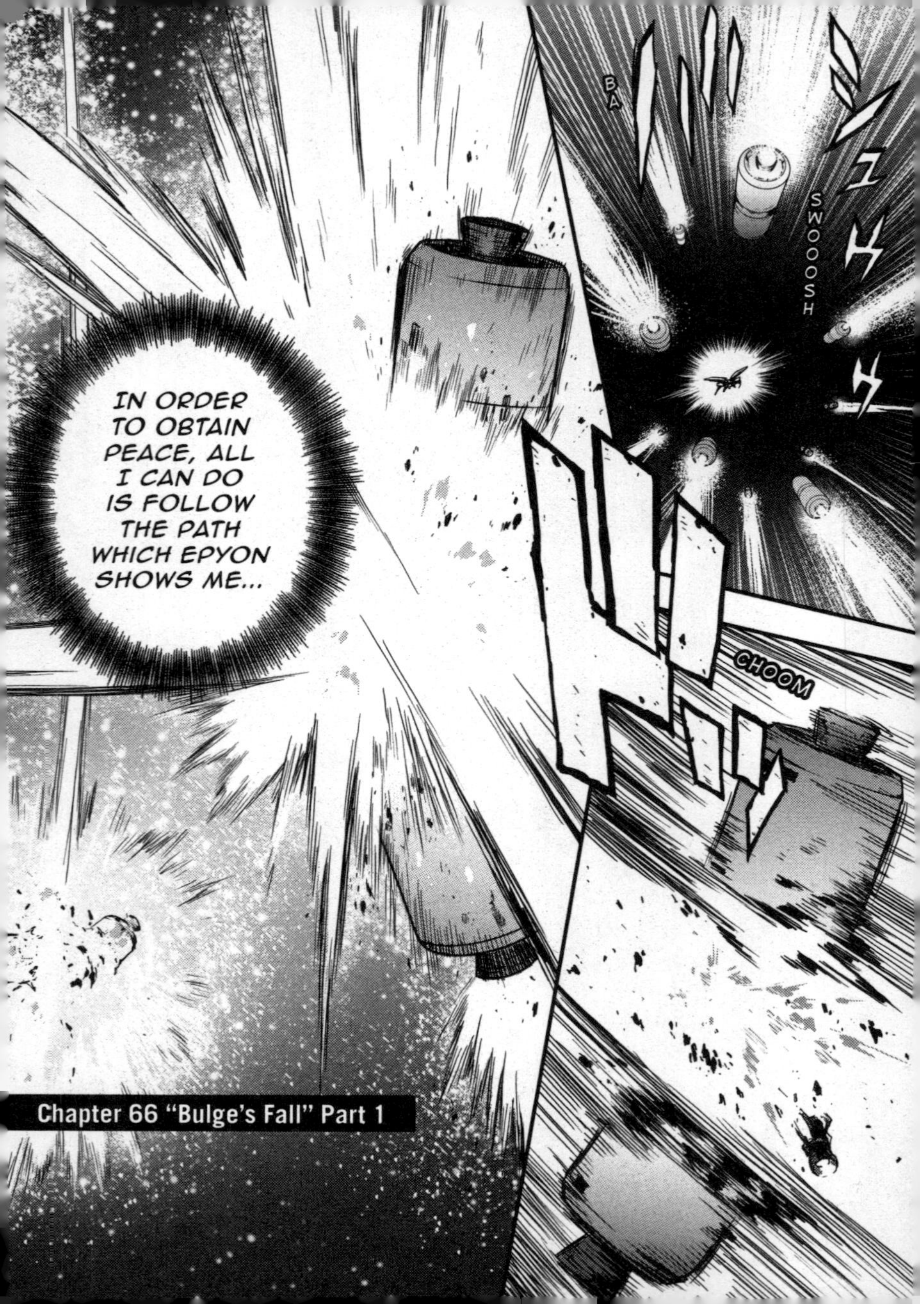
BA
SWOOOSH
CHOOM
IN ORDER TO OBTAIN PEACE, ALL I CAN DO IS FOLLOW THE PATH WHICH EPYON SHOWS ME...
Chapter 66 "Bulge's Fall" Part 1

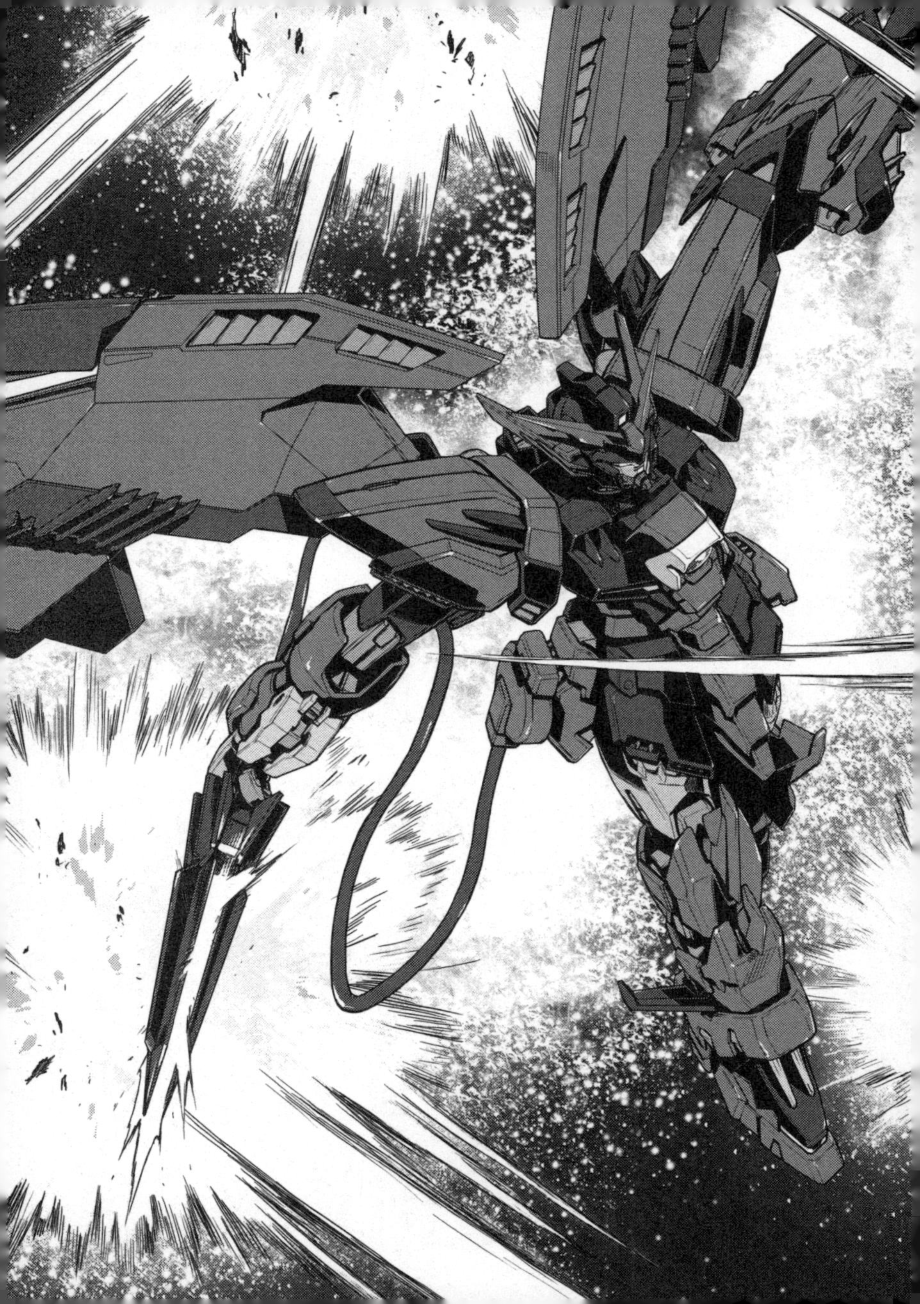

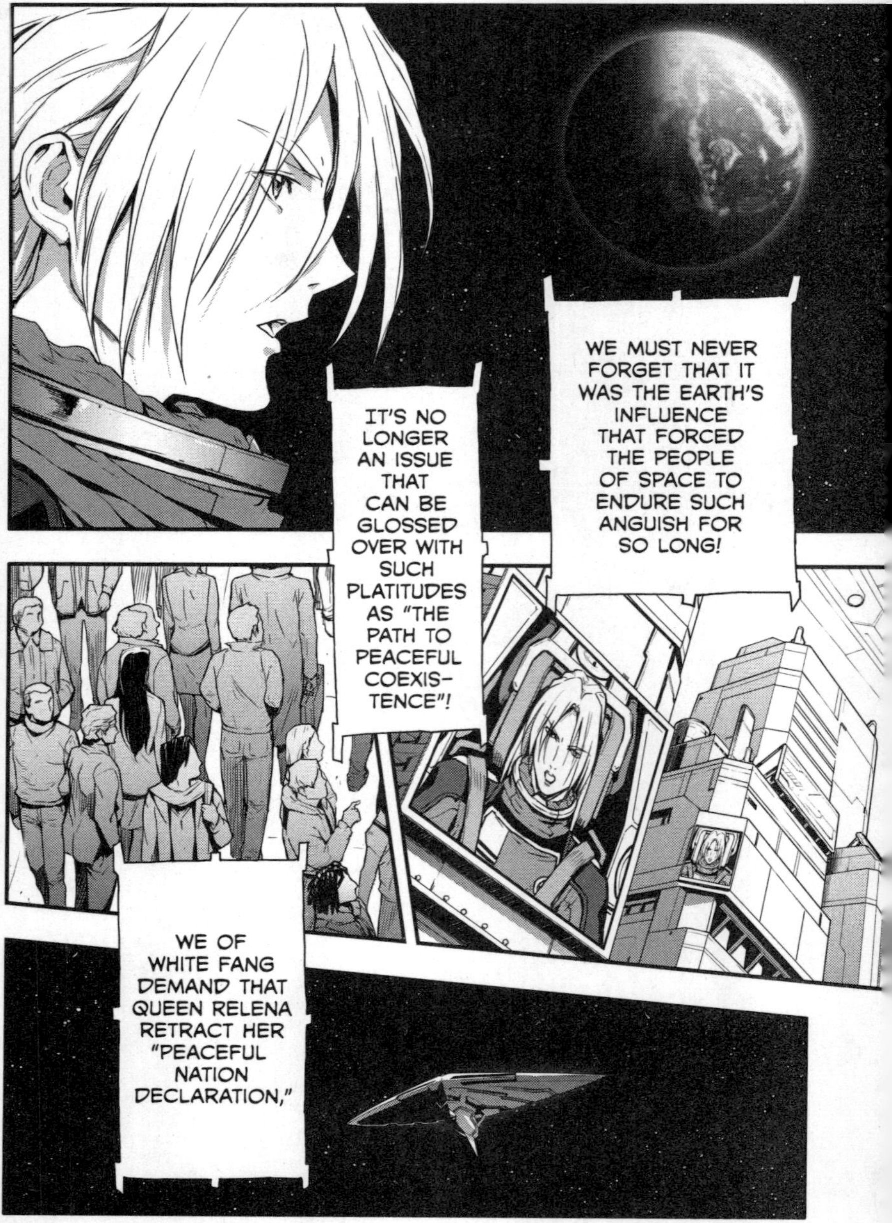
WE MUST NEVER FORGET THAT IT WAS THE EARTH'S INFLUENCE THAT FORCED THE PEOPLE OF SPACE TO ENDURE SUCH ANGUISH FOR SO LONG!
IT'S NO LONGER AN ISSUE THAT CAN BE GLOSSED OVER WITH SUCH PLATITUDES AS "THE PATH TO PEACEFUL COEXIS-TENCE"!
WE OF WHITE FANG DEMAND THAT QUEEN RELENA RETRACT HER "PEACEFUL NATION DECLARATION,"

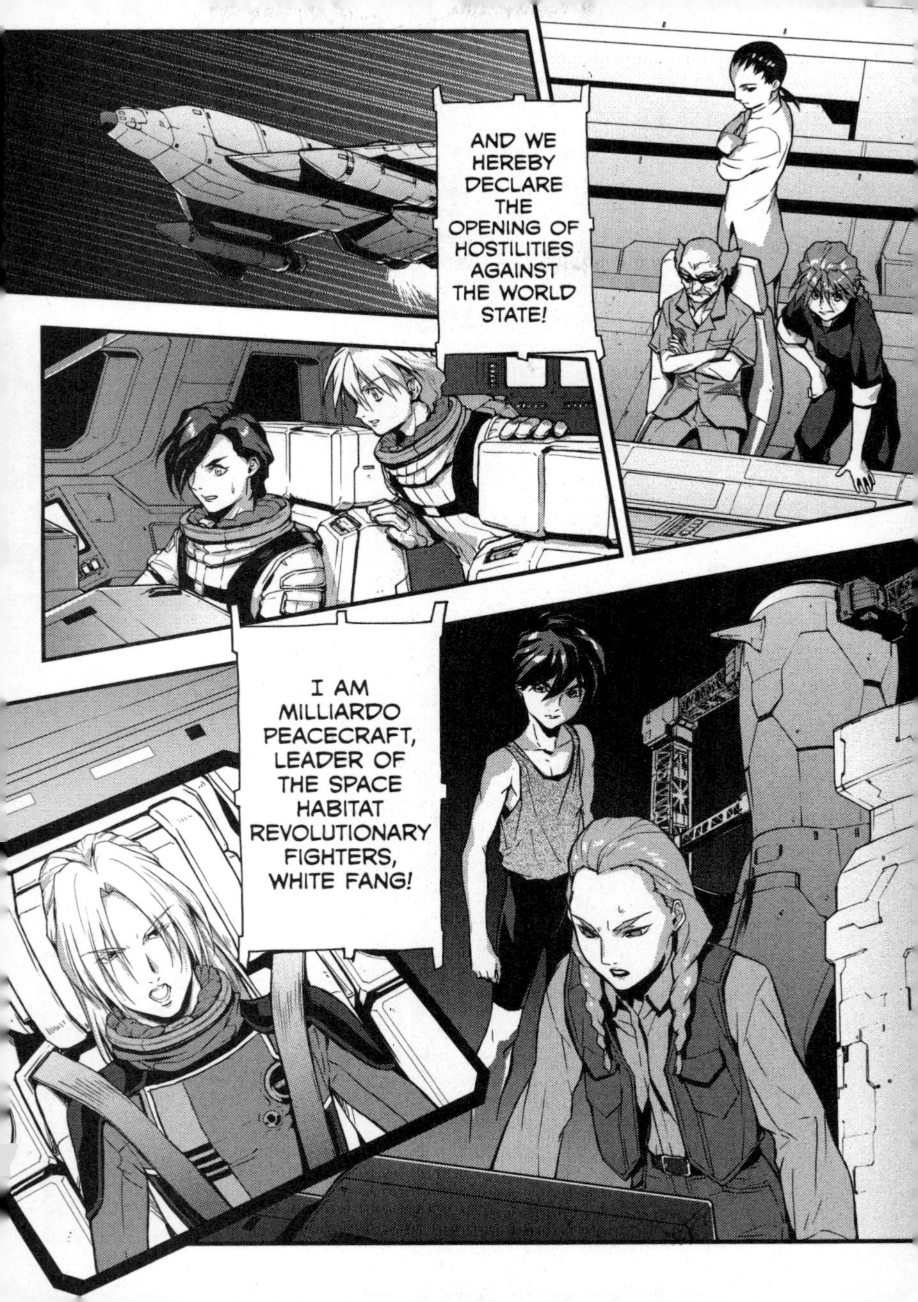
AND WE HEREBY DECLARE THE OPENING OF HOSTILITIES AGAINST THE WORLD STATE!
I AM MILLIARDO PEACECRAFT, LEADER OF THE SPACE HABITAT REVOLUTIONARY FIGHTERS, WHITE FANG!

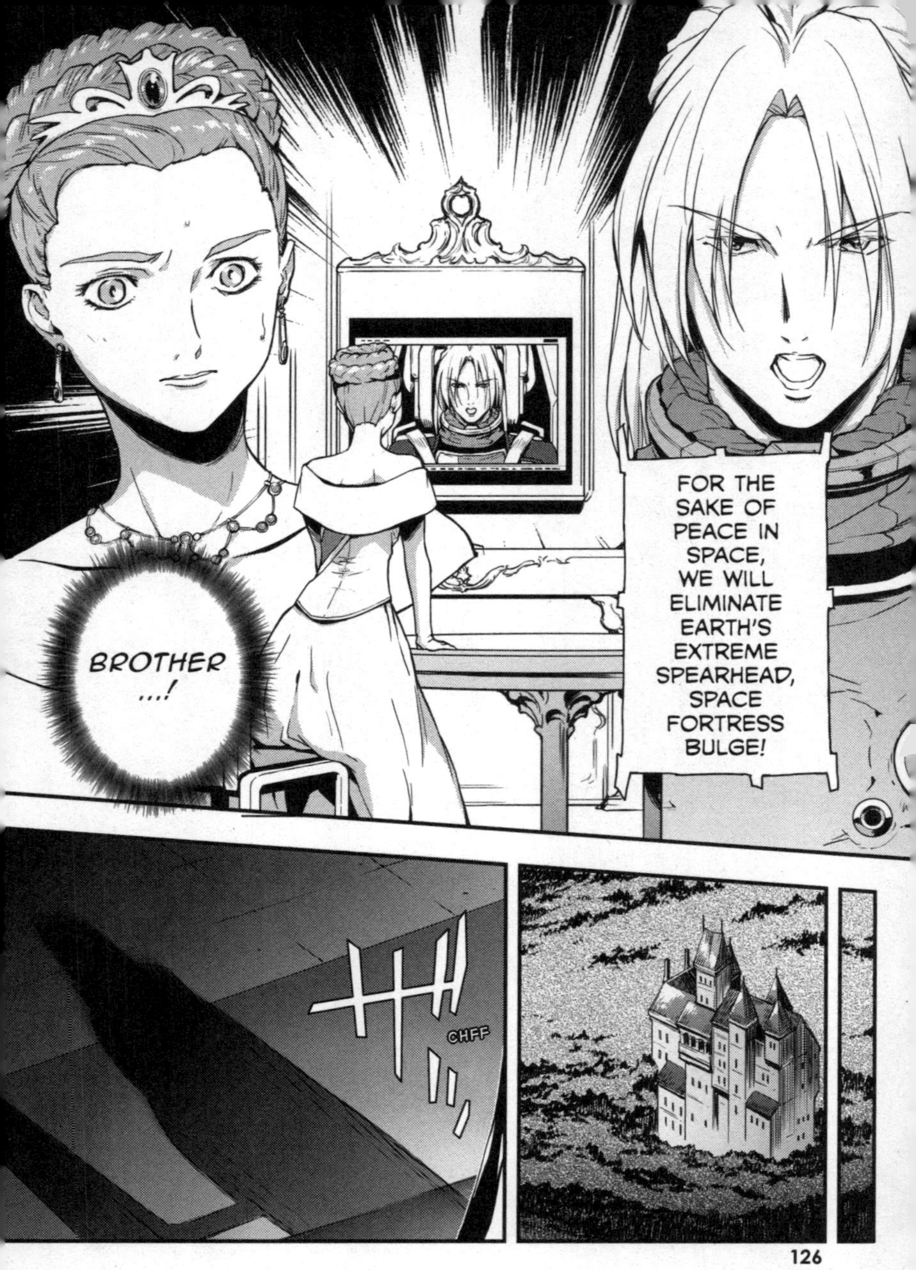
FOR THE SAKE OF PEACE IN SPACE, WE WILL ELIMINATE EARTH'S EXTREME SPEARHEAD, SPACE FORTRESS BULGE!
BROTHER ...!
CHFF

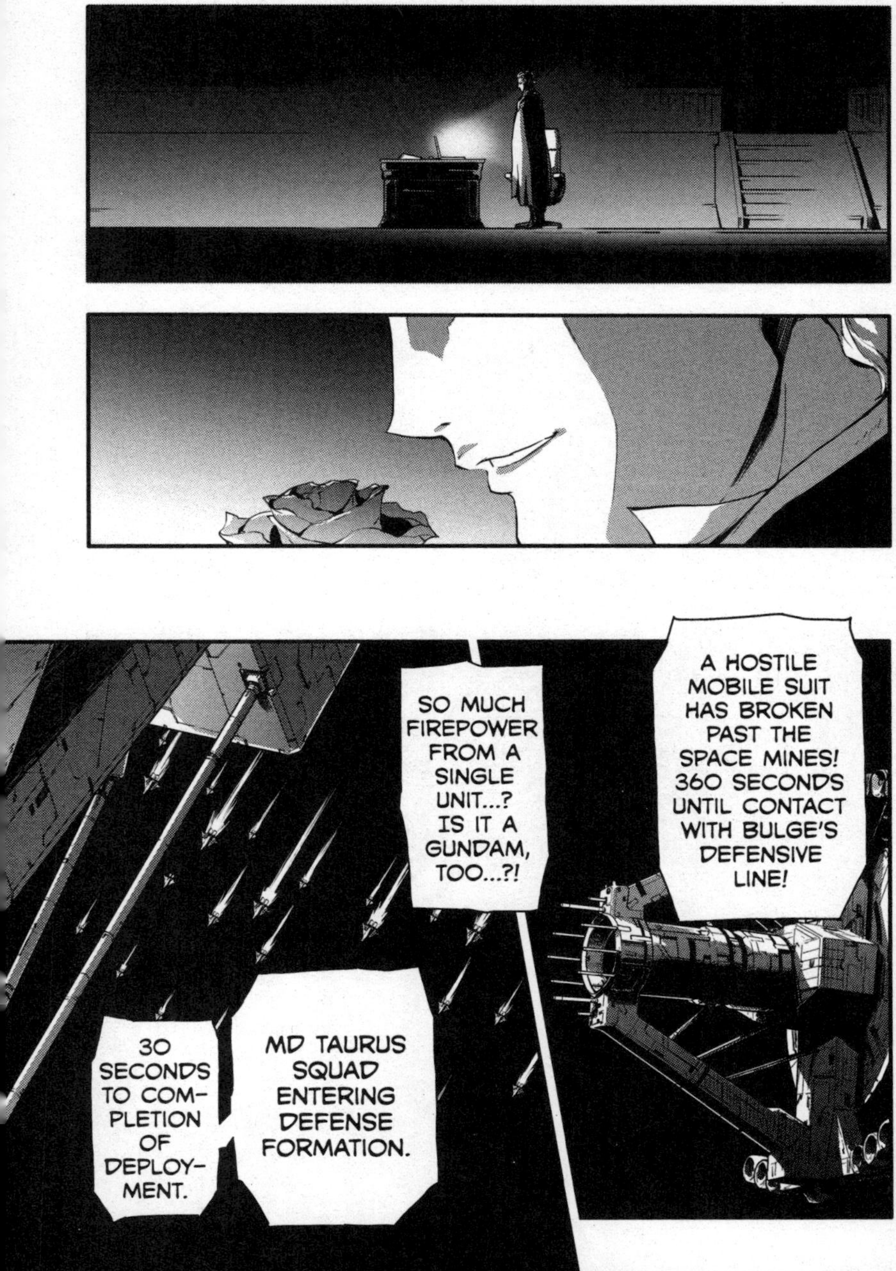
A HOSTILE MOBILE SUIT HAS BROKEN PAST THE SPACE MINES! 360 SECONDS UNTIL CONTACT WITH BULGE'S DEFENSIVE LINE!
SO MUCH FIREPOWER FROM A SINGLE UNIT...? IS IT A GUNDAM, TOO...?!
MD TAURUS SQUAD ENTERING DEFENSE FORMATION.
30 SECONDS TO COM-PLETION OF DEPLOY-MENT.

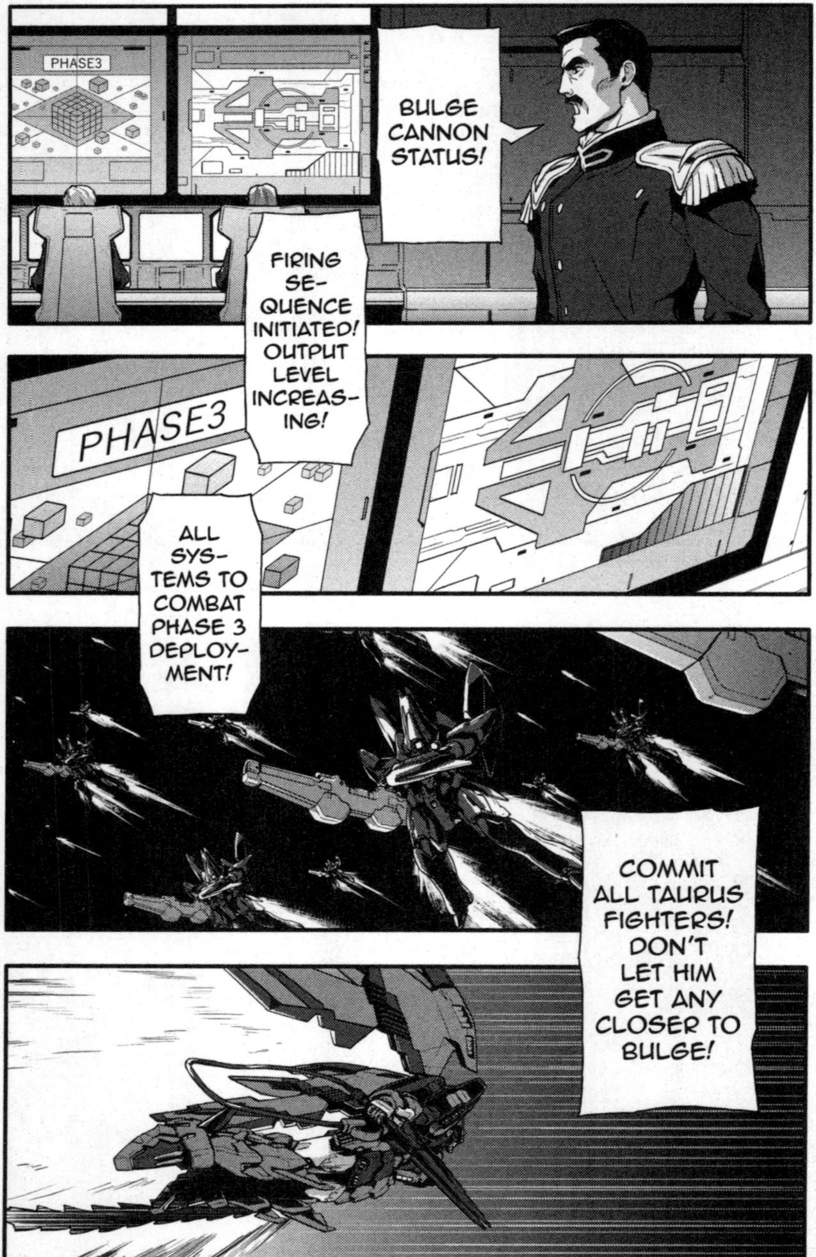
PHASE3
BULGE CANNON STATUS!
FIRING SEQUENCE INITIATED! OUTPUT LEVEL INCREASING!
PHASE3
ALL SYSTEMS TO COMBAT PHASE 3 DEPLOYMENT!
COMMIT ALL TAURUS FIGHTERS! DON'T LET HIM GET ANY CLOSER TO BULGE!

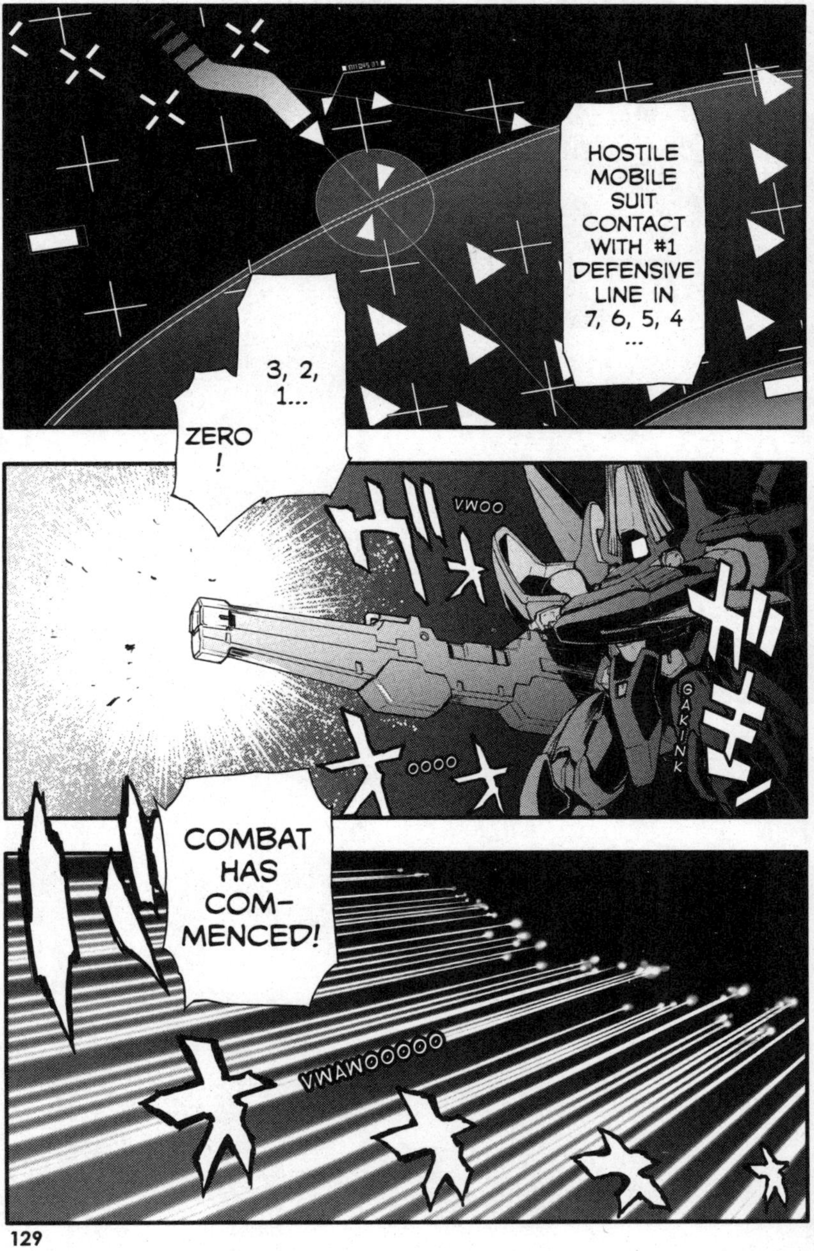
HOSTILE MOBILE SUIT CONTACT WITH #1 DEFENSIVE LINE IN 7, 6, 5, 4 ...
3, 2, 1... ZERO!
VWOO
OOOO
GAKINK
COMBAT HAS COM-MENCED!
VWAWOOOOOO

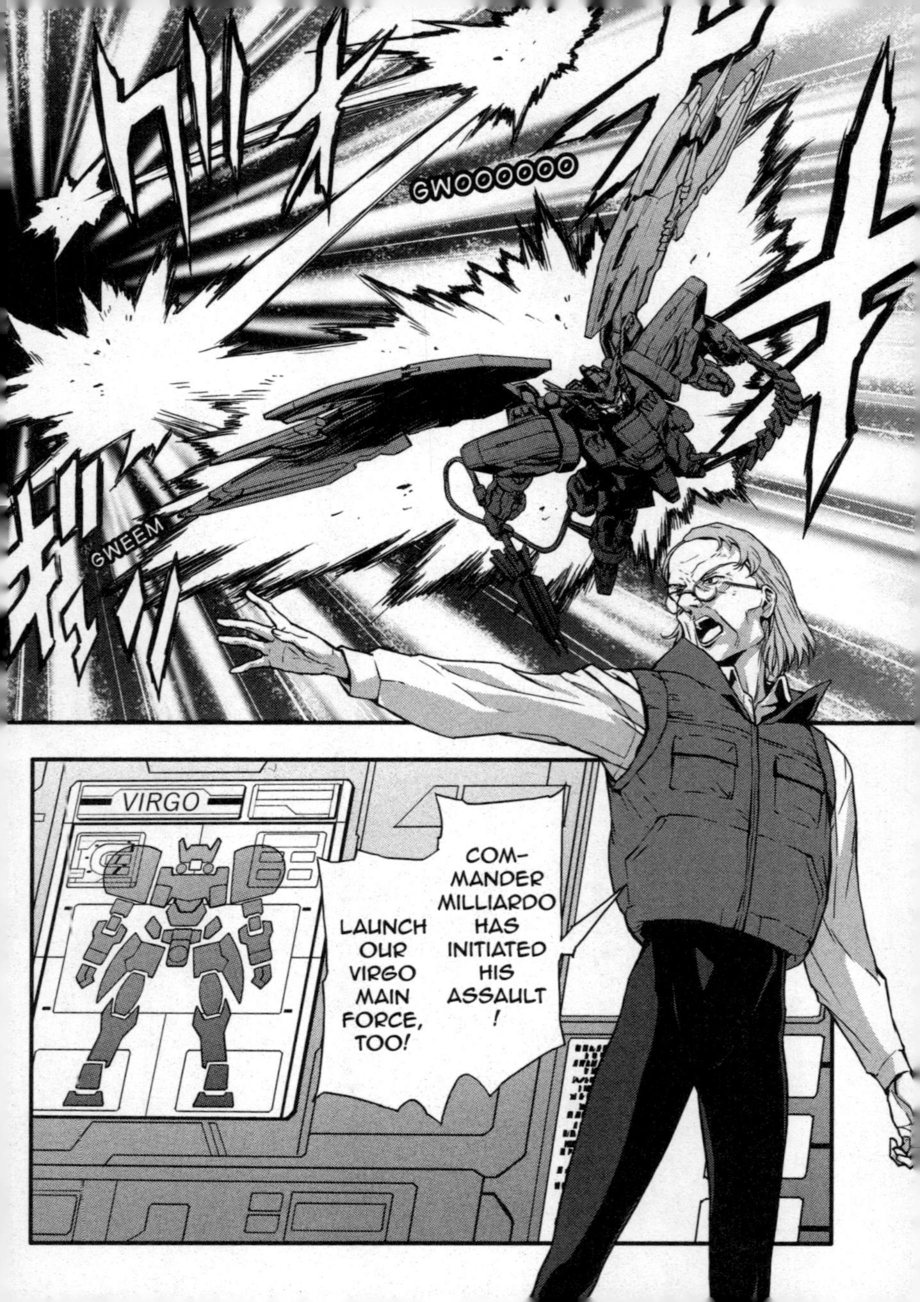
GWOOOOOO
GWEEM
VIRGO
COMMANDER MILLIARDO HAS INITIATED HIS ASSAULT!
LAUNCH OUR VIRGO MAIN FORCE, TOO!

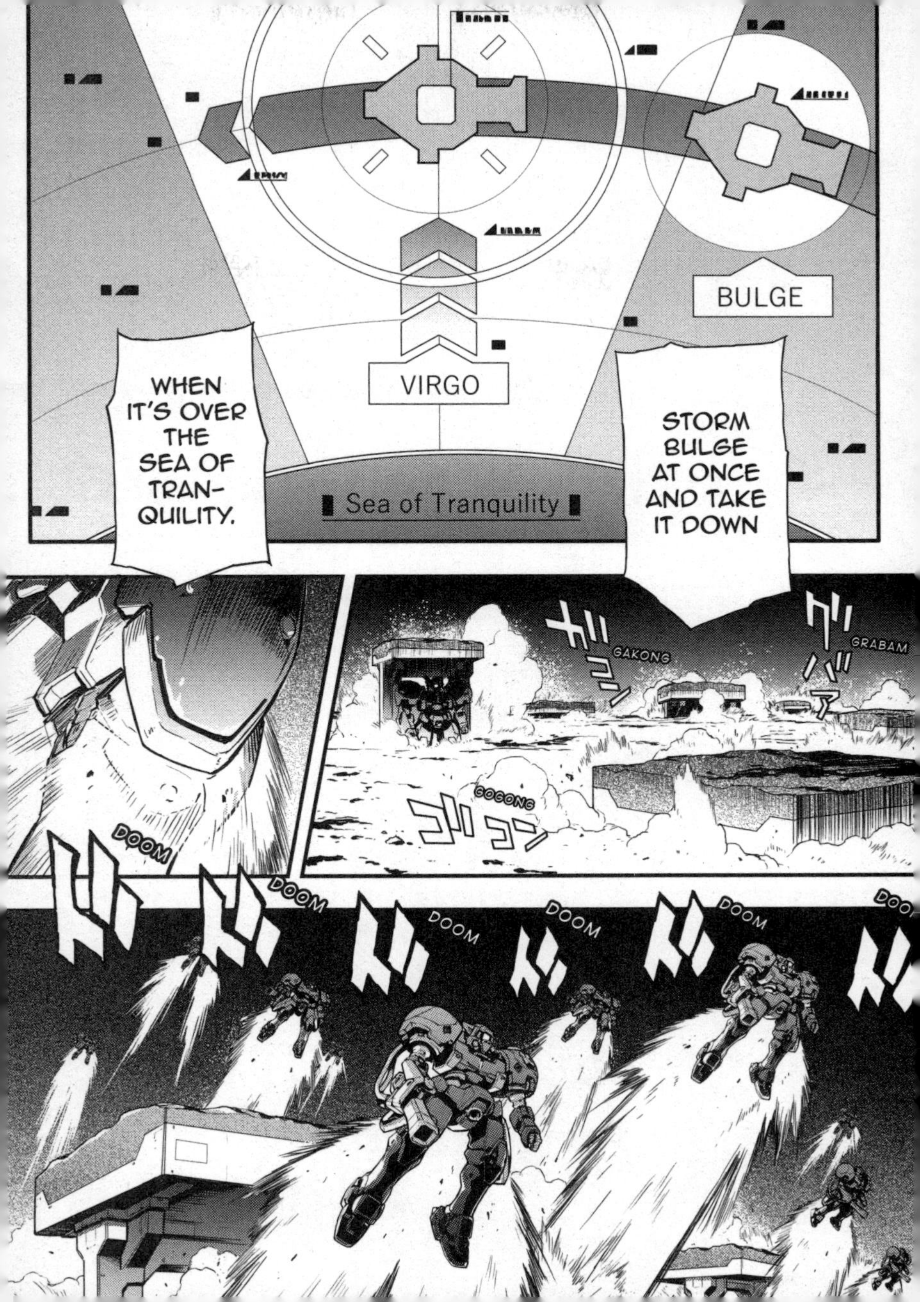
BULGE
STORM BULGE AT ONCE AND TAKE IT DOWN
VIRGO
WHEN IT'S OVER THE SEA OF TRAN-QUILITY.
Sea of Tranquility
GRABAM
GAKONG
GOGONG
DOOM
DOOM
DOOM
DOOM
DOOM
DOOM

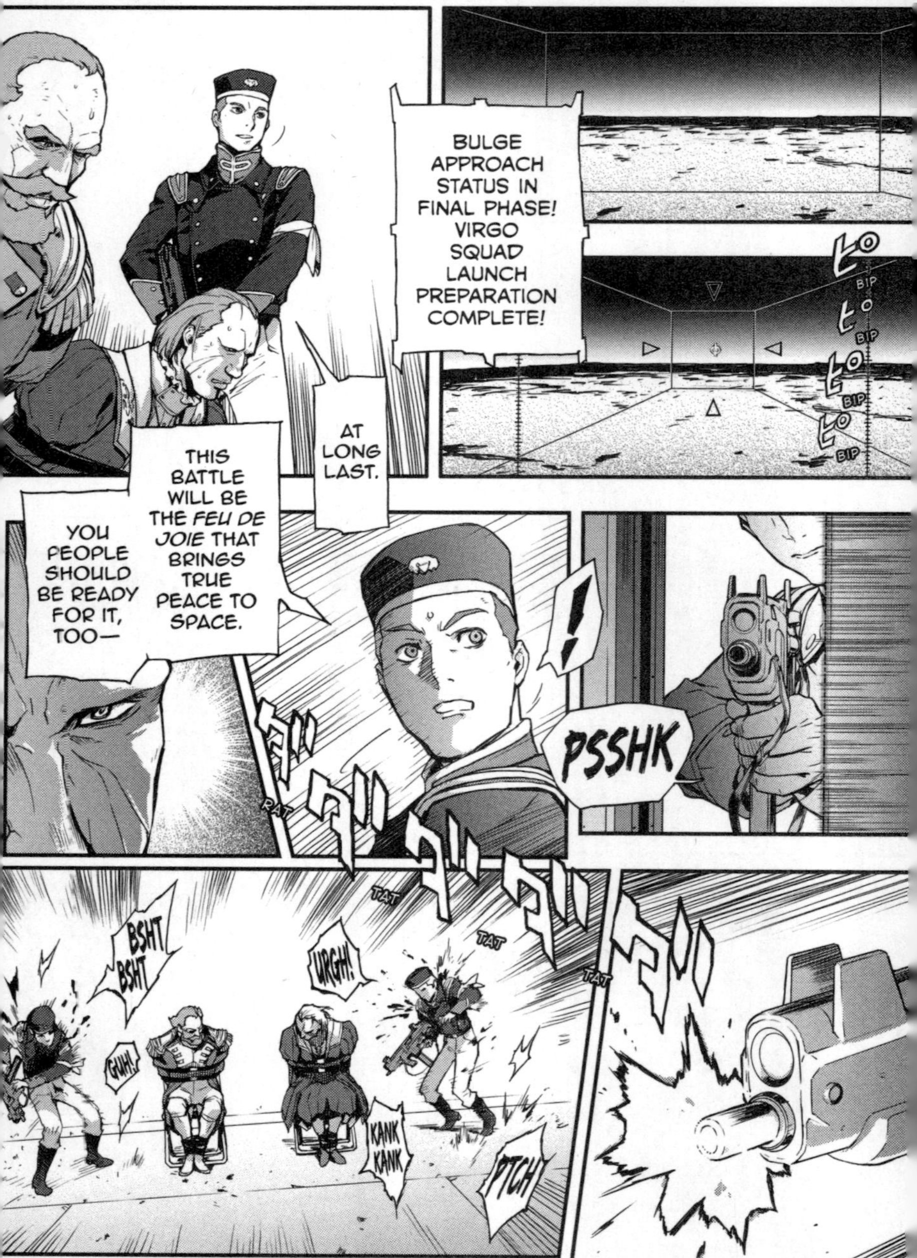
BULGE APPROACH STATUS IN FINAL PHASE! VIRGO SQUAD LAUNCH PREPARATION COMPLETE!
BIP
BIP
BIP
BIP
AT LONG LAST.
THIS BATTLE WILL BE THE *FEU DE JOIE* THAT BRINGS TRUE PEACE TO SPACE.
YOU PEOPLE SHOULD BE READY FOR IT, TOO—
PSSHK
!
RAT
TAT
TAT
TAT
URGH!
BSHT BSHT
GUH!
KANK KANK
PTCH

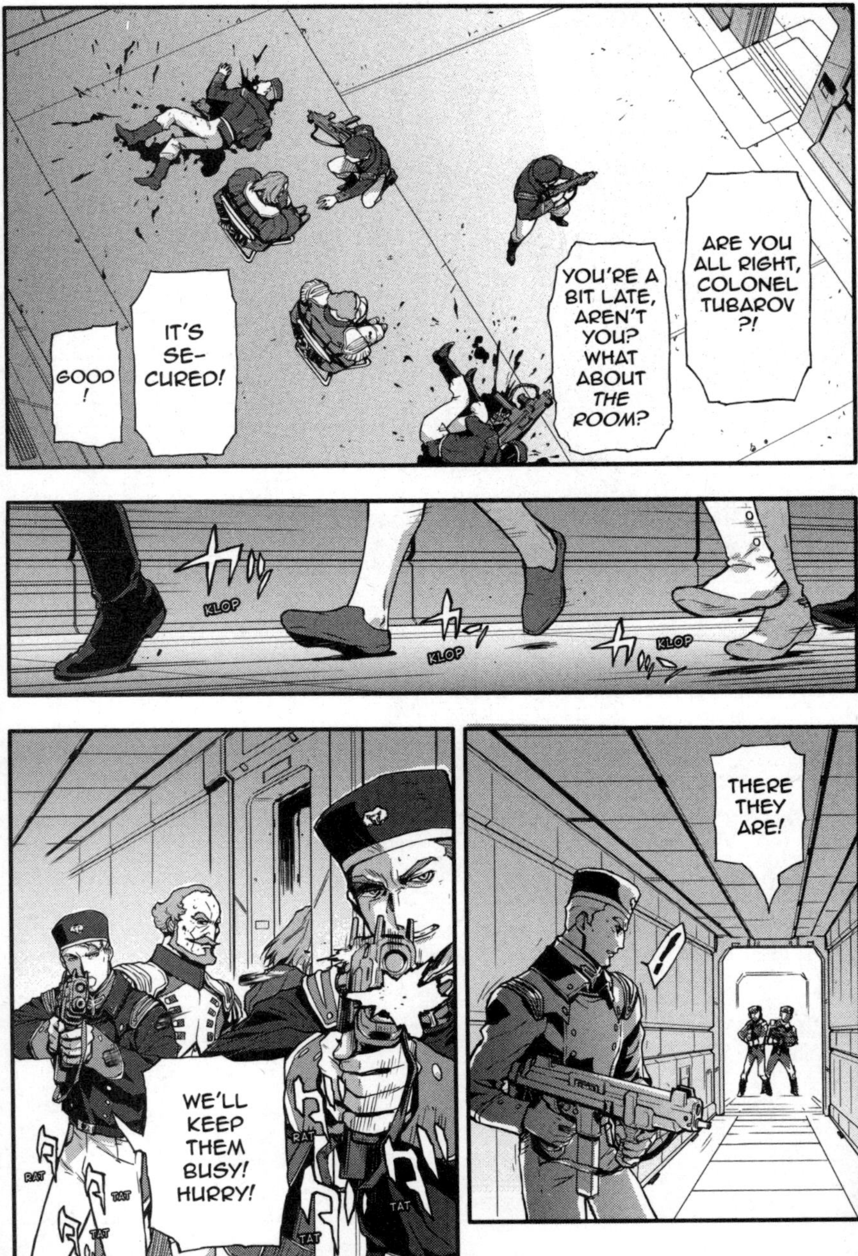
ARE YOU ALL RIGHT, COLONEL TUBAROV?!
YOU'RE A BIT LATE, AREN'T YOU? WHAT ABOUT THE ROOM?
IT'S SE-CURED!
GOOD!
KLOP
KLOP
KLOP
THERE THEY ARE!
!
WE'LL KEEP THEM BUSY! HURRY!
RAT
RAT
TAT
TAT
TAT
TAT

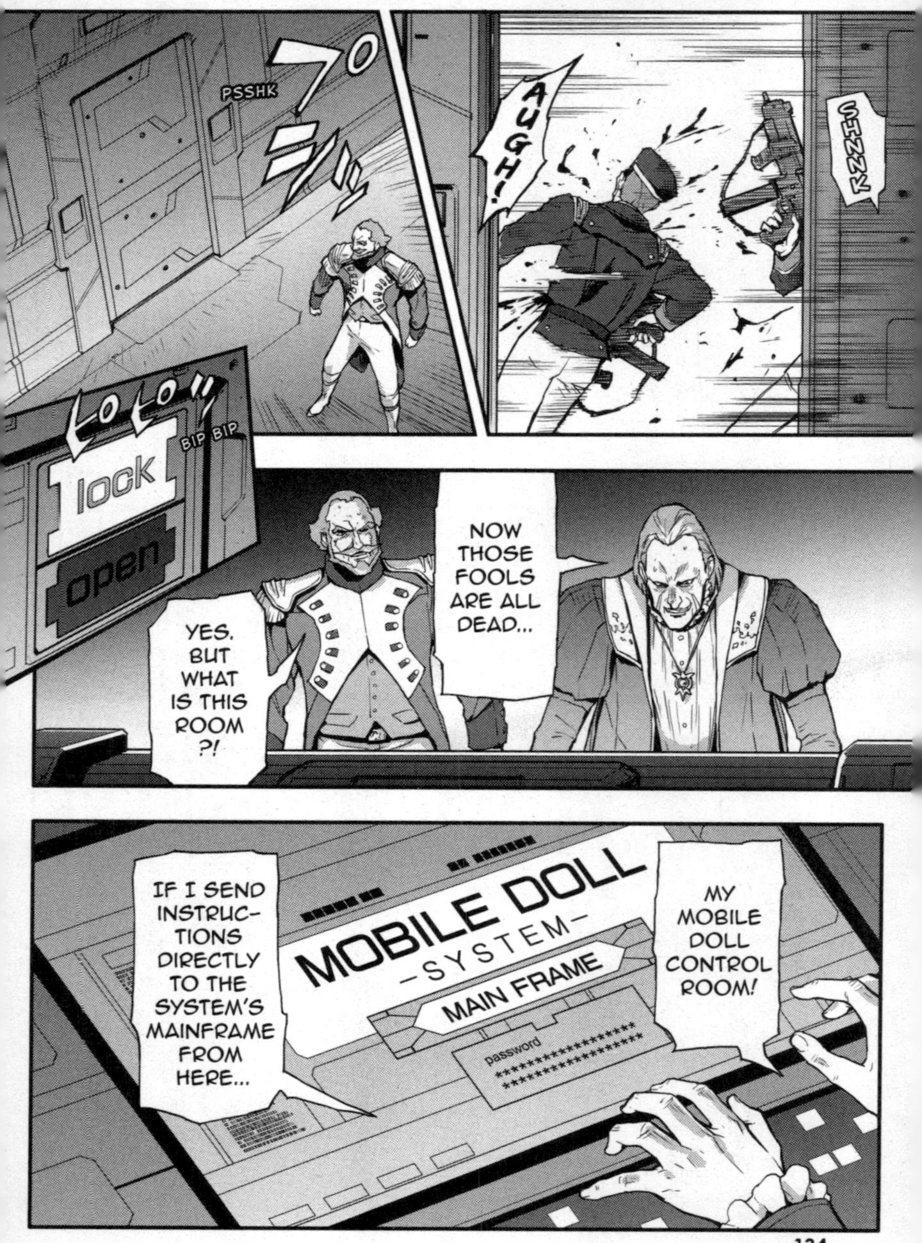
SHNNK
AUGH!
PSSHK
BIP BIP
lock
open
NOW THOSE FOOLS ARE ALL DEAD...
YES. BUT WHAT IS THIS ROOM ?!
MY MOBILE DOLL CONTROL ROOM!
MOBILE DOLL
-SYSTEM-
MAIN FRAME
password
IF I SEND INSTRUCTIONS DIRECTLY TO THE SYSTEM'S MAINFRAME FROM HERE...

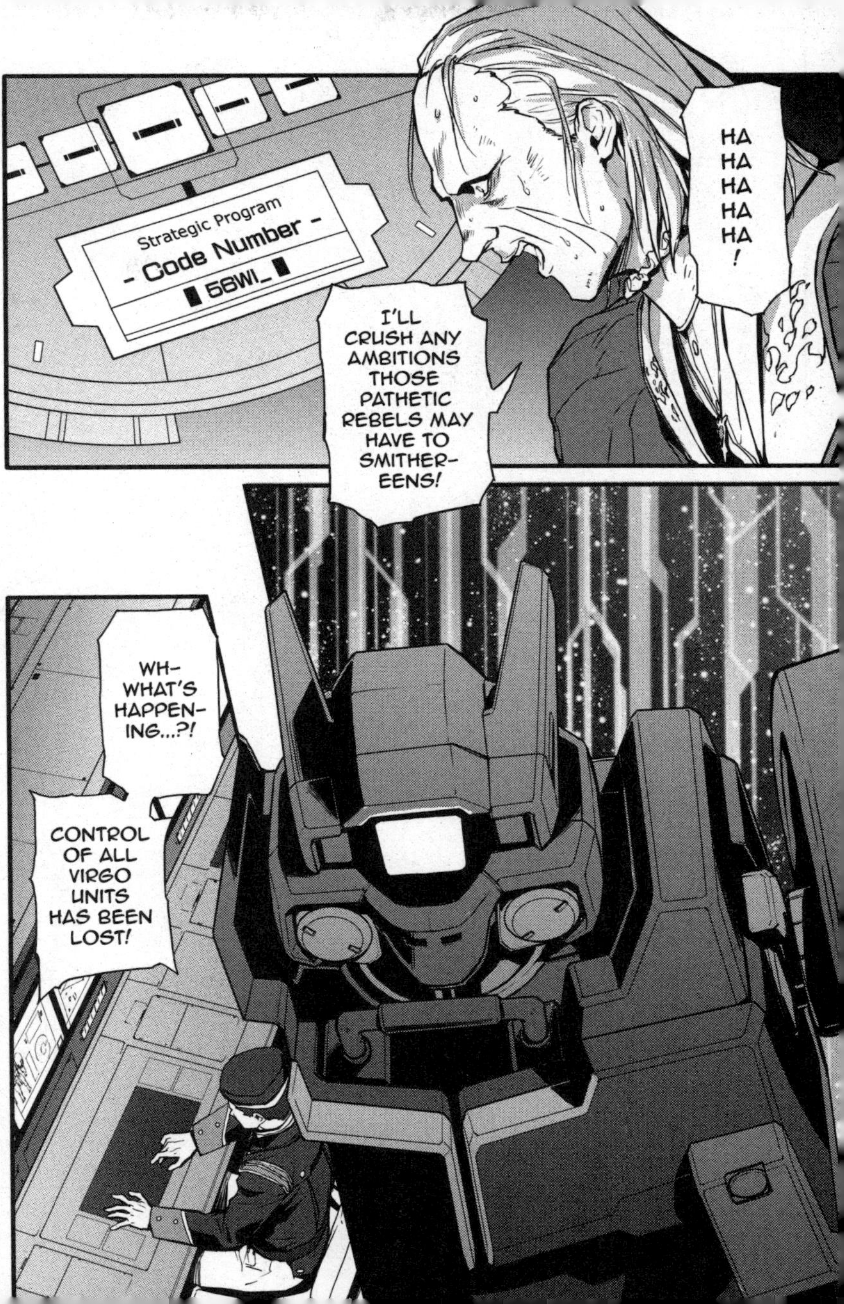
HA HA HA HA HA!
I'LL CRUSH ANY AMBITIONS THOSE PATHETIC REBELS MAY HAVE TO SMITHEREENS!
Strategic Program
- Code Number -
56WI_
WH-WHAT'S HAPPENING...?!
CONTROL OF ALL VIRGO UNITS HAS BEEN LOST!

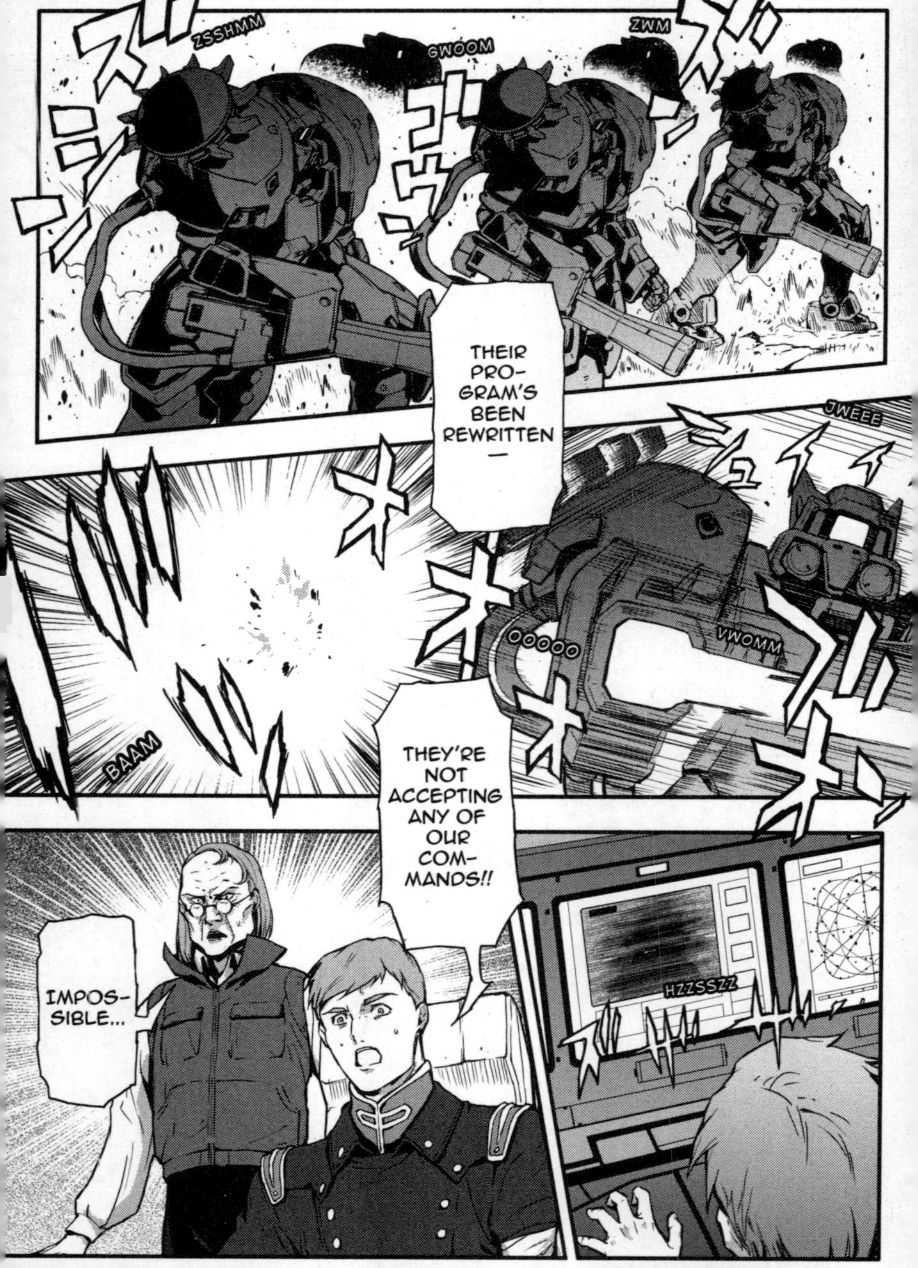
ZWM
GWOOM
ZSSHMM
THEIR PRO-GRAM'S BEEN REWRITTEN—
JWEEE
VWOMM
OOOOO
BAAM
THEY'RE NOT ACCEPTING ANY OF OUR COM-MANDS!!
HZZSSZZ
IMPOS-SIBLE...

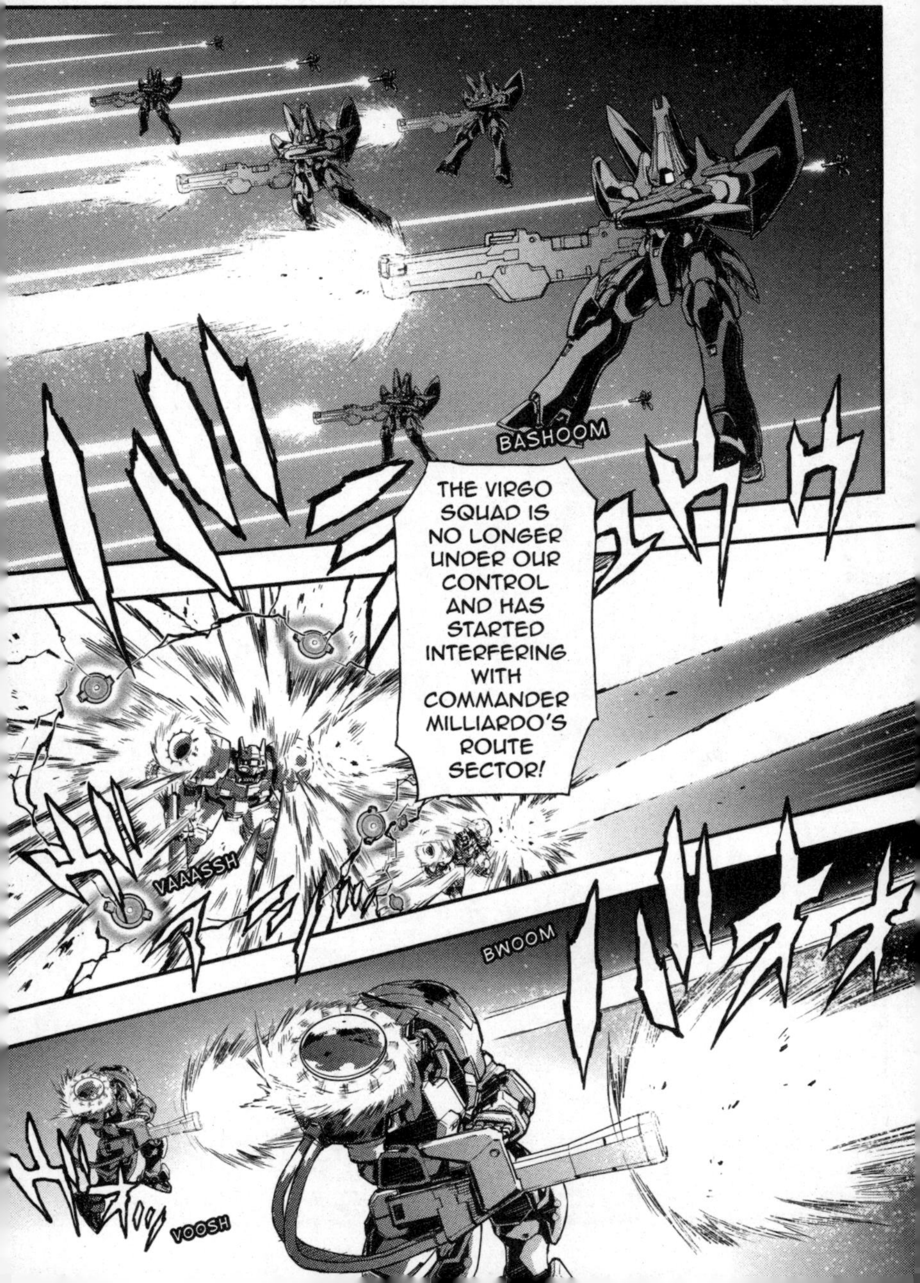
BASHOOM
THE VIRGO SQUAD IS NO LONGER UNDER OUR CONTROL AND HAS STARTED INTERFERING WITH COMMANDER MILLIARDO'S ROUTE SECTOR!
VAAASSH
BWOOM
VOOSH

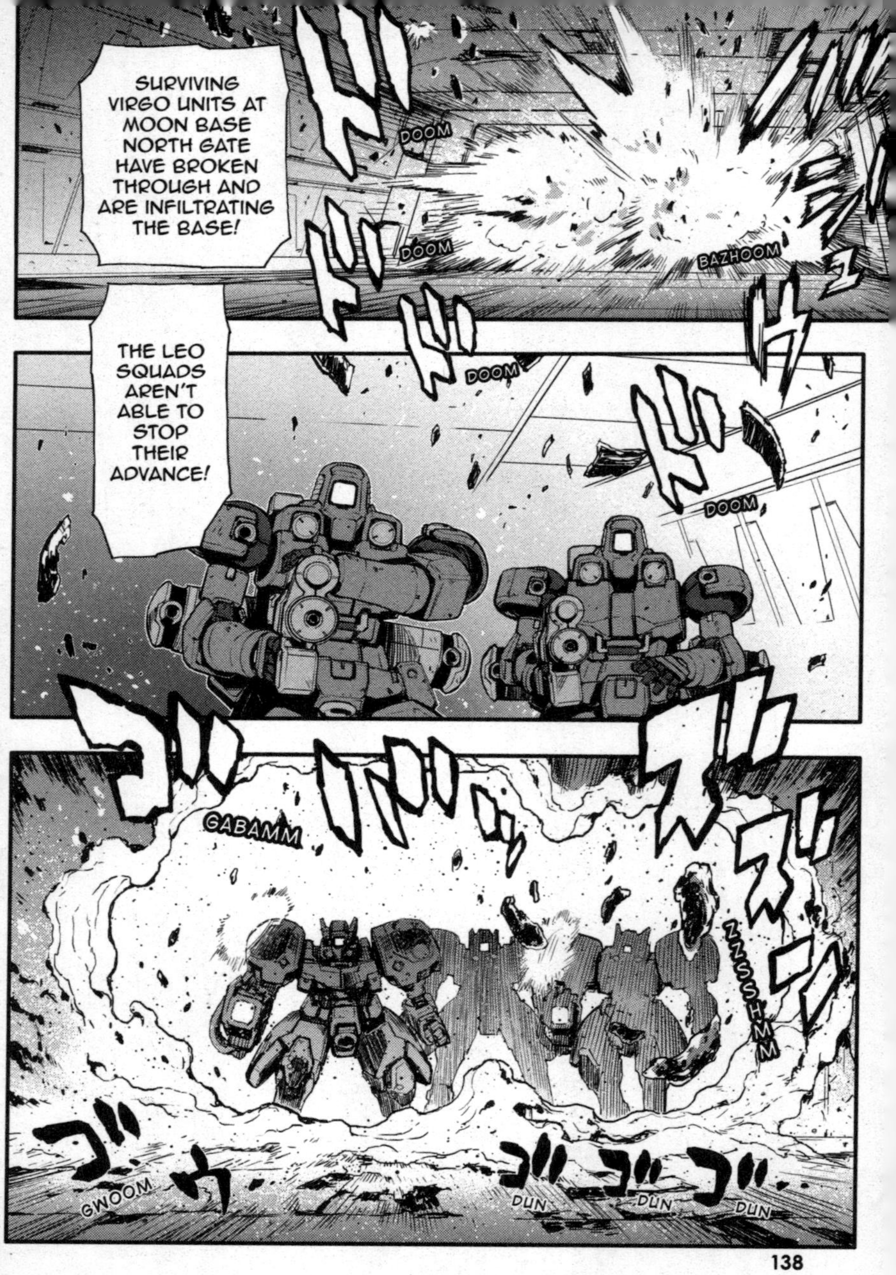
SURVIVING VIRGO UNITS AT MOON BASE NORTH GATE HAVE BROKEN THROUGH AND ARE INFILTRATING THE BASE!
BAZHOOM
DOOM
DOOM
DOOM
DOOM
THE LEO SQUADS AREN'T ABLE TO STOP THEIR ADVANCE!
ZZSSHMM
GABAMM
DUN
DUN
DUN
GWOOM

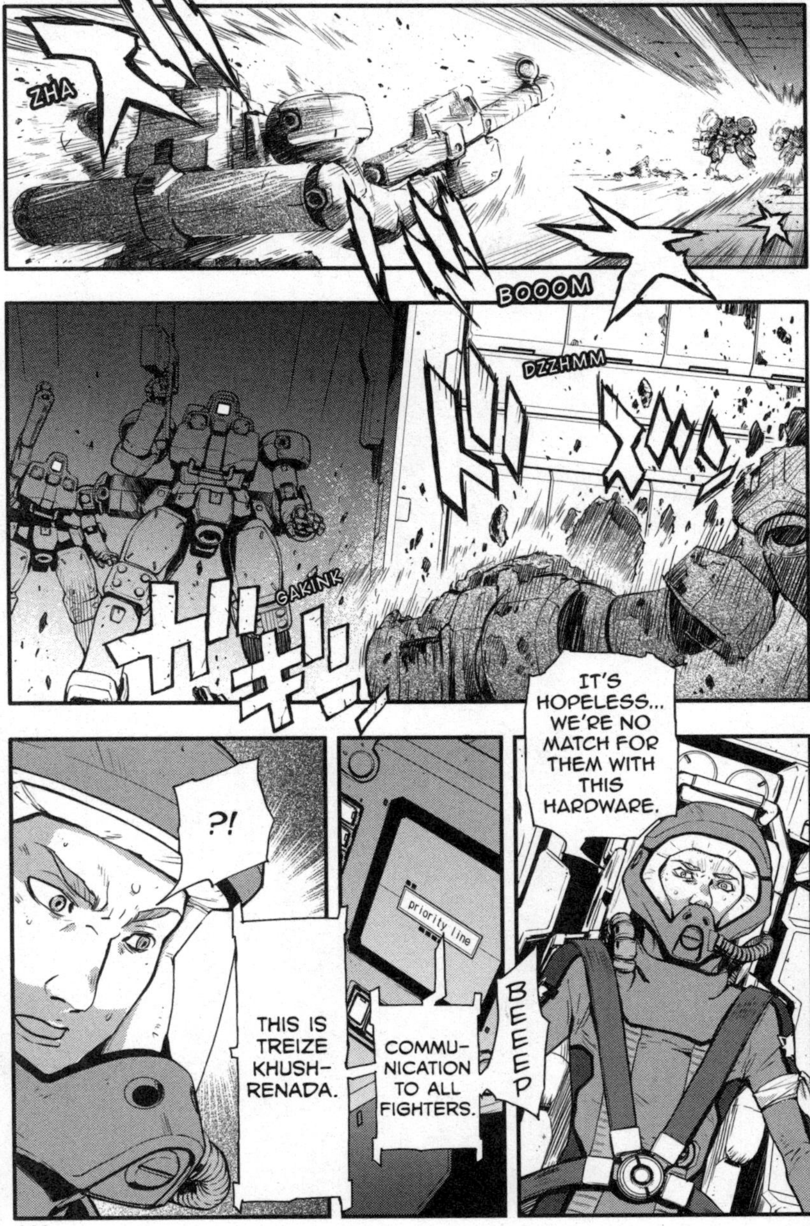
ZHA
BOOOM
DZZHMM
GAKINK
IT'S HOPELESS... WE'RE NO MATCH FOR THEM WITH THIS HARDWARE.
BEEEP
priority line
COMMU-NICATION TO ALL FIGHTERS.
?!
THIS IS TREIZE KHUSH-RENADA.

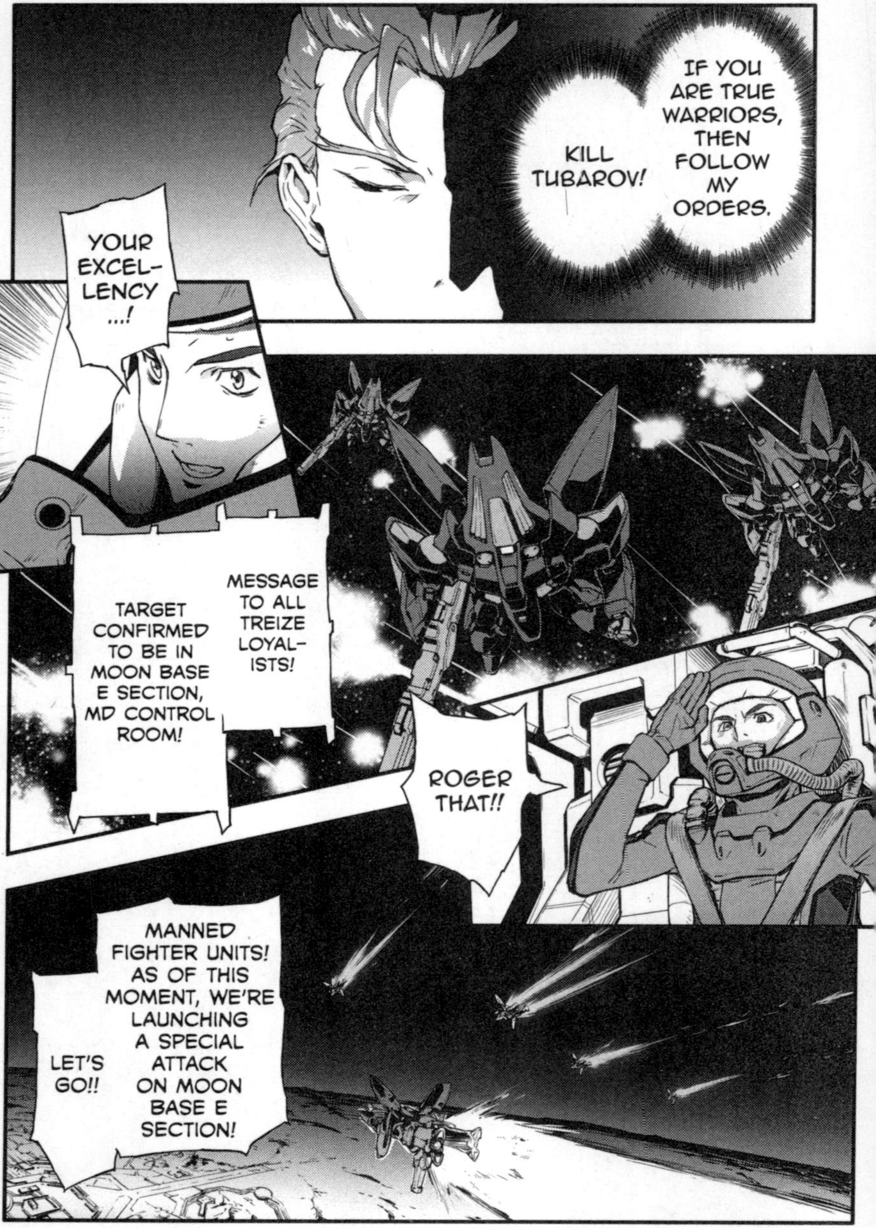
IF YOU ARE TRUE WARRIORS, THEN FOLLOW MY ORDERS.
KILL TUBAROV!
YOUR EXCEL-LENCY ...!
MESSAGE TO ALL TREIZE LOYAL-ISTS!
TARGET CONFIRMED TO BE IN MOON BASE E SECTION, MD CONTROL ROOM!
ROGER THAT!!
MANNED FIGHTER UNITS! AS OF THIS MOMENT, WE'RE LAUNCHING A SPECIAL ATTACK ON MOON BASE E SECTION!
LET'S GO!!

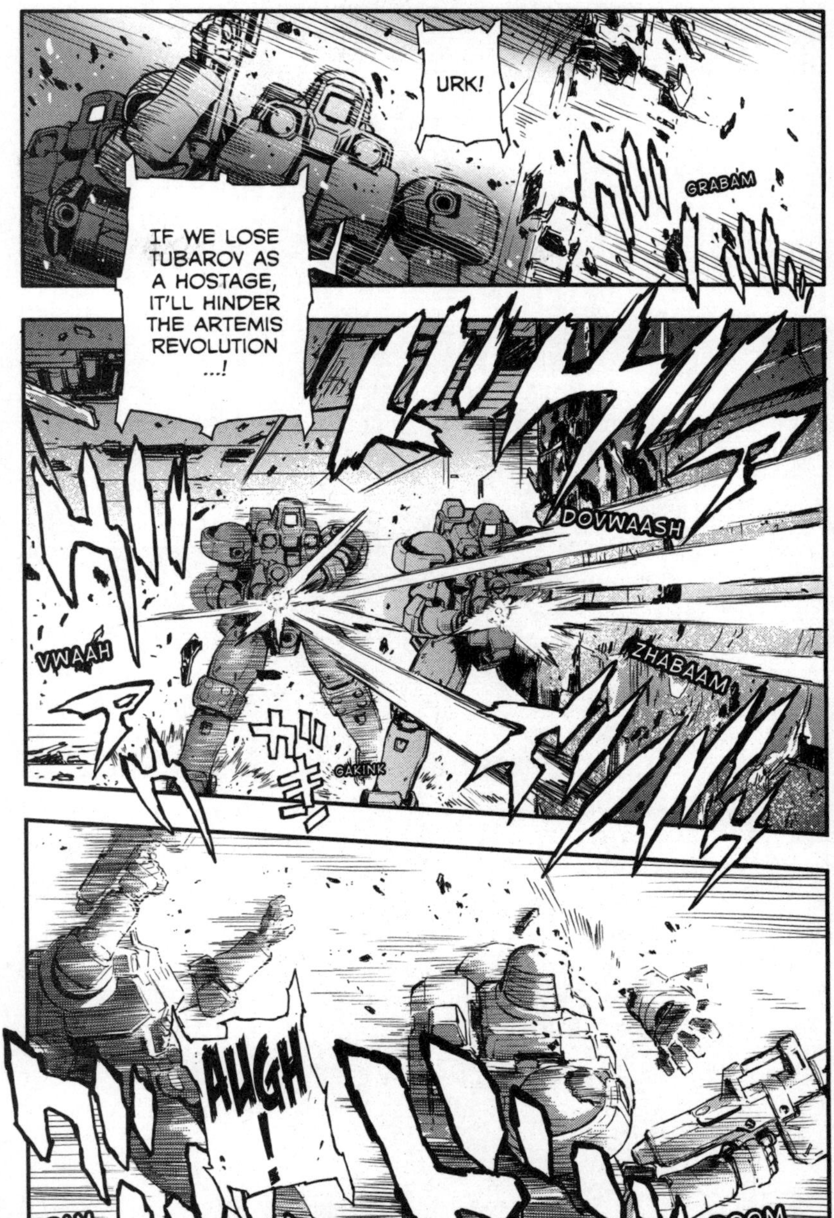
URK!
GRABAM
IF WE LOSE TUBAROV AS A HOSTAGE, IT'LL HINDER THE ARTEMIS REVOLUTION ...!
DOVWAASH
ZHABAAM
VWAAH
GAKINK
AUGH!
DOOM
GRABAM

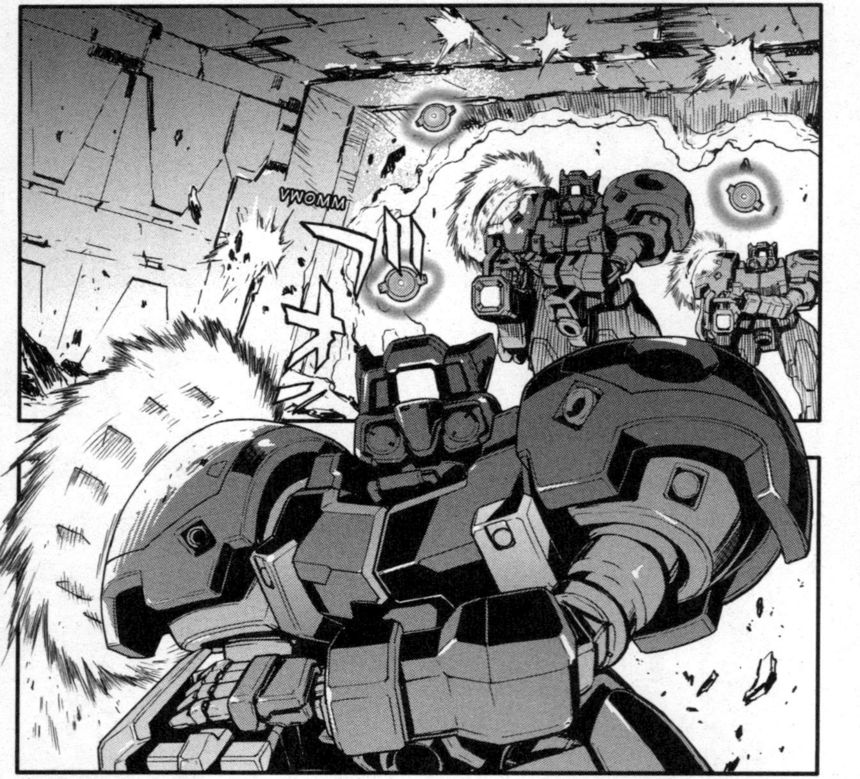
VWOMM

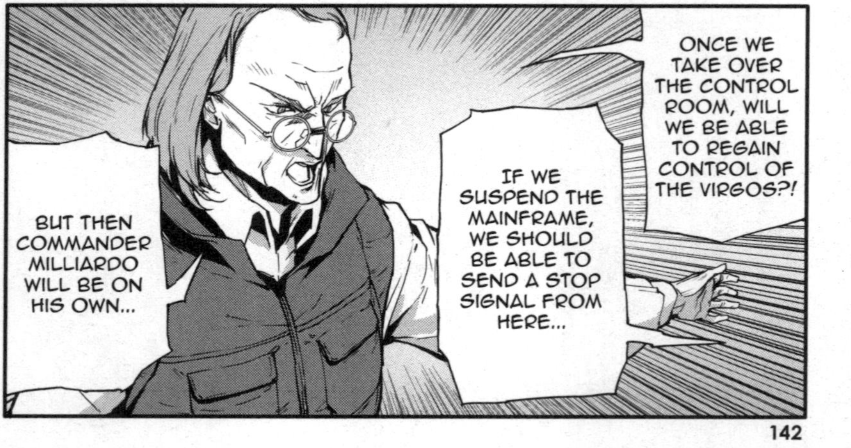
ONCE WE TAKE OVER THE CONTROL ROOM, WILL WE BE ABLE TO REGAIN CONTROL OF THE VIRGOS?!
IF WE SUSPEND THE MAINFRAME, WE SHOULD BE ABLE TO SEND A STOP SIGNAL FROM HERE...
BUT THEN COMMANDER MILLIARDO WILL BE ON HIS OWN...

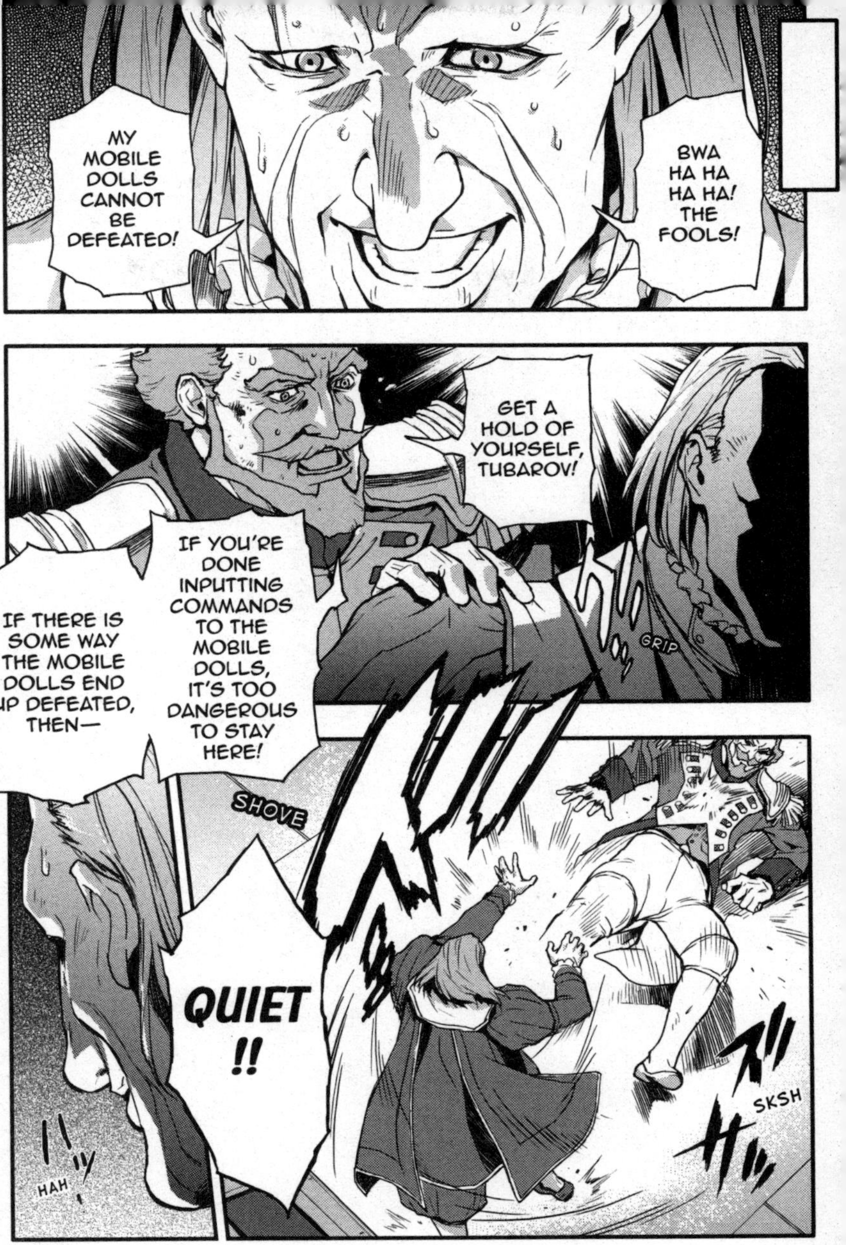
BWA HA HA HA HA! THE FOOLS!
MY MOBILE DOLLS CANNOT BE DEFEATED!
GET A HOLD OF YOURSELF, TUBAROV!
GRIP
IF YOU'RE DONE INPUTTING COMMANDS TO THE MOBILE DOLLS, IT'S TOO DANGEROUS TO STAY HERE!
IF THERE IS SOME WAY THE MOBILE DOLLS END UP DEFEATED, THEN—
SKSH
QUIET !!
SHOVE
HAH

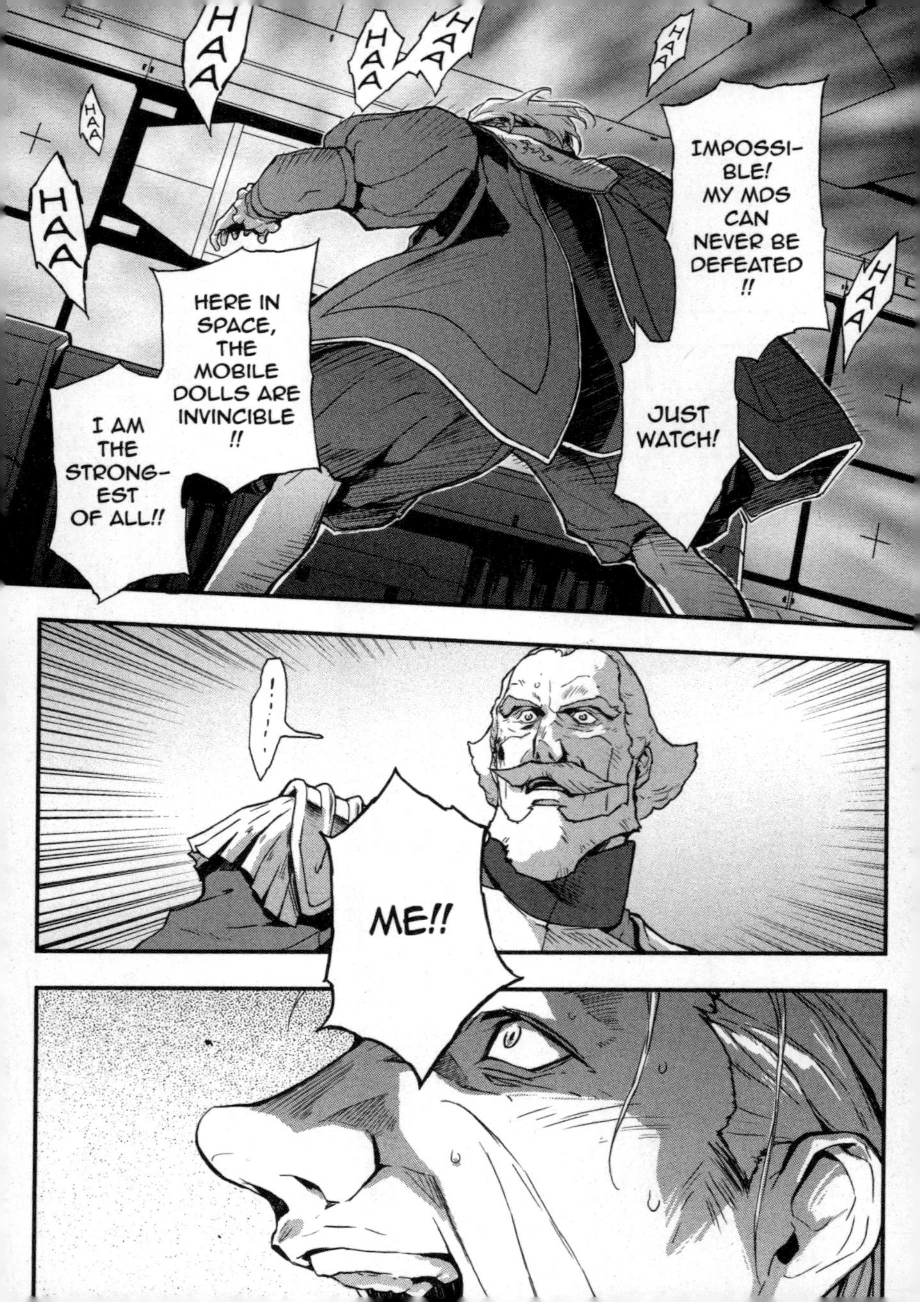
HAA
HAA
IMPOSSI-BLE! MY MDS CAN NEVER BE DEFEATED!!
JUST WATCH!
HAA
HAA
HAA
HAA
HAA
HERE IN SPACE, THE MOBILE DOLLS ARE INVINCIBLE!!
I AM THE STRONG-EST OF ALL!!
ME!!
...!

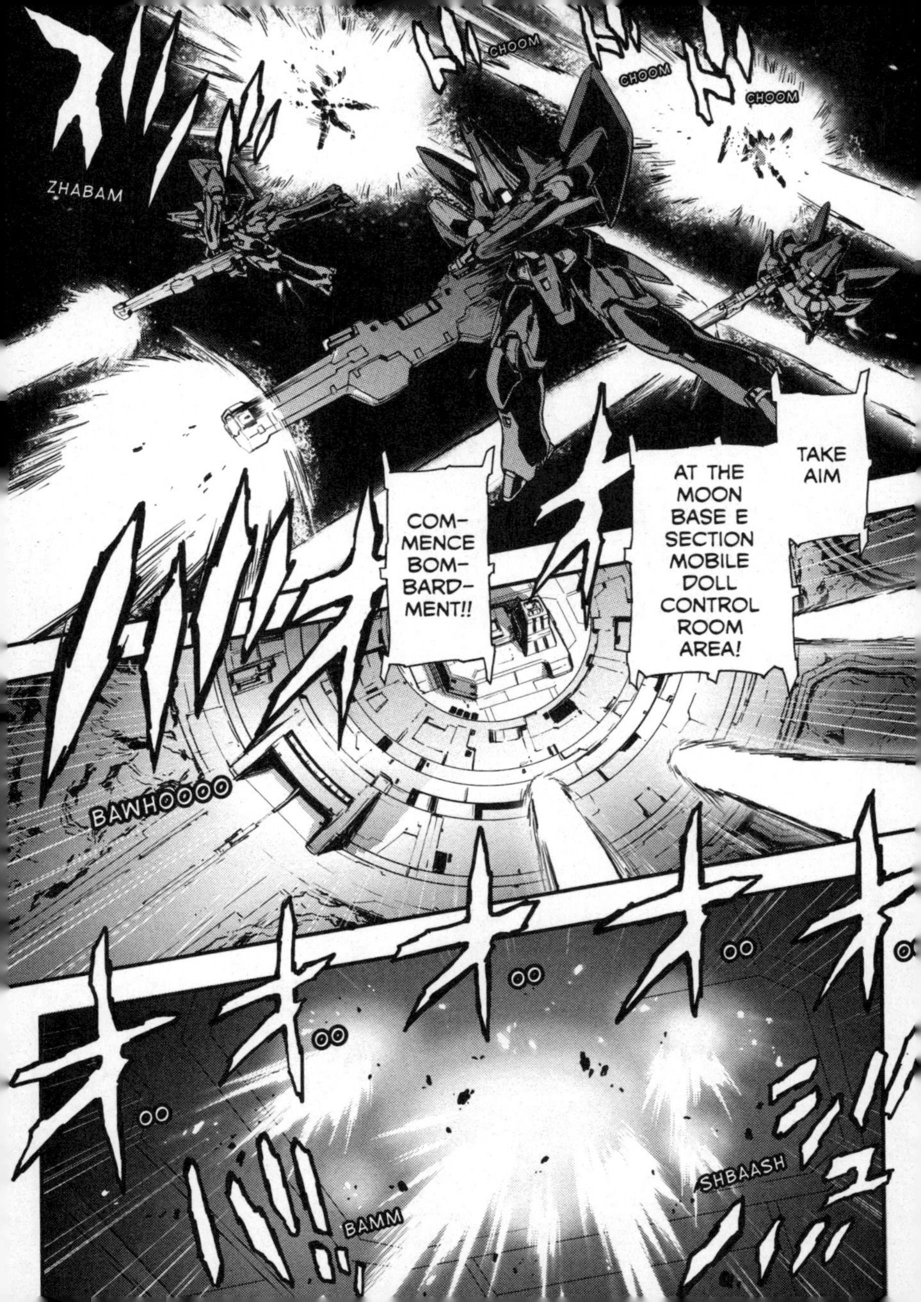
CHOOM
CHOOM
CHOOM
ZHABAM
TAKE AIM
AT THE MOON BASE E SECTION MOBILE DOLL CONTROL ROOM AREA!
COM-MENCE BOM-BARD-MENT!!
BAWHOOOO
SHBAASH
BAMM

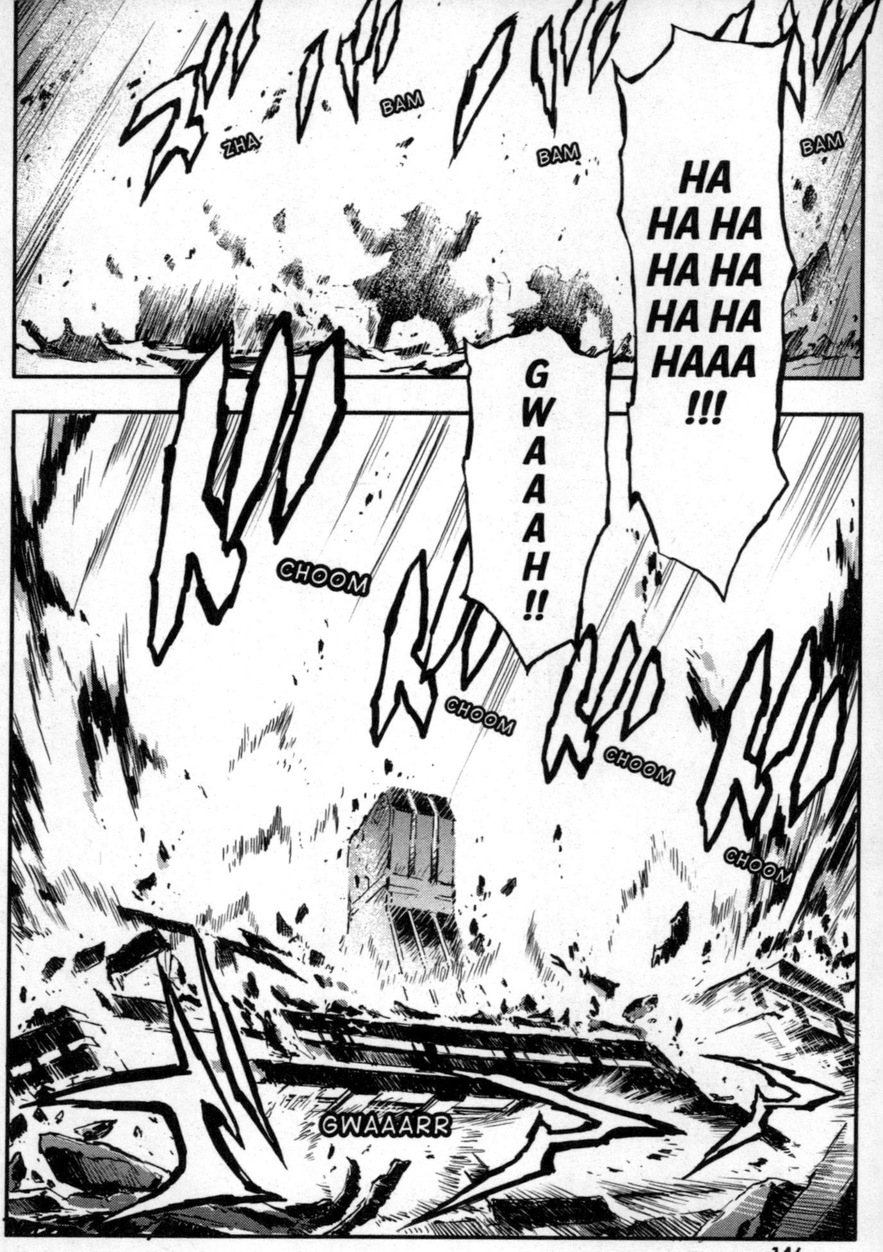
BAM
HA HA HA HA HA HA HA HA HAAA !!!
BAM
BAM
ZHA
GWAAAAAH!!
CHOOM
CHOOM
CHOOM
CHOOM
GWAAARR

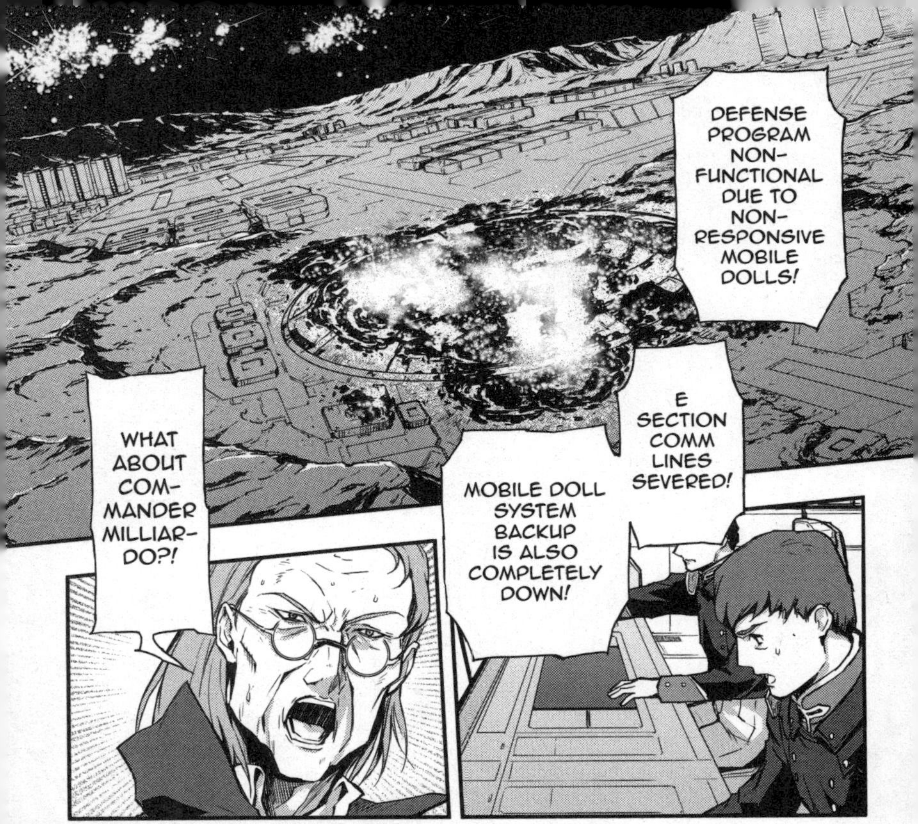
DEFENSE PROGRAM NON-FUNCTIONAL DUE TO NON-RESPONSIVE MOBILE DOLLS!
E SECTION COMM LINES SEVERED!
MOBILE DOLL SYSTEM BACKUP IS ALSO COMPLETELY DOWN!
WHAT ABOUT COM-MANDER MILLIARDO?!

Chapter 67 "Bulge's Fall" Part 2

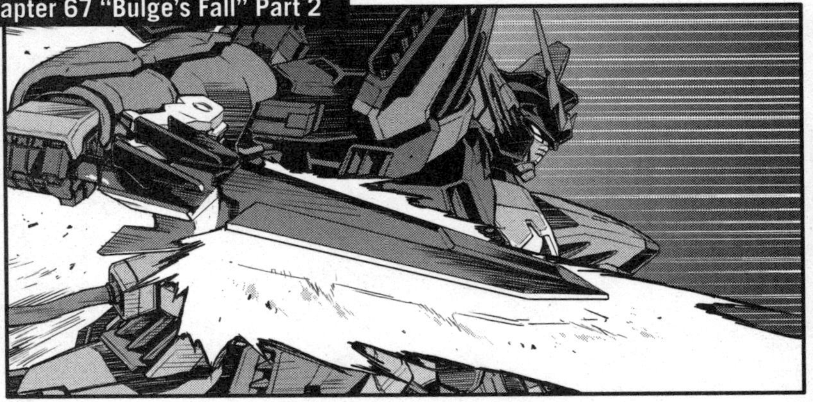

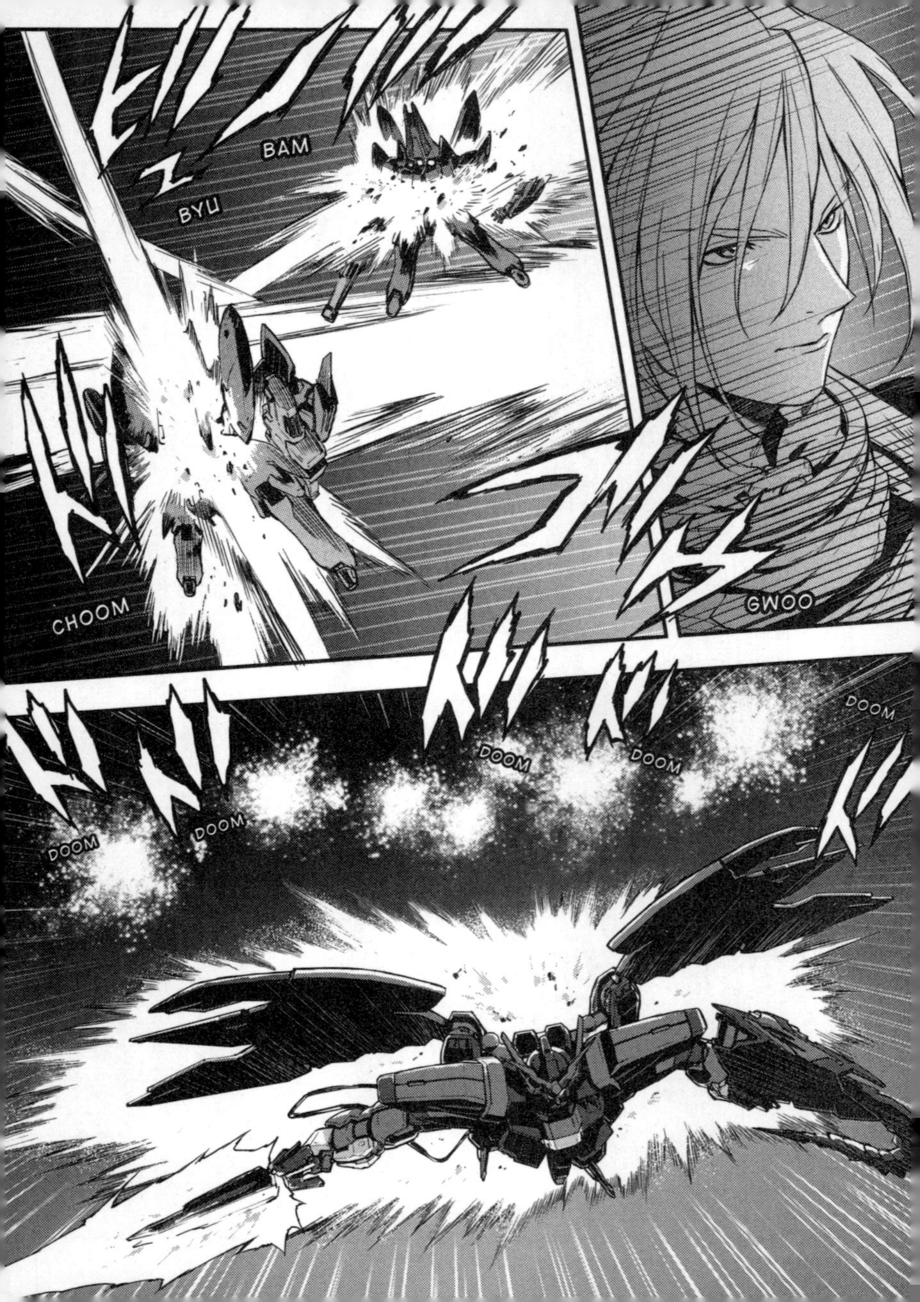
GWOO
BAM
BYU
CHOOM
DOOM
DOOM
DOOM
DOOM
DOOM

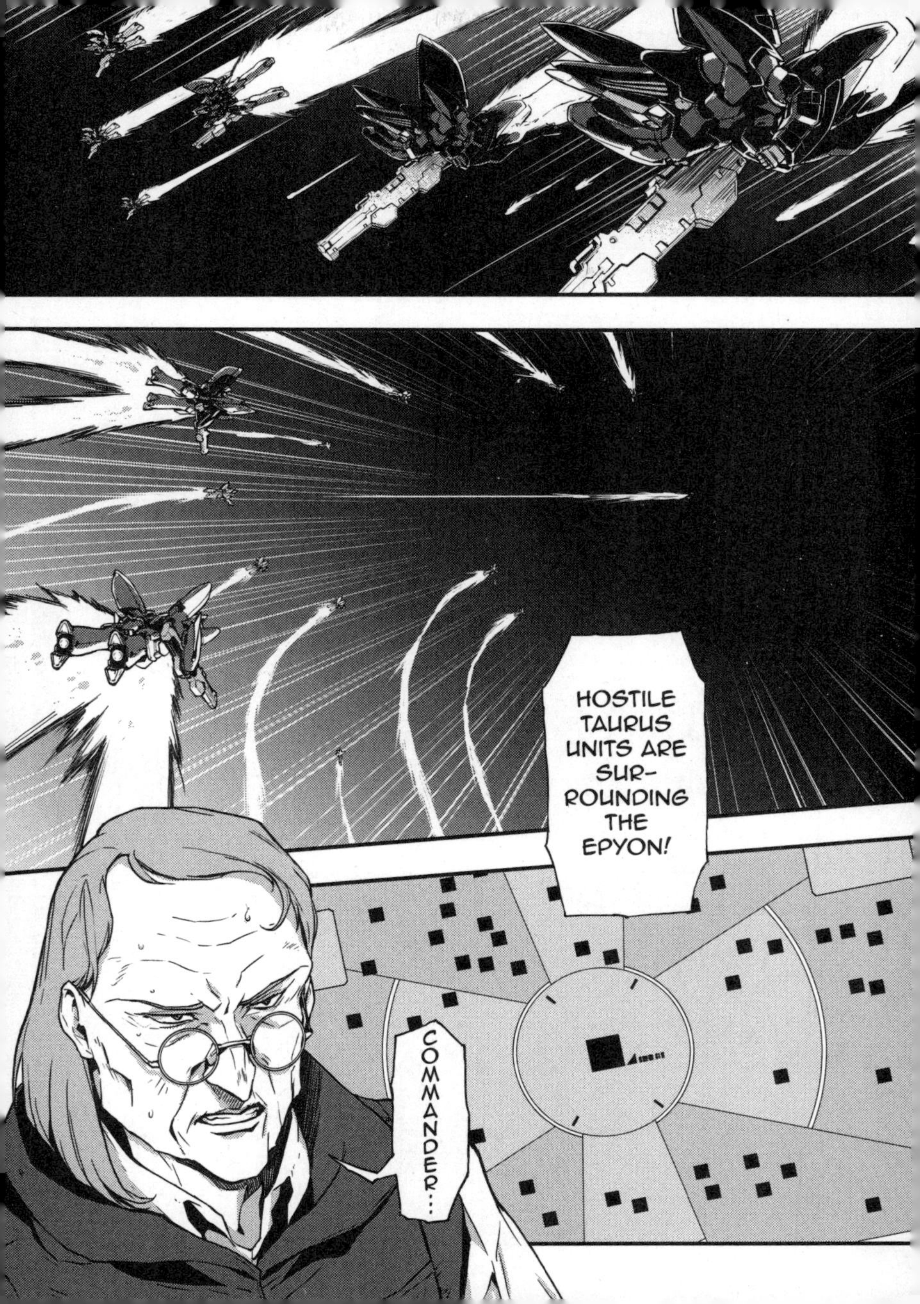
HOSTILE TAURUS UNITS ARE SUR-ROUNDING THE EPYON!
COMMANDER...

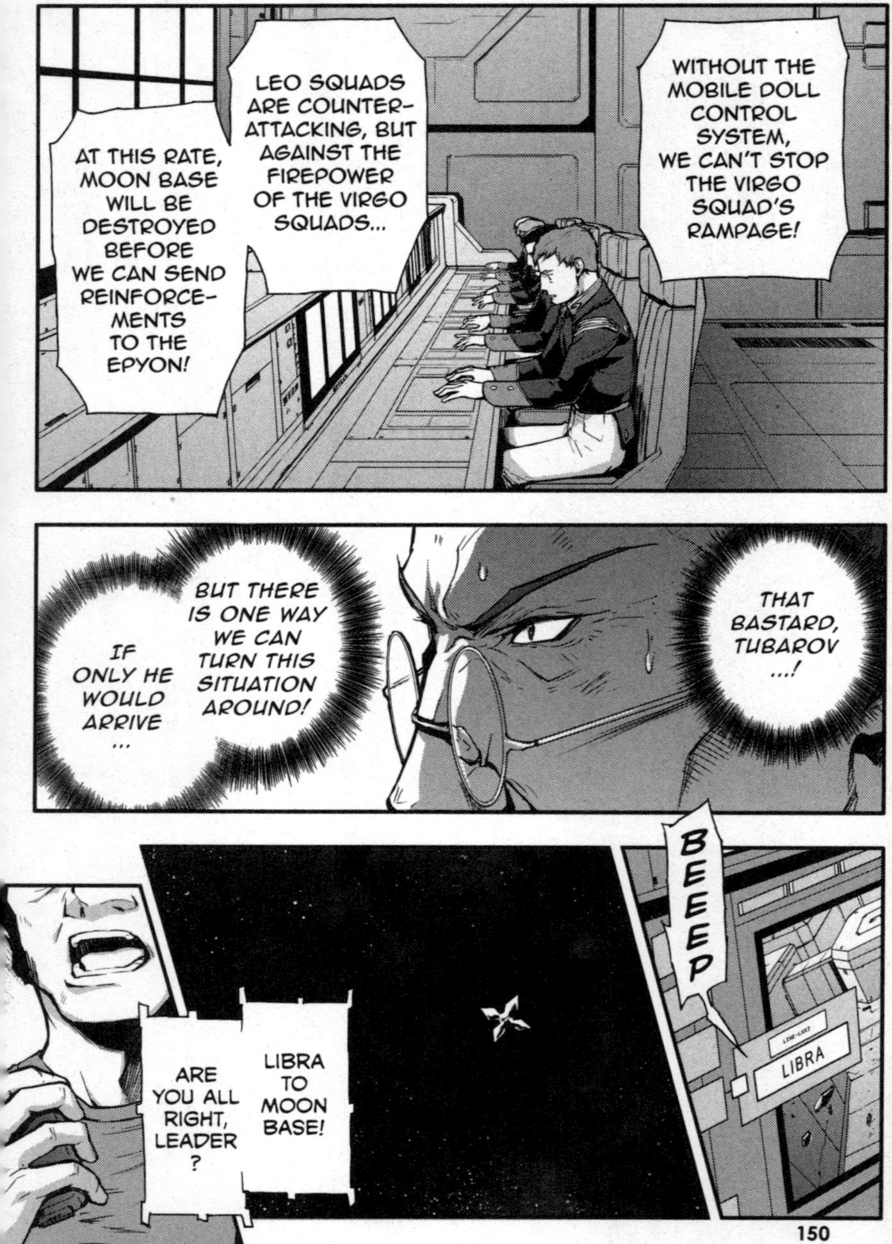
WITHOUT THE MOBILE DOLL CONTROL SYSTEM, WE CAN'T STOP THE VIRGO SQUAD'S RAMPAGE!
LEO SQUADS ARE COUNTER-ATTACKING, BUT AGAINST THE FIREPOWER OF THE VIRGO SQUADS...
AT THIS RATE, MOON BASE WILL BE DESTROYED BEFORE WE CAN SEND REINFORCE-MENTS TO THE EPYON!
THAT BASTARD, TUBAROV ...!
BUT THERE IS ONE WAY WE CAN TURN THIS SITUATION AROUND!
IF ONLY HE WOULD ARRIVE ...
BEEEP
LIBRA
LIBRA TO MOON BASE!
ARE YOU ALL RIGHT, LEADER ?

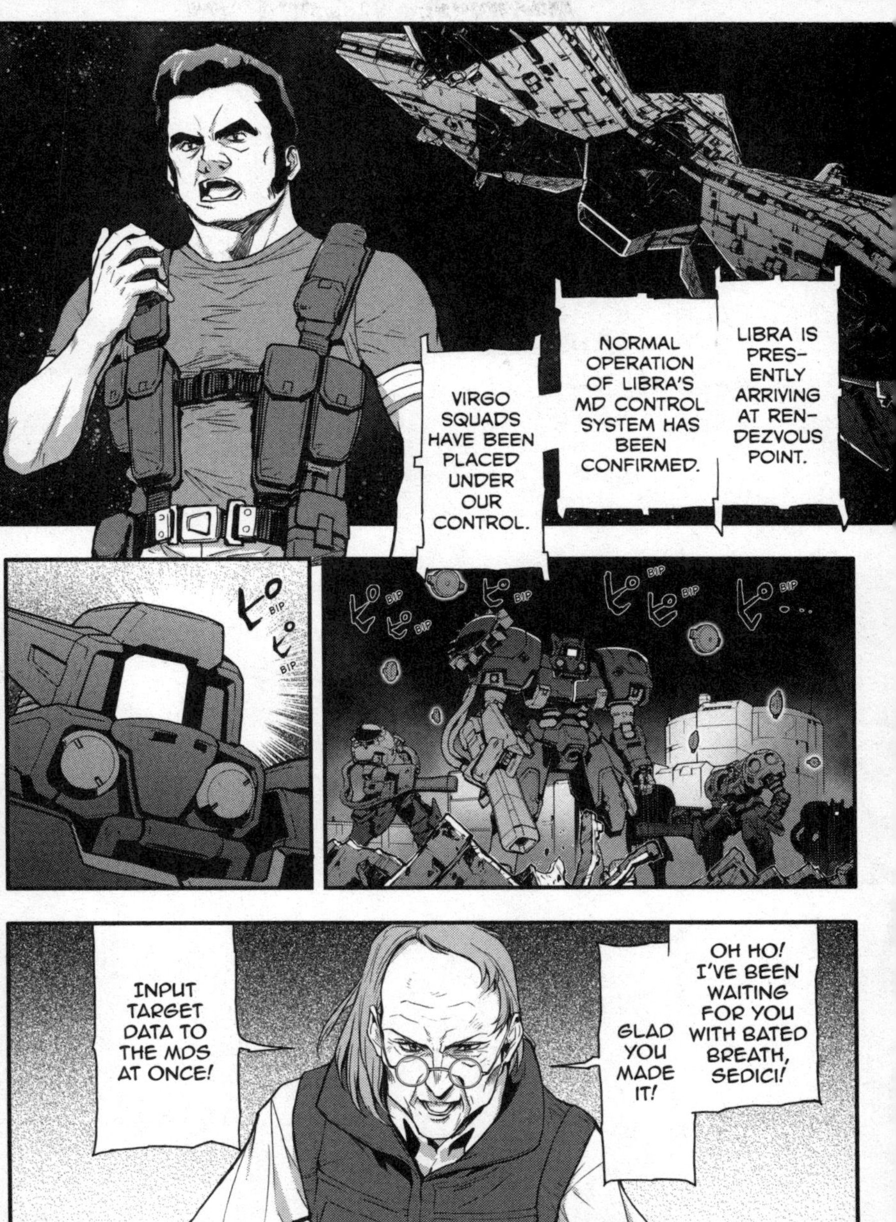
LIBRA IS PRES-ENTLY ARRIVING AT REN-DEZVOUS POINT.
NORMAL OPERATION OF LIBRA'S MD CONTROL SYSTEM HAS BEEN CONFIRMED.
VIRGO SQUADS HAVE BEEN PLACED UNDER OUR CONTROL.
ピ BIP ピ BIP ピ BIP ピ BIP ピ BIP ピ BIP
ピ BIP ピ BIP
OH HO! I'VE BEEN WAITING FOR YOU WITH BATED BREATH, SEDICI!
GLAD YOU MADE IT!
INPUT TARGET DATA TO THE MDS AT ONCE!

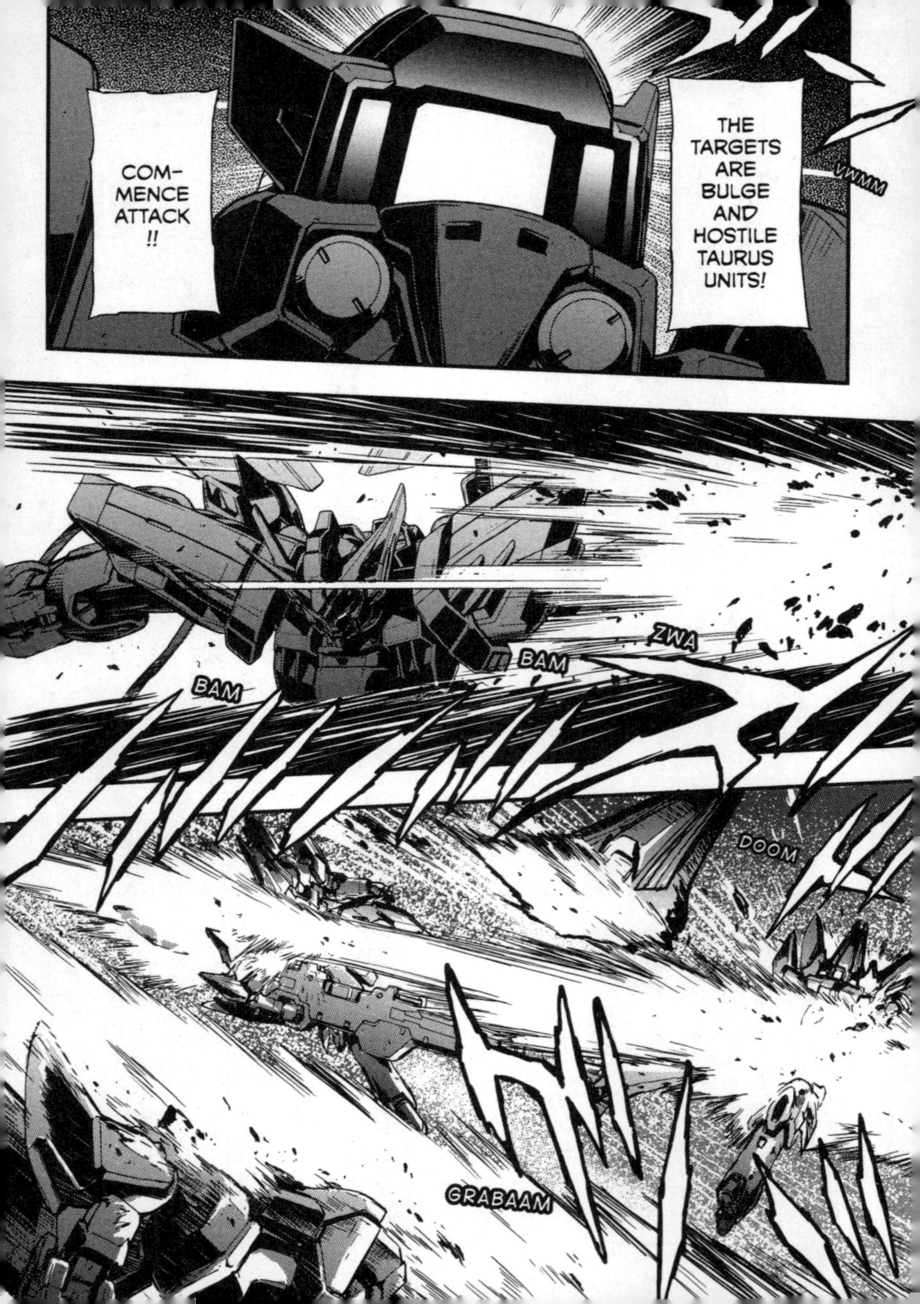
THE TARGETS ARE BULGE AND HOSTILE TAURUS UNITS!
VWMM
COM-MENCE ATTACK !!
ZWA
BAM
BAM
DOOM
GRABAAM

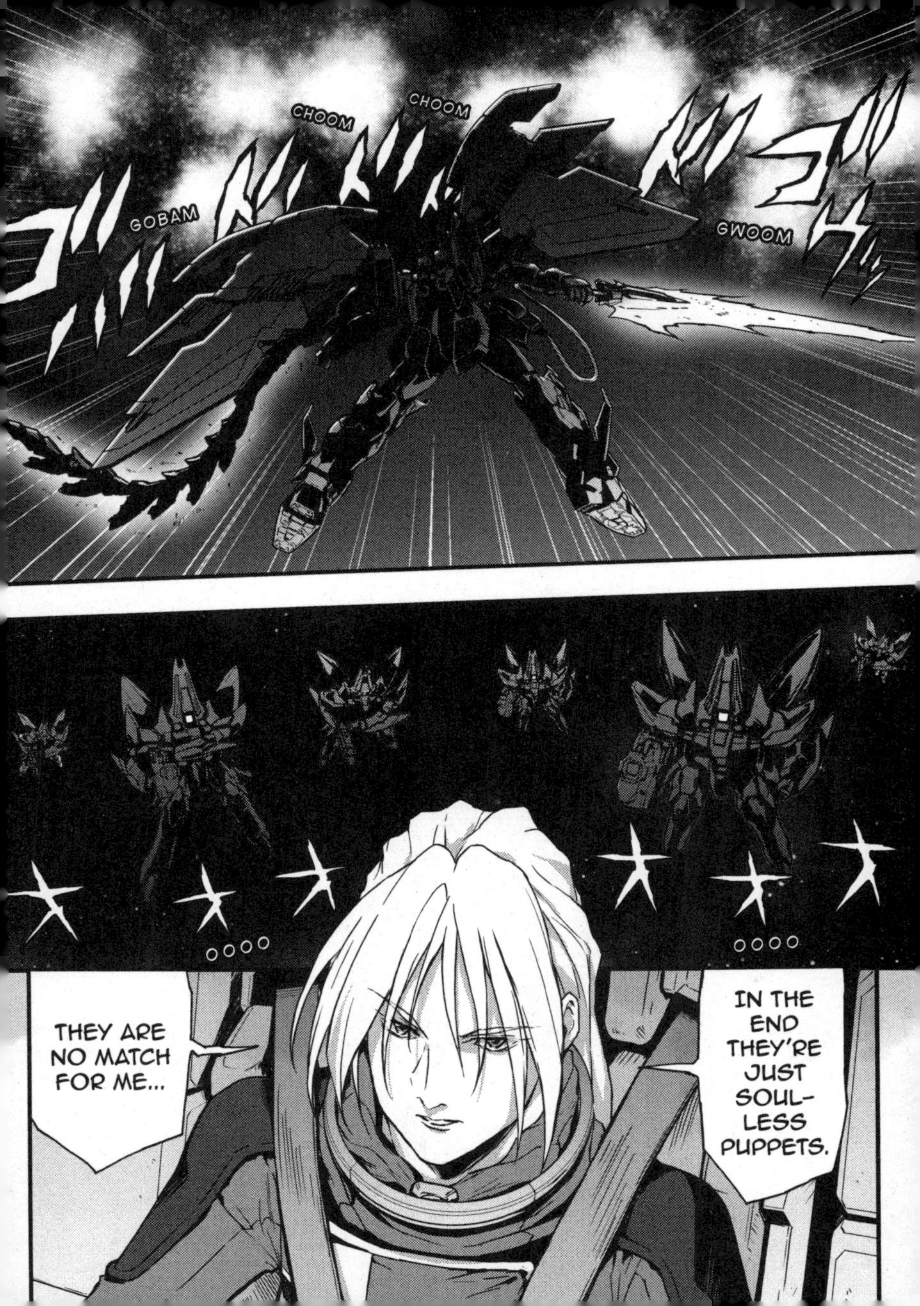
GWOOM
CHOOM
CHOOM
GOBAM
IN THE END THEY'RE JUST SOUL-LESS PUPPETS.
THEY ARE NO MATCH FOR ME...

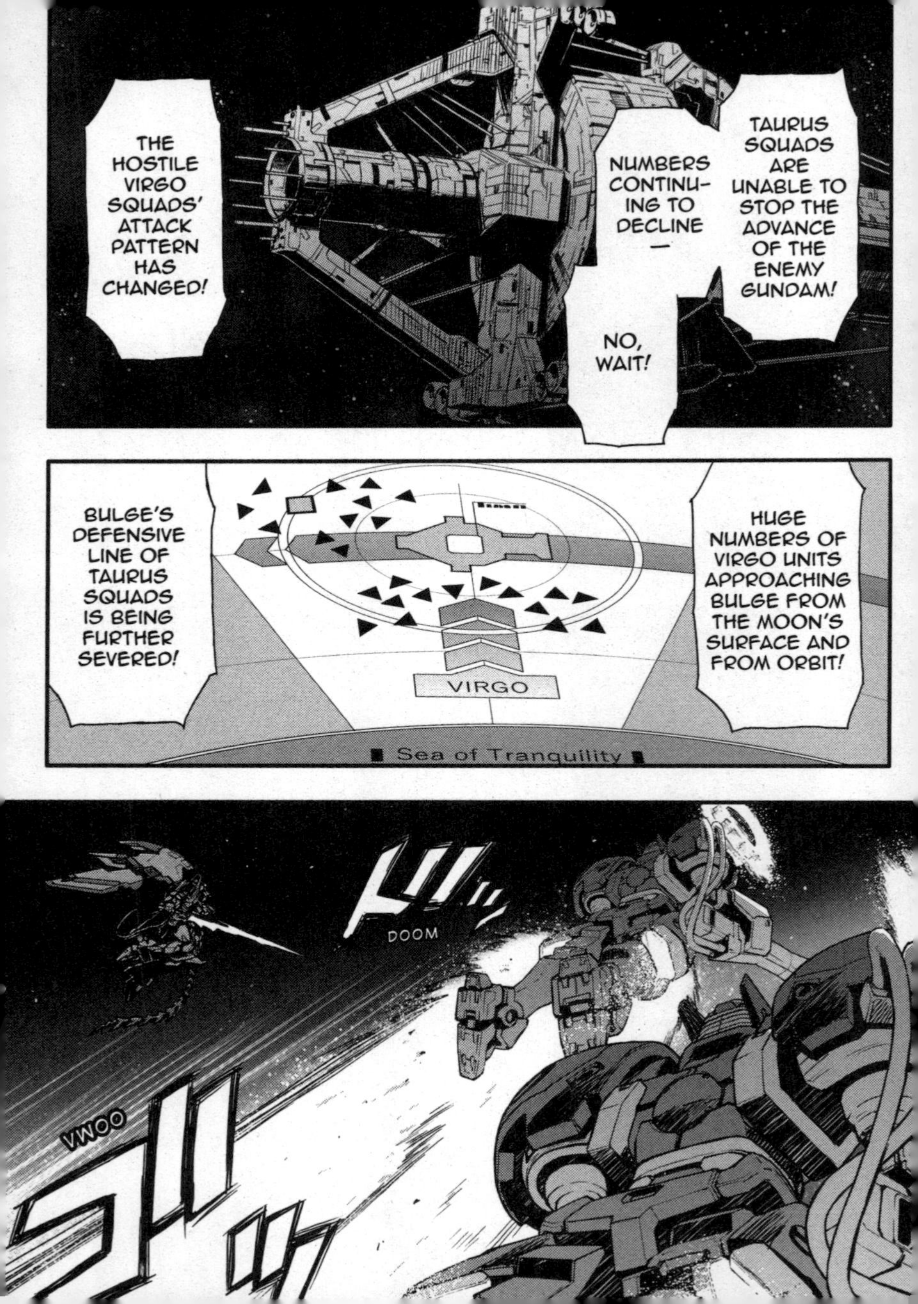
THE HOSTILE VIRGO SQUADS' ATTACK PATTERN HAS CHANGED!
NUMBERS CONTINUING TO DECLINE —
TAURUS SQUADS ARE UNABLE TO STOP THE ADVANCE OF THE ENEMY GUNDAM!
NO, WAIT!
BULGE'S DEFENSIVE LINE OF TAURUS SQUADS IS BEING FURTHER SEVERED!
VIRGO
Sea of Tranquility
HUGE NUMBERS OF VIRGO UNITS APPROACHING BULGE FROM THE MOON'S SURFACE AND FROM ORBIT!
DOOM
VWOO

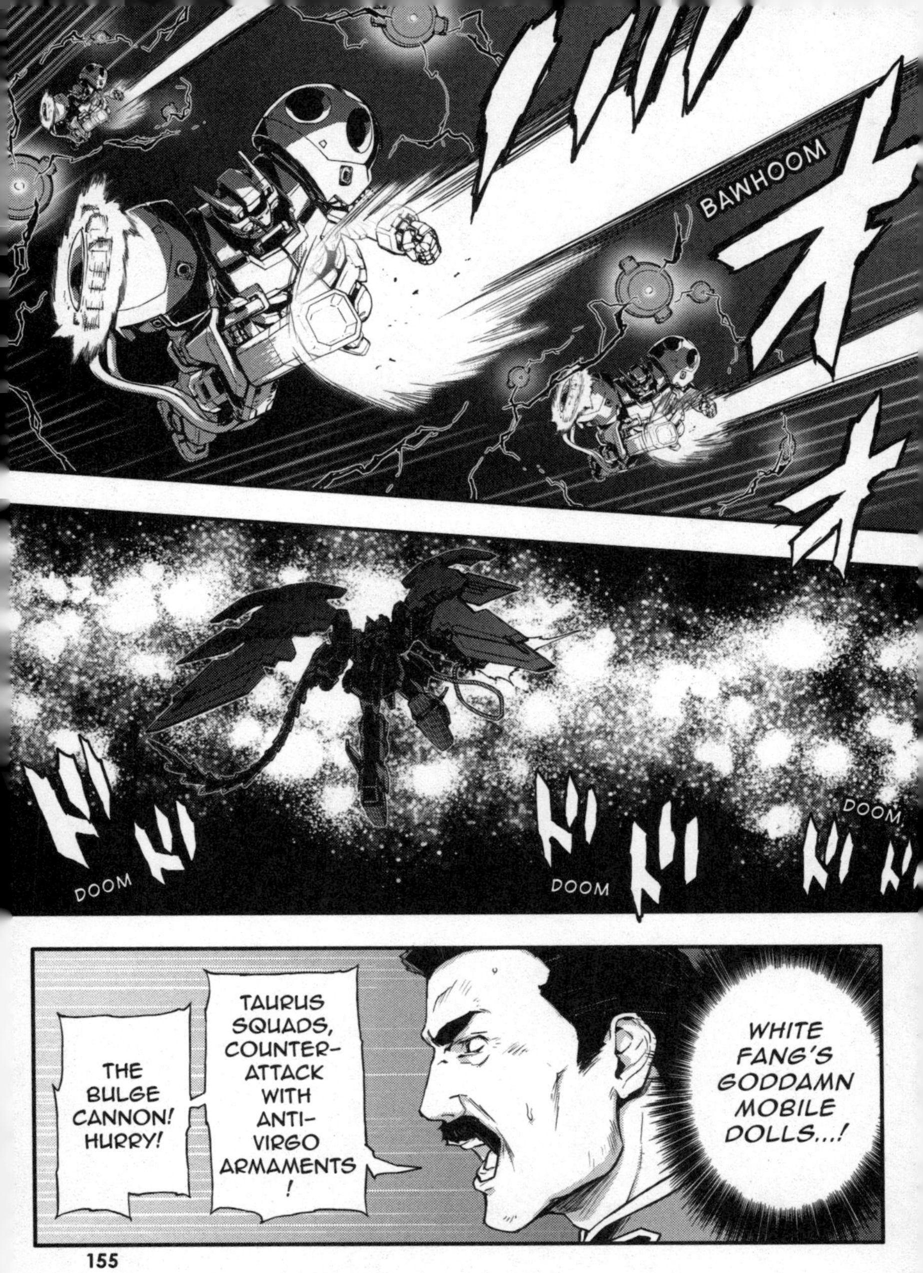
BAWHOOM
DOOM
DOOM
DOOM
WHITE FANG'S GODDAMN MOBILE DOLLS...!
TAURUS SQUADS, COUNTER-ATTACK WITH ANTI-VIRGO ARMAMENTS!
THE BULGE CANNON! HURRY!

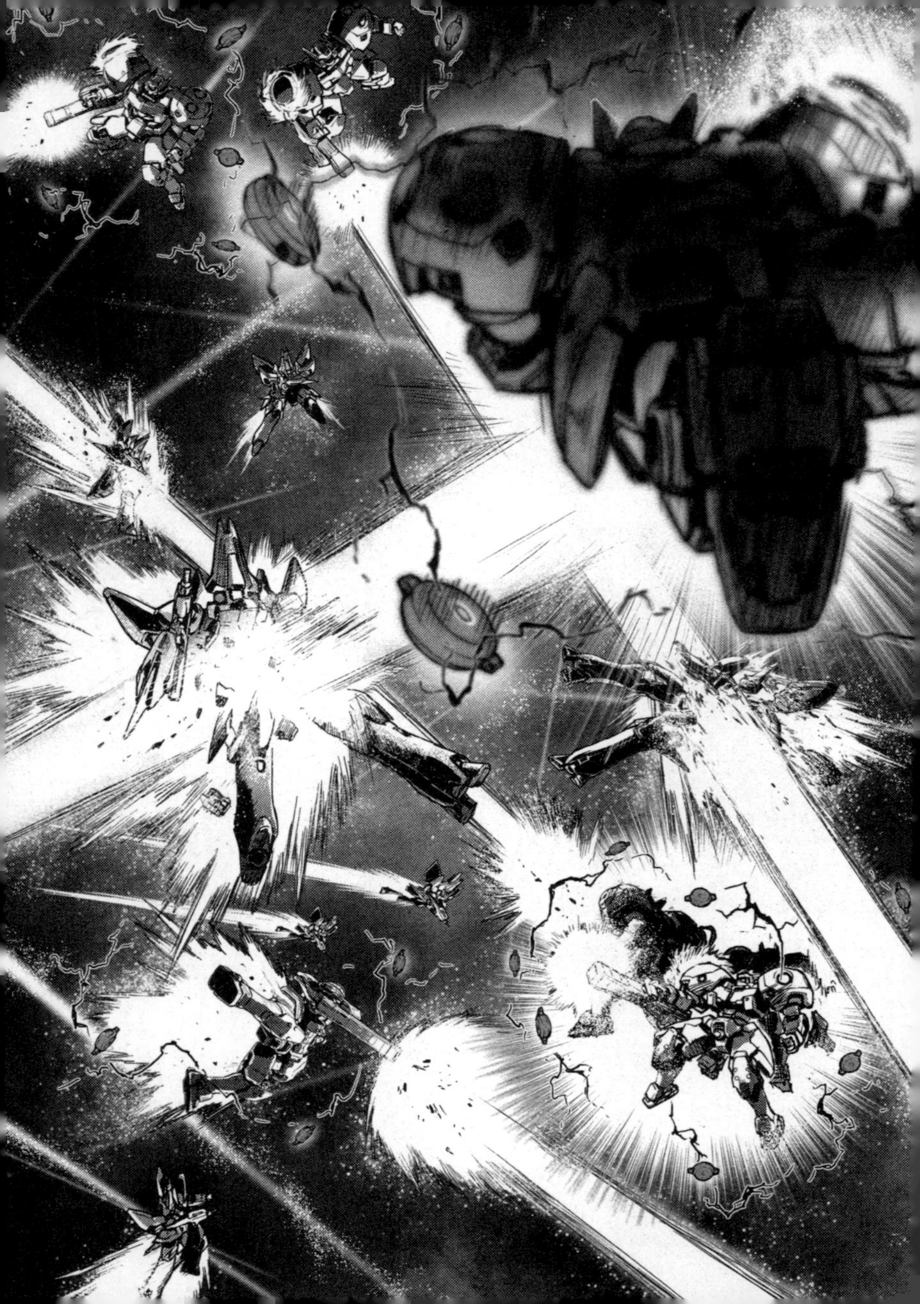

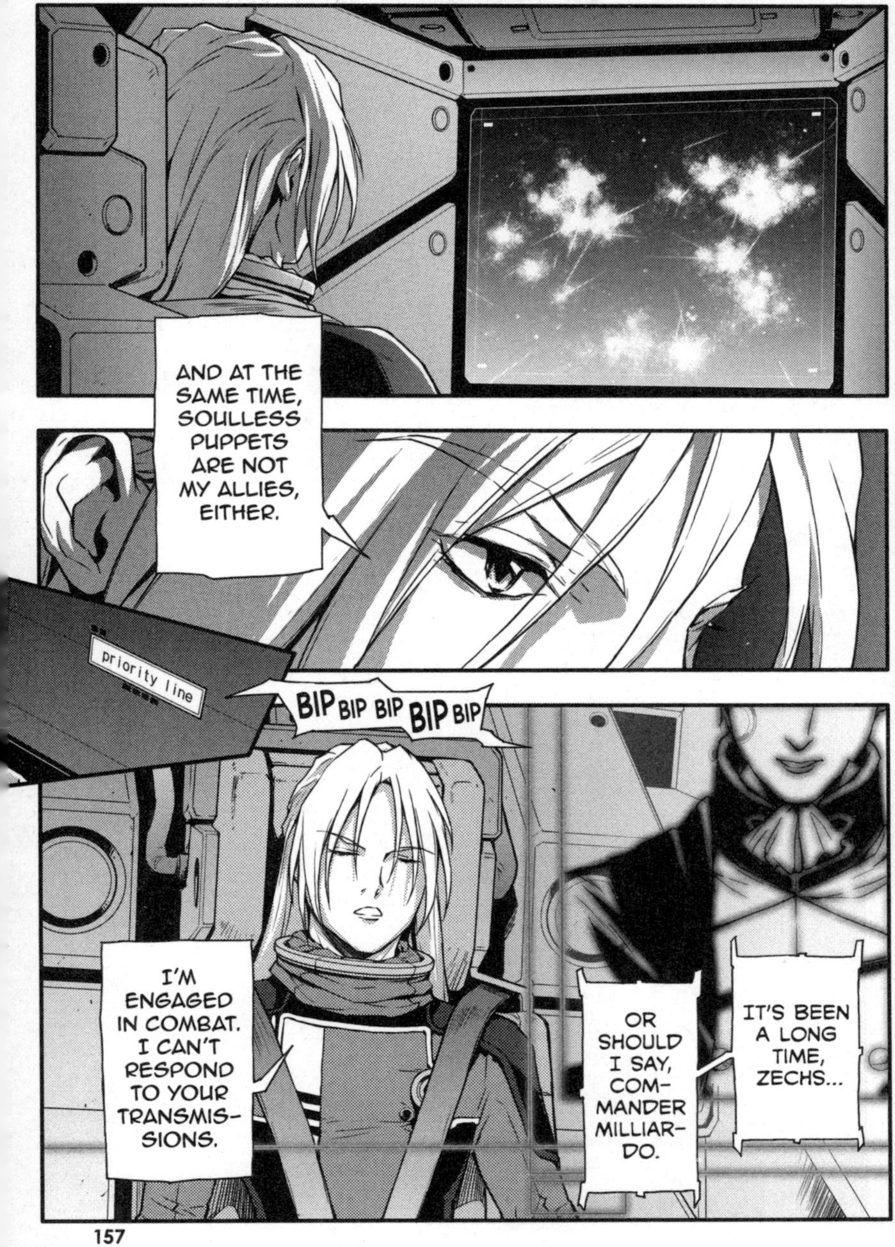
AND AT THE SAME TIME, SOULLESS PUPPETS ARE NOT MY ALLIES, EITHER.
priority line
BIP BIP BIP BIP BIP
IT'S BEEN A LONG TIME, ZECHS...
OR SHOULD I SAY, COM-MANDER MILLIAR-DO.
I'M ENGAGED IN COMBAT. I CAN'T RESPOND TO YOUR TRANSMIS-SIONS.

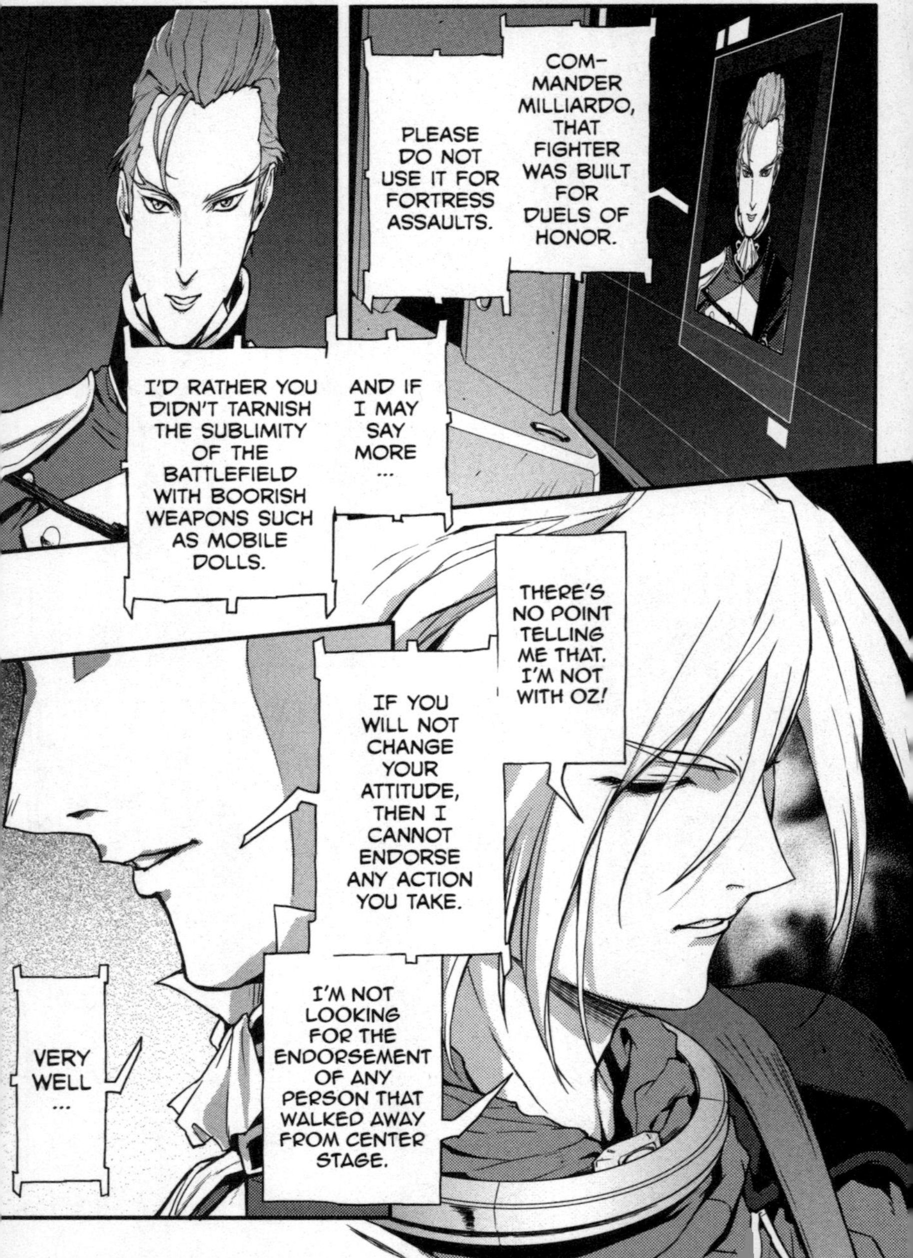
COM-MANDER MILLIARDO, THAT FIGHTER WAS BUILT FOR DUELS OF HONOR.
PLEASE DO NOT USE IT FOR FORTRESS ASSAULTS.
AND IF I MAY SAY MORE ...
I'D RATHER YOU DIDN'T TARNISH THE SUBLIMITY OF THE BATTLEFIELD WITH BOORISH WEAPONS SUCH AS MOBILE DOLLS.
THERE'S NO POINT TELLING ME THAT. I'M NOT WITH OZ!
IF YOU WILL NOT CHANGE YOUR ATTITUDE, THEN I CANNOT ENDORSE ANY ACTION YOU TAKE.
I'M NOT LOOKING FOR THE ENDORSEMENT OF ANY PERSON THAT WALKED AWAY FROM CENTER STAGE.
VERY WELL ...

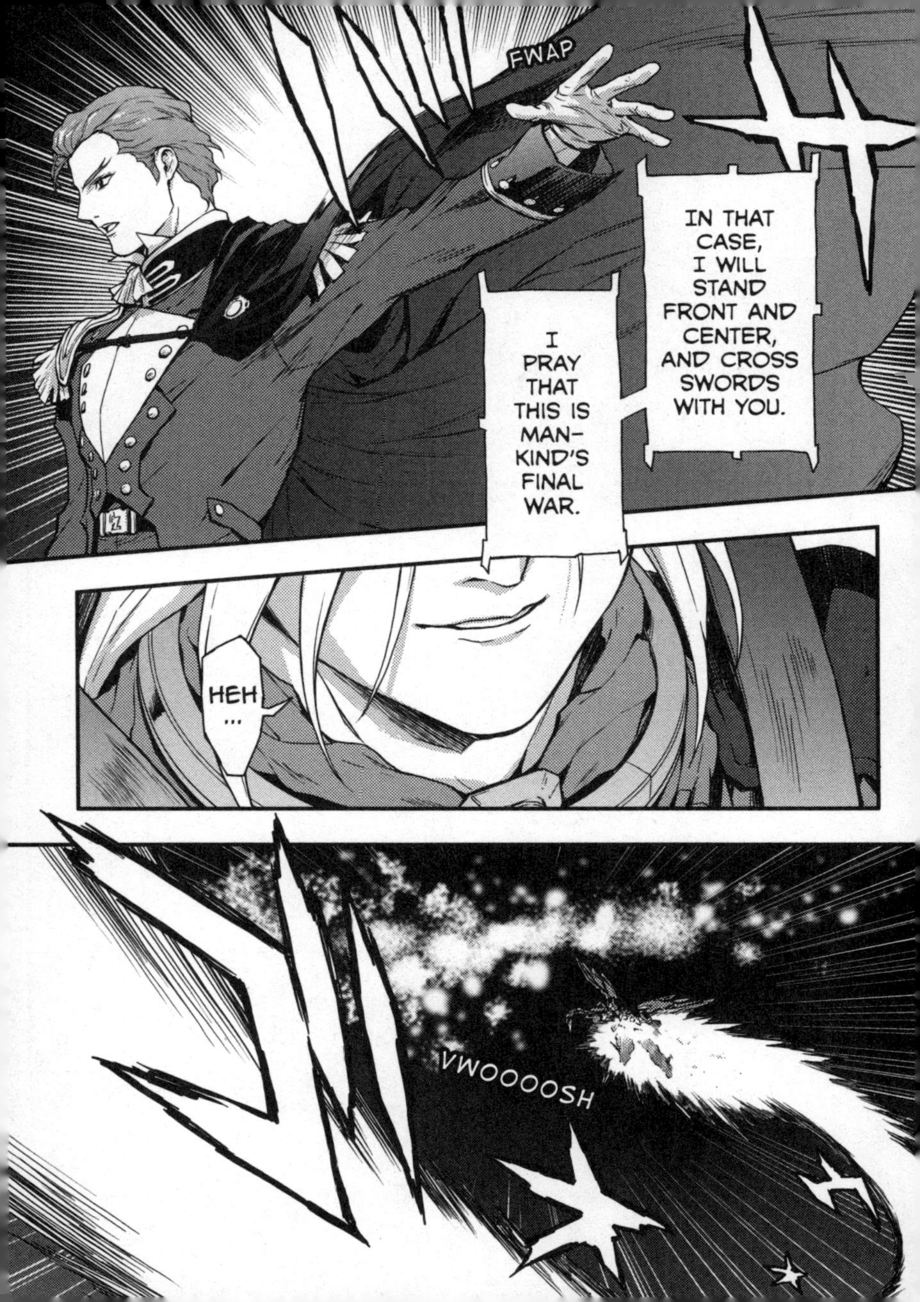
FWAP
IN THAT CASE, I WILL STAND FRONT AND CENTER, AND CROSS SWORDS WITH YOU.
I PRAY THAT THIS IS MAN-KIND'S FINAL WAR.
HEH ...
VWOOOOSH

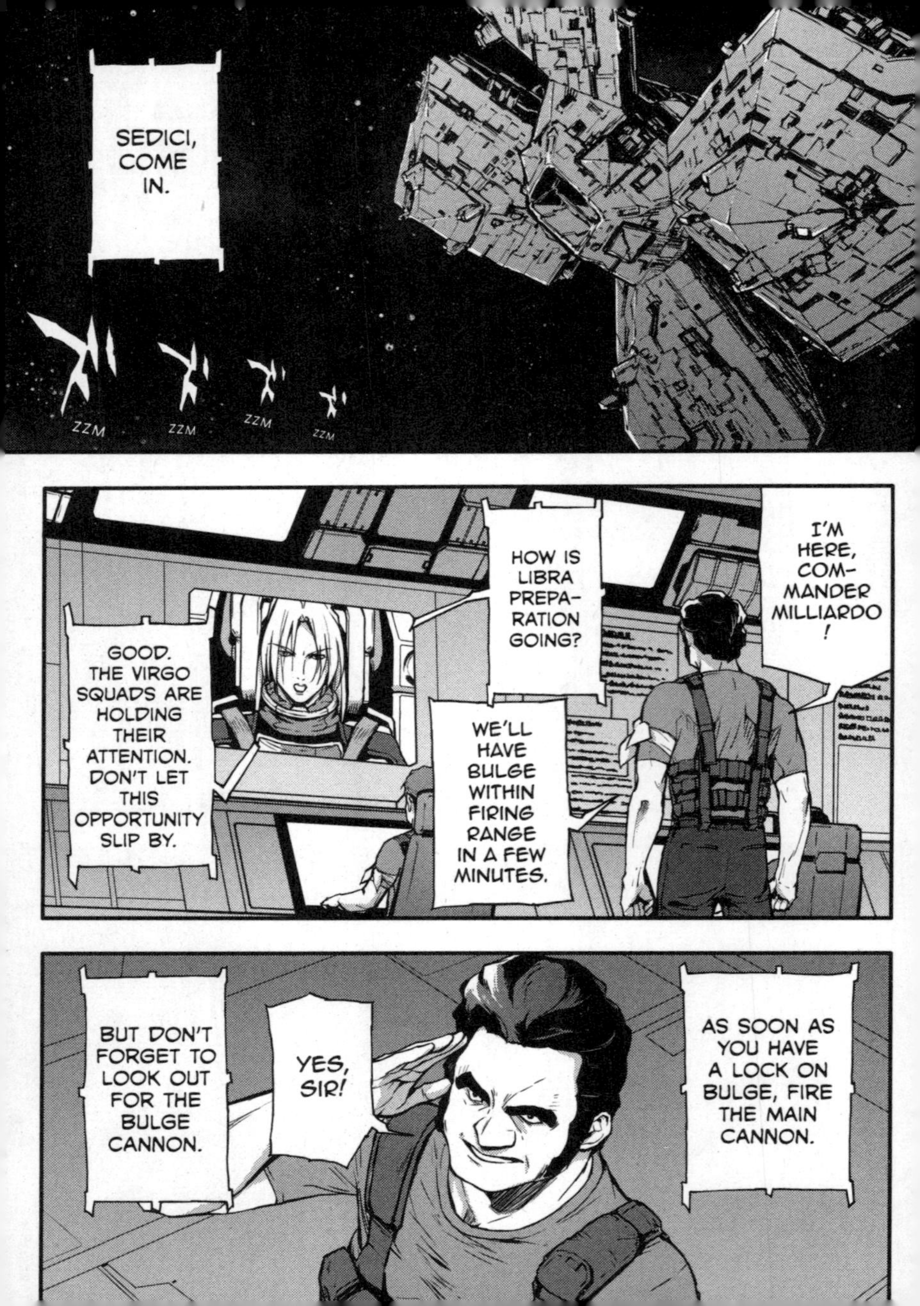
SEDICI, COME IN.
ZZM
ZZM
ZZM
ZZM
I'M HERE, COMMANDER MILLIARDO!
HOW IS LIBRA PREPARATION GOING?
WE'LL HAVE BULGE WITHIN FIRING RANGE IN A FEW MINUTES.
GOOD. THE VIRGO SQUADS ARE HOLDING THEIR ATTENTION. DON'T LET THIS OPPORTUNITY SLIP BY.
AS SOON AS YOU HAVE A LOCK ON BULGE, FIRE THE MAIN CANNON.
YES, SIR!
BUT DON'T FORGET TO LOOK OUT FOR THE BULGE CANNON.

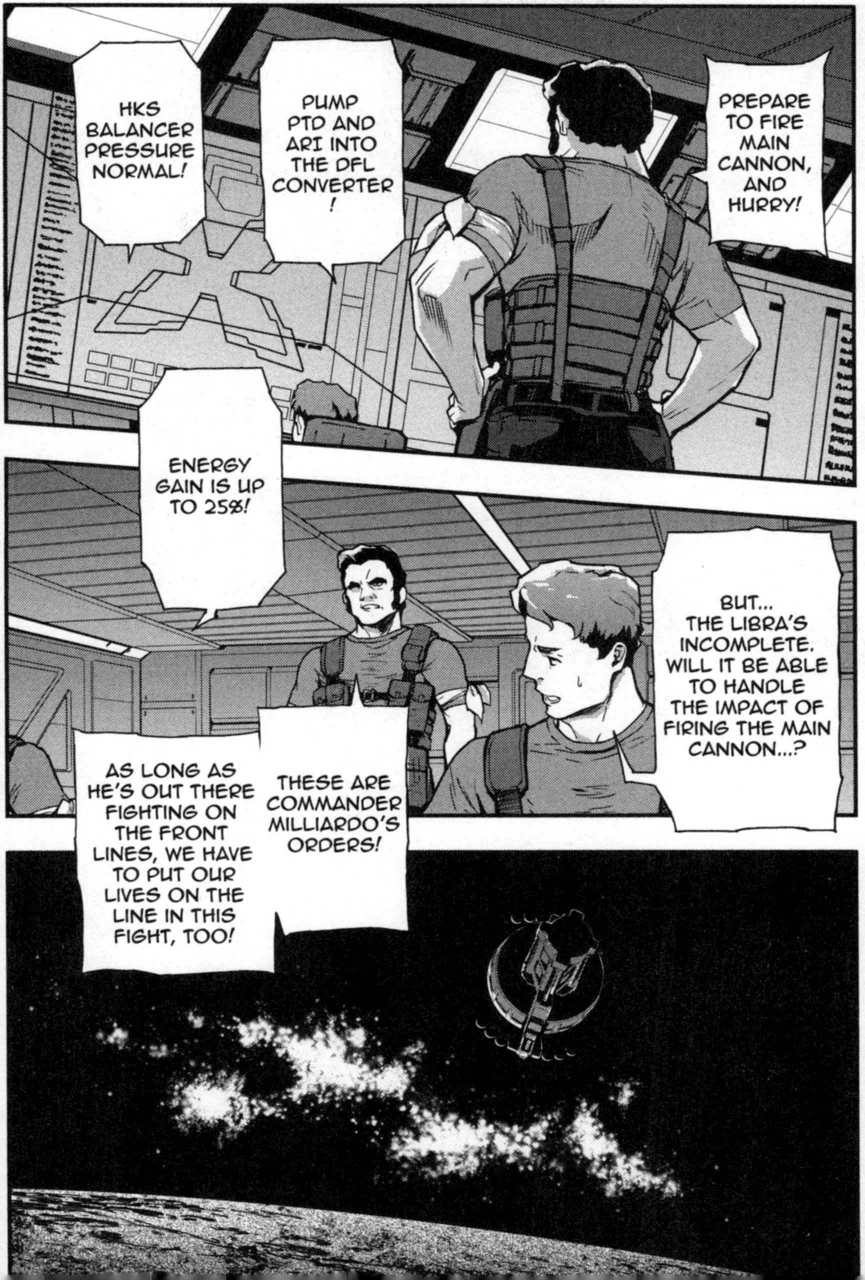
PREPARE TO FIRE MAIN CANNON, AND HURRY!
PUMP PTD AND ARI INTO THE DFL CONVERTER!
HKS BALANCER PRESSURE NORMAL!
ENERGY GAIN IS UP TO 25%!
BUT... THE LIBRA'S INCOMPLETE. WILL IT BE ABLE TO HANDLE THE IMPACT OF FIRING THE MAIN CANNON...?
THESE ARE COMMANDER MILLIARDO'S ORDERS!
AS LONG AS HE'S OUT THERE FIGHTING ON THE FRONT LINES, WE HAVE TO PUT OUR LIVES ON THE LINE IN THIS FIGHT, TOO!

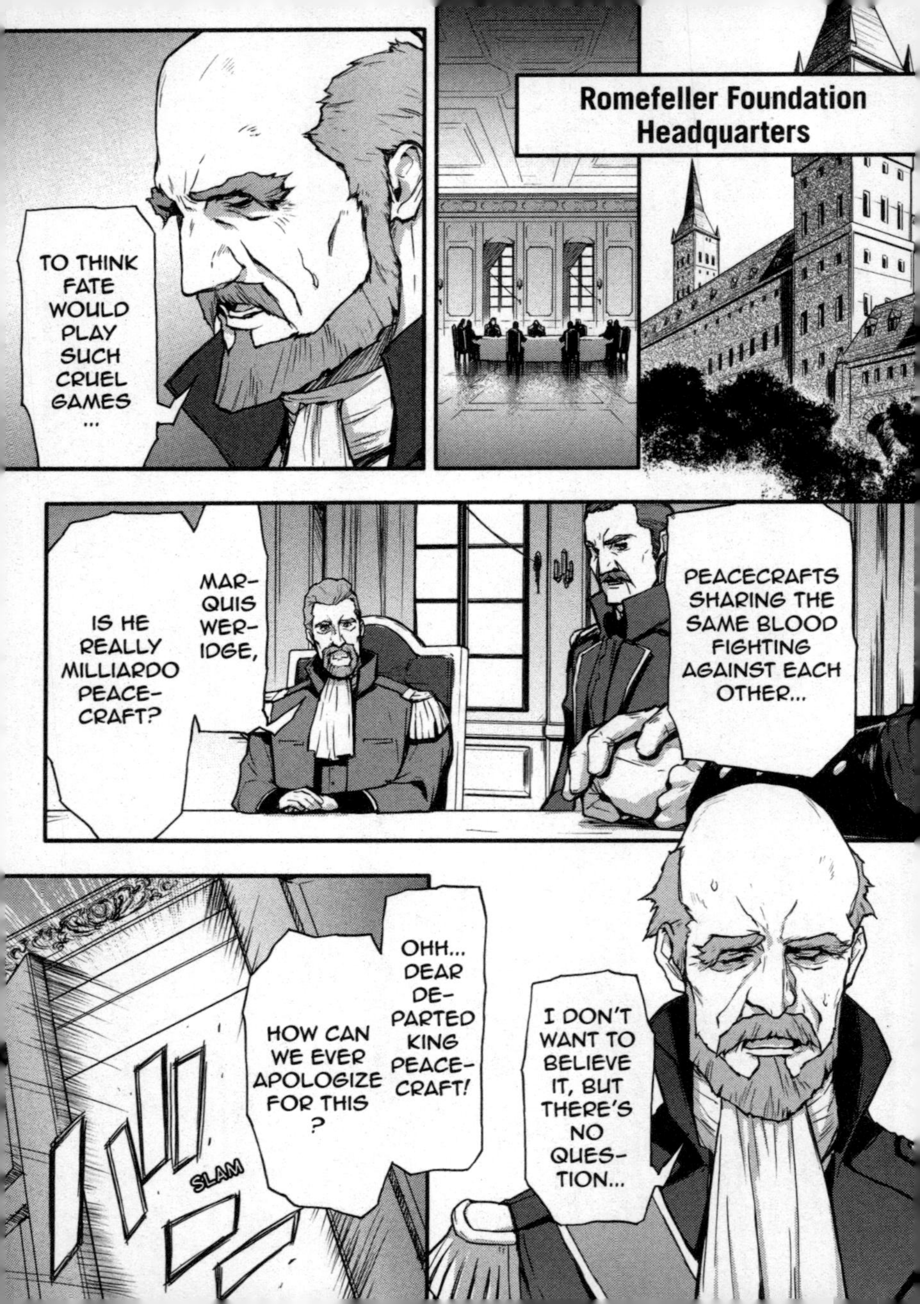
Romefeller Foundation Headquarters
TO THINK FATE WOULD PLAY SUCH CRUEL GAMES...
PEACECRAFTS SHARING THE SAME BLOOD FIGHTING AGAINST EACH OTHER...
MARQUIS WERIDGE,
IS HE REALLY MILLIARDO PEACECRAFT?
I DON'T WANT TO BELIEVE IT, BUT THERE'S NO QUESTION...
OHH... DEAR DEPARTED KING PEACECRAFT!
HOW CAN WE EVER APOLOGIZE FOR THIS?
SLAM

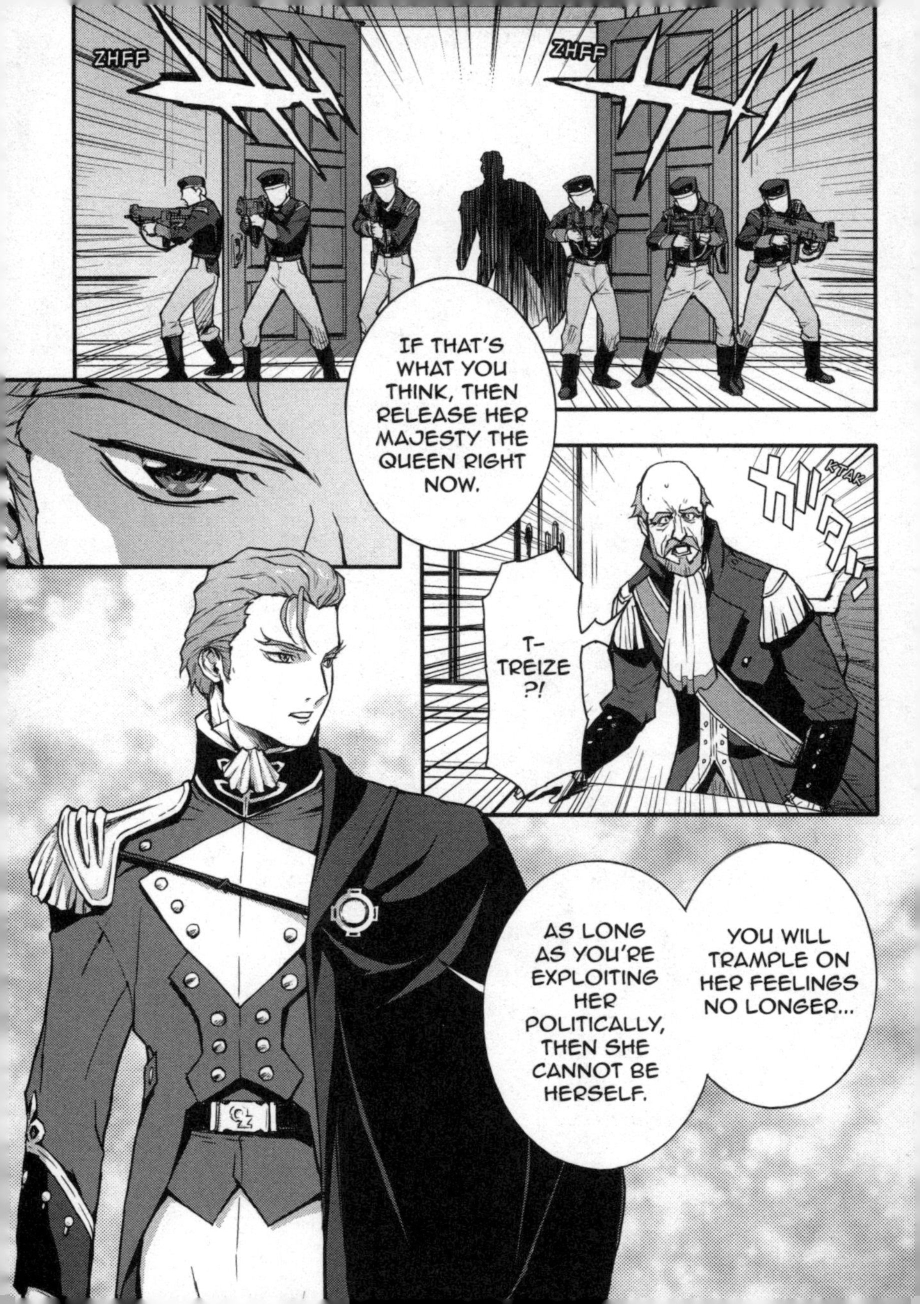
ZHFF
ZHFF
IF THAT'S WHAT YOU THINK, THEN RELEASE HER MAJESTY THE QUEEN RIGHT NOW.
KTAK
T-TREIZE?!
YOU WILL TRAMPLE ON HER FEELINGS NO LONGER...
AS LONG AS YOU'RE EXPLOITING HER POLITICALLY, THEN SHE CANNOT BE HERSELF.

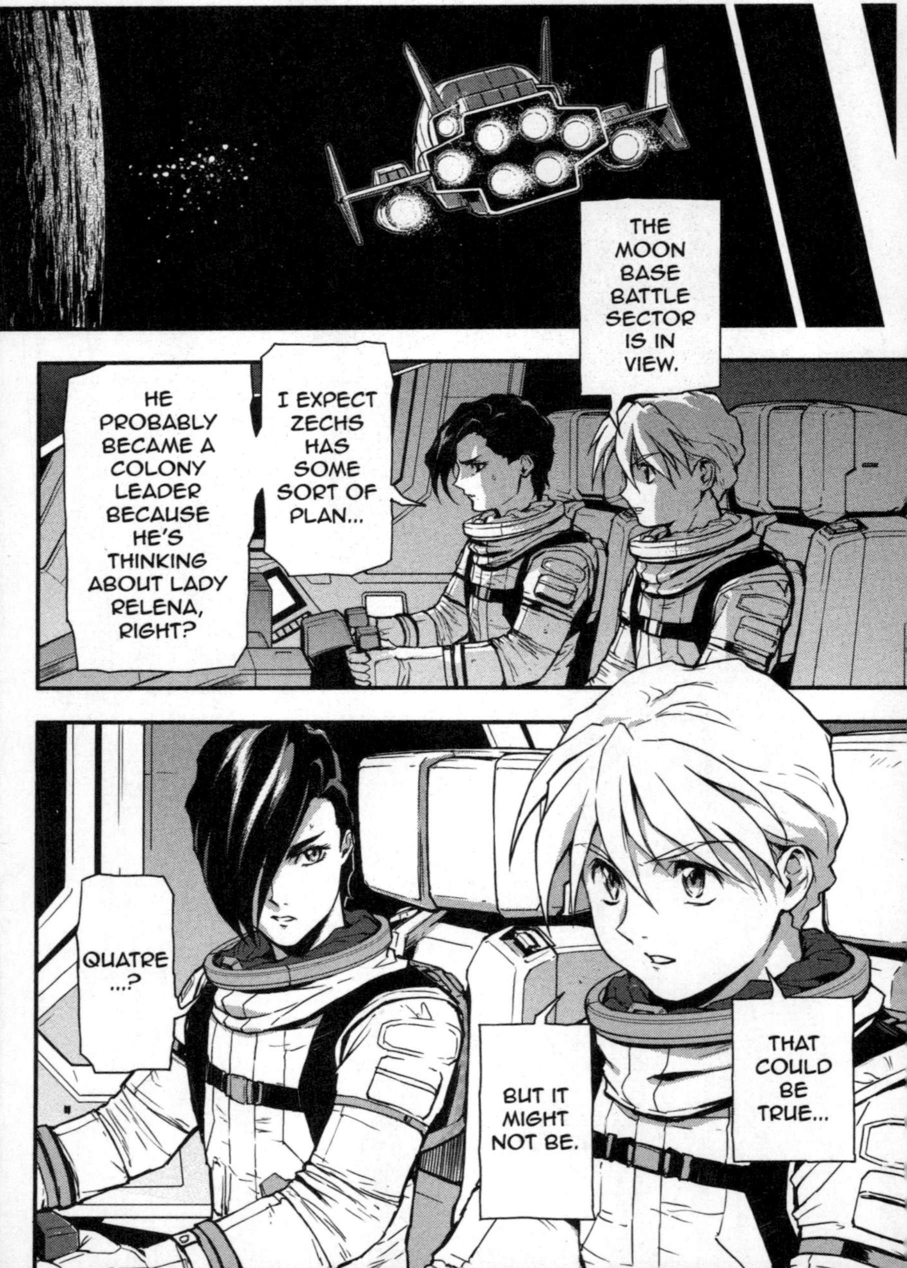
THE MOON BASE BATTLE SECTOR IS IN VIEW.
I EXPECT ZECHS HAS SOME SORT OF PLAN...
HE PROBABLY BECAME A COLONY LEADER BECAUSE HE'S THINKING ABOUT LADY RELENA, RIGHT?
THAT COULD BE TRUE...
BUT IT MIGHT NOT BE.
QUATRE ...?

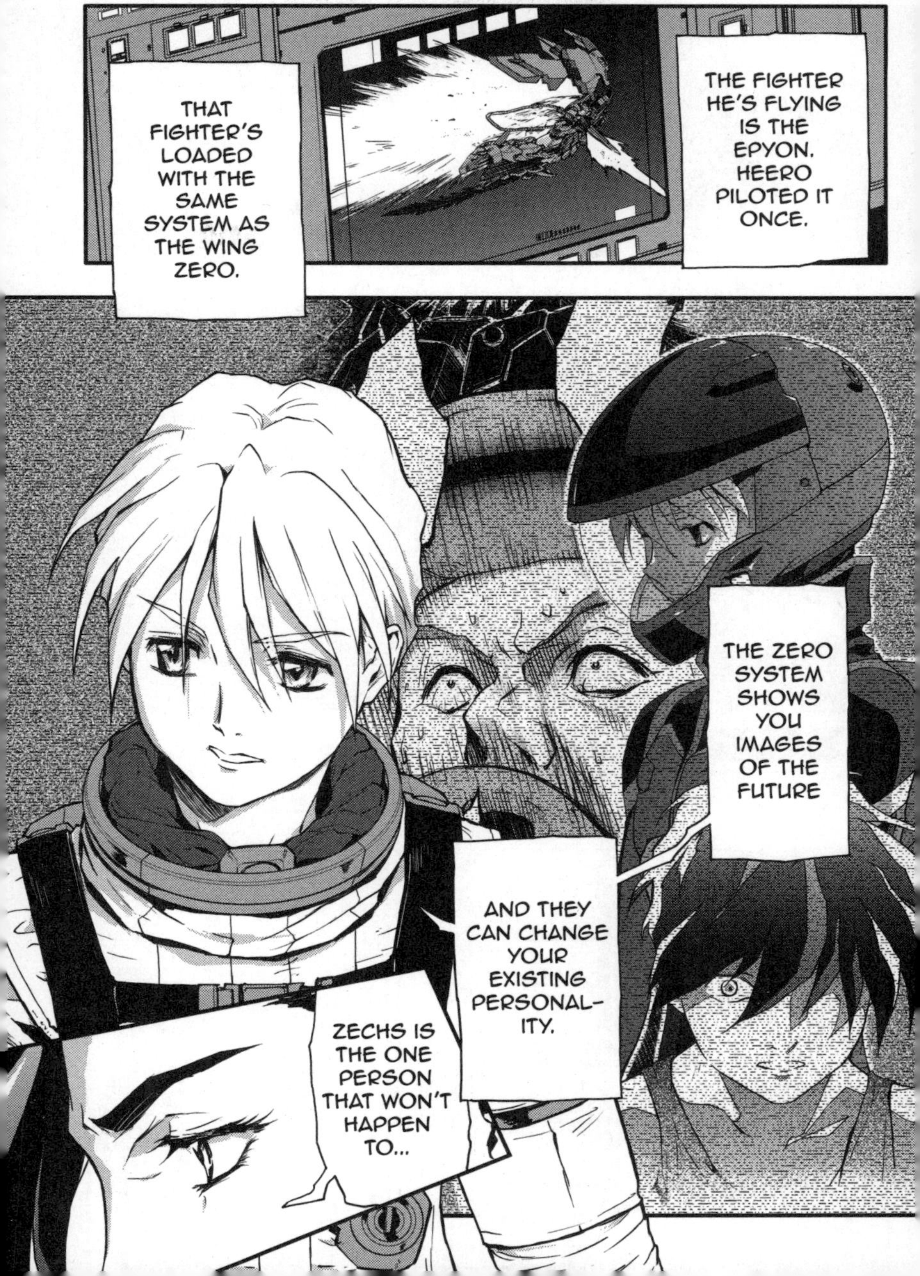
THE FIGHTER HE'S FLYING IS THE EPYON. HEERO PILOTED IT ONCE.
THAT FIGHTER'S LOADED WITH THE SAME SYSTEM AS THE WING ZERO.
THE ZERO SYSTEM SHOWS YOU IMAGES OF THE FUTURE
AND THEY CAN CHANGE YOUR EXISTING PERSONAL-ITY.
ZECHS IS THE ONE PERSON THAT WON'T HAPPEN TO...

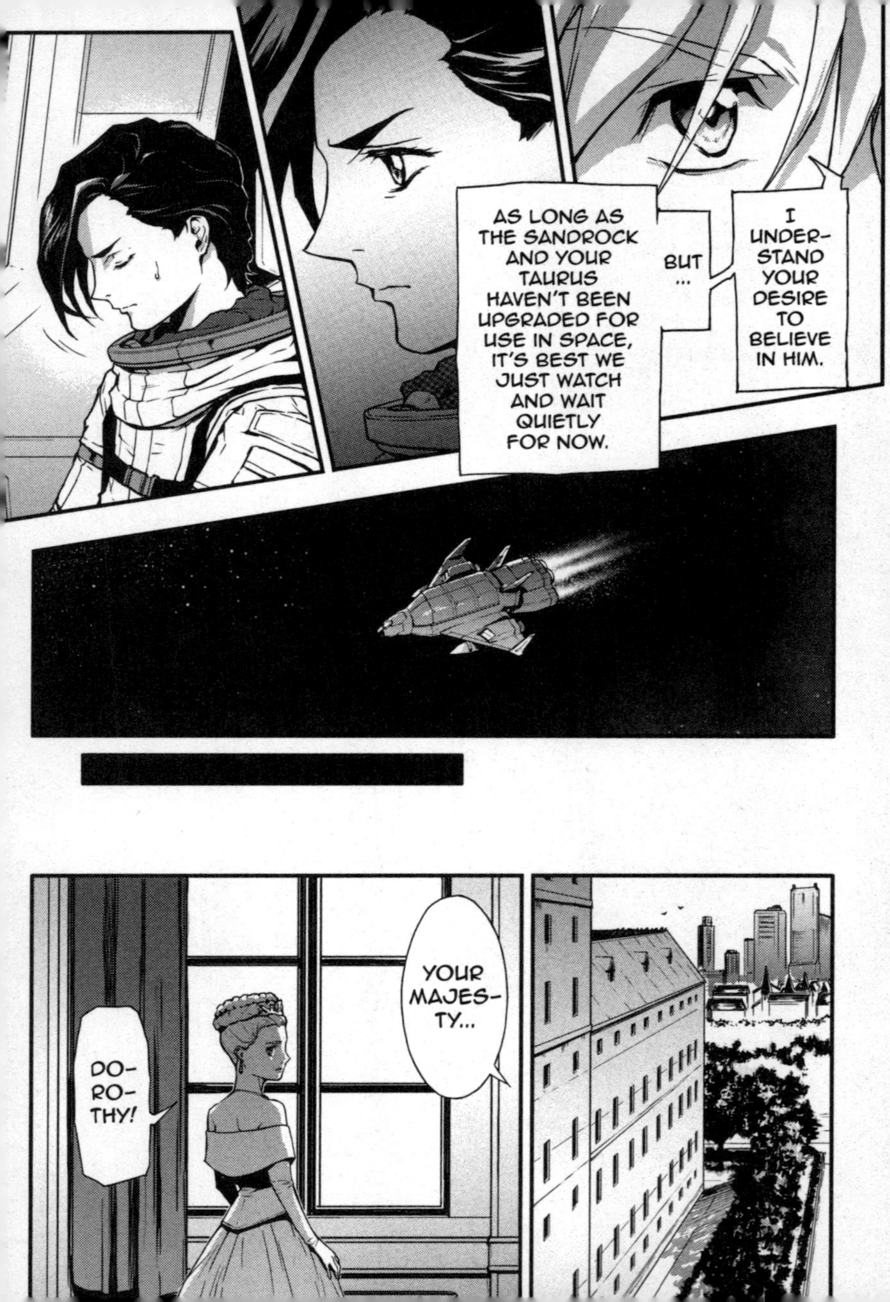
I UNDER-STAND YOUR DESIRE TO BELIEVE IN HIM.
BUT ...
AS LONG AS THE SANDROCK AND YOUR TAURUS HAVEN'T BEEN UPGRADED FOR USE IN SPACE, IT'S BEST WE JUST WATCH AND WAIT QUIETLY FOR NOW.
YOUR MAJES-TY...
DO-RO-THY!

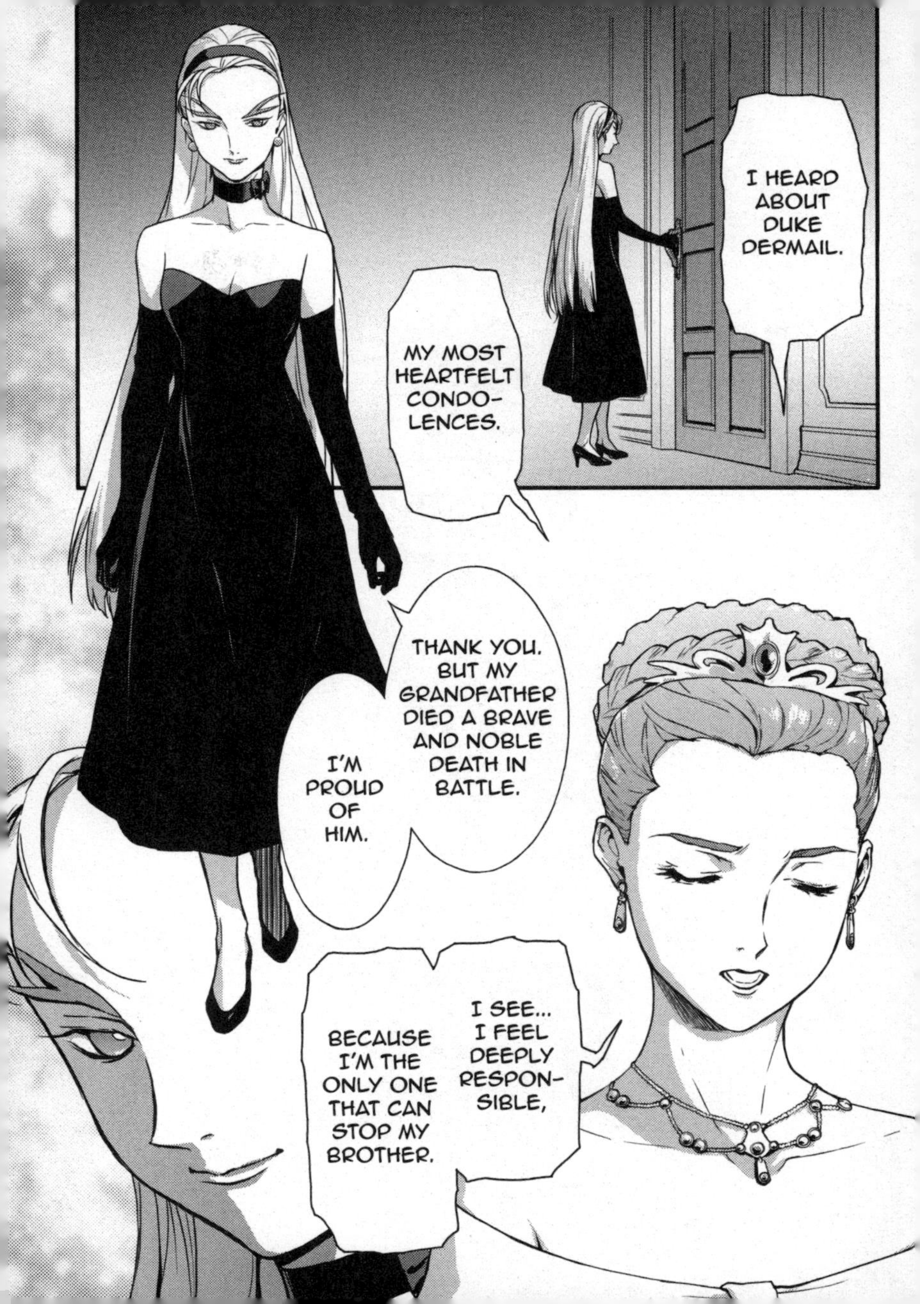
I HEARD ABOUT DUKE DERMAIL.
MY MOST HEARTFELT CONDO-LENCES.
THANK YOU. BUT MY GRANDFATHER DIED A BRAVE AND NOBLE DEATH IN BATTLE.
I'M PROUD OF HIM.
I SEE... I FEEL DEEPLY RESPON-SIBLE,
BECAUSE I'M THE ONLY ONE THAT CAN STOP MY BROTHER.

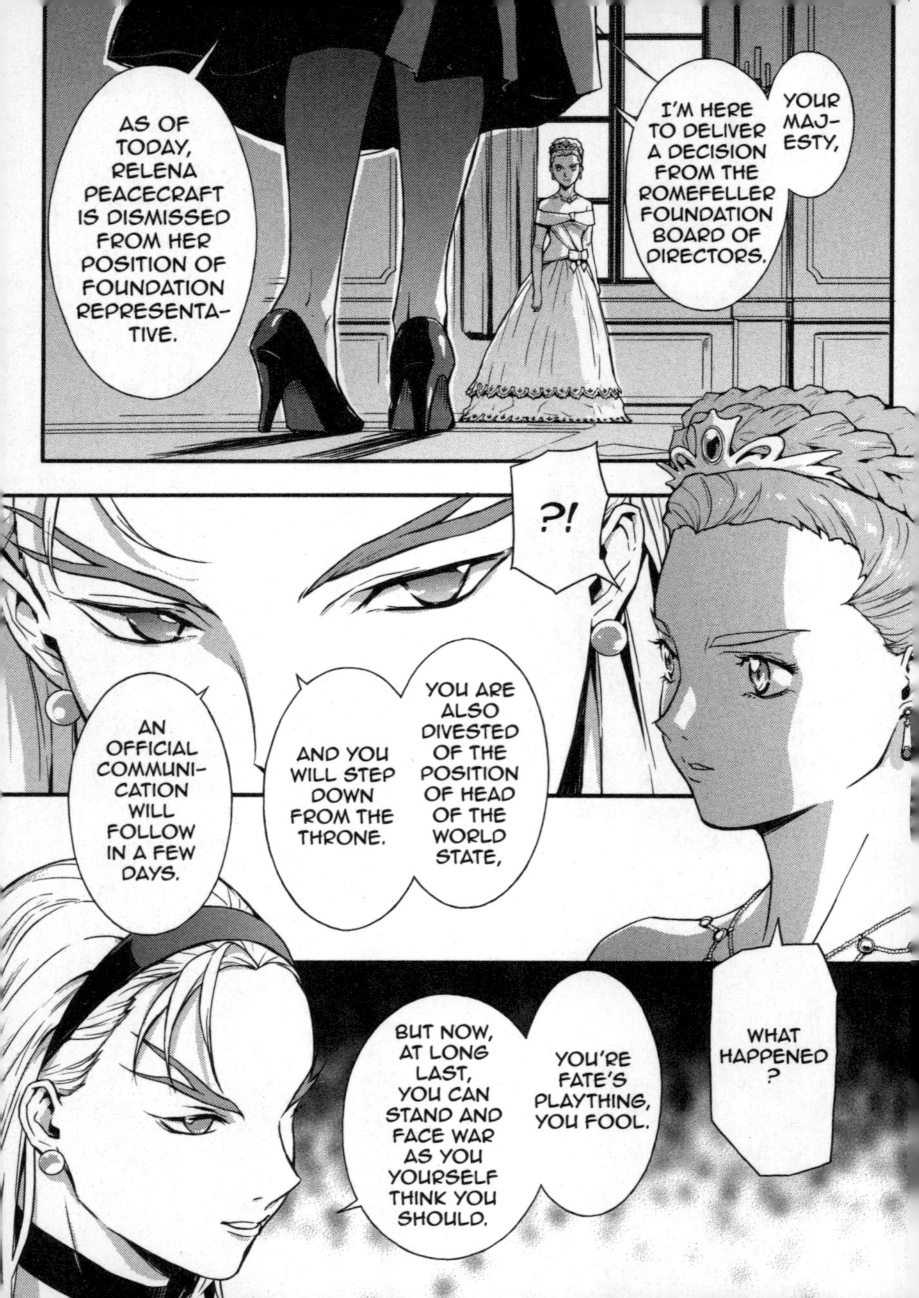
YOUR MAJ-ESTY,
I'M HERE TO DELIVER A DECISION FROM THE ROMEFELLER FOUNDATION BOARD OF DIRECTORS.
AS OF TODAY, RELENA PEACECRAFT IS DISMISSED FROM HER POSITION OF FOUNDATION REPRESENTA-TIVE.
?!
YOU ARE ALSO DIVESTED OF THE POSITION OF HEAD OF THE WORLD STATE,
AND YOU WILL STEP DOWN FROM THE THRONE.
AN OFFICIAL COMMUNI-CATION WILL FOLLOW IN A FEW DAYS.
WHAT HAPPENED?
YOU'RE FATE'S PLAYTHING, YOU FOOL.
BUT NOW, AT LONG LAST, YOU CAN STAND AND FACE WAR AS YOU YOURSELF THINK YOU SHOULD.

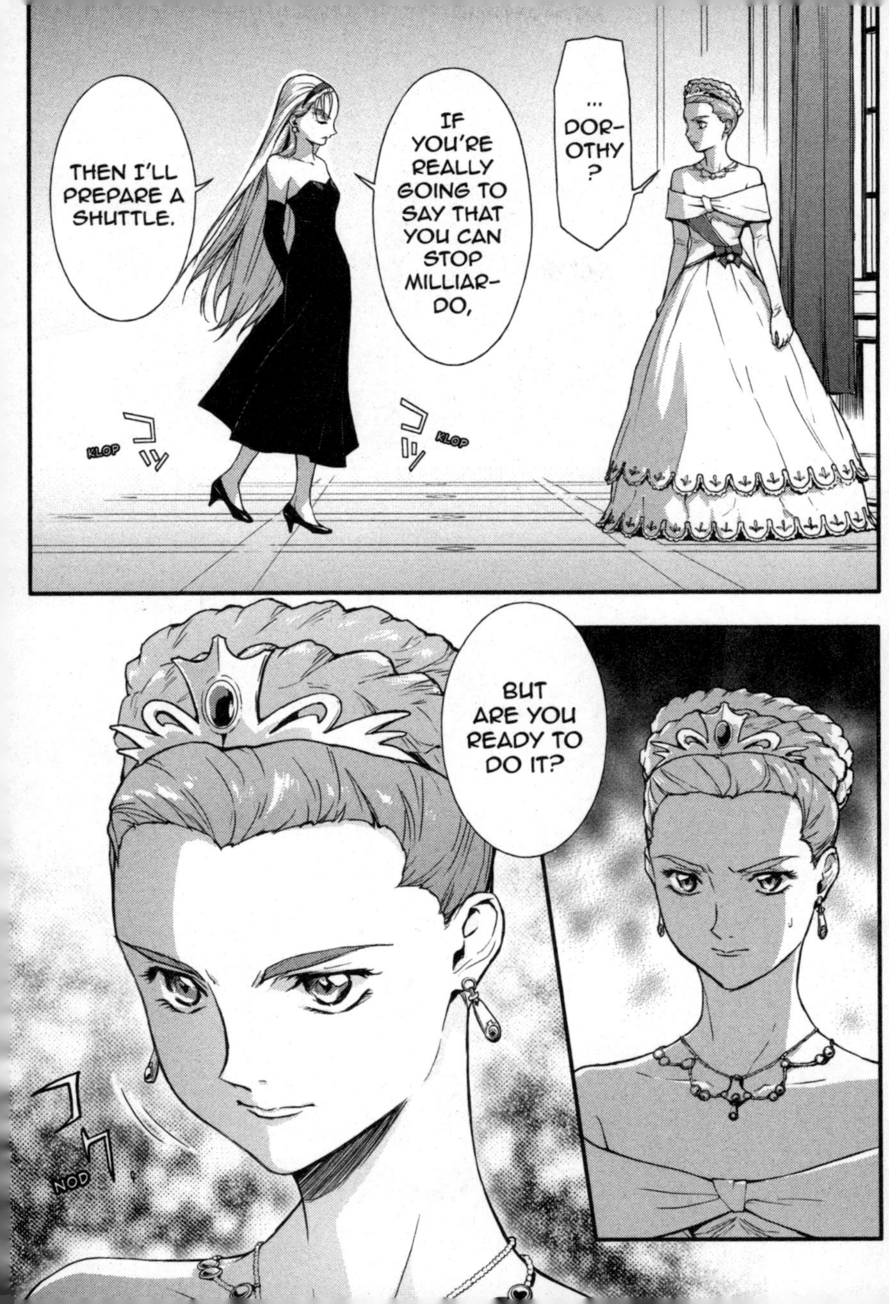
... DOR-OTHY ?
IF YOU'RE REALLY GOING TO SAY THAT YOU CAN STOP MILLIAR-DO,
KLOP
KLOP
THEN I'LL PREPARE A SHUTTLE.
BUT ARE YOU READY TO DO IT?
NOD

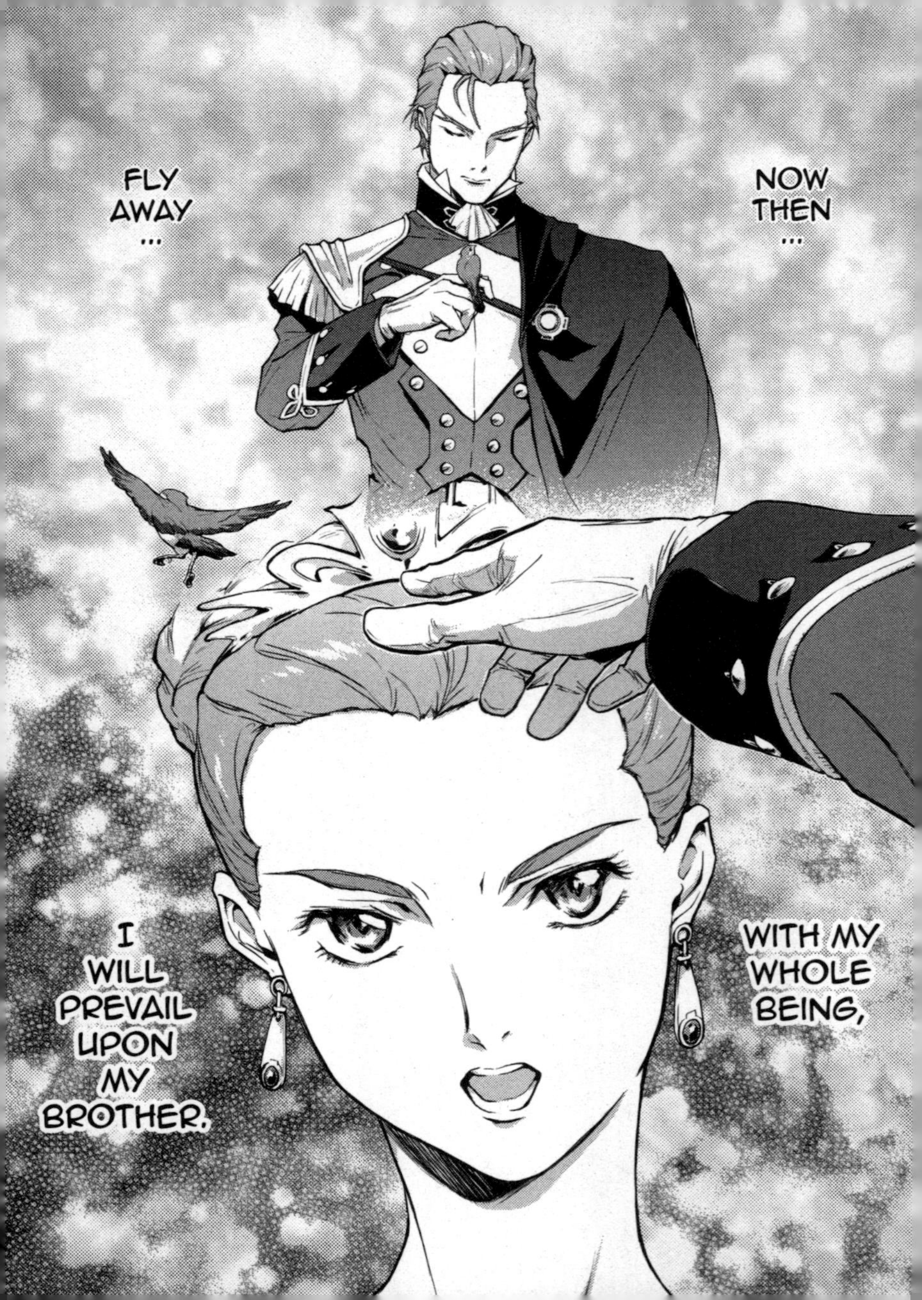
NOW THEN ...
FLY AWAY ...
WITH MY WHOLE BEING,
I WILL PREVAIL UPON MY BROTHER.

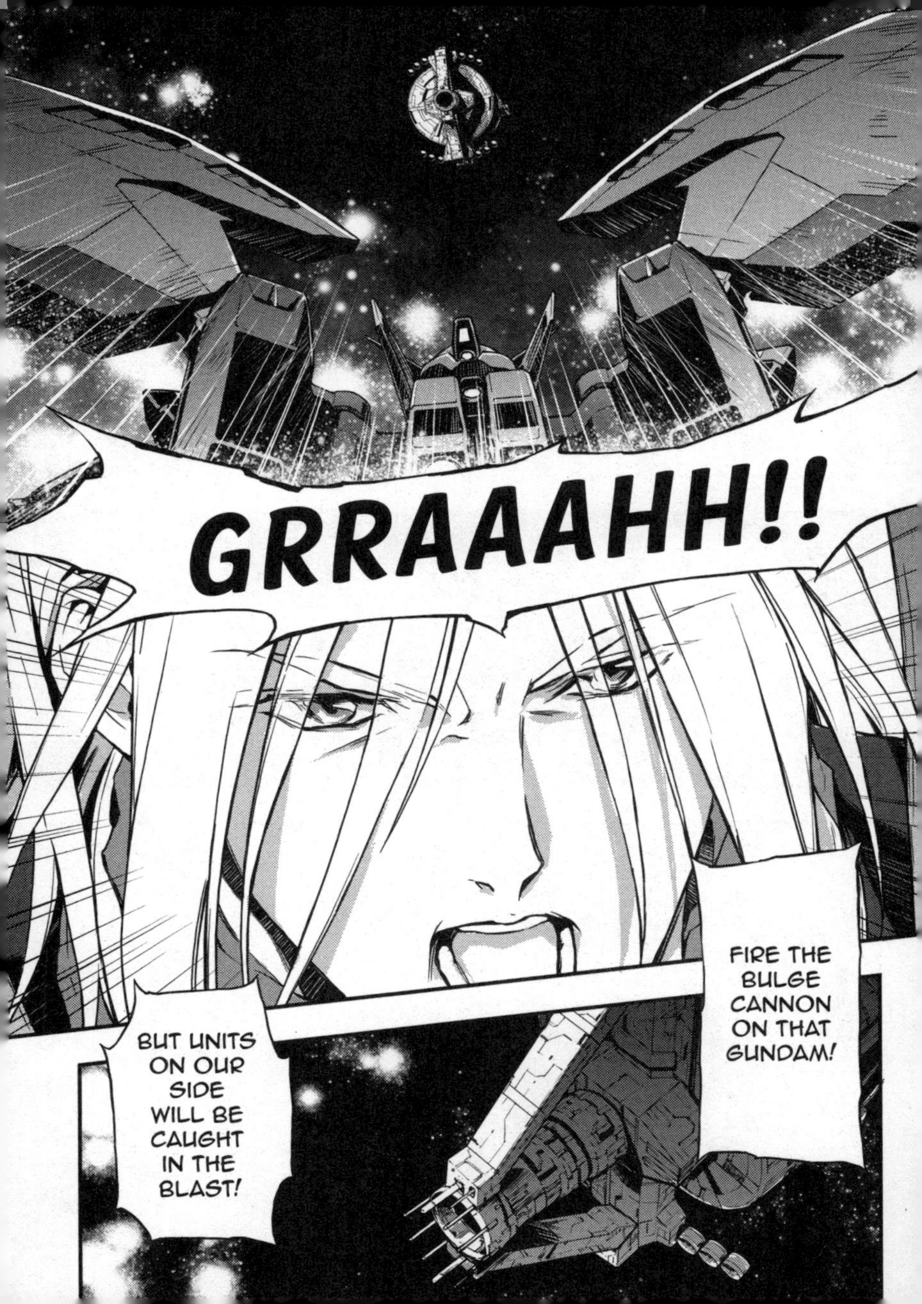
GRRAAAHH!!
FIRE THE BULGE CANNON ON THAT GUNDAM!
BUT UNITS ON OUR SIDE WILL BE CAUGHT IN THE BLAST!

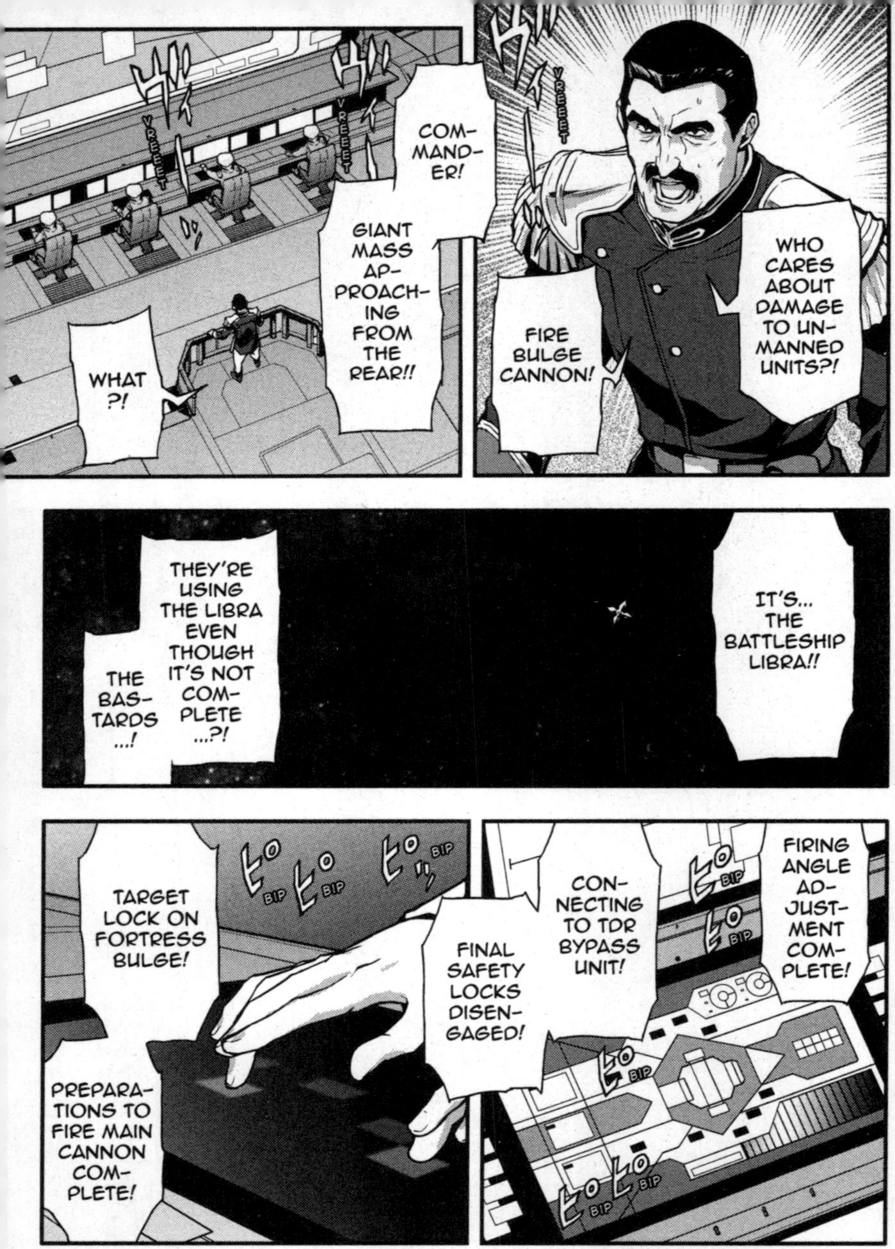
VREEET
WHO CARES ABOUT DAMAGE TO UNMANNED UNITS?!
FIRE BULGE CANNON!
VREEET
VREEET
COMMANDER!
GIANT MASS APPROACHING FROM THE REAR!!
WHAT?!
IT'S... THE BATTLESHIP LIBRA!!
THEY'RE USING THE LIBRA EVEN THOUGH IT'S NOT COMPLETE...?!
THE BASTARDS...!
BIP
BIP
FIRING ANGLE ADJUSTMENT COMPLETE!
CONNECTING TO TDR BYPASS UNIT!
BIP
BIP
BIP
FINAL SAFETY LOCKS DISENGAGED!
BIP
BIP
BIP
TARGET LOCK ON FORTRESS BULGE!
PREPARATIONS TO FIRE MAIN CANNON COMPLETE!

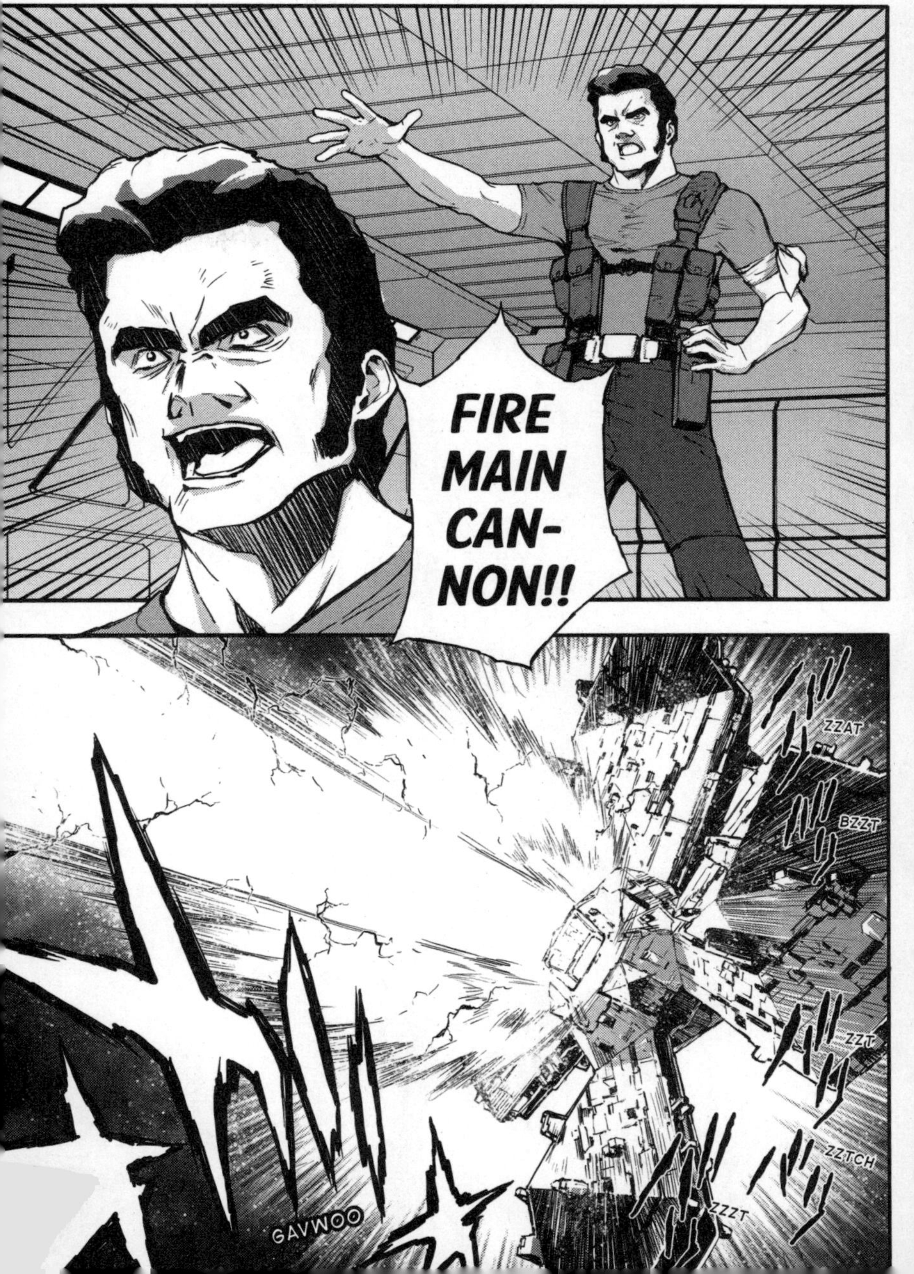
FIRE MAIN CAN-NON!!
ZZAT
BZZT
ZZT
ZZTCH
ZZZT
GAVWOO

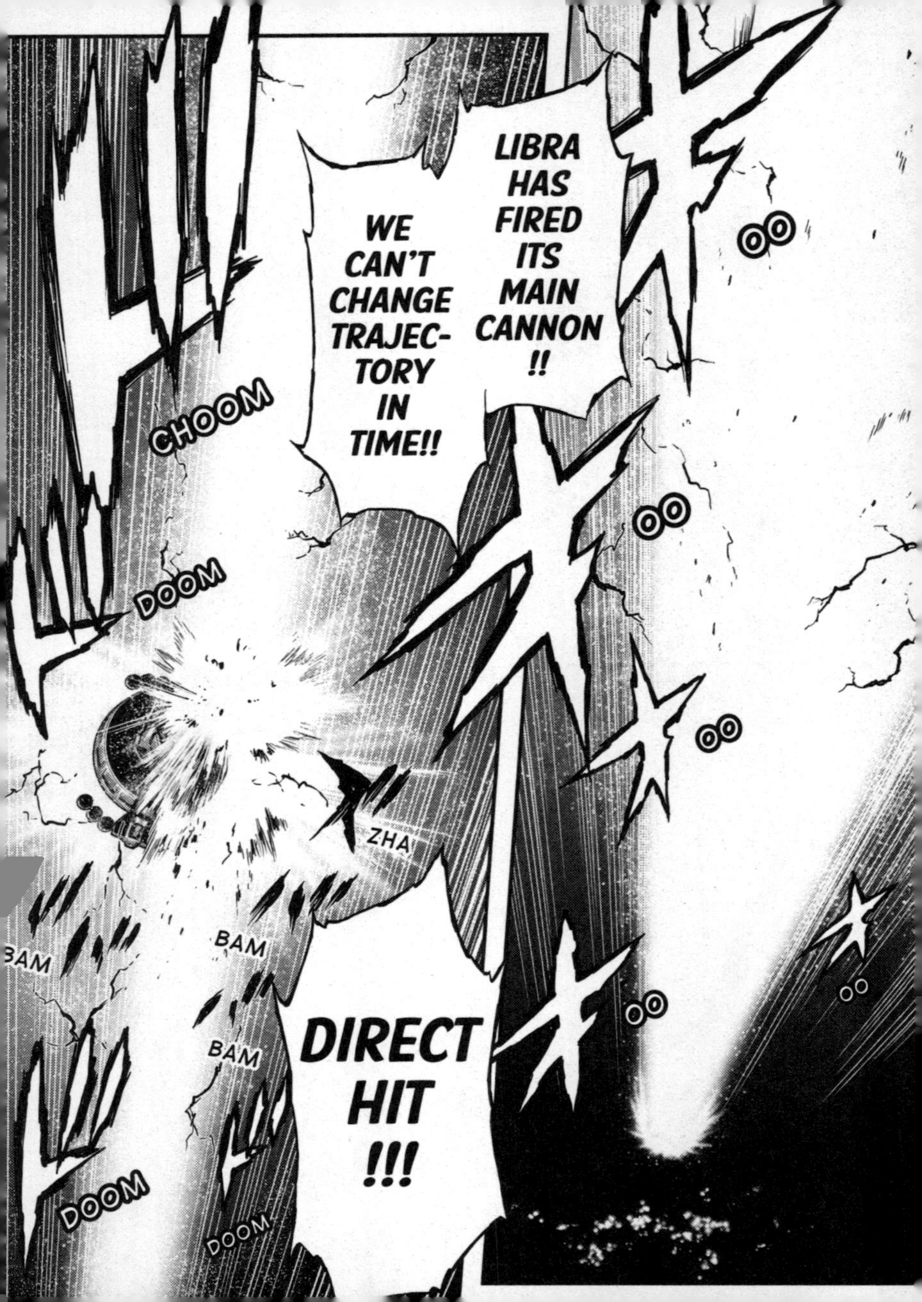
LIBRA HAS FIRED ITS MAIN CANNON!!
WE CAN'T CHANGE TRAJECTORY IN TIME!!
OO
OO
CHOOM
OO
DOOM
ZHA
OO
OO
DIRECT HIT!!!
BAM
BAM
DOOM
DOOM

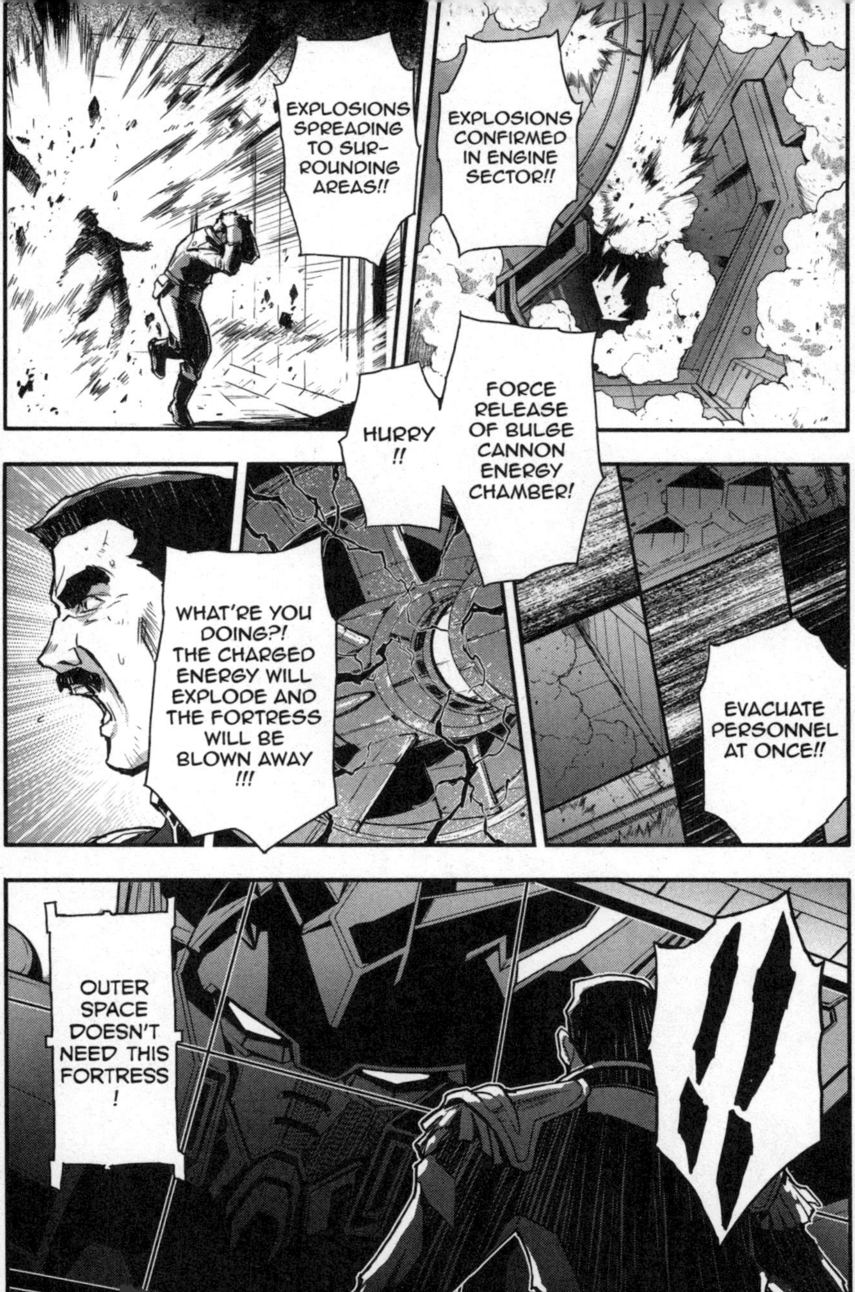
EXPLOSIONS CONFIRMED IN ENGINE SECTOR!!
EXPLOSIONS SPREADING TO SUR-ROUNDING AREAS!!
FORCE RELEASE OF BULGE CANNON ENERGY CHAMBER!
HURRY!!
EVACUATE PERSONNEL AT ONCE!!
WHAT'RE YOU DOING?! THE CHARGED ENERGY WILL EXPLODE AND THE FORTRESS WILL BE BLOWN AWAY!!!
OUTER SPACE DOESN'T NEED THIS FORTRESS!

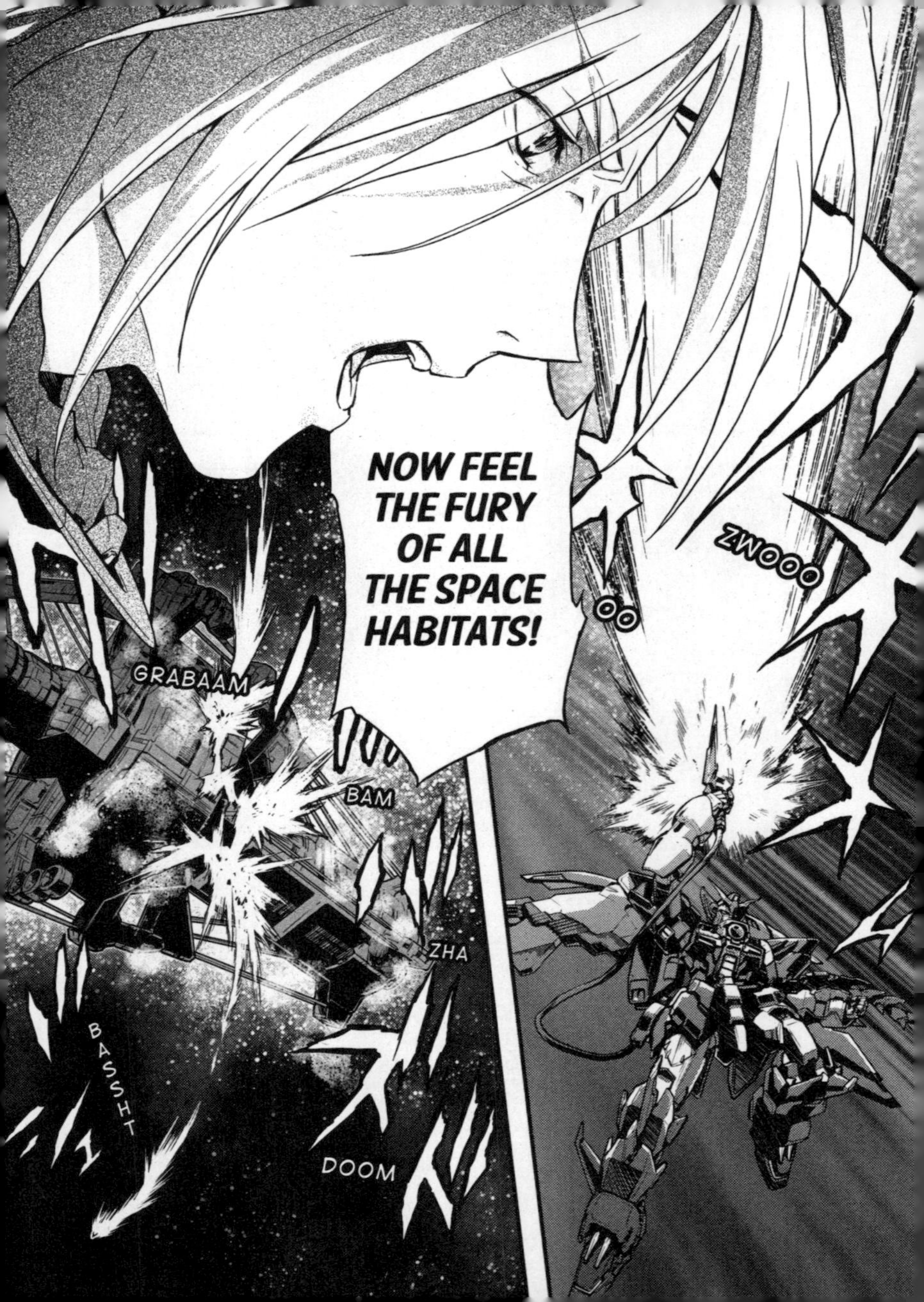
NOW FEEL THE FURY OF ALL THE SPACE HABITATS!
ZWOOOOOO
GRABAAM
BAM
ZHA
BASSHT
DOOM

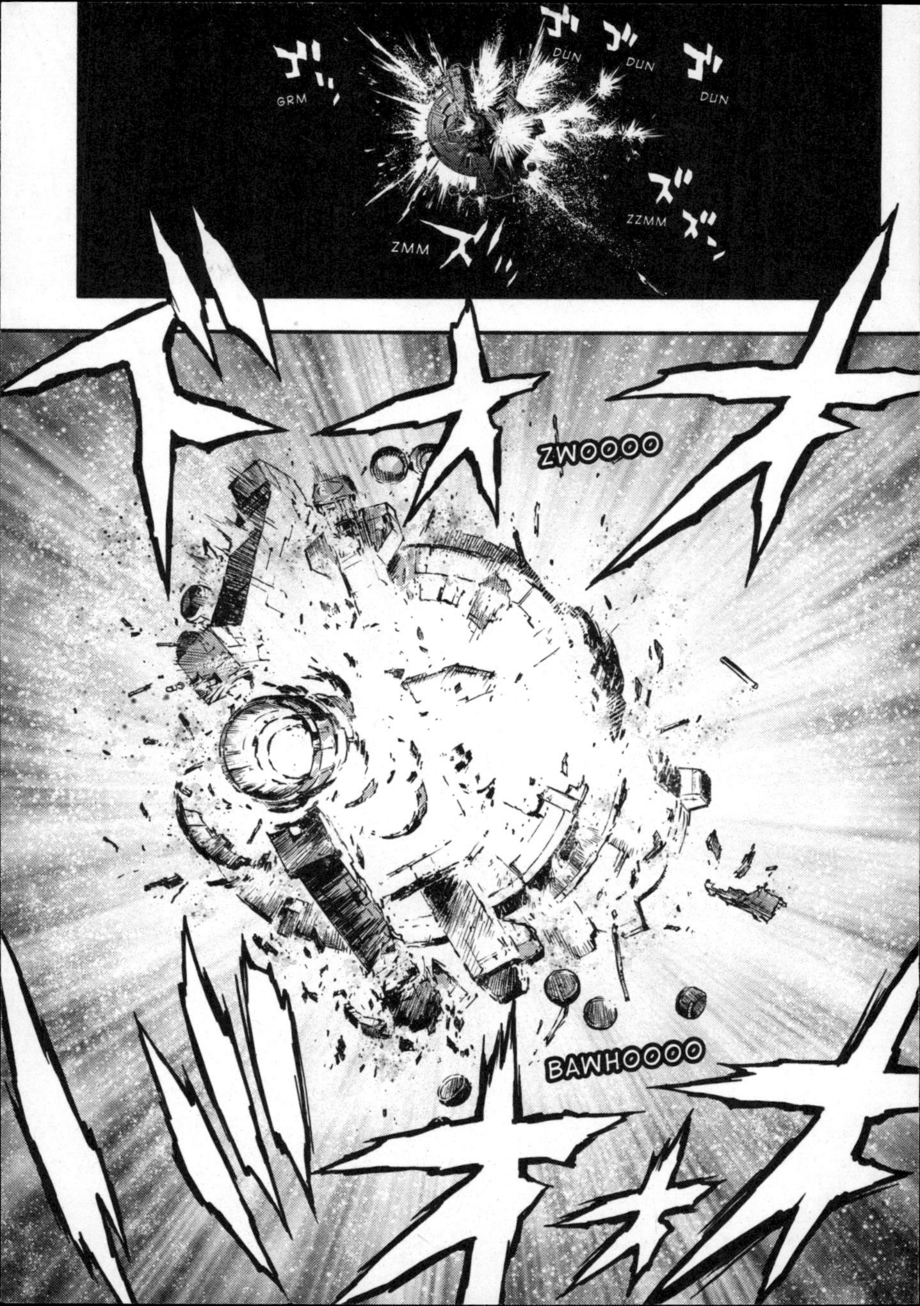
DUN
DUN
DUN
GRM
ZZMM
ZMM
ZWOOOO
BAWHOOOO

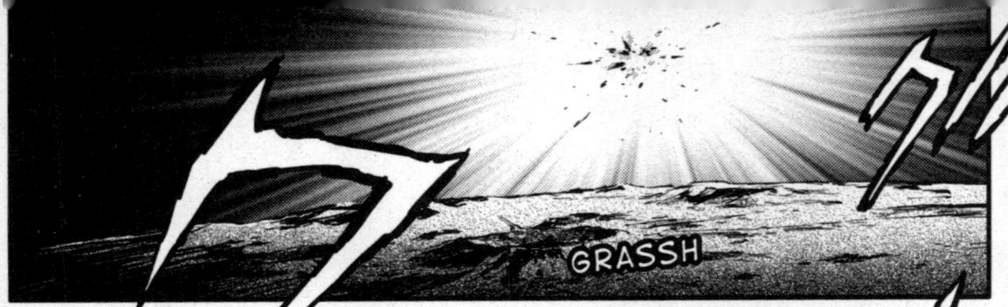
GRASSH

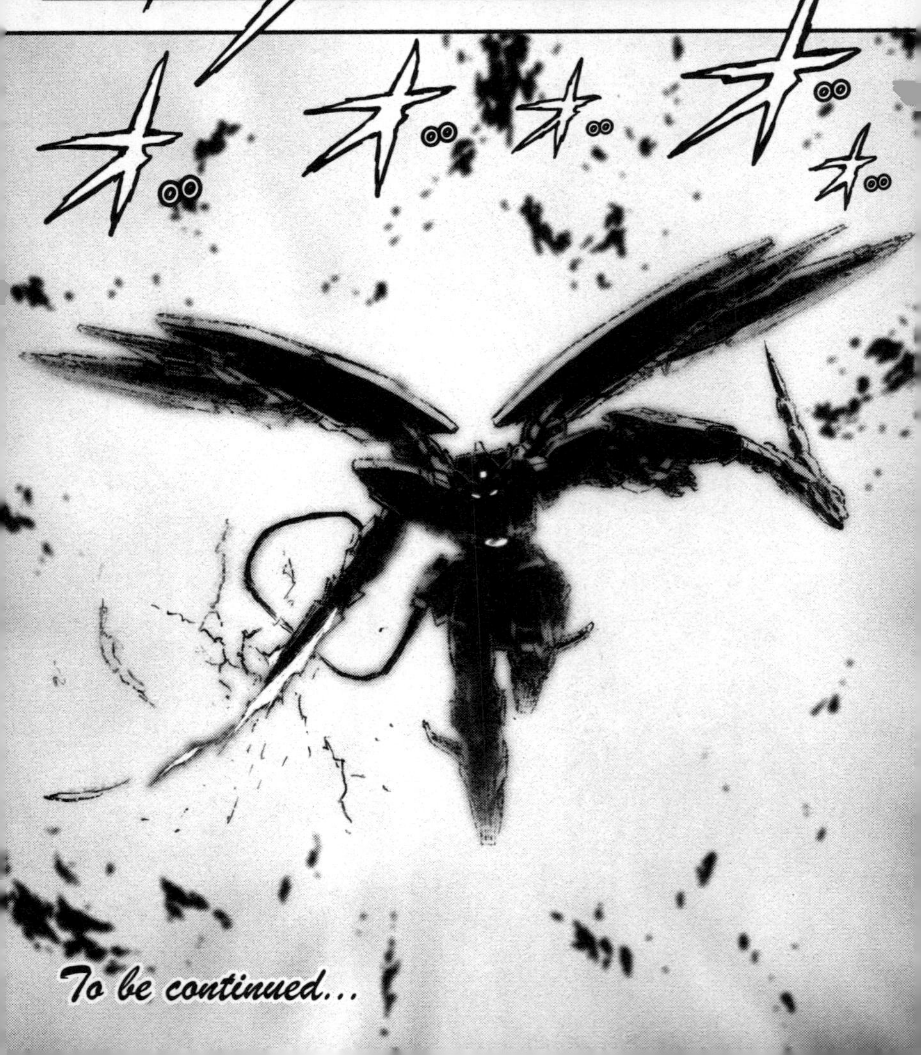
To be continued...

Mobile Suit GUNDAM WING, 11
Endless Waltz
Glory of the Losers
A Vertical Comics Edition

Translation: Kumar Sivasubramanian
Production: Grace Lu
          Hiroko Mizuno

© Katsuyuki SUMIZAWA 2016
© Tomofumi OGASAWARA 2016   © SOTSU • SUNRISE
First published in Japan in 2016 by KADOKAWA CORPORATION, Tokyo.
English translation rights arranged with KADOKAWA CORPORATION, Tokyo
through TUTTLE-MORI AGENCY, INC., Tokyo.

Translation provided by Vertical Comics, 2019
Published by Vertical Comics, an imprint of Vertical, Inc., New York

Originally published in Japanese as *Shin Kidou Senki Gandamu Wingu Endless Waltz The Glory of Losers 11* by Kadokawa Shoten, Co., Ltd.
Shin Kidou Senki Gandamu Wingu Endless Waltz The Glory of Losers
first serialized in *Gundam Ace*, Kadokawa Shoten, Co., Ltd., 2010-2017

This is a work of fiction.

ISBN: 978-1-947194-49-6

Manufactured in the United States of America

First Edition

Vertical, Inc.
451 Park Avenue South
7th Floor
New York, NY 10016
www.vertical-comics.com

Vertical books are distributed through Penguin-Random House Publisher Services.

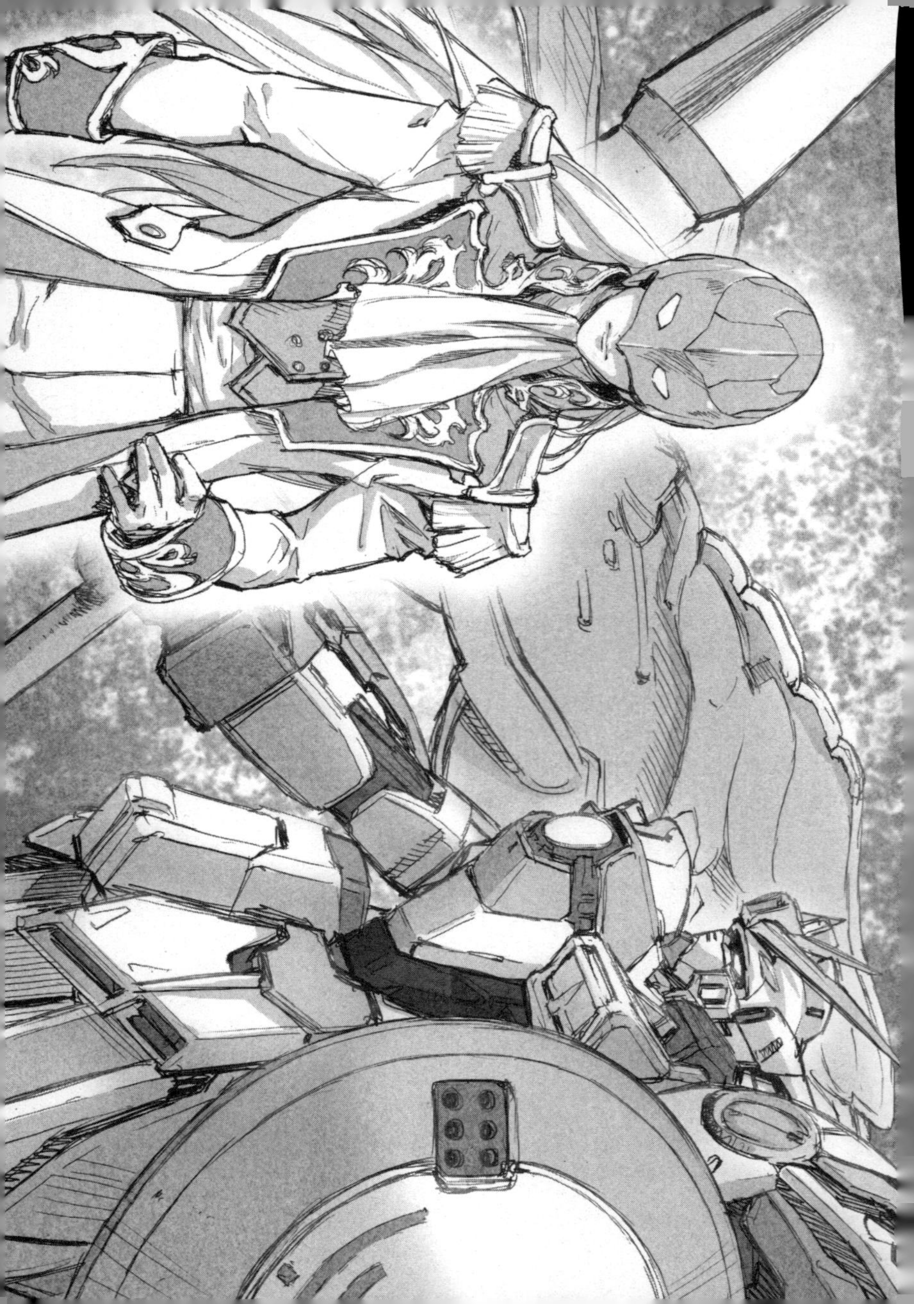